THE EMPRESS GAME

THE EMPRESS GAME

RHONDA MASON

TITAN BOOKS

The Empress Game
Print edition ISBN: 9781783295241
E-book ISBN: 9781783295265

Published by Titan Books
A division of Titan Publishing Group Ltd
144 Southwark Street, London SE1 0UP

First edition: July 2015
10 9 8 7 6 5 4 3 2 1

A CIP catalogue record for this title is available from the British Library.

Printed and bound by CPI Group (UK) Ltd, Croydon, CR0 4YY.

What did you think of this book? We love to hear from our readers. Please email us at: readerfeedback@titanemail.com, or write to us at the above address.

To receive advance information, news, competitions, and exclusive offers online, please sign up for the Titan newsletter on our website: www.titanbooks.com

To the best friends a girl could have, Jen Brooks and Diana Botsford, without whom I never would have finished this novel.

THE EMPRESS GAME

1

Shadow Panthe.

Power, grace, deadliness defined. Always cunning, never merciful, and endlessly, infinitely, victorious.

She, Kayla Reinumon, was Shadow Panthe.

And she was tired of it.

Tired of fighting, of hiding.

Perhaps her foe would end it. Kayla gripped a kris dagger in each hand and eyed the fellow occupant of the Blood Pit. This one would not kill her. Could not, had she a wish to, which she most likely did. Every woman who earned the dubious glamour of fighting in the Blood Pit wished to vanquish Shadow Panthe and claim her throne. Well, this one would not.

The girl—who possessed the ridiculous stage name Angelic Assassin—came at Kayla with knives flashing. She had technique, at least. Flawless footwork brought Angelic close, her blade descending at the perfect angle to slice a hamstring. It might have succeeded if Kayla hadn't spent her twenty-five Ordochian years training for moments such as this.

She lashed out with her booted foot and sent one of the girl's knives spinning, arcing toward the crowd that sat above the Blood Pit. It struck one of the spectators, judging by the scream that rang out, and was followed by a chorus of cheers. Kayla smiled. Hopefully the man had been killed, or at least seriously maimed.

She hated them, the men who came to this planet on the edge of Imperial Space to watch her fight. They fed off the violence, swore, sweated and screamed her name all night. She hated them, but not more than she hated herself for being Shadow Panthe. For giving them exactly what they wanted.

Angelic rolled and recovered quickly. Impressive. Kayla glanced at the wavy edge of her own kris daggers before tossing the left one away. It skittered to the limit of the pit, out of reach.

"You'll wish you had that back," Angelic called. A round of boos met her declaration—the crowd didn't believe it any more than Kayla did.

"We'll see." Kayla twirled her remaining kris. "Come."

Angelic lunged again, grabbing at Kayla's knife hand even as she stabbed at her with her long, thin blade. Clever girl. Not a worthy opponent for Shadow Panthe, but clever nonetheless.

The fight ranged across the pit floor, as Lumar liked it to. Despite her disgust for the owner of the Blood Pit, she knew who paid her prize money and how he liked things done. Lumar wanted a show. If Kayla and her brother, Corinth, didn't depend on the credits the Blood Pit fights brought in she would have ended the fight in a heartbeat, spat at the spectators and told Lumar exactly where to shove his "show."

But they did need the credits, so Kayla ignored the self-loathing and toyed with the blonde girl. If inflicting half-a-dozen minor cuts and bruises could be considered toying. Kayla herself had almost as many injuries. The fight had to look good, after all. The crowd wanted their *sport*.

Kayla closed with the girl again. Her sleek, cat-like movements and micro-fine reflexes had earned Kayla the moniker Shadow Panthe long before her nights in the Blood Pit. It had taken fighting like a caged animal in front of a crowd to make her hate the title and all the skill it implied. They chanted it now, the syllables elongated, the sound drawn out. *SHA-DOE-PANTH. SHA-DOE-PANTH.*

The crowd's mood turned. They'd seen enough sport, now

they wanted blood—Angelic's blood, never Shadow Panthe's. Not their infamous champion wench.

Screw 'em.

She'd given them enough already, and she still had a final match tonight.

Kayla sidestepped, affecting a miscalculation that appeared to put her off balance. Angelic lunged to take advantage, as many fighters would have. Of course, a better fighter would have been more cautious. The best, like Kayla's mentor, would simply have laughed at such an obvious move. Not Angelic. She dove right in.

Kayla shifted her weight, spun past the charging girl and brought the hilt of her kris down hard on Angelic's temple. The girl crumpled without a sound to the stained organoplastic floor of the pit.

The crowd roared above them, and bile stung the back of Kayla's throat. She glared at them, her adoring fans. She knew they sensed her enmity and cherished her all the more for it. What better champion had they ever seen? Who more flawless, more coldhearted than she?

None.

Nights like this made her almost thankful for her mentor's murder. If she were ever to have seen Kayla thus, fighting for money, for the pleasure of men in a pit of filth on the slum side of Altair Tri. . .

An oddity in the crowd caught her eye. Had he moved, she would never have noticed him. That he didn't stand wasn't in and of itself strange. Many men couldn't be bothered to rise for her, though they applauded and shouted as loud as any.

This man, though, didn't clap. He didn't wave his arms about, say something to his neighbor or point at the unconscious body of her latest victim. He held himself as rigid as the trinium decking and stared at her. She wanted to hate him, group him with the others. He sat in the arena, had paid to watch her fight another woman, hadn't he? One look at him and her mind refused. *Different.*

In his eyes she saw none of the admiration, none of the lust or possessiveness that shone in the others'. What she saw instead disturbed her: calculation. As if he saw past the façade, past the paint that covered her, the stage-name that shielded her.

She touched her fingers to the black *ashk* that wound around the lower half of her face, afraid she'd been unmasked. The cloth was still in place, revealing only her eyes.

The *whoosh* of pressure locks releasing tore through the crowd noise, offering her an escape. A battered section of the pit wall opened toward her, all the invitation she needed. She scooped up the dagger she'd tossed aside and fled the pit.

"What the frutt do you think you're doing, Shadow? They didn't come to see you play footsies, they came to see you *fight*."

Kayla didn't bother to look at Lumar as he ranted behind her.

"I told you to punish that upstart, but no, you let her off easy. I swear . . ."

Even if this same scene didn't play out after most of her fights, she still wouldn't have listened just then. She waited on the airway, a catwalk of trinium alloy that ringed the top of the arena and led to the fighters' dressing rooms. Lumar's uneven tread rattled the plating behind her while she peered down at the pit. Against her will, her gaze sought out the single man.

He sat as still as ever. Was he enamored with the spectacle in the pit? She glanced at the current contest—Oriala versus some unknown. All of Lumar's fighters wore skimpy costumes, and Oriala's chest threatened to burst out of her top with every breath. Kayla snorted. The look in the man's eyes must have been fanciful imagining on her part. He was just like all the rest.

Before she could decide if the revelation relieved or disappointed her, she noticed that the angle of his stare was off. His gaze was a touch high. He looked as though. . . he studied the ring of lights circling the pit. His posture indicated attentiveness, but she doubted he saw anything of what was going on in there.

Odd.

What sort of man came to the Blood Pit and didn't watch the fights? Mercenaries, smugglers, slave runners and unsavories of all sorts came to the pit to do business, but they always confined it to the intermission between matches. No one ignored the violence on display.

Except this man.

A chill crept over her, raising the fine hairs on the back of her neck. Why, then, had he been staring at her after the match? What was he doing here?

"Are you listening to me? I have had it!" Lumar grabbed her upper arm, heedless of the damage to her body paint. "Do you want to lose tonight?"

She tore her gaze away from the mysterious man in the crowd and focused her coldest stare on the pit's owner. "Shadow Panthe never loses." Kayla bared her teeth in a feral smile. "That's why they love me."

"You'll lose when I tell you to. I control every match here."

She arched a brow.

"You're a credit-whore for me, Shadow, I admit. You win because it pays for you to win, but you don't show off enough. The people want drama."

"Frutt the people. They want blood, I give them that."

"Not enough. They won't pay to watch you dance with the other bitches. Your match with Phoenix is the headliner. If you want to keep your status as golden girl of the Blood Pit I had better see some drama, I had better see some blood, and I had damn well better see Phoenix crippled before the night is over." He leaned in close. "The Blood Pit brought customers in from across the Altair System before you ever arrived, Shadow Panthe. You're not irreplaceable."

He walked away and she let him go without a reply. She *was* irreplaceable and they both knew it. The Blood Pit could only claim patrons from all corners of this star system because of its location; the slum side of Altair Tri was a catch-all for human filth. People didn't fly here to build a reputation. They didn't come to make a profit, gain a name or find their destiny. They came for one reason: to hide. As she and her brother had. Now the Blood Pit was famous on worlds beyond Altair Tri, and people came to this voidhole of a planet for another reason: to see Shadow Panthe fight. They were still the lowest of the low: murderers, rapists, slavers, but *she* brought them in. Lumar would never get rid of her as long as she continued to win.

She had no intention of losing to Phoenix tonight. The promise of four hundred credits to the victor would ensure her full efforts. The potential of another hundred as a bonus from a pleased Lumar was worth stirring up some drama.

Below, the crowd roared, drawing her attention once more to the man who sat curiously still amid the raucous spectators.

Lumar wanted a little drama, hmm?

Senior Agent Malkor Rua of the Imperial Diplomatic Corps stood in the tunnel that ran behind the Blood Pit's stands, taking a break from the violence for a moment. The place was revolting, pit to dome. The tunnel smelled like piss and ruinth smoke, ozone from the faulty lighting stung his throat and a vandalized beverage synthesizer oozed slime from a ruptured calorie pack. The stands themselves were worse, dotted with puddles of vomit and rank with body odor. The hint of the smell of semen coming from the man beside him after the last match had been enough to send him off on this momentary retreat.

He checked the feed on his mobile comm. One of his octet members, still on board Prince Ardin's starcruiser in orbit, had sent a message.

"IDs confirmed on the men following you and Hekkar. Lower-level guards in Master Dolan's employ, as suspected."

Now that was odd. As Grand Advisor of Science and Technology to the emperor, Master Dolan wielded plenty of power in the Sakien Empire. Why would he be concerned enough with the seedy goings on of such an inconsequential Protectorate Planet to send men here? And why did Malkor get the sense they were after the same thing—Shadow Panthe?

As much as Malkor had to feign interest in the Blood Pit to keep his cover as nothing more than a spectator, he didn't have to feign any of his interest in Shadow Panthe. Something about her. . .

It was in the way she moved, the defiant way she stared at the crowd, the flawless technique she wielded. She was *in* the Blood Pit but not *of* it, as so many of its denizens were. She'd been trained somewhere other than Altair Tri, and for a purpose grander than this. Where? And why?

Malkor shook off the questions. Where and why didn't matter. Who didn't matter. She was an asset, a means by which to secure Princess Isonde a win in the tournament for the crown. A fierce, feral means, and exactly what they needed. Or would be, once he convinced her to join them.

Two men lounging by the broken beverage synthesizer straightened when a third man ducked into the dark space. A glassy-eyed woman followed him, hands cuffed together in front of her, manacles connected to a metallic lead, the end of which was tucked into the man's belt.

Malkor stiffened—a slaver.

In the close confines of the tunnel, he could catch bits of the trading going on:

"Why hire a whore for a night when you could buy one for years? This one's prime blood, disease-free, brought her from Altair Prime myself."

One of the other two men muttered something Malkor couldn't catch.

"Any whore can steam up the sheets, but my girl—you can have her on her knees all night and she'll still have your breakfast ready for you in the morning. She'll spread her thighs on command, pleasure any of your other friends and still keep your house tidy." The slaver flicked a finger and the woman stepped closer. He gripped her jaw and angled her face to show off the scar behind her ear. "Discipline chip already installed, no extra charge."

Bile rose in Malkor's throat. It wasn't the first such transaction he'd overheard in the Blood Pit—more like the tenth. Though usually the "merchandise" wasn't on display. His fingers itched to draw his ion pistol and bring a definitive end to the discussion with three quick shots. He could do it, too, no one would miss them, but then he'd be ejected from the Blood Pit for making a mess. As much as it sucked, he had a larger mission at stake, and freeing this woman from her miserable existence wouldn't serve the greater good tonight.

The announcer bot boomed out a five-minute warning until the next match. Time to get back in there. Hating himself as much as the slaver and buyers in that moment, Malkor turned his shoulder and walked away. He elbowed his way through the heat and noise of the crowd to take a seat beside Hekkar, his second-in-command and backup on the mission.

"Shadow Panthe's the one, hmm?" Hekkar spoke just loud enough to be heard over the surrounding rabble.

"So it would seem." Malkor drew his thoughts back to the mission. It had to take precedence, the fate of the empire depended upon it. He forced the image of the slave's hopeless face out of his mind. "Of course we'd find Isonde's body-double in the darkest, nastiest voidhole on Altair Tri." If only Isonde knew how to fight, could win the hand-to-hand combat tournament without the need for subterfuge.

"This is a bad idea, Malk, and you know it. An IDC agent would be a better choice."

"Any agent has an excellent chance of being recognized on Falanar, no matter how long she's been undercover somewhere else. Besides, we need someone expendable if this whole thing goes to shit." Which it very likely would. How had he let Isonde and Ardin talk him into this?

"Think Shadow Panthe's good enough to win the Empress Game?" Hekkar's gaze slowly traveled over the other occupants in the arena as he spoke, never resting in any one place.

"She'll have to be. If we can't put Isonde on the throne, the empire is in serious trouble."

A bot announced the final match of the evening: Phoenix challenging Shadow Panthe. All the drug-dealing, slave-trading, gambling and bribing going on around them ground to a halt. Only one thing could hold the attention of so many disparate criminals at a time—the promise of violence. The pit drew Malkor's gaze once more. Who was this Shadow Panthe that she could rule here, thrive in this environment? A section of the wall lining the pit swung open. Malkor unconsciously leaned forward, anticipating Shadow's entrance. Every man in the room did the same.

Instead of her sleek and deadly form, flame burst forth, arcing from one end of the pit to the other. It vanished before Malkor could shield his eyes. In its place stood a voluptuous woman gowned in free-flowing fire silk. It slipped and shimmered with her every breath, giving the illusion that the woman was herself fire.

"Lady Phoenix!" the robotic voice announced, and the crowd hooted.

Phoenix raised her arms, the sleeves of her robe entwining her limbs like pyro-serpents.

"Not the most practical costume," Hekkar commented over the crowd noise. Phoenix lifted a hand to the clasp at her shoulder. One deft movement swept the robe off, revealing scads of bare skin interrupted only briefly by two strips of red-orange cloth.

The cheering increased tenfold.

"Lady Phoenix, in whose honor do you fight this eve?" The words were tradition, asked of all who fought in the Blood Pit.

"I fight for the glory of Fierenzos!" The God of Fire, how original. They'd heard many similar claims tonight. Only Shadow Panthe's answer stood out in his mind. It possessed a sincerity no one else came close to matching.

"Shadow Panthe, in whose honor do you fight this eve?"

"I fight only for myself."

No doubt this had always been her only answer.

Phoenix postured and preened, enjoying her entrance, but began to lose the crowd. From what Malkor had gathered she was a visiting challenger, champion of a rival pit come to fight the Blood Pit's reigning queen. Any woman of beauty—and scant clothing—could gain a man's attention, but it took something special to hold it against one such as Shadow Panthe. Phoenix didn't stand a chance.

The arena quieted to a hush.

A heartbeat passed.

Two.

Then she was there, standing in the doorway.

She needed no burst of flame, no flashy entrance. With only her presence, Shadow Panthe electrified the crowd. Malkor barely heard her name announced over the shouting.

"Stars be damned," Hekkar said.

Malkor could only nod.

She was painted from eyelash to hair-line, head to toe in black body paint cut through with a maze of red slashes, a stylized version of a shadow panthe's hide. The pattern continued in scarlet thread across the black halter-top and bikini bottoms she wore. The red lines scrawled across her face even, what little of it was visible above the black *ashk* she wore.

Completing the outfit were two kris daggers, one strapped to each thigh, and a gaze cold enough to burn. She strode across the pit, glaring at her admirers the whole way. They cheered her as if she were the Daughter of All.

When the gaze that raked the gathered men with such scorn turned on him, Malkor froze. Instead of contempt he read curiosity there. She weighed his appearance, judging him. Much as he had been judging her. Why had she picked him out of the crowd? Malkor cursed himself for not choosing a more shadowy spot to sit in, feeling more the hunted than the hunter as she continued to stare at him.

"Shadow Panthe," came the robotic voice, "in whose honor do you fight this eve?"

Though they all knew her reply, the crowd quieted, listening for her arrogant dismissal.

She raised a black arm until her finger pointed straight at Malkor. "I fight for him."

Frutt!

The crowd around him exploded—cheering, booing, grabbing, shouting. A dozen hands forced him from his seat and propelled him to the edge of the pit. He heard Hekkar cursing behind him, then Malkor was there, standing face to face with Shadow Panthe, who had ascended from the pit on a lift that had unfolded from the wall. A waist-high railing separated their bodies. She climbed on the barrier and crossed it slowly, one leg at a time, straddling it a moment while she checked her balance.

Around them men whistled and jeered. She didn't spare them a glance. Her eyes, a blue as bright as a flame's hottest crescent, locked on him.

Well, he *had* wanted to meet her. Somehow, though, he hadn't imagined it going like this. He'd pictured himself with the upper hand, promising a desperate pit whore a fortune of credits to do his bidding, an offer she wouldn't refuse. Instead he was caught up in the sway she held over the entire arena. Here she was not a woman to be forced or manipulated. Here, she ruled.

The noise died down again as she lowered her *ashk*, those nearest leaning in to hear what the infamous Shadow Panthe could possibly have to say to a mere mortal. Even under her *ashk*, paint obscured her features. A line of red, lurid against the black backdrop of her face, graced one cheek and cut across her lips, forcing Malkor's attention there.

Her lips moved. "A token?"

2

"For luck," Kayla forced out, when the man continued to stare at her.

Around them the crowd roared their approval. Though Lumar would no doubt be pleased, Kayla already regretted her plan to stir up drama. The man didn't have a pin or trade patch on his black duster that she could grab, or a scarf or something to tie on her arm. She couldn't go through his pockets to find a suitable token to keep up the charade.

Do something so I can get down from here, she silently urged him. *Play along.*

A red-haired man struggled through the crowd to reach his side. Despite being caught off-guard, her supposed muse looked in control and far more sober than the rest of the spectators. Choosing him from the crowd had been a mistake.

Kayla was suddenly desperate to escape. When the man simply stood there, studying her, she knew the move was hers to make. *Lumar had better give me a bonus for this.* She threaded her fingers through his hair, pulled his lips down to hers and kissed him.

It was like kissing a rock. A warm rock, maybe, but a rock nonetheless. She hadn't been kissed in five years, unless she counted attempted sexual assaults on Altair Tri, but she was pretty sure it wasn't supposed to feel like that. She released him quickly and backed away. His hand flashed out and he grabbed her wrist when she turned to flee.

"I need to speak to you. Privately." Calculation lurked in his intent gaze, and if he was shocked by her actions it didn't show. "As soon as you can manage it."

He wanted something from her, something he wouldn't leave without, and that could only mean trouble. Kayla had hidden her brother from trouble on this backwater planet for five years, she wasn't about to get caught now.

"The southeast gate. Under the launch dock, after the show." She glanced at the red-haired man who had finally reached his side. "Come alone or not at all."

Before he could answer she twisted her wrist free of his grasp and stepped away.

"Now, wish me luck." Kayla ignored the waiting lift, too anxious to endure its slow descent. She gripped the railing at her back with both hands and spun over. The instant her toes touched the ledge on the other side she jumped again, flipping backward to land in a crouch on the pit's floor.

The need to check on her brother surged through her veins. She still had the match with Phoenix ahead of her, and she'd have to wait for Lumar to settle up at the end of the evening. Now she had this stranger to evade on her way out. At least she knew where he'd be waiting and what door to avoid.

Kayla drew her kris daggers, eyeing Phoenix as the woman did the same. Despite her earlier show for the crowd Phoenix seemed to have tuned them out entirely and now focused laser-like on Kayla. No bit of fluff, this fighter, she had the potential to be a worthy opponent.

Kayla pushed her worry for Corinth to the back of her mind. There was no room for him in the pit.

Kayla strode down the airway, anxious to get her makeup off and return home. It was late, later than she usually finished, and the Blood Pit was empty. Normally she preferred the pit this way, with the lights down and filled with quiet shadows. She felt safer, more concealed. Tonight, though, the stranger in the crowd wouldn't leave her mind, setting her on edge.

It was possible he was only interested in Shadow Panthe, not Kayla Reinumon and the younger brother she kept hidden kilometers outside of the pit district. Any hint of trouble had her fearing for Corinth, though. She couldn't help it, it was in her genes, in her blood. She was Corinth's *ro'haar*, now that both of their twins were dead, and he was her *il'haar*. Her responsibility, her life's purpose, was to protect her *il'haar*. And protect him she would.

She clenched then shook her hands, trying to rid them of the numbness caused by a medstick's ministrations. With quickness and skill Phoenix had landed several cuts on Kayla, mostly on her hands and arms, though one stung across her face. They'd needed healing and Kayla had no time to wait for her body to regenerate naturally. Still, she resented the numbness that could take up to a day to fade as it made her much less effective with her knives, which she couldn't afford. A sonic shower would help with the numbness as well as flake the stage-paint from her body. The sooner she got home to Corinth, the better.

She had the shower on her mind and a hand on her kris when she entered her dressing room. The lights didn't come on with her first step in the room, which wasn't unusual. Lumar was too cheap to replace faulty motion sensors. When they didn't come on after a second step, the hair on the back of her neck rose. She tapped the pad by the door, bringing the lights up.

A shadow uncurled itself from the corner.

She had her kris out of its sheath before she recognized the man she'd kissed in the stands.

"A word of advice, Shadow. Next time you intend to stand a man up, don't agree to the meeting so easily. Makes a naturally cautious person like myself suspicious."

Kayla shrugged a shoulder in a careless gesture but didn't sheath her knife. "You seemed pleased enough with my answer."

"The famously reclusive Shadow Panthe, who doesn't even acknowledge her admirers—let alone speak to them—agrees to meet with me simply because I asked? If I seemed pleased it was only because I'd eliminated one exit from my search for you tonight. I knew you wouldn't be where you'd said."

"Where's your friend?"

"Checking the most likely exits, in case I missed you here."

She tried to play it light. "You've gone to quite a lot of effort for one little Shadow Panthe." Not that she qualified as "little" at her height, just shy of two meters. Did he have just the one man with him? Were they aware of Corinth, or was this truly about her pit whore persona? Could she make it home without being followed, or would she lead trouble right to her *il'haar*?

He watched her, seeming to evaluate whether or not she intended to use the kris she held on him. Kayla considered it, fingering the hilt of her second dagger as she studied him. Unlike the men of her homeworld in Wyrd Space he was impressively tall, at least two meters, and built to be a threat. He stood with his weight balanced primarily on the balls of his feet and his hands loose at his sides, alert, prepared for anything.

When he did nothing more than watch her, Kayla relaxed a fraction. If he'd meant to attack her he'd lost his best opportunity by not ambushing her when she entered her room. He looked like a man who understood that, so he must have something else in mind. She flipped her kris into its sheath and leaned against the wall beside the door, hands resting on the pommels of her daggers. The room was close quarters for a fight, should it come to that, and such a location favored the more agile fighter. She was safe enough, for the moment.

"What do you want?"

He hooked a booted foot under the single chair in the room and dragged it toward him. He flipped it around and straddled it, facing her. The hand he draped casually over the chair's back didn't fool her. She was sure that he could stand and lift the chair like a weapon in an instant, should he need to.

Smart man.

"I have a proposition for you," he said.

"Not interested."

"I assure you it is well worth it."

His boots were scuffed and well-worn, but not cheap. His clothes were a higher-quality synth fabric than typically seen in pit row. He wore a vest that could conceal any manner of weapon and a floor-length duster as black as the vacuum of space. The style favored slavers and illegal merch-runners but he was cleaner than either and more alert.

The owner of a rival pit, come to lure her away? They were rarely ballsy enough to court her at the Blood Pit after hours, and typically came with more pomp.

"Still not interested." She nodded to the door. "Now go find your friend and save him some trouble. I guarantee he hasn't located all of the exits."

"Look," he said, "I'll pay you ten times what you make for a headlining match."

"Why would you pay me that much for a single fight?" Any pit whore should clutch the chance to earn that many credits, no matter the risk, but Kayla had other things to worry about. True, she and Corinth needed the credits badly. It would put them much closer to bribing a runner to risk the unlawful journey to the Wyrd Worlds.

"It's a tournament. You'd be facing some of the top fighters in the empire."

If that was all there was to it she might have been interested. A tournament she could win, especially against imperials. The Sakien Empire had nothing on the Wyrd Worlds when it came to training their women to fight. "It's not here on Altair Tri or I would have heard of it."

His gaze flicked away. "We'd have to travel."

When he left it at that Kayla's unease grew. There was something here, something unusual about this tournament.

"Not interested."

"Can you afford not to be interested?"

"I'm a pit whore, not a slave. I fight when I want or not at all." Pride she'd locked down tight leaked past her control. "I don't *need* your credits." Damned if she couldn't use them, though.

"Phoenix gave you something of a challenge tonight."

Kayla tried not to think about it, about what she'd been forced to do. Phoenix wouldn't have stopped with anything short of Kayla's dead body if Kayla hadn't disabled her. So Phoenix's prize for the honor of fighting Shadow Panthe had been broken tarsals and metatarsals, a fractured collarbone, broken nose, a puncture wound above her hip—she had tried to keep it shallow—a dozen lacerations and a severed tendon in her wrist. It would be months before Phoenix could fight again, and she'd probably never be as dexterous with a weapon as she'd been, if she could even grip one. That assumed she found top-quality treatment for the injury, which she certainly wouldn't at the Blood Pit.

She would have done it to me, Kayla reminded herself. The thought didn't ease her guilt.

"Someday you're going to be off or someone's going to get lucky," the man said. "Either way the outcome would be the same. It's only a matter of time." His words echoed her own fears. None of the pit whores she encountered were her equal in the ring. One off-day, though, one random slip and Corinth would be completely alone without a *ro'haar* to protect him.

"I'll give you twenty times what you make. Enough to start over, leave all of this behind." His voice dropped to something more persuasive. "I'm offering you the chance at a new life."

His words provoked the faintest tug, an unconscious pull that made her want to agree. She pressed back into the wall, raising her chin against the unwanted feeling. "There's no new life waiting for me, no matter how many credits are in my pocket." Just the same broken life, somewhere else. Her home was destroyed, her psi powers gone and no amount of credits could ever buy her life back.

They could, however, buy her and Corinth passage to Wyrd Space, where he could get the psionic training he desperately needed among their own kind. They could stop hiding, stop living in fear of being discovered.

"Where is the tournament to be held?" she asked.

"For that many credits, where wouldn't you go?"

Any other planet in the Sakien Empire. At least Altair Tri sat on the edge of Wyrd Space.

"I could find someone else—" he started.

"Then do it, and stop wasting my time." Kayla toed the door open, leaving her hands on her daggers. "If you don't mind, this paint's starting to itch."

"Falanar. The tournament's on Falanar."

The word fell like a stalled hoverlift. Falanar, the Royal Seat of the Sakien Empire. The Imperial Homeworld itself. All the pieces clicked into place: elite imperial fighters, the outrageous payday. . . "An Empress Game has been called?"

He nodded.

"You want me to impersonate one of the princesses and win her the crown?" Kayla laughed, a short, harsh sound that echoed in the room. "You've got spacesickness if you think anyone would agree to that, no matter what price you're offering. The IDC would eat you alive."

That brought a smile to his lips. Anyone who could smile at the mention of the IDC was more trouble than she needed. She kicked the door open fully. "I heard your offer and I'm not interested. Get out."

The chair scraped across the floor when he rose and pushed it out of the way. "If you change your mind—"

"I won't."

He came toward her, his height eating up the available space in the room. Even five years on Altair Tri hadn't accustomed her to men who towered over her, not at her height. Among her people, the males tended to be the shorter of the gender.

This close, she caught the scent of his skin: old-fashioned imperial soap. A scent sadly lacking on Altair Tri.

He held his hands up—away from his sides, fingers spread— keeping a careful eye on her daggers.

"I mean to make you an offer you can't refuse, Shadow."

"And I mean to sheathe my kris in something soft if you don't back the frutt up and get out of my room. Now."

"We'll finish this later." He slipped out before she could reply.

3

Kayla was halfway home when Corinth's psionic voice sounded in her head.

::Kayla? Where are you?::

He usually waited for her to contact him on fight nights for fear of distracting her.

::Kayla?::

She fished through her bag, searching for the mobile comm she kept with her whenever separated from Corinth. Her fingers brushed several familiar items but the mobile comm was not among them.

"Damnit." She stopped walking long enough to glance inside the bag. It wasn't there. How could she have left it behind? She pictured where she'd last seen it, on her table in her dressing room before her last match. Before, but not after. "That frutter!"

::Please, Kayla.::

She growled low in her throat like a wounded cat, aching with the fear she heard in his mental voice. She couldn't answer him, not without a comm device of some sort. The familiar frustration of losing the psionic powers necessary to communicate with him at a distance rose up to choke her.

She broke into a run, still kilometers from home.

Her path brought her west out of the slums and into the polluted no-man's-land of Fengar Swamp. When they'd initially escaped to Altair Tri they'd rented rooms in the city, close to the Blood Pit. Kayla hadn't wanted to be any farther away from Corinth than necessary. With the number of break-ins and murders, though, it would only have been a matter of time before something happened to her *il'haar* if she left him alone in the slums at night. They'd moved to the swamp, constructing a home bit by bit from materials she scavenged, stole, or occasionally purchased. The place had a nauseating stench and more pitfalls than Ilmena's royal court—perfect for hiding out.

She reached the edge of the copse that sheltered their makeshift house and paused, alert for any anomaly. The shack looked as it always did, depressing and inadequate. The motion sensors she had surrounded it with were silent—potentially a good sign—but Kayla drew a dagger anyway and crept around the exterior.

No strange footprints bruised the muck and the tufts of grass appeared undamaged. She circled to the door. The pressure locks were still sealed. She punched in her access code and the locks released with a hiss of hydraulics.

"Corinth?"

::I'm here.::

"Are you all right?" Their shack consisted of three rooms. She crossed the common area and glanced in his room—nothing. Not that she'd expected to find him there. When scared, spooked or lonely on fight nights, Corinth went to the same place. His head peeked out from beneath her bed when she entered her room. It was so low to the ground that even with his small size, he still barely fit under there.

::I'm all right. You were gone so long.::

She scanned the room, searching for anything out of place. "Lumar kept me." No need for Corinth to learn about her strange conversation with an even stranger man. "The nightmares again?"

Kayla sheathed her dagger. She stripped off her *ashk* before taking a seat on the floor. "Come on out and tell me about it. I'll synth us some soup."

He might eat, but he wouldn't discuss his nightmares.

Neither would she.

They both knew what haunted the other. Memories of the day the rest of their family had been murdered, the day their twins had died and left them half-whole.

Corinth reached out to her with his mind, a whisper-light brush against her mental shields. He wanted the mind-to-mind connection only Wyrds shared. He wanted to feel her essence close and convince himself he wasn't alone. She couldn't handle it tonight.

::*Speak* with me.:: He didn't mean with her physical voice. Corinth hadn't spoken aloud since the attack on their homeworld. Nothing seemed to be physically wrong with him, but he just couldn't. Or wouldn't. She never knew which.

Corinth could still *speak* to her through her mental shields with his psi voice, but Kayla, who had lost the use of her psi powers in the attack on their family, couldn't reply. With her shields down, though, Corinth—or any well-trained psionic—could actually occupy her mind at close range. He would feel what she felt, see what she saw and hear her active thoughts. If she relinquished enough control he could even animate her body and speak for her. Kayla had never allowed anyone that much access.

Normally she would lower her mental shields and let Corinth partially into her mind so they could *speak*. Tonight she had too many troubles to hide from him and too little energy to try. She pulled her shields tighter together.

"It was a tough night at the pit, Corinth, you don't need to see that."

::I hate what you do there.::

"I know you do."

::You're so much better than that. You're a *ro'haar* and an Ordochian princess.::

"And you are a prince, but tonight we both live in a hovel and need to eat. Come out from there and sit with me a while."

She offered him her hand. Even if it was the middle of the night and she was exhausted, a *ro'haar* lived to protect her *il'haar*, and right now Corinth needed protection from his dreams. He finally edged out from under the bed, using her hand to pull himself up.

Night above, he's so small. He had barely grown at all in the five years since they'd escaped the overthrow on Ordoch. At thirteen years he looked more like ten. His head came no higher than her last rib, and his build was slender even for a male Wyrd.

"You need two bowls of soup, I think. Don't you eat when I'm away? I purchased the food synthesizer for a reason, you know."

Corinth wrapped both arms around her hips in a tight hug. ::I'm glad you're home.::

Kayla ruffled his dye-blackened hair and soaked in the love. Though kin, they'd spent little time together growing up. She'd mostly been psi training with her twin or learning to fight under the guidance of her untwinned aunts. Corinth had been busy with his own twin and psi training. He and Kayla had practically been strangers when they escaped the Ordoch massacre together.

Now he was more precious to her than anything, and even if he looked so much like a younger version of her twin, Vayne, that it hurt to even glance at him, well, she could take it.

She synthesized two bowls of broth that provided more comfort than sustenance and wouldn't tax their calorie pack reserves overmuch. They synthesized all their food from the matrix in the calorie packs, so even low-quality ones like these had to be rationed in their straitened circumstances.

::Did you win many credits tonight?::

"I did, it was a big night."

He sipped the broth, his huge blue eyes on her. ::Why were you so late, honestly?::

"I told you—"

::Lumar never keeps you this late. Why didn't you answer when I called?::

"I lost my comm."

::You never lose anything.:: She'd known he wouldn't buy it. ::Did something happen?::

"It was nothing. A man came to see me at the pit, wanted me to fight for him somewhere else."

::He was looking for you specifically?:: His features remained blank but Kayla knew how to read the energies inherent in a mental voice. Corinth sounded tense, his question laced with trepidation.

"Only as Shadow Panthe. Why, what happened?" She set her soup bowl down.

::Probably nothing. When I woke in the middle of the night and you weren't home, I thought I heard something. Outside.::

"Starfire, Corinth!"

::It could have been anything! The motion sensors hadn't even tripped.::

"What are you supposed to do if you think you hear something—anything at all? Damnit Corinth, damnit." Fear washed through her, making her furious. First the men at the Blood Pit, now this. What the void was going on? Had their true identities been discovered?

::I'm supposed to hide in the shielded hole and call for you until you come:: he recited.

"What did it sound like?" Her thoughts turned over almost too quickly to follow. The look in the stranger's eye when he saw her in the pit, his ridiculous offer, his missing partner, someone all the way out here in the swamp, Corinth home alone, unprotected except for a ring of motion sensors and an antiquated pressure lock on the door. Frutt.

Corinth shrugged. ::It was a low hum, constant and steady. It seemed to pass close but not too near the house.::

He was right, it could be anything. A swarm of marsh insects, energy feedback in the sensor lines, even the residuals of his nightmare fading away when he woke. It could be anything, but she knew it was trouble. She saw again the determination of the stranger waiting for her in her dressing room.

Trouble.

"I'll check it out in the morning, once the sun's up." She wanted to grip him by the shoulders and shake him. "You need to promise me that if you hear something again you'll dive right for the hidey-hole."

She studied his features, so pale, and looking tired despite the conversation. "Promise me."

::I promise. I'm sorry, Kayla, I just don't like it down there.::

"It could save you if anyone comes looking for us."

::No one has in five years.::

"And hopefully they never will." Or they might be on Altair Tri right now. "Come on, I'm tired and you look ready to drop. Finish that soup and we'll go to bed."

::Can I sleep with you tonight?::

She wanted to sprawl on her cot and rest her bones, not cling to the edge of it while Corinth hogged the rest. But she didn't even hesitate.

"Of course you can."

"Shadow Panthe."

Kayla's eyes flashed open. She lay in the darkness of her room, holding her breath, senses alert for the tiniest input. The voice came again, dragging her attention to the comm unit in the next room.

"Shadow?"

That bastard. Even if she didn't recognize his voice, with her mobile comm swiped earlier in the evening she knew exactly who was ballsy enough to comm her now.

"Corinth." She shook him awake.

::What's going on?::

"The hidey-hole. Now." Kayla pulled the antiquated blaster from under her pillow and lifted Corinth from the bed by one arm. "Quickly." She hustled him into his room and stripped the blanket from his bed as he slid back a panel in the corner of his floor. He dropped into the hole and she tossed the blanket in with him. "Stay here until I come to get you. Do not *think* of climbing out on your own, understand?"

He nodded.

She clicked on the small electro-torch they left in the hole, then slid the panel into place. It snapped shut and the seam melted away, hidden by a minor holographic field.

"Shadow, I know you can hear me." The comm buzzed, still switched on as if he considered his next words while leaving the channel open. "I'm sorry about swiping your comm, but. . . We need you. Let me make you another offer."

Kayla checked the charge on her blaster—low. She cursed herself for not splurging on another ion cell.

"Meet with me. Any place of your choosing," he said.

She waited in her night-darkened common room, gripping her pistol, listening to the stranger's voice.

"Meet with me or I'm coming to you. Right now."

Too late she realized her mistake. She slammed a hand on the comm system, deactivating it, but the damage had already been done. With the right equipment he could triangulate her position. "Frutt!"

The lights on the sensor grid panel winked on and off at her, green all the way. Maybe he'd been bluffing. *And maybe he was already on his way here.*

Kayla activated the light strip beside the door, leaving the rest of the room dark. She hunkered down in the deepest well of shadow, eyes on the sensor grid, and hoped the stranger decided she was more trouble than he could handle.

One hour later, she'd almost convinced herself the stranger's threat had been a bluff when the first sensor went dark. She'd been drifting closer to sleep by the minute, but that single light switching from green to orange woke her like an electric shock.

SENSOR 7—OFFLINE, her console flashed.

Shit.

In rapid succession, the remaining lights turned orange, all without a single alarm going off. They hadn't been tripped, they were simply offline. *Who in space is this guy?*

She rose, blaster ready.

She'd built their home like a bunker with only the front door for access, so she didn't have to worry about other entrances or windows to guard. With nothing more than twenty centimeters of organoplastic between her and whoever stood outside, that thought didn't give her much comfort.

Kayla flicked off her blaster's safety and the pistol hummed, drawing full charge.

Let's see what you've got.

Malkor studied Shadow Panthe's misshapen shanty. The woman provided surprise, he'd give her that. Fengar Swamp was the last place he would have looked if Hekkar hadn't tailed her to its edge. Even then he might have assumed she ran clandestine errands to this wretched place if Rigger, his octet's tech specialist, hadn't tracked her comm unit to this copse.

What a dismal place.

He tried not to inhale the swamp gases too deeply while his people finished deactivating the sensors. So. . . she was more than a pit whore, but he'd known that already. No one in her situation should have rejected his offer. What was she hiding? Only mortal fear of discovery or irreconcilable xenophobia would compel a person to live here.

Hekkar approached him. "Trinan and Vid are finishing the last two sensors now, then it looks like there's just the door to worry about. No other defenses." He glanced back at the pressure lock on the door. "Who the void is this girl, Malk?"

"No idea. It's too late to find someone else, though." Hopefully her secrets wouldn't catch up to her until after the Empress Game was won. "Ardin got confirmation an hour ago—someone 'officially' called the Game since we've been away. The first princesses have already arrived on Falanar to compete. We would have known sooner if news didn't take an eternity to reach this voidhole."

"Ardin himself didn't call it, though."

"The whole empire thinks he did. Someone crafted the speech from old holovids and it has been playing on every Sovereign and Protectorate Planet for three weeks. We need a fighter now and Shadow Panthe's it, shady background or not."

Preferably not, but he didn't hold out hope.

Trinan and Vid came around the corner of the home, each giving Malkor a nod—the sensor grid was down. He motioned for them to spread out, flanking the door. He'd initially felt silly bringing four of his team to hunt down one woman, and had only let Trinan and Vid come because they needed some exercise. Now, staring at a makeshift bunker in the middle of Fengar Swamp, surrounded by motion sensor lines and staring dead-on at a pressure lock strong enough to keep out an angry bull, he wondered if it would have been smarter to bring his whole octet.

"Rigger, can you handle this?" Malkor pointed at the lock. His tech specialist, datapad in hand, was already approaching the door. She pulled a knife and pried the cover off of the control before interfacing directly with the system.

The lock hissed open, the sound loud in the pre-dawn air.

Malkor drew his ion pistol. "Let's see what sort of trouble we're in for." He crept up to the door and Hekkar did the same on the hinge side. When they were in position, Hekkar gave the door a slight pull.

Blaster fire shot through the opening, singeing the air half a meter from Malkor's head.

Looks like Little Miss Twin Kris has more than one trick in her bag.

Malkor pulled a stunner grenade from his vest pocket. No way would he risk entry with her conscious. He depressed the trip and knelt, nodding at Hekkar to crack the door again. He rolled the grenade through the nanosecond the opening was wide enough, then snatched his hand back as blaster fire answered his delivery.

A three-second count and the familiar hum of a sonic burst

resonated through the walls. A thud, a noise that sounded like a boneless body crumpling to the floor, followed.

Hekkar grinned. "She is not going to be happy when she wakes up."

The shanty was only slightly more inviting on the inside than on the exterior. The three small rooms could have easily fit into Malkor's cabin aboard Ardin's starcruiser. An outdated food synthesizer and a battered table furnished one corner of the common room, and an amalgam of electronic equipment was amassed in the other corner, probably the source of the sensor grid.

Two equally sparse bedrooms completed the place. Shadow shared the space with a child, judging by the size of the clothes in one dresser. She struck him as a solitary hunter—it never occurred to him that the female fighter he'd seen in the ring would have a child in her life. A complication he didn't need.

The woman in question lay unconscious on her bed where he'd placed her, looking nothing like he'd remembered. Without her costume and body paint he couldn't be certain it was her. The kris strapped to her thighs convinced him, though, as did the lean muscles of her arms and the way she curled her hands, as if gripping a dagger even in sleep. She was younger than he'd anticipated, mid-twenties by imperial standards.

"Are you sure that's her?" Hekkar asked.

Rigger spoke up from the other room. "Are you questioning my tracking abilities? You told me to pinpoint her comm signal and this is where it ended."

Malkor drew her kris from their sheaths, setting the daggers on the nearby dresser. "It's her." He called to his teammates in the other bedroom. "Vid, Trinan, set up outside. I don't want to be surprised when the child arrives." He reentered the common room in time to see Rigger smack the complink console. "Anything?"

"She hasn't set up more defenses beyond the sensor grid. This piece of shit can barely maintain an open comm link from here to the Blood Pit, and does little else. It is generating some sort of EM field, though, in that room." She pointed to the room Shadow didn't occupy. "Not sure what it is, it barely registers on my scans. Designed to read as background sensor trash. I'll let you know what I find."

A scuffle sounded in the next room. "She's awake," Hekkar called, sounding muffled.

Malkor left Rigger abusing the ancient console and returned to the bedroom. He paused in the doorway, taking in the scene.

Shadow sat cross-legged on the bed, hands on her empty sheaths and a furious gleam in her eyes. Hekkar stood an arm's distance away, hand clamped to his bleeding nose, ion pistol trained on her.

Malkor looked to Hekkar, who nodded that he was all right. "Go see if Rigger needs any help. And take those," he motioned to Shadow's daggers, "with you." He waited until Hekkar had cleared out before taking up position in the doorway.

"Sleep well?" he asked.

She glared at him.

"I thought we'd finish that conversation we started earlier."

"Believe me, we're finished."

"Let's start off again, then. I'm Malkor." He offered her an opening that she ignored. "And you are. . .?"

"Shadow Panthe."

"That's somewhat unwieldy. Stage names aside, what does the kid who shares this fort call you?"

"What kid?"

"The kid who sleeps in the other bedroom. Unless those are your tiny clothes."

"I don't know what you're talking about."

He let it slide. It didn't matter who the kid was, as long as she was willing to ditch him for the trip to Falanar.

"Regardless, what should I call you?"

"Shadow Panthe. Now leave."

"Not until you hear my latest offer."

She cocked her head, unnaturally black hair sliding past her shoulder. "How did you deactivate my sensor grid?"

"What's your real name?"

"How did you do it?"

"I have my ways."

"In other words, you have no idea. That woman hunched over my complink in the next room did it?"

"Sure." Malkor left it at that. No need for her to know how many team members he had at his disposal.

"Who the void are you guys?"

"Specialists." He refused to out himself as IDC yet. He needed Shadow's goodwill, needed her to trust him. The Imperial Diplomatic Corps met with everything from respect to fear to hatred on their missions, but rarely with any warm feelings. They had near-limitless jurisdiction and the authority to do, well, whatever they wanted. The IDC got its way but it rarely made friends. Malkor didn't tolerate misuse of power within his octet, but the tarnished reputation other IDC teams had earned for the whole agency had hurt him on more than one legitimately diplomatic mission.

"Look. I know coming here like this wasn't exactly sporting. I'm under something of a time constraint, and unless I missed my guess back in the Blood Pit, you're under pressure, too."

Her face became more guarded.

"You're hiding out here, I get it. You should know I'm not the only man looking for you, though." That got her attention. And it was the truth. Dolan's men had been busy. "There are others asking around, interested in things like where you stay when you aren't at the Blood Pit, who you run with, what sort of weapon you seem to favor. Details a girl like you likes to keep to herself."

Her eyes darted to the doorway beyond him. "Who were they?"

The change was minute, but Malkor noted it. He was just a nuisance to her, someone she intended to brush off until he lost interest. Whoever she feared might be after her was a different matter entirely. This was of real concern to her.

"I don't personally know the men involved, but I know who they work for."

"Who?" She didn't bother to pretend it didn't matter to her. Her honesty surprised him and made him answer with the same, even though he'd originally intended to barter the information.

"An exiled Wyrd known as Master Dolan. Technology Advisor to the Emperor."

His words flipped a switch in her. She rose from the bed, suddenly in motion. He rested a hand on his pistol grip but all she did was slide a bag out from under the bed. "You're certain?"

"We've encountered his men before. I'm certain."

She grabbed her *ashk* from the dresser and tied it on before pulling clothes out and stuffing them haphazardly into the bag.

"Does this mean—"

"You can get us off this planet?" she interrupted. "You can get us away from them?"

"Yes, but—"

"Then I've decided to accept your offer—with conditions."

However he had hoped the night would go he had never imagined things being this easy. He needed to know who this woman was—stat. For Dolan to send men out to the farthest reaches of the empire she had to be important. A double agent? A council spy? An informant who'd double-crossed him? And why was she so terrified of them?

"Firstly, I want half again what you promised me."

"Done."

"I want to leave tonight. And I want us to be taken wherever we wish to go after the Empress Game—no questions asked, no place too far."

"Done."

"And one more thing." She glanced up, a half-full bag in her hands and a hint of steel in her eyes. "I am bringing someone else with me."

"I don't think—"

"He's coming, or no deal."

"So there is a kid after all."

"Yes."

"Is he trouble? Because I'll have about all that I can handle with you on board."

The question brought a sad smile to one corner of her mouth. "You won't hear a peep out of him."

4

Kayla brushed past Malkor and made her way to the complink console.

No doubt the noise Corinth had heard earlier had been Dolan's men searching the swamp for their hideout. Thank the stars they hadn't located it while she was gone.

She could always escape Malkor later but she had to get Corinth off Altair Tri right now, tonight. Or this morning, or whatever time it was.

The woman muttering over her console stared as she approached. Kayla glimpsed a very sophisticated—by imperial standards—datapad before she tucked the device away.

"I take it you couldn't figure it out, Rigger?" Malkor asked from behind her.

Kayla reached past Rigger and tapped a sequence into the keypad. She didn't wait for the command to finish running before entering Corinth's room. The holo field surrounding the hidey-hole melted away and Kayla hesitated. Had she made the right call? What did she even know about these people? What if they themselves worked for Dolan?

Just the thought of Dolan, the *kin'shaa*—an exiled Wyrd ritually stripped of his psi powers—sent a shiver through her. He had betrayed his own people. He had given the empire the coordinates to her homeworld of Ordoch in Wyrd Space. Had come pretending to be a mediator between the two sides and had instead helped the empire kill her family and take over her planet when talks failed.

However, if they did work for Dolan, she'd know it. Malkor clearly had no idea of her true identity, or that she and the "kid" she lived with were Ordoch's last heirs. Dolan wouldn't cook up the Empress Game plot to lure her with, he would simply grab them as prisoners of war, or, more likely, kill them.

As bizarre as it sounded, Malkor was probably telling the truth about his plan for her. And as Malkor was the only one of the two men who actually wanted her alive, she'd choose him over Dolan any day.

She slid the panel off the hidey-hole. "Come on out, we're leaving." She reached a hand to help Corinth up and out.

::I was sleeping:: his mental voice grumbled, before it abruptly changed when he caught sight of Malkor and his team. ::Kayla! Who are these people? What's happening?::

"It's all right. We need to get out of here quickly and they're going to help."

::Imperials don't help Wyrds.:: His gaze fell on Malkor. ::Is he the one you mentioned, who approached you at the pit?::

Malkor looked at her strangely, reminding her that Corinth spoke only in her head, and that no one else must know about his psi powers. She gave Corinth a slight nod.

"Pack what you want to bring that will fit in one bag."

"He doesn't speak?" Malkor asked.

Not to you. "Nope."

Malkor glanced at Corinth, who looked even smaller and frailer beside the impressive forms of the two specialists. "A word, please. Rigger, you stay with the boy."

"No," she snapped. "Rigger can watch him from the doorway, but stay away from him."

Rigger raised her hands, palms out, away from her body. "I'll stay over here." She backed as far away from Corinth as she could in the cramped room. "I won't go near him, I promise."

::I'll be all right, Kay, they're a little afraid of you.:: Corinth tried to sound brave, but times of stress showed just how under-trained he was. Fear laced his mental voice. She placed her hand on his shoulder, willing strength into him.

"I'll be right out here. Let me know if you need me." She stepped out of the room after Malkor, never taking her eyes from Corinth.

Malkor positioned himself off-center from her, not blocking her view. Strangers hadn't been this close to Corinth since they'd moved out here, and the certainty that she'd exposed him to danger gripped her like a vise.

"Are you serious about this?"

She didn't bother to answer Malkor's question.

"You want to take a child to Falanar while you impersonate a princess at the Empress Game? Do you have any idea what the stakes are, here? Do you know what they do to people caught cheating at the game?"

"Are you trying to convince me not to take the job?"

"Starfire. You know what I mean. Isn't there someone he can stay with until this is over?"

This time she did glance at him, but only to make her point. "Do you think we'd be living out here if there was?"

"Who are you hiding him from? Dolan? Someone else? Who is he?"

"He's my brother, and that's all you need to know." *Brother*— such an inadequate word. Her *il'haar* was everything to her. An imperial wouldn't understand that.

"What if we left him with one of my contacts. I could—"

"No. I don't know why this is hard to understand. You want me to fight, he comes with me. It's either that or find yourself a new girl."

"Damnit, Shadow. I'm trying to do the right thing here."

"By buying a fighter to cheat with at the Empress Game? Could've fooled me."

::He wants you to do what?!::

A half-smile came to her lips at Corinth's outrage.

::My *ro'haar* never cheats! You don't have to. Tell him, Kay.::

"We need to pack," she said instead, brushing past Malkor. "And I want my daggers back."

Dawn brushed the eastern edge of the sky when they exited the shanty for the last time. Two more of Malkor's team greeted them outside. Introduced as Trinan and Vid, they completed the box of guards surrounding Kayla and Corinth.

She studied Malkor's back as he led the group in a northeast direction. Without a doubt he was in charge. Most criminal groups on Tri worked in smaller units of two or three men, yet here Malkor had four very competent-looking people with him, and Trinan had mentioned meeting up with more at a ship. Just how many people Malkor commanded, and what sort of specialist he was exactly, were the questions front-most in her mind.

The team traveled well for people unused to Fengar Swamp, but Corinth faltered often between the channels of murky water, muddy hillocks and patches of sludge. Kayla kept a constant hand on his arm to keep him from going down.

With the exception of her time at the Blood Pit, Kayla stayed away from imperial men. They made her uneasy with their size, physical strength and aggression. Oddly, however, she didn't feel threatened by the men of this group. At least, not currently. They and Rigger had spread out in a protective formation with her and Corinth at the center. For the moment she had allies, albeit temporary ones. She let them watch the swamp for signs of Dolan's men while she concentrated on Corinth.

"Are you doing all right?"

::I'm fine, Kay.:: Corinth's foot sank deep into the soft earth as he spoke, wrenching him to a stop. He made no sound of exasperation, simply pried his foot free and took another step. He looked tired already. The earlier nightmare had robbed him of sleep, and he'd had similar nights this week. He hadn't been eating enough lately and the trek was tough even for someone in healthy, athletic shape.

"Do you need me to carry you?" she asked Corinth. Malkor turned his head at her words. He looked a question at her as if asking if she needed help. Kayla waved him on.

::I'll be all right for a bit more. I've never been out here at this hour, it's spooky. *Speak* with me?::

Corinth's presence approached the edge of her mind, brushing against her shields lightly, the way a feline might barely touch its nose to her hand when first scenting her. Kayla ordered her thoughts, directing them into neat mental compartments and sectioning them off. The practice was still second nature to her despite barely using it since they'd left Wyrd Space.

She took a deep breath and struggled against her deepest will to lower the mental shields protecting her mind. Though she loved Corinth and had been his *ro'haar* for the last five years, she still found it tough to open herself up to him. He rushed inside her head, too quickly. It caused an instant ache between her eyes.

::Sorry, I didn't mean it.::

I know you didn't, she thought, knowing he could hear her active thoughts. She pushed the pain to a corner of her mind and blocked it there, away from his reach. Little extra room remained. Corinth coiled himself inside her mind, filling her head near to bursting.

::Do you trust these people?::

How to answer that? She couldn't exactly lie to him, but she could hide some facts by burying them behind inner shields.

I can't say I know them well enough to trust them. I do think they're telling the truth about wanting me to fight in the Empress Game.

::Because they know you're a princess?:: His voice held a mix of horror that they might have been discovered and pride.

Only because they've seen me fight. I'm supposed to impersonate someone else, I think. They don't know who we are and we need to keep it that way.

::Where are we going?::

Falanar.

::But— The military. Dolan. The IDC. You said they might be searching for us.::

We'll have to be extra careful. She kept the knowledge that the *kin'shaa* Dolan was after them locked tightly away. Hopefully they would elude Dolan altogether and never have to worry about him again.

::Why did you agree to help them? We don't need them, we're doing fine on our own.::

We are not doing fine. You need psi training that I can't give you. The sooner I get you to Ilmena or another Wyrd World the better. I know you hate this life. I hate this life. The isolation ate away at her. Once she had had friends. Family. People in her life. *And I hate fighting in the Blood Pit.* Gods, how she hated it. Hated herself and what she had become. *It would have taken me at least another year to earn enough credits to buy passage back to Wyrd Space.* Finding a pilot willing to fly into Wyrd territory against violation of Universal Occupation Laws would require an exorbitant amount of credits.

I made a deal with Malkor. I fight in the Empress Game and he takes us wherever we want to go afterward, no questions asked.

::And you trust this imperial to keep his end of the bargain?::

That was the question, now, wasn't it?

Corinth stumbled again, falling to his knees in the watery channel. His shin connected with something hard and the pain shot straight through Kayla.

Enough of this, Corinth. You don't have to prove yourself to anyone. You are an Ordochian prince, and you have skills that go beyond the physical. Come here. Without waiting for him to comply she bent and lifted him up. Stars, but he was thin. She should have done more physical training with him. Vayne had begged her to teach him some of her hand-to-hand combat arts, and had prided himself on his limited but hard-earned physical strength. Corinth preferred to exercise his mind almost exclusively, like most male Wyrds. She should have—

::It's not your fault, Kayla, stop blaming yourself for everything.::

She set Corinth on his feet long enough to turn around and hike him onto her back. *Hang on.*

His arms closed about her neck and his legs looped over her hips like a human backpack. Thankfulness seeped into her from their mental link as he settled himself.

Around her the team kept moving, but Malkor took one look over his shoulder and dropped back beside her. "Let me carry him."

"No."

"I understand that you're protective, but he's going to get heavy real quick."

"I'll be fine." Kayla continued to walk. Corinth's added weight upset her center of balance and made her sink farther into the muck with each step.

Malkor walked beside her in silence. She glanced at him when Corinth's attention split and partly focused on Malkor. There was a note of concern on Malkor's face.

"I won't slow you down," she said.

::He doesn't believe you.::

Thank you, Corinth, I can see that.

"Let me know if you need me to take him," Malkor said. His gaze dropped from her eyes to the *ashk* that covered the rest of her face for a second.

::What does he mean you kissed him?!::

Corinth Reinumon, get out of his head this instant.

::Kayla—::

Now.

Just what she needed, a thirteen-year-old boy dabbling in the mind of a man like Malkor. Corinth's curiosity seeped into her.

I refuse to discuss this with you.

::You're no fun.::

Kayla shifted his weight higher on her back and settled in for a long hike.

*   *   *

Corinth's weight rivaled that of a fully loaded hoverpack on her back, and each step was a small triumph over her tired body. When they finally hit the grassy outskirts that marked the edge of the swamp, she gratefully set Corinth on his feet. She steadied him when his numbed legs didn't want to hold his weight.

The hike through the swamp, her second in the last eight hours, on top of a night spent in the pit, wiped her out. They walked on a few hundred yards toward two strange depressions in the landscape, and it wasn't until they reached the flattened-out sections of grass that Kayla realized what she was looking at: the landing spots of cloaked ships. The inside of a ship revealed itself from the air when the outer hatch opened. Another of Malkor's team jumped out.

"'Bout time, boss. Ardin's been comming every fifteen minutes for way too long." His gaze shifted from Malkor to Kayla. "This our girl?"

His too curious look had her resting a hand on one of her daggers.

"This is not *our girl*, this is Shadow Panthe, who will be working with us for the next few weeks." Malkor turned toward her. "Shadow, this is Gio. You have my permission to hurt him if he gives you any trouble."

Gio grinned.

"Just, don't kill him," Malkor said. "He's somewhat useful to me." He called to the rest of his team. "Load up."

The cloaks of the hidden ships dropped, revealing two sleek interatmosphere shuttles. It had been years since she'd seen any advanced imperial space vehicles, but she was certain the empire hadn't achieved this level of sophistication on their own. The shuttle design, though imperialized, still had a basic Wyrd feel that Kayla recognized, even if no one else did.

No doubt this was Dolan's influence.

"Tell me you stole these," she said to Malkor, as he hefted Corinth's bag into the closest shuttle.

From the look on his face, he'd expected some sort of question. "No."

"Who do you work for?" She put a hand on Corinth's shoulder, a signal to be ready. He tensed at her motion.

Malkor eyed her hand, not missing her intent. "We're working with a princess who wants to win the Game, no one else."

Few people had access to shuttles such as this, and all of them were men she'd need to avoid. The IDC and imperial military sprang to mind, as they'd arrived on Ordoch in this vessel's predecessor. Rigging the Empress Game, though? What motive would either have for that? Kayla considered her options. Alone, she might have made a break for it, but she couldn't run with Corinth in tow. He couldn't sprint past the people loosely guarding them and even if he could, he wouldn't be able to keep up the pace.

Say they did manage to escape Malkor and his team, what then? With Dolan searching Altair Tri no place could be considered safe. Like it or not, Malkor was still their best bet for survival. She helped Corinth into the nearest shuttle and climbed in after him.

5

Kayla's fears about the breadth of Malkor's influence were confirmed when the shuttle approached a luxury-class starcruiser that could only house a high-ranking member of the empire.

Damn. Now we're into it.

Still, being in space again, seeing the stars and escaping the oppressive atmosphere of Altair Tri, lightened her heart. They were infinitely closer to Wyrd Space once off the ground.

The shuttles docked with precision and Malkor ushered them into the starcruiser. Malkor's people peeled off, heading in different directions until only Corinth and Kayla followed him through the passageways. They entered a dead-end wing that contained living quarters of some sort, based on the evenly spaced door pattern.

"I only had one room readied."

"We'll share." Corinth seemed asleep on his feet and Kayla felt scarcely far behind.

Malkor placed his index finger on the scanner beside the door and the panels hissed open. The room surpassed the hovel they'd left behind in every detail, and it had a bed large enough for the two of them to sleep comfortably. The room was efficient and uncluttered, with most of the storage and furnishing units built into the walls. Two chairs created a sitting area to the right of the door and a console that appeared to become a desk when pulled out took up a large section of one wall.

What drew her attention, though, and what Corinth had already drifted toward as she'd studied the room, was the window port revealing a blaze of stars. Corinth's chin barely reached the sill but he drank in the sight.

Malkor motioned for her to join him in the hall. She glanced at the doors in this wing as she followed, counting quickly.

Eight. A well-trained team of eight people, a luxury-class starcruiser, shuttles at the top level of imperial tech. . .

She pitched her voice low, hoping it wouldn't carry to Corinth. "You're IDC, aren't you?" He must be the leader of an IDC octet. "When were you going to mention that?"

"Would you have agreed to work for me if you knew?"

She shook her head. "Given the choice I would never help the IDC achieve a goal, no matter how insignificant."

"You're helping me right now."

"I had a choice?" She stepped closer to Malkor, until she was less than arm's length away. "Tell me that if I had refused you when you came to the swamp you would have let me walk away. Tell me that it was my choice to be here."

Seconds passed with no response from Malkor. He stared at her, his lips pursed as if ready to speak the words, but they didn't come.

"I thought not."

"You are perfect for the mission," he offered finally, half compliment, half apology.

"And what the IDC wants. . ."

"Hey," he said, taking a half-step forward so they were toe to toe. "You're making a fortune on this deal, don't act like you're a victim."

"Yeah? Then where're my credits? So far I've got nothing but a promise from you."

"I'll give you half now, half when this is over. Deal?"

"Done."

"Done." He grinned as if he had trapped her into something. "Just give me your iden chip and I'll transfer the credits to you."

Tricky bastard. She grinned right back, with about as much friendliness. "I'll take the down payment in quad cubes, I don't mind carrying around that money."

"I *will* find out who you are." The certainty in his voice worried her. With the resources of the IDC at his disposal, how long could she keep her secret? And once he found out, what would happen to her and Corinth?

"Don't waste your time. I'm a pit whore from the slum side, that's all."

Before he could reply, a woman's voice interrupted from the open end of their wing.

"Malkor? What is going on?"

He stared at Kayla one last second before stepping back and turning his attention to the newcomer. "Princess Isonde." He inclined his head in greeting. "May I present Shadow Panthe? She has agreed to work with us."

Kayla shook off the worry about her identity, there was nothing she could do at the moment. Instead, she assessed the woman she'd be impersonating at the Empress Game. Isonde was tall and slender, nearly as tall as Kayla herself, and statuesque, with her auburn hair coiled neatly atop her head. She wore flowing white pants and a matching knee-length tunic, made from a material finer than anything Kayla had seen in the last five years. Slippers covered her feet. Considering the morning hour it was possible she had come straight from bed, though she looked as neat as a row of neuro-circuits.

Her gaze swept Kayla from head to toe. Pale blue eyes seemed to miss nothing, making Kayla acutely aware of her shabby clothing, the mud stains knee-high on her legs and the stink of the swamp clinging to her.

The princess did not offer a greeting and Kayla felt disinclined to be friendly. Malkor cleared his throat in the awkward silence that followed, drawing Isonde's attention once more.

"A word, Agent Rua, if you please."

Malkor didn't exactly hop at Isonde's request, but he did as she asked without hesitation. They shifted out of the octet's wing and into the main hall, though still within Kayla's earshot. Isonde didn't seem to care. Malkor, at least, kept his voice low.

"What have you done?" Isonde asked. "Why did you bring her here?"

"It wasn't my call, you know Ardin demanded it."

"He asked that you find someone to fight for me, but a pit whore, Malkor? A pit whore? For the love of— What were you thinking?"

"I was *thinking* that if you and Ardin want this insane scheme of yours to work, you need the best fighter. Shadow Panthe can win."

"I thought we agreed that one of the female IDC agents would work better."

"No," Malkor said definitively. "I'll not ask them to jeopardize their careers and their lives by being involved."

Did being a pit whore make her that expendable, that inconsequential? Where was the concern for her career, her life? And who did they think would look after Corinth if this entire fiasco went supernova?

"Besides," he continued, "Ardin wanted Shadow specifically."

"Only because you recommended her."

"The Empress Game is less than a month away now. Who else do you expect to find in time?"

Isonde glanced at her then, clearly unconcerned that she was listening. "Someone more respectable, at least. Damnit, Malkor, she's sleeping in the room right next to yours."

Did the woman think her a threat to Malkor's life or his chilly sheets? Maybe both.

Malkor sighed. "It's late. Or early, rather. Either way, it's been a long night and we all need to rest. I know you're stressed about the whole thing." He placed a hand on Isonde's arm in a familiar gesture and Kayla felt an odd dip in her stomach. Five years of loneliness, loss and homesickness hit her all at once. "Trust me," Malkor was saying, but Kayla couldn't watch the two of them together any longer.

She ducked inside the room she shared with Corinth. All her family in the universe stood at the viewport, soaking in the stars. Her whole world. She crossed the room and joined him.

Kayla came to consciousness like a bear waking from hibernation. Despite the strange environs and the uncertainty of her future, she'd just had her best rest in five years. The viewport showed the green-pink wash of a hyperspace stream as the starcruiser sped toward Falanar.

Her body told her it was late afternoon. The chronometer embedded in the wall indicated it was morning in the palace on the imperial homeworld. Her head declared it time for more information. Any plan to rig the Empress Game would require delicate maneuvering, thorough planning and more luck than she liked to depend on. Best learn all the details now.

She grabbed a clean outfit from her bag and headed to the bathroom. As she enjoyed the rippling sensation of the sonic shower she kept one thought in mind—that was the last time she'd have to settle for smelling like swamp fungus.

She dressed quickly, checking the mirror to make sure the shower hadn't stripped away too much of the oily black dye that hid her blue hair. She wrapped a clean *ashk* around her face, pulling the top edge up to just below her eyes. The garment was common on the slum side of Altair Tri. What once had felt odd and restrictive now felt like a shield. When she exited the bathroom, Corinth still lay sleeping on the bed, one hand fisted in the plush covers as if to keep someone from stealing them. At least he slept peacefully. Kayla couldn't be certain how long it would last, but she was glad of it. Her *il'haar* needed the rest.

She moved to the touch panel on the wall that controlled the doors' lock features. Advanced by imperial design, relatively rudimentary to a Wyrd. She pried the faceplate off with one of her kris, exposing the delicate interface beneath. She'd need finer tools than the point of her dagger to recalibrate the ID priority code, but Kayla never left home without such tools. One never knew where one might be required to break out of—or into—on any given day on the slum side.

Kayla fished the instruments from her pack and quickly realigned the allowable IDs. Satisfied the doors would only open for her—verified by a print scan—and that her fix wouldn't be as easily undone as the original programming, she snapped the faceplate back into place. Now she felt slightly more at ease leaving Corinth alone on a ship crawling with IDC agents.

Only very slightly.

She unfolded the complink console unit from the wall and typed Corinth a brief message. He'd had nothing more sophisticated to play with than the glorified abacus they'd rigged together. The complink unit, even with limited access to the imperial data field, would keep Corinth amused until she returned.

The minute she stepped out of her room the doors directly across from hers opened. Malkor filled the space, hands crossed over his chest.

"Going somewhere?"

He'd abandoned the illegal merch-runner outfit and looked at ease in what must be his IDC casuals: boots and loose black pants topped with a gray T-shirt. Pity. The merch-runner getup suited him.

"Looking for you."

He seemed skeptical.

"Are we going to chat in the hallway, or. . .?"

He pivoted on one foot, allowing her access to his quarters. Kayla slipped past him, tucking her arm in close to avoid touching him as she did.

"I'd ask if you want me to keep my door open," he gestured with a thumb toward her closed doors, "but I doubt you left your brother in there without rigging something first." Even still, he left his stance open and took a seat at his desk. "What should I call him?"

Kayla hadn't considered that. Corinth rarely left the swamp so he'd never needed an alias.

"Rinth." The word slipped out. Vayne had called their younger brother that.

"Rinth." Even as Malkor tried out the name, Kayla heard Vayne saying it and the familiar pang hit her chest. "And I can call you. . .?"

She gave him a flat look.

"Figured I'd ask one more time. Shadow Panthe is a bit much for everyday conversation, so we'll use your alias." He called up a file on his complink. It was no standard imperial citizen ID. She would be Lady Evelyn Broch, cousin to the ruling family on Piran—one of the Sovereign Planets, the six planets that had comprised the Sakien Empire at its inception. Other than the gray box where her picture would go, the ID looked complete.

"Lady Evelyn it is," he said. "We'll have to finalize it today so I can send the packet to IDC headquarters." His gaze took in the *ashk* that shielded her face, her rough tunic and serviceable, if drab, pants. "I'll also find something more appropriate for you to wear."

A flush crept up her neck. Urban vagrants didn't dress this poorly on Ordoch, and the needy were given cast-offs of higher quality than the clothing she and Corinth owned. Nothing like scrounging on the slum side for five years to really lower her standards.

"The same goes for Rinth. He'll need an ID badge if he's going to move about on Falanar."

Kayla shook her head. "I don't want him on the planet."

"I didn't think you'd want to be away from him. He could stay on the ship, I suppose. It'll be in orbit at the royal space dock."

Damnit. Neither option suited her. She didn't want to be separated from Corinth by kilometers of atmosphere, but they increased their risk of discovery ten-fold by being seen together.

"Let me think about it," she said.

"I could have one of my team watch him."

"Having an IDC agent oversee my brother's care doesn't give me a warm, fuzzy feeling."

Malkor frowned. "You're the one who insisted I bring him."

She paced away from the console, hands resting on the hilts of her kris. Same frustration, different day—how to keep her *il'haar* safe while doing what needed to be done to get them home.

"Lady Evelyn? Evelyn."

It took Kayla a minute to realize Malkor meant her. "What?"

His gaze dropped to her hands, now curled around the hilts of her kris. "Can I trust you loose on the ship, armed, without escort?"

"You mean, was I planning to assassinate one or several of the high-ranking guests on board?"

"Don't start with me, Shadow. Evelyn," he corrected. "Do I need to keep you under guard?"

"You could try, but I doubt they'd fare very well."

One touch on his complink and his doors hissed closed like the jaws of a hungry beast. Kayla forced herself not to react to the implied imprisonment. She released her grip on her daggers, though it went against the grain, and lowered herself into the nearest chair.

"I made a deal with you on Altair Tri," she said. "My participation in your mad scheme in exchange for a cargo-hold's worth of credits and a free ride to the planet of my choosing. I don't intend to break our deal." At least, not until a better option presented itself. "And I'm not about to harm anyone on board. . . unless it becomes necessary." Let him eat that.

"Your word?"

It was on her tongue to ask what the word of a pit whore was worth to an IDC agent, but his tone halted the sarcasm. For the first time since the massacre of her family someone offered to value whatever honor she possessed. Her much-abused pride refused to make a mockery of even so small a moment.

"You have it."

He touched the panel again and the doors slid open.

"Now that that's out of the way, what did you want to discuss?"

6

What was with the ashk? Malkor wondered. They were common on Altair Tri but it was hardly effective camouflage now that she was the only person wearing one.

"Tell me how you plan to pull off this ridiculous scheme of yours," she said.

Shadow—*Lady Evelyn*, he had to start thinking of her that way—perched on the edge of her chair. She didn't seem at ease, but he doubted she ever seemed at ease, even in that filthy hovel she'd called a home.

"I've set you up as a noble from Piran, Isonde's homeworld. You're her political ally, old friend and attendant for the Empress Game. We want it to seem natural for you to go everywhere Isonde does. The attendant is the only one allowed access to the pit with the contestants."

He lifted a canister from his desk and tipped the contents into his palm: a thin, flexible bioelectric strip about the width and length of his index finger. Rigger had dropped the prototype off less than an hour ago—still a work in progress. "We're counting on a high-quality hologram to allow you and Isonde to switch places for the actual fighting."

Shadow scrutinized the biostrip, and even without seeing the rest of her features he sensed her hesitation. He placed the strip across the base of his throat and it stuck there. It felt warm at first, while the organic membrane adhered to the skin, then nothing.

He glanced down. Sure enough, Isonde sat in his place, wearing his IDC casuals. He knew too well the shape of her, by sight and feel, not to recognize her form.

"Very pretty," Shadow murmured dryly.

"Rigger is good." The words came out in Isonde's alto timbre. "Very good." Malkor had heard her voice a million times, recognized every nuance of her tone. Rigger's voice replicant program matched perfectly.

Kayla rose and approached. "That hologram will fool everyone at a distance and most people up close, especially since the princess and I are very similar in size." She lifted her arm but paused with her fingers outstretched. The hesitation lasted only a moment, then she placed her hand on his shoulder. Heat radiated from her palm and fingers where they curled lightly over him. He glanced at her hand, resting on the empty air ten centimeters above the image of Isonde's shoulder.

"It would be less pronounced on me, but I am still a hair taller than the princess. Any fighter skilled enough to compete in the Empress Game will notice that. Or this." She moved her hand to just above Isonde's elbow, landing on his actual forearm. She angled her fingers to slide beneath the sleeve of his T-shirt but the fabric remained undisturbed as she passed through it.

She snorted. "Apparently Rigger isn't that good. Clothing often gets rearranged in a fight. One match in this hologram and we'd be finished."

Malkor peeled the strip from his neck, breaking the illusion, and she backed away.

"Obviously it's not finished yet," he said.

"I hope not. Assuming you have top-level technology at your disposal, I recommend a multi-layer, stress-reactive, integrated living matter replicant."

He could only stare. Of course he knew what she meant, but never in a hundred light-years had he expected those words to come out of her mouth. His suspicion that there was more to this pit whore than a love of kris daggers was irrevocably confirmed.

"Who are you, really?"

"Apparently I'm Lady Evelyn Broch, of the Sovereign Planet Piran."

She had to have sky-high clearance to have experience with that kind of tech. A deep-cover spy? "Where were you before the Blood Pit?"

"None of your damn business. I agreed to help your princess win the Empress Game, not answer all of your questions." She put her hands on her hips. "What other security measures are there? It can't be as easy as a hologram or every princess would have her own body-double."

"No, the hologram is only one part of it. Each contestant is both routinely and randomly scanned to confirm their ID. The scan consists of a palm-print analysis, retinal scan and DNA verification."

"Before and after each fight?"

He nodded. "And randomly, any time day or night, at the IDC's discretion."

"The IDC is in charge of the Game?"

"Being the diplomatic arm of the imperial government, we have the most experience with each of the contestants. The IDC is responsible for ensuring the Game's validity by confirming entrant IDs."

"The scan before the fight would be easy enough to defeat," she said. "A biofilm composed of the princess's DNA and stamped with her handprint would work."

"The IDC will be looking for just such a thing. Anything thick enough to prevent your DNA from contaminating the palm-print would be noticed."

"Depends what it's made out of," she said offhand, as though her mind were absorbed by another problem. "Certain synthetic polymer combinations are virtually undetectable." She shook her head. "That wouldn't solve the problem of the scan after the match, though. Those polymers dissolve within thirty minutes of skin contact and there's no telling how soon before the fight you'd have to apply it."

He'd never heard of such technology, and if the IDC wasn't employing it he wasn't sure it existed. Although, the criminal element within the empire was always on the cutting edge of ID hijacking...

"Our plan for the print scan is more long term," he said. "Once you've been initially identified as Lady Evelyn, Rigger will access your file and set up a looping pathway between yours and Princess Isonde's IDs that will temporarily switch your DNA, retinal and print information whenever the pathway is activated."

"Activated how?"

"By applying the biostrip hologram. The IDs switch back when you remove it."

She nodded, apparently approving that part of the plan. "At least you've thought this out. Why am I not surprised that an IDC agent has a plan to fix the very game he's supposed to be keeping cheat-free?" She glanced toward the closed door that led to her quarters, formerly Hekkar's room. "I should go, my brother will likely wake soon. You'll talk to Rigger about the new hologram?"

"She'll be hearing plenty from me, don't you worry."

"She certainly showed you up, didn't she?" Ardin said.

Malkor glanced at his long-time friend and future emperor, Prince Ardin de Soliqual. He had summarized his earlier meeting with Shadow Panthe for Ardin, who seemed rather amused by the entire hologram episode.

"You should offer her a position with the IDC, Malk. Fighting skills, advanced technical knowledge, thinks quick on her feet—she'd be an asset."

Malkor frowned, recalling their earlier conversation. "There's the small fact that she, in her words, 'would never help the IDC achieve a goal, no matter how insignificant.'"

The prince sobered. "Can she be trusted? If our plan fails, the balance of power in the Council of Seven swings back to my father. Isonde's life will be forfeit for her part in the deception. I—" Ardin halted, taking a deep breath. "That can't happen. You must be absolutely certain."

"I'm as certain as we're going to get. Anyone who's motivated by something *other* than a fervent desire to place the best empress on the throne is a liability," Malkor said. "Shadow has much to gain by helping us, and she seems to have committed to the scheme. All we can do is wait and see."

"That does not ease my mind."

"If it helps, I trust her intention is to keep the deal." For now. She had accepted his terms under duress. He was prepared for her loyalty to switch if a similar pressure was applied again.

"You, the ever-suspicious, oh-so-cautious Malkor trusts someone from Altair Tri's slum side?" A speculative gleam came into Ardin's eyes that Malkor didn't appreciate. "I'll have to meet this pit whore for myself."

"Don't call her that."

Ardin arched a brow at Malkor's tone.

"Her fighting skills are only part of the equation. We need to convince everyone that she's Lady Evelyn, Isonde's attendant, or it won't matter how well she fights. Start treating her that way now so it's more natural when we arrive on Falanar."

That and hearing someone else call Shadow a pit whore irritated him. She was more—he just had to figure out if that was a good or a bad thing.

"Fair enough, though you know Isonde won't like it."

Malkor shrugged. "She'll get over it. I don't know who she thought we were going to find for a body-double, Shadow Panthe was always our best bet. Same size and body shape, excellent fighting skills, anonymous outside of her own sphere on Altair Tri, and willing to risk everything for the right amount of credits." That last wasn't strictly true, which begged the question: why had she been hiding out in the Blood Pit?

"She'll—" Ardin broke off when the door to his chambers opened. Even without looking Malkor knew who had arrived. The reverent expression on Ardin's face said it all.

Isonde.

Malkor himself had worn that same look, longing mixed with furtive hope, when Isonde had walked into the room so many times before. She greeted them casually, as elegant and refined as ever in an emerald gown. Her auburn hair was pulled in a loose chignon at the nape of her neck and a single silver chain encircled her throat.

She chose a seat halfway between the two of them. "What have we been discussing?"

"Your newest attendant, Lady Evelyn Broch," Malkor said. She gave him a blank look. "The fighter we hired on Altair Tri."

"Oh, the pit whore?"

Malkor frowned. "The fighter. Her identity is Lady Evelyn."

"Quite the jump in position. I think Miss Evelyn would do fine."

After days of recon on Altair Tri, nights spent at the Blood Pit and a trek through Fengar Swamp, Malkor was in no mood to be diplomatic. "You're not usually such an uptight snob, Isonde. What's your problem with the lady?"

He had the satisfaction of seeing Ardin wince. Isonde seemed taken aback, but they had grown up together in the emperor's court. He'd known her too long—and too intimately—to dance around a subject.

"Did you want to do your own fighting at the Empress Game?" he asked. "I assure you that though she agreed to my terms, *Lady Evelyn* is by no means excited about the prospect."

"Don't be ridiculous," Isonde snapped. "I don't stand a chance and you know it."

"Then what's the problem?"

"I just—" She made a frustrated sound. "It's this whole thing."

Malkor held up a hand. "Hey, you two cooked up this plan. I'm happy to scrap it."

"There's no other way," Isonde said.

"I still don't see why the two of you don't just marry," the word stuck in his throat, but he forced it out, "and damn the Empress Game."

"We already put forth several proposals to both the Sovereign and Protectorate Councils to suspend the Game," Ardin said. "No one liked the idea of the heir choosing his own mate. The empress-apparent wields too much power in the Council of Seven for them to give up the hope of placing one of their own daughters in the role."

Ardin had dreamed of wedding Isonde as long as the three had known each other, almost as long as Malkor had. If there was a way around Isonde needing to win the Empress Game to validate a marriage, Ardin would have found it.

"The plan is fine," Isonde said, "but how can we trust this. . . fighter? She's from a Protectorate Planet, for starters. Most have only been in the empire for one or two generations, their loyalty is tentative at best. And she's a pit whore. She brutalizes people for money. You want to let a woman like that run loose?"

She glanced from Malkor to Ardin, seeking support.

"You don't know how she became a pit whore," Malkor found himself arguing. "It's likely she had no other choice."

Ardin agreed. "There aren't many honorable professions available to a woman on Altair Tri."

"Is this the kind of woman you want to entrust the fate of the empire to?" Isonde asked.

"I am entrusting the fate of the empire to you and Ardin," Malkor countered. "*That's* why I agreed to this outrageous scheme in the first place, because I believe the two of you, working together to control the Council of Seven, are the only chance the empire has to become something worth believing in again.

"If you're asking me if I believe Lady Evelyn can be trusted to win the Empress Game for us, then my answer is yes." Or something close to yes, at this point.

Malkor switched his gaze to Ardin. "You both need to let me do my job and trust that I know what I'm doing or this will never work."

One of Ardin's guards commed the room. "My prince? There's someone here to speak to Senior Agent Rua."

Malkor looked at his two closest friends, gauging their moods. "Are we good here?"

Ardin nodded right away, but it was Isonde that Malkor watched. She'd have plenty to say later. Isonde was as verbose as she was intelligent, and would have strong opinions on how a scheme that could end in her own death was run. Opinions he valued, but he needed to know that she would back him, trust him to handle the details.

She finally nodded.

Ardin tapped the comm panel. "Send them in."

The doors opened to reveal Shadow Panthe standing in the gap. She looked even shabbier next to the two royals than she had earlier in his room. Her posture, however, was every bit as proud.

Ardin's guards came in behind her, their attention split between the prince and the daggers Shadow's hands rested on. Ardin waved the guards back outside.

"Agent Rua. I require a place to train."

Well, she certainly doesn't waste any time.

"Lady Evelyn, may I present Prince Ardin de Soliqual, eldest son of Emperor Rengal, heir to the Sakien Empire. I believe you've met Princess Isonde already."

Shadow Panthe's gaze barely skimmed Isonde. She studied Ardin longer, then gave him the barest of nods. She immediately returned her attention to Malkor. From the corner of his eye he caught Ardin's surprise at being so easily dismissed.

"I'm assuming you have a suitable space on board?"

"With Isonde available, now is a good time to go over some other aspects of your role. What's expected of an attendant, the people you're likely to meet, who to avoid—"

"No."

Isonde blinked. "Pardon?"

Shadow shrugged one shoulder. "We can go over that later. Right now I need to train."

"This is important," Isonde said.

Shadow finally turned her full attention on Isonde, who sat straighter when that cold blue gaze fell on her. "No doubt. All the subterfuge in the world won't win you your emperor, though. When it comes down to it, the only thing that matters is if I can beat your opponents in the ring, one on one."

The two women stared at each other, locked in a battle of wills. Something passed unspoken between them. Likely the determination of Shadow's stare impressed upon Isonde her dedication to the cause. Isonde gave a sharp nod and rose from her chair. "Malkor, find her some place to practice. We'll talk later."

7

Malkor escorted Shadow through the ship and into a magchute that would bring them to the recreation deck of the starcruiser. The magchute's module was a little tight for two people when one of them was intent on keeping her distance from the other. Malkor studied Shadow from the corner of his eye, trying to piece her puzzle together.

Her cheaply dyed hair was completely incongruous. Her minimalist dress code and insistence on wearing an *ashk* already played down her beauty, what did she care about her hair? Why color it? His gaze drifted lower, over her body. She needed new clothing, something more fashionable and form-fitting to pull off the Lady Evelyn disguise.

"If you want a black eye you're headed the right way." She dropped a hand to her nearest kris but remained staring directly ahead.

The module decelerated and the doors opened, saving him from comment. He motioned for her to precede him into the hallway.

She paused in the entry to the practice room when she spotted Trinan and Vid working out at the far end. Not surprising to find those two here. They had more energy between them than a pulsar. At least they burned some of it off constructively.

Vid and Trinan stopped what they were doing and there was an odd sort of standoff between them and Shadow. Then

Trinan grinned, Vid gave a short salute and they went back to working out. That seemed to relax her.

Ardin had outfitted the practice room well, with space and equipment enough for the octet.

"Use whatever you like," Malkor said.

She walked to the farthest sparring ring, stripping off her tunic as she went to reveal her muscled back and the black halter top he remembered from the pit. She pulled her hair into a high ponytail before starting a warm-up.

He'd meant to escort her and leave, stars knew he had enough work waiting. Instead he perched on a weight bench, watching her, judging the fighter he'd pinned their hopes on. Her warm-up ramped quickly, footwork sequences and light cardio transitioning to hand and foot techniques. Those gave way to full-speed punches and knifehands, spinning aerial kicks and tumbling drops. From there she pulled her daggers and began blade work. Trinan and Vid gave up pretending to work out and came to stand beside him.

Shadow finished her last kata and turned quickly, catching them staring. She lifted her chin with a look that said, "What— you think you can do better?" She twitched her ponytail over her shoulder and made her way back to them. When she reached their group she squared herself off, shoulders front, appraising them each before settling her gaze on Malkor.

"I need an opponent to spar."

Both Trinan and Vid stepped forward with their typical enthusiasm for action and Shadow shied away minutely. "A female opponent. It is the *Empress* Game, after all."

"Of course." Malkor pulled his mobile comm and entered his agent, Janeen's code. "Care to spar?" was all he needed to ask when she answered the page.

"Uh, Malk. . ." Trinan said. "You sure about this?" He glanced at Shadow. "It might be a little. . . soon."

"Janeen'll be fine."

Shadow arched a brow but remained quiet. The group waited in awkward silence until the doors to the rec room opened and Janeen Nuagyn strode through. She greeted the men with a smile that turned predatory when she spotted Shadow Panthe.

One of the three capable women in Malkor's octet, Janeen could hold her own with the boys, even best some of them, like Gio. She was tough, rough and tumble, and looked built like a boar next to Shadow's sleek frame. A shorter boar, perhaps.

She heckled Trinan and Vid good-naturedly for standing around doing nothing in the rec room, then turned her attention to Malkor.

"Are you in the mood for a match, boss?" She stood ready to offer a challenge. She'd taken him to the ground more than once.

"Not today. Would you be willing to work with Lady Evelyn?"

"Absolutely." Something of her light-heartedness faded. "I would love to spar with her."

Shadow rested her hands on the pommels of her kris, sizing Janeen up. She nodded, as if to say "she'll do," and walked back to the practice ring. "Warm up," she called over her shoulder.

With Janeen heading after Shadow, Vid closed the distance between him and Malkor. "I'm not sure this is a good idea. Janeen's still sore after your decision."

"She'll get over it. She has to learn to work with Shadow anyway."

"I thought we were going with Lady Evelyn now?"

"We are. It's just—" He gestured toward the ring. Shadow's muscled back rippled as she stretched her arms over her head. "Does she look like a Lady Evelyn?"

They fell silent as the women began to spar.

He'd seen Janeen fight a thousand times, knew her style, so he watched Shadow instead. Not because her pants rode low on perfectly curved hips or because her top left nearly every centimeter of her taut abdomen bare. He'd do well to learn her strengths and weaknesses. Any tips he might provide could make the difference in winning the Game.

She was quick, but he'd seen that. What he hadn't noticed before was her strength. She could hold her own when the fight turned to grappling, and Janeen brought to bear the maximum force a body her size could muster.

She was also aggressive. Where Janeen took her time, circling, waiting for the right moment, Shadow forced an opening. She came first, never letting Janeen get comfortable in her stance or allowing her time to plan an attack. She pounced, springing before Janeen could figure her out, overpowering her before Janeen could counter. After half an hour, Shadow had had enough.

"This is your best?" she called to him.

Malkor winced at the slight to Janeen. Shadow approached, the fabric of her *ashk* moving in and out rapidly as she breathed. Sweat gleamed on her forehead and slicked her ponytail back. "Or do you have someone else?"

"I have only my octet with me." And while Rigger and Aronse were tough, neither woman would offer her a real challenge.

"I don't suppose you have a virtual deck on board? Not the same as fighting an actual person, but I need some competition, not a playmate."

"Try me."

Her gaze snapped to him. He could only guess at her expression beneath the *ashk*.

"And lose the mask."

She brushed her fingers against the cloth as if to check its position, shaking her head.

"You'll have to lose it some time." When she didn't comply, he shot a look at Vid. His fellow agents left to check on Janeen. He stepped closer and she held her ground.

"What are you afraid of?"

"Nothing." She flexed and unflexed her right hand as if stretching her fingers. "It's just. . . comfortable."

"No it isn't. It makes me claustrophobic to look at you."

"Then don't."

"Shadow—" He caught himself before treating her like a

subordinate. "You don't need it. Whoever you hid from on Tri, whyever you buried yourself in that pit, it's over." Was it? Did he need to be looking over her shoulder?

A bitter chuckle escaped her.

"Fight me for it," he said. "You win, I won't bother you about the *ashk* until we reach Falanar. I win, you burn it."

"Deal."

"Do you need to rest first, or. . .?"

She shot him a look of disgust and headed back to the practice circle.

Kayla glanced at Malkor, who walked beside her. She rarely fought an opponent so large, and never males as well-trained as she assumed he was. How tough would he be to beat?

"Shall we say barehanded, first takedown?" he asked, when they stopped opposite each other in the ring.

With his greater mass he'd have that all over her. One bull-rush and his momentum alone would win him the day.

"Best of five."

He raised his eyebrows. "Sure you have that in you?"

"Do you?"

"Five it is."

The others might have gathered to watch but they faded from her mind. Only Malkor remained, drawing all of her attention when he sank into a casual but ready stance, arms up, hands loose.

She nodded to indicate she was ready and he lunged forward, driving into her with the force of a maglev train, knocking her on her ass.

Ugh. Nice to know she'd been right about the bull-rush.

She ignored the hand-up he offered and sprang to her feet, resisting the urge to rub her stinging rump.

First point, Malkor.

When he tried the same thing a second time, she was ready. She sidestepped, swept his leg and shoved him between the shoulder blades as he passed. *Wham*—one IDC agent face-down on the mat.

Now *that* was satisfying. *Did she need time to rest?* Pfft.

He sprang to his feet, looking surprised enough that she almost laughed. "Got that out of your system?" she asked. "Maybe we can use some actual technique now?"

He smiled, a little ruefully. "I suppose so." He readied himself again and this time Kayla settled in for a more serious contest. He was big, but not heavy on his feet. He had a lightness to his step that she could admire. They circled, trading blows here and there, testing each other.

"I watched you with Janeen," he said, "how you controlled that fight. Not every opponent is going to be shorter than you." He double-stepped and made a grab for her wrist but she evaded and sent him back with a kick to the ribs.

"I know that." She looked him in the eyes, watching his footwork, waiting for an off-balance step.

"Do you? You're used to the women on Altair Tri, but they grow them big on some of the Sovereign Planets." He shifted stances, flowing from one to the next.

She followed his movements. "Are you *lecturing* me?" His guard was excellent, there didn't seem to be an opening.

"Let's call it 'helping.'"

"You can take your help and—"

He shifted to a weaker stance to dodge a fist to the temple and she had him on his counter. He attacked off his lead foot and as he stepped forward she blocked, turned into him and wrapped an arm behind his back. She gripped the back of his belt in one hand, his forearm in the other and bent forward at the knees, using his own force to hoist him on to her back for a nanosecond. She straightened her legs and torqued away from him at the waist, throwing him off one hip.

Stars, he was solid. She'd barely gotten him off his feet long enough to down him.

"—shove it up your ass," she finished, panting with more effort than she wanted to admit to.

He rolled with it when he hit the mat and she heard a chuckle. "So you don't like advice. Noted." He took a minute to catch his breath, and this time when he pushed to his feet he looked ready for a serious fight. A leave-them-on-the-floor-wondering-where-half-their-teeth-went kind of fight.

Now we're talking.

It was something of a joy to her to be sparring again. To be fighting with her full capabilities without fear of killing or maiming someone, without the jeers of spectators deafening her, without the threat of death looming over every move. There was something pure in it.

Just her, him, and the overwhelming need to kick someone's ass.

Her mentor might have bided her time and waited for the perfect opening, but Kayla had never been that patient. She took the fight to Malkor in a series of spinning kicks, backing him around the ring as he moved to avoid them. He had her backing off just as quickly with his return kicks. One kick glanced off her block with bone-jarring force and she grinned. He showed the true measure of his respect for her skills by coming at her full-force.

Kayla closed with him, trading punches, overhand strikes and elbows almost faster than they could block, and all the while she looked for the chance to hook his lead leg and pull it out from under him. When the opening came, she stepped into it, only to be clocked in the face by a knifehand that hit her cheek so hard her world blanked for a second. Then, he tilted.

No, she tilted, as he hooked *her* leg out from under *her* and flipped her on her ass.

He leaned over her where she lay on her back. "You okay?"

Pain pulsed in her cheek and her head hurt from striking the mat. Man, that was going to need some ice. "I like your order of operations there: score the point, *then* ask if I'm okay."

His lips quirked. "Priorities."

She took the hand-up he offered, letting him anchor her while she got to her feet.

"Last point," he said. "You still up for it?"

She dropped back into a ready stance. "If you ask me if I'm okay one more time, I'm going to kick you in the balls."

He shook his head, getting set in his own stance. "That's dirty."

"You'll have it coming."

They circled, more cautious than before. She considered and rejected techniques she normally used. Several depended on a superior height and reach to be most effective. With his higher center of gravity, how good was his balance? Exactly how much stronger was he? Did he rely more on his upper or lower body? These were things she didn't know how to gauge in a man.

They traded a few blows, deflected automatically as they each tried to find an opening.

Maybe if she. . . She shook her head.

How about. . . That wouldn't work either.

Last point. She'd be damned if she'd lose this fight.

He feinted in her direction and she skittered away. His gaze followed her every step, practically radiating anticipation as he threw jabs with enough speed to daze her should they connect. She offered a half-hearted side-piercing kick to keep him at bay, not finding anything to work with.

Time ticked away in the fight, and like always for her, the minutes lost were painful. She should have won by now. *Patience*, she imagined her mentor muttering.

Frutt patience.

She stabbed with her right, a spearhand to the throat intended to knock the breath from him. He caught her wrist, yanking her off-balance and spinning her around so her arm wrapped across her own neck. When she tried to elbow him in the ribs he pinned it between them by snaking his other arm around her waist and pulling her tight to him. He placed his knee at the back of hers, ready to push forward and take her leg out from under her in a second.

He pulled down on her right wrist, the arm across her throat tilting her head back until it rested against his shoulder.

With her head trapped she couldn't drop her weight and slip out of his grasp. With his knee behind hers she couldn't risk lifting her free leg to kick back because he'd take her down in an instant.

His breath at her ear rasped in time with hers. She tensed for one last struggle and his grip tightened.

"Don't make me down you, Shadow."

He was definitely quicker than she'd anticipated—something to remember when their alliance eventually dissolved.

If she could get a heel strike off on his instep, she might surprise him just enough to break free. There was a less than one percent chance of that, she reasoned, but a *ro'haar* never surrendered willingly. She shifted her weight in preparation for the move and he sensed it. His knee slammed into the back of hers, crumpling her leg. She pitched all her weight into the forward motion of her collapse and dragged him down with her until they crashed into the ground, his weight crushing her into the mat.

"I win," he said.

The wind had been knocked from her lungs in the fall and it took her a second to reply. "How do you figure?" she croaked out.

"I downed you, last point to me." He rolled off of her into a sitting position.

She took a few deeper breaths before pushing herself up to squat on her haunches. "If you'll notice, we're both down."

"Ah, but I came out on top."

"A technicality." She wiped sweat from her forehead with the back of her wrist. "I never concede defeat on a technicality." He'd plastered her to the mat on that one and they both knew it. A lucky break, on his part. If he hadn't caught her spearhand before it struck his throat he'd have been bent over, gasping for air when she kneed him in the face and knocked him to the ground. This close and she'd have won outright.

"You're calling a draw, then?" he asked with a smile.

She smiled in return, but of course he couldn't see it with her *ashk* covering her mouth. "Seems only fair."

Quiet settled between them while they caught their breath. His arms were marked up and down with red welts from blocking her attacks, and she was no less marked by him. It had been an even fight. A satisfying fight, she realized with surprise.

She rose and stepped away from him at the unsettling thought. He got to his feet, clearly catching something of her mood change.

"We don't have to be adversaries," he said.

"What would you call us, then?" The question hung so long she thought he wouldn't answer.

"Would partners be so far out of the question?"

She arched a brow. Partners. With this man? *With the IDC*, she reminded herself.

"Allies, at least," he said, with a hint of persuasion. "We're in this together now, working toward the same goal."

True. And as much as she hated to admit it, she needed him. Needed his credits and his promise of transportation to Wyrd Space. Needed to trust him, if only a little, now that she'd thrown in her lot with his. She'd need an ally once they landed on Falanar.

She reached for the ties that held her *ashk* in place, fingers hesitant as she worked at the knots. Five years she had worn this mask like a shield, five years it had protected her. She took a deep breath as the last knot slipped free and the black fabric fell to the ground. "Allies it is."

Their unexpected camaraderie lasted until they arrived at the wing that housed the octet.

"Why don't we—" Malkor started, but she shut out his voice. The doors to her room down the corridor were open.

She exploded into a sprint to the doorway.

"Corinth!"

Corinth sat at the complink terminal, a single IDC agent looming over him. She launched herself at the agent and tackled her to the ground. Kayla drew a kris from its thigh sheath and pressed it to the agent's throat in one smooth motion.

"What are you doing here!" she shouted.

"Shadow!"

::Kayla!::

Malkor and Corinth's voices overlapped with matching tones of alarm, heard only distantly.

"Why are you here!" She recognized the agent as Rigger, probably the most benign of the octet. She pinned the woman's body beneath hers with her weight and drew back her free hand to punch Rigger when she didn't answer quickly enough. Someone grabbed Kayla's elbow from behind before she could, but that wasn't what stopped her.

Corinth stopped her. He was there. Ephemeral. He hadn't moved, but she *felt* him, pushing on her with no more force than the weight of a stone in her hand.

His telekinetic powers had emerged? And he used them to protect the IDC agent?

She looked up, searching Corinth for any sign of harm.

::It's all right, Kayla, I'm fine. She wasn't trying to hurt me.::

The fingers on her elbow tightened like a vise. "Shadow."

She looked down at Rigger, who seemed stunned more than anything else.

::It's okay, please don't hurt her.::

She jerked her arm from Malkor's grasp and leveraged herself off of Rigger, dagger still in hand.

Rigger sprang to her feet as quickly. "What the frutt was that all about?" She brought one hand to her neck, testing for blood. "Are you insane, woman?" She looked at Malkor. "You have to be frutting kidding me with this bullshit. I was just talking to the kid."

"Why?" Malkor barked.

"I thought he might be lonely." Rigger turned her attention back to Kayla. "I was keeping him company, which I would have explained if you'd given me two seconds before attacking, you banshee."

::She means it, Kayla.::

Corinth's voice cut off her angry retort. "How did you get in?" Kayla asked instead.

Rigger pointed to Corinth. "He—"

::I let her in.::

"You did what?!"

::Kayla—::

"Everyone out. Now." Her gaze locked on her brother. She felt the agents hesitate, then make their way out, eyes on her the whole way. Malkor murmured, "We'll talk later," as he passed. The doors to her room shut after them, leaving silence in their wake.

Kayla's bloodlust raged. Her heartbeat slammed her ribs and she gripped her kris until her knuckles turned white. Even seeing Corinth there, unmolested, couldn't quell the choking fear. An IDC agent had been here, in her room, with her *il'haar* while she'd left him alone. Anything could have happened.

::She didn't want to hurt me.::

"You don't know that."

Corinth was again eight years old in her mind, clinging to her in terror when she'd found him beneath the bodies of his twin and his aunt. They'd died saving him, and he'd watched every second.

The image dissolved and she saw him as he was now: thirteen, nervous, but unafraid.

::Yes, I do. She doesn't know to guard her thoughts from me. When she commed the door I sensed only curiosity and an underlying empathy, nothing more.::

"You can't trust them, Corinth."

::You're the one who told me I need to have faith in my abilities. Should I not have trusted myself?::

He needed her validation now, her approval. She wanted to protest that her instincts were superior and that he should rely on hers, but that wouldn't be fair. He was a Wyrd. He had his psi powers even if hers were gone. Something had made him trust Rigger enough to open the door.

She sheathed her dagger, drawing a deep breath and trying to expel her adrenaline on the exhale. Her hands shook the slightest bit.

"What did she want, then?"

::She thought I might be lonely. She honestly came to look in on me.::

"Nothing more?"

He shook his head. ::She was. . . nice. And!:: He scurried back to the complink. ::She gave me access to more of the ship's database!::

Kayla scoffed, her tension easing. "You could have gotten that on your own."

::I don't know, she had some pretty sophisticated counter-looping blocking the pathway algorithms. They siphoned the code into nanosections that intersected at irregular intervals to form the basecode for the security. It reminds me of the time Vayne—:: He looked over his shoulder at her. ::Sorry.::

She shook her head, using the motion to cover the stab of pain. "It's all right." But it wasn't. And it would never be.

::Did you. . . feel anything? When you attacked her?:: His voice held a guarded hope.

She released the last of her worries and focused her full attention on Corinth. "I did. Did you reach out?"

::Yes! Just like we'd discussed. It was hard. And tiring. But, you felt it? I've been trying for so long.::

She needed to get him back to Wyrd Space. His telekinetic powers should have manifested long before this, and he should already be very comfortable with them, able to affect objects and even unsuspecting humans. His force should have stopped her, not just surprised her.

"Tell me about it."

8

"**N**o Match Found."

The nil query results didn't surprise Malkor. The criminal database on Altair Tri resembled mesh, with more holes than substance. He tapped his finger on his desk, considering his next query. A database search for "Blood Pit" this morning had turned up dozens of citations for violations on every health and safety concern imaginable, but only the owner was listed on the complaints. A search of the criminal activity logs for "Shadow Panthe" came back empty. The slum side was policed in such a desultory fashion it was amazing they kept a database at all.

Where to go from here? He'd snapped an image of Shadow earlier for her imperial ID and run facial recognition comparisons on it, trying to match anything in Altair Tri's criminal or registered citizens databases—nothing. "Corinth" was such a common name as to be useless without anything beyond a rough age range to compare.

Time to expand the parameters.

His mobile comm chirped, reminding him he was late for a meeting with Isonde. He set up a search for Shadow throughout the entire registered imperial citizens database, in case Altair Tri hadn't synched their list with central lately. That would take the better part of an hour—he would have to wait to sate his curiosity about her identity, especially if he had to gain clearance to search higher-level, restricted personal files.

One last glance at her picture provided only more questions. *Who are you?*

Kayla stared unseeing at the pink-green blur of the hyperstream through space as she rested on the viewport sill in her chambers. *Blip-chirp*s from the complink were familiar and reassuring, and she didn't have to worry about Corinth for once, knowing he was happily engaged raiding the ship's system logs.

Their conversation yesterday came to mind. Apparently Rigger *had* truly come to keep Corinth company. She hadn't minded that Corinth didn't speak. She'd carried on a conversation for the two of them, talking aloud without expecting responses while she showed Corinth how to access the ship's databanks. She'd been natural and friendly, and, from what Kayla could gather, Corinth actually *liked* her.

Liked. IDC.

She shook her head. Her *il'haar* would be on his own for a large portion of this escapade. More than just protection, he needed interaction. Mental stimulation. They'd lived like prisoners of war for the last five years despite having escaped the enemy, and being deprived of simple human company had hurt them both. Spending that time with Rigger, little though it was, had been novel and fascinating for Corinth. He wanted more. He had, in an unprecedented show of temper, demanded it. He needed someone other than Kayla for company. Someone who could challenge him in ways she couldn't, who could teach him things she hadn't the knowledge or the time for.

Damnit. Now she'd have to apologize to Rigger.

And, worse than that, allow the agent access to her *il'haar*, if indeed she even wanted to spend time with Corinth after Kayla's reaction earlier. At least Rigger, as part of an IDC octet, was not completely useless as a bodyguard.

Their comm unit issued a high-pitched *beep*, making Kayla jump.

"Lady Evelyn?"

Octet leader and IDC Senior Agent Malkor Rua. Her new ally.

"Are you available to meet with me and Princess Isonde?"

::Go ahead:: Corinth smiled at her. ::I'm happy here.::

She nodded to indicate she'd heard, then crossed her chamber to the comm unit. "Sure. I need to have a word with Rigger first, though."

Malkor and Kayla stopped at Rigger's quarters where she scraped out an apology and offered an invitation for the agent to join them for dinner after her meeting. Kayla was as surprised that she agreed as Rigger clearly was that she'd asked. They could both thank Corinth for that bit of awkwardness.

Kayla followed Malkor down the hall and let the reality that she'd just invited an IDC agent to dinner with her *il'haar* sink in, trying not to feel like she had bared him to enemy fire. Corinth had a "good feeling" about Rigger, he'd said. Though Vayne had said that many times and he'd always been right, Corinth's assertion didn't calm her nerves.

Vayne she trusted. Vayne knew people. Vayne had been trained since birth to use his impressive psi powers.

But Corinth?

This was the IDC. The same IDC who had come to Ordoch with Dolan under the pretense of requesting aid. The IDC who had instead killed her parents when they refused to help. The IDC who had staged a coup, murdered her elder brother and sister, Corinth's twin, her untwinned aunts and sisters, and ripped half of her soul from her when they executed Vayne.

A warm hand touched her arm and she jerked away.

"Are you all right?"

Malkor's voice. She'd fallen into the past and forgotten where she was. Her face must have betrayed her emotions.

She took a deep breath, trying to expel the festering hurt, to shake loose the memories. Malkor hadn't killed her family. *He is IDC*, part of her mind argued. *Were they all to blame?* she argued back.

"Sorry," she said.

"No, my fault. I startled you." He hesitated, then rested his hand gently on her arm again, watching her face for any warning sign. His touch centered her firmly in the present.

"I'm fine," she said, as much to herself as to him.

"You're not fine, Shadow."

"You have to stop calling me that."

"Tell me your name."

"Evelyn. Lady Evelyn of Piran."

He frowned, looking ready to push the issue. Instead his fingers slid down her arm as his hand fell aside. They regained their former distance. "My apologies, *Lady Evelyn*. We shouldn't keep Isonde waiting."

They walked in silence to the royal lounge and Kayla wrestled the past to the darkest corner of her mind, where it belonged. Her mission loomed in front of her: win the Empress Game.

Malkor nodded to the guards at the door who commed the room to announce them.

What passed for a royal lounge on Prince Ardin's starcruiser was not what she expected. There were no fountains, menageries, VR platforms, draka tables or cliques of courtiers. It was deficient in opulence, aroma, atmosphere and decadence.

She found she liked it.

The rectangular room might have been as large as her bedchamber and Malkor's combined. Soft cream walls, paired with a maroon cane-fiber carpet and helio light sconces, made for a warm, almost cozy, interior. A bank of couches lined one corner, fronted by a low table covered with datapads and the remainder of a meal. A cluster of hoverchairs sat together nearby, currently at rest, and a large meeting table dominated the other end of the room. Immense viewports showcasing the pink-green hyperstream lightened the wall opposite the door.

All of this she noted peripherally, her attention focused on the woman commanding Malkor's attention in the center of the room.

Her doppelganger, Princess Isonde.

Isonde scanned her head to toe, seeming to look for anything out of place. Kayla gained satisfaction from knowing she looked immaculate. A garmenter had outfitted her this morning with clothes befitting her new station, and she'd dressed with more care today than she'd employed in the last five years combined. When Kayla arched a brow as if to say, "done?" Isonde looked away, tilting her face toward Malkor.

"So that's where you've been," she said.

"I thought now would be a good time to discuss some of the particulars with Lady Evelyn."

Isonde gave him a flat look. "Planning our advances with the policy makers of the Sovereign Council is more important. I found the Caetcha files while you were on your errand, we should get back to it."

"That's better left to a time when Ardin can attend. You two know more of council politics."

"Malkor—"

"Should I leave you two alone?" Kayla shifted her weight to one foot, putting her hand on her hip. "Because I have better things to do than listen to this bickering."

Isonde's attention snapped back to her. Malkor intervened before the princess recovered her voice.

"Evelyn's right, the Sovereign Council can wait." He gestured toward the table. "Shall we sit?"

Kayla took the seat closest to the door. Best get this started so they could get it over with. Malkor chose his seat next to her almost as quickly, leaving Isonde alone to further protest or join them. The princess sank gracefully into a chair across from Kayla.

Malkor waited until she settled to begin. "Playing the role of Lady Evelyn at the Empress Game will require more than fighting as Isonde. As her principal companion you'll go everywhere with her, attend every function, meeting, dinner, party and so on. There's much more to the Empress Game than the tournament for the crown. At no other time do so many of the empire's sovereigns, leading families, councilors, trade magnates and elite gather in one location. The amount of business being transacted, the number of alliances formed—and broken—at a game is staggering. As Lady Evelyn, you'll represent Princess Isonde's and Piran's political position. It's vital you have a strong grasp of what we're trying to accomplish at the Game, and do your best to support that."

"Politics?" Kayla sighed. She'd expected to dress up, speak politely when spoken to and blend into the background. She could accomplish that in her sleep while keeping an eye on her *il'haar*, thanks to years at her family's court. This, though, was becoming more involved than she liked.

"We have dozens of alliances with different members of both the Sovereign and Protectorate Councils, and a dozen more tentative friendships in the works," Isonde said. "Beyond winning the Game, we need to secure each of these potential alliances and strengthen our standing in the councils if we want to achieve our ends."

"And those ends would be. . .?" Kayla's interest piqued. A senior IDC agent, the princess of Piran and the heir to the Sakien Empire working together, all for. . . what?

"An end to the Ordochian occupation and an alliance with the Wyrds."

Isonde's words hit her square in the chest. "What?"

"With enough support in the two lesser councils, we can influence the Council of Seven to vote for a withdrawal from Wyrd Space. That is," Isonde added, "if the Wyrds will agree to create the counter-nanovirus we've been asking for."

Kayla thought she must have hallucinated. Did a leader of one of the empire's most powerful planets suggest freeing Ordoch?

"Wait. Wasn't Piran involved in the original attack?" Kayla reached back in her memory to the weeks leading up to the coup. Emissaries from the empire had come, a contingent made up largely of IDC agents and diplomats from several of the Sovereign Planets. There had been meetings. Talks. Hours upon hours of talk over a nanoplague that the empire had accidentally unleashed on itself and the technology they demanded the Wyrds provide them with to stop it. Dangerous technology. Technology forbidden in Wyrd Space for its insidiousness and unpredictability. Technology that, in the hands of the aggressive empire, could just as easily be used as a weapon against the Wyrds, rather than as a cure.

"We were under pressure to approve the use of more. . . persuasive measures with the Wyrds, if talks did not go as hoped."

"Assassinating the ruling family was your idea of 'persuasive measures?'"

"Not initially, no," Isonde said, with a coolness that made Kayla want to slap her. "But it became necessary.

"The current situation on Ordoch is tenuous at best," Isonde continued. "It's only a matter of time before the other Wyrd Worlds refit their ancient battleships and mount an offensive. We've only held the planet this long because interplanetary warfare between the Wyrds ended generations ago and their armadas had fallen into disrepair.

"We can't afford the manpower and resources it would take to hold Ordoch against the combined might of the Wyrds, not when the Tetratock Nanovirus plague is still advancing."

The TNV. Kayla thought the same thing about the plague now as she did back then—serves them right. But news that it raged on unabated surprised her.

"Still?"

Isonde nodded. "Our designers are useless. All they've managed to do is speed up the destruction in the Tanaki sector."

"The Ordochians can't deactivate it?"

"Won't. We captured their major tech installations with minimal casualties, but many of the brightest scientists and designers slipped our net. They've been in hiding since.

"It comes down to simple numbers," Isonde said. "We can hold the capital city, control most of the power grid and tech centers and keep the highest ranking Wyrds hostage, but we can't do a door-to-door search of the planet. What scientists

we did manage to capture have been uncooperative, despite. . .
pressure being applied."

"We never should have gone there," Malkor murmured.

Kayla struggled to rein in her anger, to sound as disinterested
as a pit whore would be about something so far beyond her
sphere of influence. "And now you—what? Want to do the
right thing? After five years?"

Malkor looked pained. "We want the same thing as always:
to deactivate the TNV before it spreads farther among the
planets of the empire."

"And you think that if you return control of Ordoch to the
Wyrds, they'll be so thankful that they'll agree to help you
neutralize your super weapon gone awry?"

"We don't have another choice," Malkor said. "The Wyrds
will eventually reclaim the planet. Even trying to hold it this
long is draining resources needed elsewhere. Agreeing to
withdraw now, and avoiding what could be another half-decade
of occupation for them, is our most attractive offer. Something
they might consider worth designing a counter-nanovirus for."

"If holding the planet is so obviously bad for the empire,"
Kayla asked, "why do you need me to help solidify your stance
against continued occupation at the Game?"

Isonde tapped her fingers on the table in obvious impatience.
"Not everyone sees the situation as we do. Most don't realize
how tenuous our hold is there. Some think the empire should
devote more resources to the occupation, make Ordoch our
foothold in a ludicrous bid to take over Wyrd Space. Some
like the glamour and prestige of besting one of the ancient psi
races. Others, like many of the Protectorate Planets on the far
side of the galaxy, don't give a damn what happens in Wyrd
Space or the rest of the empire, but will vote our way if certain
trade demands are met. It's complicated."

"Regardless," Malkor said, "we need to return sovereignty
to the Ordochians." His lips formed a hard line.

"Eradication of the TNV is the top goal," Isonde said.
"Freeing Ordoch is in line with that, so—"

"No. Freeing Ordoch *has* to happen. You and Ardin assured me you would pursue that agenda with or without the Wyrds' help on the TNV." His gaze bored into Isonde. The air seemed to heat between them, their words ringing of an oft-held discussion. "I am not going forward with this charade otherwise."

Isonde met him stare for stare. "Of course we'll push for a full withdrawal from Wyrd Space. But—" she raised her finger to emphasize her point, "the coup was the right call at the time and you know it, no matter your guilt now."

Holy— Kayla's gaze flashed to Malkor. What guilt? The general sort that came from being part of an unethical organization like the IDC, or the specific kind, the kind that came from bloody hands?

She, along with her brothers and sisters, had been kept apart from the proceedings on Ordoch that led up to the take-over. They'd been segregated from the diplomats, IDC agents and imperial military personnel that had arrived, so she had seen very few of the people involved. Malkor could have been right there, on her homeworld, and she might never have seen him.

Had he murdered her family without provocation, or was he just an agent with a conscience?

"We can finish this debate later," Isonde said, shooting a pointed look Kayla's way. "For now, let's get Evelyn up to speed on politics."

9

Kayla sat at the table in her room, Corinth on one side, Rigger on the other, making stilted small talk with the agent while Corinth watched avidly.

"Sorry about . . . yesterday."

Rigger smiled, easing some of Kayla's tension at having the agent so near her *il'haar*.

"No harm." Rigger waved her hand. "I'd be protective too." She seemed like she meant it.

"Corinth, is it?" Rigger looked to Kayla for confirmation. No use trying to hide Corinth's name after she'd shouted it. Hopefully it was a common name in the empire. Rigger turned her attention to Corinth. She'd brought a datapad, some sort of device and a toolset with her. "I've been thinking about the holofield you generated on Altair Tri," she said to Corinth, "the one that ran as background sensor trash. Thought maybe you'd like to reconfigure this more sophisticated holofield generator with me, see what we can get it to do."

::Oooo. Kay, do you mind?::

Rigger's tone held genuine interest and Corinth eyed the generator like a new toy.

"I'll get dinner," she said, trying not to cringe when Corinth slid closer to the agent and the offered electronics. The two were already absorbed in manipulating the field generator when she returned with food.

Kayla stayed with them while she ate, her mind consumed by a single question: who was Malkor? IDC, yes, a senior agent and an octet leader, but beyond that? Who was she working for, and just how deep did his involvement with the Ordochian coup go?

She'd had Corinth run a search for any information on him as soon as she'd gotten back from the meeting, to no avail. The ship lacked access to the imperial data stream while in hyperspace, and sensitive IDC documents weren't stored in the starcruiser's database. They'd have to wait until they reached Falanar to gain any insights. That didn't mean the question didn't sit heavily on her when she considered her new alliance, though.

Kayla sat near the engrossed Corinth and Rigger for a few more minutes, feeling like an unnecessary bodyguard, but once Corinth assured her—again—that he was fine and happy, she shifted into gear. She had survived the meeting with Isonde earlier and had gotten both a lesson on the political structure of the empire and a homework assignment.

Despite having an emperor, the Sakien Empire was ruled in large part by councils. The planets of the empire were divided into two groups of disparate size. The smaller of the two was the group called the Sovereign Planets. They were the original six planets that defined the empire at its founding, and the Sovereign Council was made up of their number exclusively. The Sovereign Planets were the most advanced, wealthy and powerful planets in the empire, and their council's decisions dictated much of the goings on within the empire.

The Protectorate Planets were, on the other hand, only loosely confederated, made up of those planets added one by one to the empire as it expanded. The Protectorate Council ruled over matters between the Protectorate Planets, but had scant power to exercise change at the imperial level. The greatest power, however, lay with the Council of Seven. They had ultimate rule over the entire empire, and as the premier governing body decided the fate of the empire. The seven council seats were filled by, at any one time: the current emperor and empress; the heir to the throne—in this case, Ardin—and his wife, the empress-apparent, who would be chosen at the Empress Game; two members of the Sovereign Council; and one member of the Protectorate Council. Each had one vote on any decision and the majority won.

With Ardin unmarried, his future wife's seat was taken by a second member of the Protectorate Council. The Empress Game would mark a significant power shift in the Council of Seven.

Kayla drifted over to the complink. With all the talk of political structures and influential members of government today, she hadn't had a chance to ask one of her biggest questions: why an Empress Game at all? In an empire ruled by an overlap of councils, why was one of the seats on the Council of Seven chosen by means of a hand-to-hand sparring tournament?

She accessed the ship's databank, looking for answers. A thousand articles met her query for "Empress Game Origins," but one came from a book titled, *How the Wyrds Shaped Our Identity*, so she started there.

Section 4: The Empress Game

Time and again we've seen how the Wyrds, in the short five months they spent in the empire before returning to isolation in Wyrd Space, influenced our traditions. Perhaps their largest contribution to imperial politics comes in the form of the Empress Game.

When the Wyrds first made contact with the empire generations ago, the then-emperor, Shazni Tirefel, became enamored with them, as did the rest of his court. Their culture, fashion, mannerisms and customs were studied to the last detail and anything "Wyrd" became the fad.

The emperor was especially impressed by the fighting prowess of the *ro'haar* among the group.

The *ro'haars* competed against each other in friendly tournaments to demonstrate their skills and teach the empire something of *ro'haar* customs. In Wyrd Space these tournaments were common at festivals and holiday celebrations, and were often held when visiting foreign courts. It was a way for *ro'haars* to measure themselves, show off, trade techniques and earn acknowledgement for their skills.

The emperor was so in love with these strong, dedicated and deadly women that when his son Ghirit came of age, he passed an edict that the boy's bride would be determined in the style of a *ro'haar* tournament. Considering that any female with a claim to power in the empire would be allowed to enter the tournament, the councils adopted the edict immediately. Everyone imagined their sister, niece or daughter winning and becoming the next empress.

The Empress Game has persisted since.

Imperials. Kayla shook her head at the idiocy. No wonder her people had decided relations with the empire were not worth pursuing and had cut ties. They were like children, aping something they didn't understand.

She reached for the datapad Malkor had given her—crammed full of information on the influential citizens in the empire. She had to be ready to talk politics with as many of them as possible once they reached Falanar.

With Rigger's quiet stream of one-way conversation as a background and the excited energy emanating from her *il'haar* lulling her to ease, Kayla settled into the chair for a long, boring night of biography reading.

Malkor paused in the bathroom, toothbrush halfway to his mouth, staring at the faucet unseeing. His earlier conversation with Isonde played in his head.

"The coup was the right call at the time and you know it, no matter your guilt now."

He'd rather touch an energy conversion coil than examine his sense of guilt, or even worse, his role in the coup, but couldn't get those words out of his head. They brought back a similar question raised by his superior, Commander Parrel, when they'd debated the IDC's actions in the coup.

"If it had turned out successfully, if the Wyrds had agreed to create a counter-nanovirus for us once we'd taken over their planet, would you still feel guilty over what was done?"

Yes. Frutt yes.

. . . right?

Fizzled gel dripped from his mouth and he spat before finishing his tooth brushing.

Shadow had surprised him with her pointed questions about the coup. She wasn't the first person to express a negative opinion of the empire's handling of the Ordoch occupation, and was certainly not alone in her disapproval, but she was the first he'd met outside of the imperial elite who cared one way or the other. At least now he understood where some of her animosity toward the IDC came from. She might have—

A massive shock rippled through the walls and across the floor, staggering him. He fell to one knee, smashing his forehead on the edge of the sink.

"Frutting—" Another wave crashed through.

What the void? The fingers he pressed to his forehead came back bloodied but he pushed to his feet. He sprinted through the blackness of his cabin with one arm out, catching himself from slamming into his door by picometers. The portals of his room were vacant of the hyperspace glow. Two fumbling attempts at the doorpad opened neither the door nor a comm channel. He slid his hands along the wall, fingertips skimming for a seam.

Thank the stars for remnant mechanical systems.

He found the emergency panel, forced the pressure switch and reached inside the console for the manual door release. Yanking on the lever produced a split between his doors just wide enough to let in an eerie, pulsing blue glow. He pumped the lever again and they spread apart a few centimeters. Three more pumps exhausted the hydraulics of the system, leaving him with a twenty centimeter wide opening and the acrid taste of burning organoplastic.

"Malkor?"

Shadow's voice came to him over the wailing of alarms.

"Malkor!" Her hands appeared against the edges of his door. He could barely make out her face in the spasmodic light. She managed to slip a shoulder inside, bracing herself against one door panel while she pushed against the other.

He stepped forward to help. "I'm here."

Her eyes were huge in the dark as she assessed him, gaze flitting to his forehead before refocusing on the doors.

"I have no idea what happened," she said. She looked fresh from bed in a sleeping tunic and bare feet, one kris strapped to her thigh.

"Is anyone else out yet?" She'd escaped her room before he'd managed to get his doors open. Impressive.

"I don't know, I looked for you first." She heaved and he braced a palm against the opposite door, together forcing the two panels apart.

"You all right?" they asked each other at the same time.

Corinth lurked behind her, gripping one of her kris still sheathed. The dagger looked more like a shield than a weapon in his hands.

"Malk?" Hekkar shouted from down the corridor. His second-in-command jogged up and Shadow sidled away.

"I'm good," Malkor said. "Let's check on the others."

All around his octet fought through the frozen doors like divers searching for air. Janeen was already in the hallway, pulling at Vid's doors, noticeably keeping her weight off one ankle.

"Gio?" he shouted. A mass of twisted wreckage marked Gio's quarters and blocked the end of the hall. Flaring blue light crested over the pile, offering the only illumination amid the chaos. Various snapping, popping and sparking sounds emanated from beyond the destruction and smoke billowed down the corridor.

"Not sure he's home, boss," Hekkar said.

Shadow was yanking on the other side of Vid's door so Malkor set himself to helping Trinan while Hekkar went for Rigger. Aronse, his last IDC agent, spilled into the hallway as they freed the others.

"What do you know?" Malkor asked.

Janeen replied from where she sat propped up against a bulkhead with Aronse examining her ankle. "Last I heard the hyperdrive was acting twitchy and the captain wanted to drop stream to cool it off."

"Any idea whose space we're in?" With so many other things going on he hadn't followed their stream course.

"None."

"I think we're in the Mine Field," Hekkar shouted.

Wonderful.

The Mine Field was dead space, the wreckage of a war long lost by both sides. It stretched in a void between the farthest Sovereign Planet and the closest Protectorate Planet. A freak exception to kinetic laws drew all of the hyperspace streams in the area through the point, and the same energy anomaly caused disruptions in hyperspace such that fifty percent of ships dropped stream there. Normally they'd have avoided this area of space altogether. Anyone deposited in the Mine Field would have to navigate through the scattered debris with a precision some ships just weren't capable of, until they reached one edge of the field and had the jumping room for a hyperstream launch.

And then there were the rooks.

An explosion on the other side of the debris wall sent them all to the floor. The concussion subsided into an angry sizzle and another wave of the fumes of burnt organoplastic washed over them.

"We have to get to an undamaged section and find out what the void is going on," he said.

The corridor dead-ended in a viewport but two maintenance shafts ran in opposite perpendiculars, opening at floor level. "Half and half," he shouted. Better to split his team in case either escape became a death trap. Hekkar and Vid set to popping the panels off the openings.

Rigger approached. "If we can get to a section with emergency power I can tap into the ship's systems and get a sense of the damage."

"We're gonna need Rigger to bypass the security if any of the crisis lockdown protocols are in place," Hekkar said.

Shit. Both teams needed Rigger.

"We can do it." Shadow crouched beneath the acrid smoke layer, pushing Corinth's head down. "We can hack the systems. Hang on." She left the boy long enough to sprint back into her room, then returned clutching a slim case. She gripped Corinth's arm, clearly ready to spur him to motion.

Malkor didn't want to send his whole team in the same direction in case things went to shit, but without Rigger. . .

"Trust me," Shadow shouted.

Her confidence convinced him.

"Trinan, Vid, with me." The rest scrambled to follow Hekkar's lead as he dove into the other maintenance shaft. A shower of sparks illuminated Aronse helping the limping Janeen over, then they were all just silver outlines in the pulsing light. Before he could duck into the opposite tunnel, Shadow darted past him, Corinth in tow, and disappeared inside.

"Wait," Malkor said.

Kayla ignored him and crawled into the tunnel. Corinth scampered in beside her, despite the passage being barely large enough for an imperial male. She didn't have the damnedest idea where to go. It was doubtful Malkor had a greater understanding of starcruiser schematics than she did, though, and his debating their options wasn't helping her get Corinth to safety. Who knew how much structural damage their wing had sustained, or when the smoke would kill them.

Away and down. That was her only plan as she crawled

blindly. Corinth gripped at her with his mind, holding on like he might have clung to her hand if they weren't crawling. She pressed on, hearing the others behind her. The textured surface of the passage met her palms as she passed one junction in an effort to gain more distance. When she came to a second, she reached for the rungs of the ladder that led to a lower level. Kayla descended quickly, Corinth all but stepping on her hands as he followed. She dropped two levels and hit the bottom of the shaft. Everything was darkness still and she led them farther down the next tunnel. A slow rumble started as no more than a tremor, then built to a jarring vibration through the floor and walls as they advanced.

Damnit.

::Kayla!::

I know, I know. Of course he couldn't hear her. It was too late to turn back and find another junction. All they could do was press on into the worsening situation. They hit a branching finally and she chose left. Relief surged when she slammed into the dead end of the tunnel.

"Release is at the top," Malkor said.

She heaved the hatch open and spilled into a corridor painted with a gray glow. Around a bend the promise of light beckoned even as another explosion sounded nearby. She took off at a run, hauling Corinth along. His unblocked fear buffeted her.

One hundred paces later they came face to face with a containment door sealing the corridor. The panel indicated it had enough reserve power to keep itself in lockdown, no more. She went for the panel but Malkor stopped her, one hand on the door. She pressed her hand to the metal—hot to the touch.

He glanced back the way they'd come. "No other choice."

Malkor led the way back to the life or death gamble of the tunnel and they crawled inside. She lost track of time as they scurried down and away, aware only of her stinging knees and Corinth struggling to keep up as he crawled beside her. When the air heated and filled with the tang of smoke she was ready to take on anything rather than stay in what promised to become a tomb.

They dropped down several levels and landed in a tunnel that ended in a pressure-locked, heavy-construction door with a barely active panel beside it. Only the brief interruptions of light told her Malkor's fingers worked on the panel, attempting exit.

"Damnit!" He slammed a palm against the door. Behind her Trinan and Vid cursed in similar frustration.

"Get out of the way." She squeezed past Malkor, Corinth following. She retrieved the slim case she had jammed under the band holding a kris to her thigh and selected one of her tools. Prying the panel's face off revealed a complex mass of circuits glowing beneath.

So. Slightly more complex than she'd expected. She studied the design, trying to identify the circuits controlling the locking mechanism. The others' harsh breathing echoed in her ears.

Hmm. . . It might be that one. Or. . . it could be that. . . She reached out slowly.

::No.:: Corinth grabbed her hand. The dim light painted his face, lighting his wide eyes. His pupils darted back and forth, watching the flashing patterns.

::Here. This one.:: He pointed but she couldn't differentiate his directions. Corinth took her tools before she could pass them. He delicately disrupted the flow of one circuit while he reached for a second tool to twitch the activation of another. She held her breath while he worked, time grinding by.

::Almost—:: Sparks flared. Corinth spasmed hard against the tunnel wall as the security door whooshed open. Kayla crawled out and tugged Corinth's unconscious body from the shaft. Her fingers found a pulse in his throat as the others climbed out.

Malkor crouched beside her. "Is he—"

"Alive, I don't know how bad." She held Corinth to her.

Malkor's voice was firm. "We have to keep moving. We can rest him someplace safe once we get to the powered sections of the ship and find out what's going on."

She nodded, rising to stand on stiff legs and heaving Corinth's dead weight up. Without a word Malkor took him from her, hoisting her *il'haar* onto a shoulder and taking off down the corridor.

"He'll be all right," Vid said.

Her eyes were full of Corinth's still form as she jogged after Malkor automatically.

Corinth hadn't roused by the time they reached a fully powered section. Malkor handed Corinth to Trinan, who cradled him like a baby in his arms. Adrenaline's burn-off bled the strength from Kayla's body, and though she knew Corinth was her responsibility, she let the impressively muscled Trinan continue to hold him as if he weighed no more than a leaf.

The ship's damage hadn't been fully assessed, but conversations with the bridge crew and security team revealed fairly localized destruction. Several sections on multiple decks were still black though, and no one could account for the situation in those areas.

That was the least of their worries.

They'd dropped stream in the Mine Field and the rooks had already spotted them. The mechanized sentinels prowled in their direction. The ship was on frantic alert, trying to make their way to the edge of the Mine Field without appearing to be fleeing. Desperate movement, it was rumored, drew the rooks' attention like an electromagnet.

More immediately, though, they were under attack. Two smaller ships that must have been lurking in the Mine Field dogged their retreat, taxing the starcruiser's superior shields with an array of weaponry, some more effective than others.

"Hekkar's team made it through all right, we're rendezvousing at Ardin's quarters, near the bridge," Malkor said. He touched her shoulder. She'd been staring at the ruins of the ship's medical station, useless to the still unconscious Corinth. "I don't want to leave you here. You'll be safest with the rest of us."

The group started into a jog, heading down the corridor to the magchute that would bring them to Ardin's floor.

"What kind of weaponry does the ship have?" she asked Malkor.

"Very little. It's a private luxury vessel, not a gunship."

"Ion cannons?"

He shook his head.

"Frag missiles?"

"A few."

She huffed out a breath. "We could be in serious trouble."

They made it to Ardin's wing without further incident and met up with Ardin, Isonde, the rest of the IDC agents, including Gio, and half of the ship's security force.

Trinan carried the still unconscious Corinth to one of the couches. Janeen sat nearby, her ankle elevated on a table and a frustrated look on her face. Kayla perched next to Corinth and rested her hand on his shoulder.

An open comm link to the bridge gave them a stream of information on the assault and their progress out of the Mine Field, and a debate arose.

"We have to stop running and fight those ships."

"We don't have the firepower for it."

"If they manage to get microbolts through the shields in the aft we run the risk of losing the engines. We'll be sitting ducks for the rooks."

"Jumping a hyperstream is our best chance of escape."

"If we take much more damage, we won't be able to open a stream."

"We could detonate a concussive charge off our bow, which might give us enough running time to make it to the edge of the field."

"That'll bring the rooks for sure."

Whatever threat their attackers presented, it was agreed that any action that would further provoke the rooks was too risky.

Corinth stirred. He raised a shaky hand to his head in a

semiconscious gesture to ward off pain. His eyelids peeled back slowly.

"I'm here," she said, before he could panic.

::I know. You'd never leave me.:: His mind voice was groggy.

Conscious of Janeen watching them, Kayla kept her words short. "How do you feel?"

He flexed his hands, then shifted his legs and feet. ::I'm fine, just. . .:: He shook his head. ::Knocked me out, that's all.::

She brushed a hand over his brow. "You did well."

He smiled at that, looking up at her. ::So did you.:: She felt his pride.

Vid approached. "How is he?"

"Okay, I think."

He looked over at Janeen. "How 'bout you? Aronse said she thought the ankle was broken."

"Damn medstick's useless on this. I'd be up and about in a stabilizer splint if we were planet-side."

"Gonna have to heal the hard way." He gave Janeen an apologetic smile. "Probably best Malk refused to give you the assignment after all."

The look she shot Kayla said exactly which assignment Janeen had wanted.

Activity from the comm caught everyone's attention when the ship rocked with another impact. Only the tangle of debris that made a maze of this quadrant saved them from an all-out assault by the other two ships. The captain directed a duck-and-weave course through the dangerous cover.

"The rooks have mobilized!" The transmitted shout brought silence to the room. She wrapped one arm around Corinth and pulled him closer.

The attacks on the ship ceased, the other two ships apparently trying to mimic the starcruiser's flight path to screen themselves from the rooks, balancing stealth with speed as they shot for the edge of the field. One of the two ships dropped off radar, melting into the background sensor noise of the field. The other fled alongside as the rooks hopped space to reach them.

How the rooks made their attack, what happened and where the rest of the rooks were Kayla didn't know. One minute Ardin's whole starcruiser held its breath, the next everyone broke into shouting.

"The rooks got the other ship!"

"Oh shit, they tore it apart!"

"Hit the engines. Now! Everything!"

The starcruiser burst toward the edge, tore open a hyperstream and launched into it. Silence reigned for a heartbeat, then, cheering erupted.

10

The next morning their ship limped along under half power while the crew worked to fix damage to the hyperdrive.

Power remained down in the damaged sections, and with their wing off limits, crew quarters were tight among the octet. Kayla stayed with Isonde, a situation that pleased neither of them, but made the most sense considering they'd be sharing the small apartment allocated to them at the Empress Game soon enough.

Not only was Kayla now subjected to Isonde's haughty disdain on an hourly basis, but she had nowhere to hide when the etiquette lessons began. Kayla came back from that morning's training session to find Isonde seated in the cabin's lounge area, apparently waiting for her.

Fantastic.

"We need to discuss the role you'll be playing at the Game beyond the tournament itself," Isonde said, her gaze sweeping over Kayla's sweaty form as if cataloguing her faults.

"Can I shower first, at least?" Kayla asked. She walked off without waiting for a reply.

Isonde was sitting in the same spot when Kayla returned. The princess looked perfectly composed, sitting at ease without looking too stiff or too casual. Must be a royal talent of hers, that poise.

"As Lady Evelyn, you'll be moving in some exalted circles, representing Piran while under a microscope. I need to know you can get on in such company without embarrassing yourself." Isonde's tone made it sound unlikely.

"If you're going to tell me which fork goes on which side of the plate, I'm out of here."

"I wasn't aware pit whores used forks," Isonde countered, in a perfectly civil tone.

So, the princess had claws. Kayla smirked. "I usually prefer to shovel food into my mouth bare-handed, but I suppose I could make an exception for the Game."

Isonde was too well-mannered to roll her eyes, but Kayla sensed the impulse wasn't far off. "Sit."

Kayla hadn't needed one gram of her royal court manners while on Altair Tri, but she was an Ordochian princess, and etiquette was bred in the bone. She sank into a seat opposite Isonde with perfect posture and schooled her features into an expression of bland politeness.

Isonde raised a brow. "Not bad."

"Do your worst." And so began her lessons on the social aspects of her charade as Lady Evelyn—in minute, excruciating detail. Isonde was an exacting instructor, annoyingly patient and obsessively thorough. Kayla took great pleasure in surprising the look of superiority right off Isonde's face as often as possible.

The days fell into a pattern after that.

In the remaining week of their journey, Kayla focused all her energy on training, polishing her schmoozing skills, memorizing the names and faces of the empire's leaders and studying their politics.

Somewhere along the way Trinan and Vid had become Corinth's unofficial bodyguards. The two seemed to have bonded with her *il'haar* and spent most of their time with him. Much like Rigger, who visited in her free time, they kept up a steady stream of chat, including Corinth in the conversation without expecting a reply. They never questioned him directly, they never pressured him or made him uncomfortable, they merely. . . talked.

Corinth loved it.

He convinced Kayla to let him bunk down with the agents in their makeshift quarters beside Isonde's. The men promised her he would be safe. Corinth echoed their assurance, and conveyed to her the protective feelings coming from Trinan and Vid. It was hard for her to argue with two impressive bodyguards, especially when she had so much else to focus on.

The IDC agents brought Corinth with them to the rec room while they sparred and worked out, and he was already starting to hero-worship them. The animation on his face, the engaged way he listened to the men, filled her heart to see. He looked alive. Alive in a way he hadn't since they'd escaped Ordoch. It eased her mind, and for the first time in five years she was relieved of her constant fear for his safety.

While the guys sparred among themselves, Malkor became her training partner. Their sessions, sometimes three a day, were more intense than anything she'd experienced since leaving Ordoch. It was exhausting in the best of ways. He pushed her limits, forcing her to develop tactics she'd never employed before and find new ways to handle larger opponents.

He learned from her as well, and he was a quick study. They'd taken to hanging around after a session to discuss the tactics of the day, what worked, what didn't, and why. Long after the others filtered out, when Corinth assured her he was fine and was off to tinker with the ship's damage with Rigger for the afternoon, she and Malkor would sit and talk while the sweat cooled on their bodies. His analysis of fighting was impressive, their talk easy and natural.

Kayla sat with him now after a particularly fierce workout, each stretching tender muscles in silence. Across the length of the rec room Janeen heckled Trinan and Vid, much to Corinth's delight. The woman seemed friendly enough with the rest of the octet, but Kayla had had enough of her sour looks. Kayla felt oddly competitive with the woman, driven to prove that she was the better choice even though Malkor had already rejected Janeen. She trained harder and spent that much more time studying imperial politics.

::Kay?:: Corinth brushed against her shields. She dropped them just enough to allow him into her most conscious mind. She bent her right leg into her body and pretended to concentrate on stretching over her left.

::You were fierce today.::

She hid a smile at his pride. *Am I not fierce every day?*

::Especially today! He didn't hurt you though, did he?:: She felt his intention to explore the rest of her body for injury. She held him in place, only allowing him access to her thoughts.

Never.

::Rigger's going to check the progress the tech team is making on the engines and she said I could come along. After some lunch. Is it all right if I go?::

She hated being away from him, but the alternative was locking him in their room like a prisoner.

You still feel safe with them?

::Trinan thinks I need more meat on my bones and plans to feed me a shuttle's worth of food when we get back, and Vid is trying to think of a way to get me to try some exercise without pressuring me.:: The surprised and delighted feel of his mental voice came through. Five years with no one to talk to besides her, no one else looking after him, taking an interest in him. No wonder the agents fascinated him.

You call for me the nanosecond you need me. Before that, if you even think *you might need me. I'll come running.*

::I know you will.:: He swirled in her head, his mental hug, and withdrew as the agents packed up to leave.

How much trouble could he get into on a ship this size? She reasoned against her anxiety. He waved as they filed out, and Janeen was the last to go. It looked like she might hang around, watching Kayla and Malkor with that poorly hidden frown, but Trinan jibed her for slowing them down and she headed out, hobbled by her healing ankle.

The room settled into silence.

"We should be arriving in Falanar's orbit by tomorrow

night," Malkor said, breaking the calm between them.

"So it begins then, the charade?"

"I'm afraid so. These are your last hours as Shadow Panthe." He searched her face as if looking for a reaction.

Unexpected fear rose up. Shadow Panthe—the hated persona, the comforting disguise. The lifting should have been a relief, and it was, but she had worn the mantle so long. It had kept them safe until now. One mask ripped off to assume another. Was it opaque enough? Could she shield her *il'haar* beneath it? Could she stand the weight of it?

"I'm ready." She would have to be.

She gained confidence from the certainty of his expression. He thought she could do this. Or at least, he didn't consider the plan a total failure before it began.

"And we are agreed, Corinth will stay with Trinan and Vid for the most part, positioned ás a refugee from one of our latest missions?"

That had been hardest to decide. Her role as Isonde's attendant would leave her little time to watch over Corinth. In her absence, he was safest with the two agents and she had no one else she could trust him to. She couldn't take him everywhere she went, and leaving him on the starcruiser, out of her grasp, hadn't been acceptable even before it had been damaged. In the end, this was her only choice.

"Yes, provided I get to see him often."

Malkor chuckled. "I doubt anyone could stop you."

"What of you and the octet, once we land?"

"I'll be with you. At least, as much as possible." He shifted his weight. "I'm not leaving you alone in this."

The words gave her an odd sense of relief. "Thank you."

"You don't need to thank me. I brought you into this mad scheme. What kind of man would I be if I abandoned you to it?"

Malkor might be IDC, but she trusted him on a superficial level. More than anyone else on this ship, and certainly more than anyone on Falanar. She could use his analysis of opponents' techniques in the fighting to come. That and. . . it was perversely pleasurable to have someone—anyone—to talk to again. Someone who spoke out loud, who occasionally offered a wry chuckle. Someone with a sarcastic tongue who could give as good as he caught.

"My octet has duties during the Game, mostly of the diplomatic sort. Facilitating relations between visiting dignitaries, playing host to all of our foreign contacts, and of course, validating the ID of every Empress Game participant."

"A full schedule."

"I'll make time. It's not. . . unusual, for me to be seen in Isonde's company." He glanced away. "She and I. . . Ardin, Isonde and I grew up at the emperor's court, for the most part. Her uncle and my father both sit on the Sovereign Council, and we spent the majority of our time on Falanar. It will not seem odd for me to visit with you and her."

"Just how familiar are the two of you?" She could tell her question put an end to their post-sparring closeness.

"Why were you hiding on Altair Tri?" he asked instead of answering.

"We're back to that, I see."

"Always." And she was back to hiding. As always.

"You'll not get an answer from me." Despite the distance now between them she wanted to stay, try to reclaim the few minutes of closeness she got to share with anyone. Instead she forced herself to stand. "Don't waste your time. Or mine."

11

Malkor stood in the giant customs block on Falanar, expelling annoyance with every breath. They'd arrived on the imperial homeworld mere hours ago and already his octet was swamped. An unprecedented number of guests had come for the Empress Game. All available tech and security officers had been enlisted for the enormous task of confirming the identity of every last person who came through the port. Meanwhile, the IDC was responsible for identifying every participant in the Game. An agent personally oversaw the palm print analysis, DNA assay, retinal scan and visual confirmation of identity for each participant and their attendant. Of course, all of that happened only after each visitor had tested negative for the Tetratock Nanovirus while still on board their own ship.

Malkor had a stack of assignments just as large as the rest of his agents, and had been running around like a bot on overdrive since he got there. Already he'd logged princesses, sovereigns, governors and priestesses from every planet in the empire. Who *wasn't* making a bid for the empress-apparent's seat on the Council of Seven?

Beyond identifying the contestants, the IDC had a secondary list of people to investigate. The techs handling the registration of spectators compiled lists of suspicious persons who had been allowed entrance with special circumstances attached.

These people formed the watch list of persons of interest who might attempt to fix the Game.

The IDC had received hundreds of allegations of cheating already, and more would pour in after the first round of fighting when people started getting eliminated. The hours it would take to wade through the illegitimate claims would prevent a thorough investigation into each, giving any real threats to the Game's validity a greater chance of slipping through.

He hoped.

Malkor checked his datapad again, the lists upon endless lists, and made mental notes. He'd heard from the junior IDC agent he'd assigned to the de facto queen of Narden—she'd been unable to provide proof that her husband was actually dead. He'd heard from Janeen in the regen lab—the ankle was healing, but swelling from last week was hindering the cellular repair process. He'd heard from Rigger—the latest version of the Isonde hologram was ready for testing. He'd heard from Vid and Trinan—the boy was settled. He'd heard from Gio and Aronse—they'd been assigned a special detail for a party Master Dolan, Grand Advisor of Science and Technology and the only exiled Wyrd ever to live in the empire, was expecting. He hadn't, though, heard from or seen Shadow in hours. Not since before they'd arrived.

The group had split three ways when the starcruiser docked. Ardin and his contingent had been admitted without being processed. The IDC agents and Corinth had gone to their own station on the planet's surface. Isonde, her bodyguards and Shadow had joined the mass of imperial citizens in the queue at Falanar's customs block to await admittance. Even as a member of the Sovereign Council, Isonde wasn't exempt from procedure.

Malkor's first order of business had been to locate the apartment Shadow and Isonde had been assigned to and reassign it, moving them to an apartment closest to the rooms the visiting IDC teams would occupy. The IDC complex could only house so many octets. It could not accommodate the sheer number of octets returning to the homeworld from various planets where they had been stationed. Housing the rest of the octets in the buildings where the Game's participants would stay was the perfect solution.

He checked the Game's roster: Isonde hadn't been registered yet. With Isonde's high standing in the empire they should have been processed already.

Where the frutt were they?

Malkor debated his next action. Two massive sections comprised the customs block on Falanar. The identification depot was laid out in row after towering row of offices and waiting areas stacked on each other where people coming or going from Falanar were detained, searched, scanned and positively identified before being allowed on their way. Malkor occupied the second section of the block, the welcome port.

The welcome port was as big as a plaza and open from floor to arching ceiling. The setting suns sparkled through various skylights, each cut in the shape of a star and filled with prismatic birefringence gel. Maps of every aspect of Falanar lined the walls, pointing visitors toward tourist attractions, lodgings, trade sectors, business sectors and pleasure sectors.

Malkor watched the thousands of visitors crossing toward the doors at the far end of the port for one more minute before heading in the opposite direction. He pushed his way through the welcome port's entrance and headed into the multi-level maze of the main customs depot for Falanar. He walked the first floor, which contained the tech rooms where visitors were scanned and positively IDed. The hallway was just the open space between two of the many parallel columns of rooms. They rose on either side, story after story of offices, waiting areas and private lounges. Open-air walkways fronted each floor and the upper levels connected to their counterparts across the space via bridges. A multitude of brightly dressed people milled behind the glass fronts of the waiting rooms above, and staff members ushered groups on the maglifts to yet more waiting rooms even higher up.

Shadow, Isonde and their dangerous charade waited somewhere amid all this. He checked his datapad again. Next on his list of participants to validate was Ophala ut'Anani, a tribal priestess from the ruins of Mimar's Ward.

She could wait.

Kayla felt as though she might hyperventilate.

The feeling, stressful enough, was exhausting when going on its fourth hour. Isonde looked out the glass front of their waiting room, calmly surveying the bustle of the customs depot. They'd been placed in a room on the seventh floor, and Kayla could see into the glass-fronted waiting rooms across the way from theirs. Not just on their level, but on all the adjacent levels.

How could Isonde stand there like a fossil on display?

Kayla hadn't approached the glass despite being in the small room for hours. Instead she had pulled a chair into the farthest corner and sat with her back against the wall.

It didn't help.

She had felt less exposed standing in the center of the Blood Pit in her skimpy fighting outfit. Thousands of people could see her. Without her body paint. Without her *ashk*. Everywhere she looked, every time she glanced through the glass, jade and indigo uniforms passed. Imperial uniforms. She was surrounded by the official imperial security force.

Her dress might as well be on fire, as conspicuous as she felt.

"Start fidgeting," Isonde said, as she turned away from the glass.

"Excuse me?"

"Patience is one thing, it adds grace. You look like an ice sculpture ready to shatter. Have you even blinked?" She strolled to one of the empty chairs, her ivory skirts swirling in an elegant twist from her waist to her toes as she walked. She brushed her auburn hair back over her shoulder and light danced up one arm, the shimmersilk of her tight then loose double sleeve flowing with the movement. The dress, with its gold-accented neckline and subtle crystal matrix hemming, looked natural on Isonde despite probably costing a fortune of credits.

Kayla, wearing a complementary gown of the same style in black with platinum accents, made a show of just barely moving a hand to twitch the fabric of her skirts a micron. "That better?"

"Oh, much." Isonde folded herself neatly into a chair. "I realize you've probably never even worn a gown before, but at least try to look like it's not made of glass."

The condescending tone had to go, but Isonde was right. Kayla took a deep breath, trying to forget that she was in her enemy's house, and relaxed back into her chair. The action felt unnatural.

No one knows who you are.

She ignored the threat the myriad security officers, guards and IDC agents posed to her life and focused on mimicking ease. Black satin slippers peeked from beneath the crystal matrix as she crossed her feet at the ankles. She leaned casually on the arm of her chair and began to beat a staccato rhythm on the metal frame with two fingernails.

"Now you only look slightly more uptight than Joss and Rawn." Isonde nodded to her two guards.

"We never look that uptight, my lady," the one named Rawn said.

"Enough. I get it." Kayla pushed out of her chair. If she couldn't pace, she could at least stretch muscles stiff from tension. "Why are we still here and not down by the arena yet? The officer who led us here said we'd be scanned 'soon.'"

"The bureaucracy of Falanar has its own standard units of time, and none of them equal 'soon.' For a gathering as large as the Empress Game, our wait has been nothing."

Kayla forced herself to take a few steps toward the glass front of the room. She tucked against the wall as if an opaque barrier on one side offered any real concealment. She didn't look into any of the rooms across, that felt too voyeuristic. Instead she watched people walking the corridor far below.

The only people-watching Kayla had ever been interested in was the threat assessment kind, ranking everyone into a scale based on the threat they presented to Vayne. It was as natural as breathing to her, but today her scale was skewed.

Everyone presented a threat to her *il'haar*. How could she protect Corinth from so many unknowns? A stream of people wound along the floor of the depot, slower groups eddying here, more determined citizens surging there. Most ranged in groups led by imperial officers in jade and indigo uniforms, being shuffled to and from the waiting pens like livestock. Some pairs and trios strode along, clearly on business, and some collected at the edges to talk.

The predictable flow swirled with disturbance at the far end of the corridor.

People startled and parted, proving that someone unique was making their way down the corridor. Kayla couldn't pinpoint the source from seven levels up, but conversation seemed to stop and heads turned, either to stare or look away. A group of guards in matching lavender uniforms passed directly below her, revealing who was causing that level of disturbance among such a cosmopolitan group.

"*Kin'shaa*," she whispered, her fingers curling into talons at her side.

Surrounded by guards, the diminutive Master Dolan swept along the corridor at a clip. Formerly a top-level neuroengineer on the Wyrd World Ilmena who was caught experimenting on his own people, Master Dolan was now *kin'shaa*—a Wyrd whose psi powers had been stripped from him using the Kalichma Ritual. The practice had been outlawed on Ordoch, but some of the more rigid Wyrd Worlds still used it in extreme cases as a form of punishment. His physical appearance gave him away. A web of scars started at his right temple and spidered out across the right side of his face. They ran straight through his eye, and that orb was now a blank, angry red, with no visible iris. The lines crossed his nose and cheekbone and warped the corner of his mouth ever so slightly, giving him a hint of a smirk at all times. Each *kin'shaa* had the same scarring, those few who survived the procedure.

Dolan had been there during the coup on Ordoch. He had come with the empire, claiming to be an emissary of both sides wanting to bridge the distance between the planets. He had been there the night her family was murdered. He would recognize her.

She stepped back sharply from the glass wall, bumping into an accent table.

Was he coming for her? Had he already found Corinth, is that how he knew to look for her? She hadn't even been scanned yet, how could he know? Kayla turned to dash for the door, but it opened before she could take one step.

"There you are."

12

Malkor's trouble radar shot to hyperdrive at the sight of Shadow's hunted look.

"What is it?" he asked from the doorway of their waiting room.

Her chest rose with rapid breath and she stared at him uncomprehendingly. Beside her, Isonde looked calm, unconcerned, and her guards were at ease. Still, Malkor's hand went to his ion pistol.

"Lady Evelyn?"

"I. . . it's nothing. I'm fine."

She was decidedly not fine.

He glanced over his shoulder into the hallway. Aides bustled back and forth, admitting or escorting people to and from the various rooms. No one paid him the slightest attention. No one hustled furtively down the hallway, and none of the people he saw presented a threat. When he looked back at Shadow she had regained her calm, but fear lurked in her eyes. She studied him as if assuring herself he was real. What had she seen?

"Have you come to rescue us?" Isonde asked.

"Something like that. Have you been waiting this whole time, or. . ." He wouldn't put his concern into words, not in such a public place.

Isonde gave a slight shake of her head. "Just waiting."

He looked at Shadow one last time. If her past had caught up to them, he needed to know. A full-on inquisition would have to wait, though.

"Let's get you ladies out of here."

Kayla did her best to slow her breathing as Malkor led them along the airway.

His gaze swept over their surroundings, touching on people, landings and hiding spots before returning to her. He slowed his step a fraction so they walked in sync, their long legs matching their gaits.

"Do I need to be worried?" he asked in a low voice.

She shook her head, eyes darting to inspect the other visitors.

"You're not doing a very good job of convincing me," he said.

Kayla breathed. In. Out. No shouting. No guards. No one she knew. No one to recognize her.

In.

Out.

"I'm fine. Just. . . nervous." She tried on a faint smile.

"Hmm." There were questions building in him, she could tell. If they had more privacy, she didn't doubt he'd press for a more believable answer.

The *kin'shaa* would have passed on by now, they wouldn't run into him. Millions of people congregated for the Game, an endless sea she could sink into like a drop of water. Dolan wouldn't recognize her unless they came face to face, and she would make sure that never, ever happened.

Kayla sensed Malkor's strength of purpose as they strode along together, his focus on the mission. It was a focus she was becoming accustomed to. He had changed into his formal IDC uniform, with a knee-length indigo tunic over tailored slacks of dark jade. Jade piping followed the two vertical side seams and accented the short stand-up collar of the tunic. Matching thread picked out a pattern near his left collarbone and the outlines of eight hollow rectangles fanned to form a ninety degree arc, the symbol of his rank as an octet leader. The simplicity suited him, even if the uniform left her chilled.

They rode the maglift to the floor of the depot, then skirted groups of people to enter an empty identification room. The room was nondescript, the walls' synthetic stone matrix rendered unidentifiable by layers of taupe paint. A counter, atop which sat several palm scanners, a retinal scanner, a stack of datapads and two interlink terminals, dominated the room. Two techs argued about something on one of the terminals. Behind them the seal of the Sakien Empire covered the wall in brilliant jade and indigo—a ship jumping to hyperspace, surrounded by a ring of stars. A padded bench ran along two of the walls, completing the room's furnishings.

The techs had been expecting someone else and took a few minutes to pull up files, change the calibration on the scanners and sort through a series of datapads. Corinth had assured her he had every faith in Rigger's technical expertise, he didn't doubt that the ID Rigger had designed for her—"Lady Evelyn"—would hold up. Nonetheless, Kayla hesitated when they called her for a palm scan.

Malkor gave her a discreet nod and she pressed her palm to the slick aeroglass surface, plunging into her role as Lady Evelyn.

The rest of the process went smoothly, Isonde and her two guards being as easily confirmed as Kayla. The women were given credential bands to be worn at all times. The guards were then relieved of duty and sent to join the rest of Isonde's people at the townhouse she owned in Falanar's crown district. The safety of every Game entrant would be assured by the imperial security officers while they remained on the tournament grounds. A necessity. The Game complex couldn't support the amount of security and attendants each combatant would bring if a limit hadn't been set.

The techs then discharged them into the spacious welcome port. Kayla adjusted the fit of her ID bracelet as she took in the bustle of the port. Light spectrums danced across the curved walls of the enormous building, the suns casting the last of their light through what looked to be birefringent skylights. Porters, guides and shuttle drivers, both of the living and android variety, lined the walls waiting for customers. Interspersed with them were welcome kiosks where visitors could take virtual tours of the capital city and reserve accommodations, if there were any left to be had. Hundreds of temporary bots supplemented the traditional bank of translator ones. A staggering line of visitors waited at each to receive an aural implant calibrated to the exact dialect of their native language. The bots required a series of verbal examples of the wearer's speech, then adjusted generic implants to precise translation devices that would translate every known spoken language into the listener's native tongue. Visitors were on their own for the non-verbal languages.

Thank space Rigger had attuned one for her when she was still on board the ship. She spoke the five dominant languages on Ordoch, but her knowledge of empire linguistics was limited to Imperial Standard Common, the only language broad enough to serve the eclectic mix of unsavories on Altair Tri's slum side.

It took some time but they managed to wade through the port to the doors at the far end and exit into the maglev terminal. Nearly a hundred gleaming maglev trains waited in their bays, their silver ends stretching farther than Kayla could see. Passengers swarmed the arriving trains, each impatient to claim their own place. Trains filled in minutes and shot down rails, launched from reversed polarity buffers at the end of each bay.

Malkor led them past several trains toward the less crowded reaches of the platform. The near constant *whoosh* of air stirred strands of her hair and she brushed an impatient hand against them as she followed in Isonde's wake. It wasn't until they'd chosen seats on a half-empty train and the doors locked into place that the reality hit her. She was grounded on the imperial homeworld with no way off, out or away except through a horde of the empire's top fighters.

Let the Game begin.

* * *

The magrails had been diverted to run right to the Game pavilion, and it wasn't long before Kayla, Malkor and Isonde arrived at the huge housing complex designated for Empress Game participants. The credentials embedded in the lithodisc bracelet they each wore allowed them access to the floor their shared apartment was on and the suite itself. Kayla examined the room. Adequate, if not elegant. Larger than her shack on Altair Tri had been and more secure. There was the lithodisc reader and a print scan-dependent door lock, vid-recorder surveillance in the corridor and an impressive alarm system with an estimated ten-minute response time. Five if you expected the IDC agents to come from the adjoining wing in the place of guards. If the walls were thinner than she liked and the recorders too accessible—and thus too easy to manipulate—she could deal.

"He's close?" she asked Malkor, as soon as she'd finished her assessment of her bedroom off of the apartment's common area.

He followed her thinking immediately. "Corinth's staying with Trinan and Vid. The opposite end of your corridor intersects the main corridor separating contestant quarters and IDC quarters. Rigger's already tuned your creds to give you access to the IDC dorms on that level, and the print scanner on Trinan and Vid's door has been keyed to admit you. You might want to knock before you enter, though, just in case." The datapad in his hand beeped and he glanced at it impatiently. "I have to get back. Before I go, do you want me to show you where he is?"

"Yes. Please," she added as an afterthought. Malkor must be needed in a million places simultaneously. The Imperial Diplomatic Corps had been created for events like this, gatherings where cultures, traditions and races would meet, mingle, exchange and potentially clash. The IDC had been diplomats initially, and if the latest generation had become more martial, it hadn't changed the core of their training. "I'd appreciate it."

He'd already turned to the door, knowing her answer.

"The inaugural banquet is in a few hours," Isonde said. "We'll need to prepare."

More studying politics and practicing conversation.

"I'll return in time." Kayla let the door slide shut behind her and followed Malkor down the hall. Their suite was only a short walk to the security doors that opened into a broader main hallway. Two minutes of walking brought them to the security doors at the end of the IDC wing. Her bracelet unlocked the doors and Malkor escorted her into the deserted corridor. The IDC wing mirrored the layout of her own wing and it wasn't hard to locate Trinan and Vid's room. Malkor indicated that the rest of the octet was stationed in rooms to either side and across the hall. Her *il'haar* was as safe as she could make him.

Vid answered the door when they commed, but it was Corinth's voice she heard, a mix of excitement and relief in his greeting.

::You found us.::

She finally relaxed. His appearance had improved since joining forces with the octet. The nutripacks of the food synthesizers on the starcruiser were so much more complete than her supplies had been, and even the small amount of extra food Corinth had been eating had improved both his color and his energy level. He had lost his fearful wariness of the agents and looked more comfortable than she felt around the large imperials. His eyes shone with enthusiasm.

How bored he must have been on Tri, trapped with only one person for his mother, sister, psionically dead *ro'haar* and teacher.

How bored she had been.

"I'm glad you're here," Vid said with a smile. "Your brother's been busy hacking into the mainframe and manipulating stars knows what. I'm pretty sure he's already gotten us fired. . . or worse. I let him use Trinan's complink terminal, of course." He winked at Corinth and the boy's answering grin lifted her heart.

"Thank you," she said. "For looking out for him."

Malkor's datapad beeped again.

"Well, he's a bundle of trouble, as you know, but I do what I can." Vid's infectious teasing made her chuckle. "I need a break from his wild antics. Malk, a few words maybe, if you've got a second?" The two headed into the hallway.

::You won't believe the number of people we saw!:: Corinth launched into conversation as soon as the men had left. ::So many minds. And some have shields! Some people are completely closed off, like you can do, Kay. Even the octet is more guarded. I don't know if it's conscious, but Vid is shielding his thoughts somewhat, it was harder to read him than normal. Well, except when we were getting IDed. Then he was worried for me, but he didn't show it at all. No one else could tell. But the techs were so easy, and they didn't even pay attention to our scans. And then we met some other octet and Vid didn't like them. He said they were lazy. And too aggressive. He called them—:: Corinth stumbled to a halt, but not before the memory of Vid's colorful description of the octet's leader landed in her mind. ::Um, he told me not to tell you he'd taught me that phrase.::

"Corinth, if Vid's getting harder to read, I don't want you to push it."

Exasperation came through their link. ::He doesn't know I'm trying to get past his shields.::

"He might, if he's being cautious. The others might too."

::I'm careful. I've been practicing.::

She sighed, disturbed at what thoughts Corinth might dredge up in a grown male's mind. "Don't get too comfortable in there. He's not a toy or a test bot."

::I know that, Kayla. I try not to invade his privacy. Too much. Besides, Trinan's even more entertaining.:: He paused, then rushed on. ::I really like them, and I think they like me. Rigger too.:: She felt his adoration of them, blended with his pride for being someone the tough, capable IDC agents could like, and his yearning for a connection with someone who wasn't her.

"At least promise me you'll leave anyone with stronger shields alone. No practicing on them."

::They won't know if I just *try*.::

"You can try all you want—once we get home. Where it's safe." The mention of home dampened him, but for the first time she felt an easing of the familiar longing the word evoked. "Promise me you'll be careful, now more than ever. Just a little while longer."

He nodded. ::I will.::

"Did you go through the floor plans of the building yet?"

::Yup. I know exactly where you are and how to reach you there.:: He closed his eyes and his focus shifted from her. ::The princess is pretty agitated with you for taking off.::

"I need to study, there's an important gathering tonight. And apparently your *ro'haar* needs some more prettying up."

::You are beautiful, all the octet thinks so.:: His mouth cocked up in a grin so like Vayne's it hurt. ::Especially Malkor.::

"*Corinth Reinumon*. We discussed you staying out of his head."

::I can't help it. He projects when you're around. You intrigue him.::

"Please, *please* stay out of his head."

He made a noncommittal noise.

She glanced at the door, reassuring herself of their privacy. "Were you able to find out anything more about Malkor?"

Corinth shook his head. ::I didn't have much time with the complink, and I didn't want Vid to get suspicious of what I was doing.:: A thread of uncertainty crept in. ::I'll keep looking, but I doubt it'll be easy to gain access to the IDC domain. I wasn't even able to find it in my initial search.::

Her thoughts sheared against each other, the need to know exactly who she'd partnered with buffeted by her fear of that knowledge, now that their futures were inextricably linked with Malkor's.

::You do want me to keep searching, right?::

"Yes. Of course I do." Of course. There was no dodging the truth, whatever that was. Better to know now than before things went any farther.

The chronometer caught her eye. Thoughts of the council members she still had to read up on intruded, and there was that diplomat from Nixna that she had wanted to investigate. He had powerful backing among the more prosperous Sovereign Planets and actual Wyrd sympathies. He would be a good one to approach.

"Will you be okay here tonight?"

::Rigger's coming by later, she's going to let me help with the final modifications on your hologram and we're going to crack into the Game print-DNA database to add your profile to Isonde's for the switch.::

"Just, try not to impress her *too* much. I'll check on you later."

::You don't have to.:: He pulled back and looked into her eyes, his psi powers flooding her with the protectiveness that flowed from the octet members. ::They'll keep me safe while you're busy. I'm safe here, Kayla.::

If only that were true.

Kayla wandered from the dining area of their suite to the sitting room and back, giving no thought to her steps as she read. She had a datapad in each hand, memorizing a face while she scanned a brief on Archon Raorin's latest speech before the Sovereign Council. It was stirring and provocative, and introduced for major consideration the idea of a complete withdrawal from Wyrd Space. His wife—a less influential council member herself who represented a smaller colony on the same moon—had spoken immediately afterward, proposing instead a stronger presence on Ordoch and more pressure on the Wyrds to develop the cure for the TNV.

Their marriage seemed to be going well.

Satisfied she would be able to recognize Raorin on sight, Kayla ducked into her room one last time to check her appearance. She took her identity as Lady Evelyn Broch as seriously as she did her research on the current atmosphere of imperial politics. The more convincing her role, the less suspect her actions. Lady Evelyn, she decided, was confident, well-spoken and stylish, someone the refined Princess Isonde would bring as her one attendant. Knowing as she did each piece of the costume she'd donned, the combined effect in the mirror still surprised her.

Her mother stood there, entwined with Kayla's uniquely snubbed nose and long, loose, dyed black hair. The same fey eyes, their flame-bright blue a perfect match. Same rounded cheeks that had always held a smile. Kayla's were more gaunt, but the bone structure was perfectly her mother's.

For the first time in five years Kayla felt attractive. Beautiful. She wasn't just a weapon, a *ro'haar*. She was her own. A woman.

Not necessary for the mission, but damn if it didn't make her glow a little.

She turned her hip to admire her dress. The magenta "fabric" was in fact millions of microscopic links, made from the lightest known metal and interwoven with protein strands from the dhara arachnid. The deep red-violet shimmered when she shifted, and fit her body like a snake's skin. A stiff collar had been fashioned using extra protein strands, and it came up almost to her jaw line on all sides except the front of her throat. The fit of the dress hugged her body through her hips. She most appreciated the slits running up each thigh; they would have allowed perfect access to her kris daggers, if any visitors for the Game had been allowed to carry weapons. A collection of silver triangles hammered together hung from each earlobe, completing the outfit.

Kayla entered the sitting area and Isonde's pale blue gaze skimmed over her. The princess straightened her posture with the slightest smile. "Good. You might almost be able to pull this off." Kayla took that as praise.

They'd been forming an odd sort of rapport over the last week. From things she'd said, Kayla knew that Isonde's aim to become empress came not from a desire for power, but rather from a need to correct the course of an empire that she saw as having gone off the rails. She rather arrogantly assumed she was the only woman for the job, but Kayla took that in her stride. The goal, and the woman behind it, she could respect.

Isonde's initially chilly manner had thawed as Kayla demonstrated not only her ability to carry off the charade, but her determination to do the whole thing right. The disparaging remarks had disappeared as they'd both gotten down to the business of planning their political agenda for the Game.

Tonight Isonde wore an airy gown of layers of sheer white pinned at one shoulder and wrapped around her body. An opaque slip lay beneath and both fabrics floated like cloud wisps. Subtle plascrystals glowed at her ears, formed a necklace that rested on her collarbones and wrapped around the wrist not wearing her credentials bracelet. Her auburn hair was done up in curls held in place with woven copper filaments.

They made their way through the halls, seemingly in no great hurry despite the determination Kayla felt coming from Isonde.

Kayla thought she was ready. She'd practiced the traditional Piranan greeting, touching right fingertips to right shoulder before lowering the arm, palm up. She'd studied the current Piran treaties and trade agreements with Sovereign and Protectorate Planets, memorized potential allies who had yet to commit to the Ordochian situation one way or the other, made a list of council members who could potentially be brought to their side with trade, aid or other incentives, and identified those worlds most affected by the TNV.

She had not, however, been able to prepare for the sheer size of the gathering at the inaugural banquet.

Or the noise.

It was held in the arena that would house the enormity of matches the Empress Game required. The Game complex had hundreds of function rooms, none large enough to accommodate the mob of guests present—they could have populated a small city on Ordoch. The hum of chatter drowned her. Above it all rode the announcement of each guest as they

arrived, name, rank, station, holding, designation, planet. . .
the titles seemed to go on and on.

Kayla and Isonde stopped in the lower level arena seating,
by what had been dubbed the presentation steps, waiting to
be scanned for weapons and then announced. From there
they would make their entrance by descending the stairs
to the floor, or "pit," and joining the waiting throng. She
skimmed the crowd, unable to focus on a face before another
person came into view. So many. Too many. How could she
find anyone?

Indigo and jade crepe assaulted the eye from every level
of the arena. It ringed the perimeter, wound around the stair
railings and draped along the edge of the pit. Flags representing
each nation recognized by the empire lined the ceiling, hung
from rafters in row after row of fabric, too high up to even
make out their differences. Lights of a million colors shone
down, created laser shows on the walls, blinked in time to
music. The heat from the press of bodies in the pit rose into the
chilled upper levels, the breeze stirring her hair.

"Princess Isonde Veriley of Gangisha, Sovereign Planet
Piran, accompanied by Lady Evelyn Broch of Ishimi, Sovereign
Planet Piran."

The number of heads that turned at the announcement was
staggering. She descended the stairs beside Isonde, trying to
mimic the princess's elegance. Isonde casually lifted the hem
of her skirt a centimeter as if she strolled through a meadow,
and she drifted down the steps like a feather, floating into the
galaxy's most monumental social event. Kayla felt more like
an escape pod launched down a long chute into the unknown
of space.

They touched down on the arena floor and she fought
the urge to run as a swell of people met them. She was an
Ordochian princess. She had attended every royal function
since she and Vayne had come of age. None of these people
could even read a thought, let alone influence an emotion
from her. She could handle this.

She affected a smile similar to Isonde's—pleasant, confident and approachable. Kayla might battle for the crown here in the days to come, but tonight, she was in Isonde's arena.

Within an hour it became clear that the problem wouldn't be one of finding people, it would be escaping them. They'd been offered a dozen drinks Kayla had never heard of; she'd chosen a raspberry-hued cocktail for no other reason than that it matched her dress, and held it like a fashion accessory. They'd been offered enough food to feed five; she'd neglected to challenge the tight knot in her gut. They'd easily conversed with fifty people, not one of whom she recognized, and they hadn't made it farther than twenty meters into the crowd. At one point the crush of people heading in their direction actually backed up the flow of newcomers, halting introductions on the presentation steps.

Imperial functionaries in official jade tunics had politely disengaged the throng long enough to allow them to pass farther into the pit and stop jamming traffic.

"Lady Evelyn, might I engage a moment of your time?" An earnest man, the first face among the sea that she recognized, waited a polite distance away, hand over his heart.

Alunri Dega. Prince, eldest son. Protectorate Planet Uha. Her hours of memorization had paid off.

"Prince Alunri. Of course."

He looked stunned at the sound of his own name.

"You. . .?"

"I've been studying." She smiled at him, easy to do when his lips quirked self-deprecatingly.

"Of course."

"Please, take no offense. You are very memorable, I assure you."

"And you as well. Your holovid is a pale comparison to you this evening." He bowed, his hand falling away from his chest as she made her traditional greeting. "I have done some studying as well."

"Then we are even." She kept a check on Isonde's location from the corner of her eye. The two moved as a unit, never allowing themselves to be separated from each other by the ring of interested parties. The princess was just off her right hip, their backs together as each conversed. If the mass of courtiers awaiting her attention swallowed Isonde up, Kayla would never find her again.

"Can you believe this crush?" His was the typical opening, the easy ice breaker. Despite the fact that everyone was here to increase their position, station or power, either for themselves or their nation, they all insisted on acting as though it were a purely social event.

"It's more than I expected." She pretended to sip her cocktail. "I swear it's like grain price-fix day at the start of the trade window on Piran."

He chuckled. "Surely it's not *that* hectic."

"Worse, I assure you."

They shifted position as they spoke, a subtle dance that kept them close enough to be heard over the cacophony of joined conversation, distant enough to be polite, and always moving away from the presentation stairs.

"How did the dispute over fishing rights in the Utar Sea work itself out in your province?" she asked.

He raised blond eyebrows. "You *have* been studying."

She inclined her head. "Favorable, I hope?"

"Near enough. The Gethans were not pleased, but then, they never are." He said it lightly but she noticed tension in his smile. "My people will continue to fish it, as they always have. To ask otherwise had been. . . unfair."

"Of course. Original rights should be respected wherever possible."

"Thank you, my lady. I concur. And what of your people? I apologize, I have not your dedication to study and while I am aware of Princess Isonde's achievements in the Sovereign Council, I am uncertain what occurs in your nation of Ishimi."

She had to laugh at that, having only just this past week

learned the lay of the land in Ishimi herself. She played it casual, offering minor details.

He made polite chat before duty called him away, leaving Kayla and Isonde slowly making their way through the crowd toward more significant guests.

"It's not that we aren't in favor of a more balanced standing within the intergalactic trade environment. Certainly we'd like to see the Protectorate Planets develop and be allowed to flourish within their own commodities structure. But Timpania shouldn't be forced to beggar itself for the sake of fledgling nations that can't provide one hundredth the resources that Timpania has already provided to the empire. We have a right to fair trade prices on our gallenium ore."

Kayla tried to smile politely at Councilor Adai. The woman's last sentence might have been more accurate if phrased as, "We are fully committed to raising the already obscene price on a resource we know everyone needs." Timpania could bleed money for a century and still not beggar itself. They were one of only a handful of planets with natural gallenium resources, which, when refined, fueled ion weapons, ion generators, and most importantly, stardrives.

"There's some discussion," Kayla said, "of putting sanctions in place that would regulate the market, considering the essential nature of the resource."

Councilor Adai looked disgusted. "Such a proposal would never pass."

Historically most nations had been afraid to vote for imposing a price cap on gallenium, fearing Timpania would refuse to trade with them if they backed it. The balance had been shifting with the ever-rising prices, however, and looked to be approaching a critical point.

"Interplanetary travel has been harder to come by in the outer sector among the fringe Protectorates due to fuel shortage," Kayla said. "That might begin to affect transport of other necessary goods back to the Sovereign Planets."

"The Councils have more pressing issues to debate."

"A fuel shortage is a concern with many," Kayla said. "However, Piran could be convinced that other issues were of greater importance. For instance, exploring alternative avenues for finding a cure to the TNV plague might demand more of our attention within the Sovereign Council, shelving the question of sanctions on gallenium for the time being."

She had Adai's full attention now.

Some time later Kayla sipped at a fruity, non-intoxicating beverage, this time in blue. She listened to Isonde speak about a nation ravaged by the TNV. Those who had gathered to discuss with her, intimates all, nodded with the same concern her voice expressed. Names and faces whirled through Kayla's head from the hours they'd already spent at the party. Still, Isonde's recounting of the absolute devastation the TNV left in its wake arrested her. She'd seen the numbers, read the reports on estimated landmass affected, studied the numerous impacts the death toll had on the empire as a whole.

But to take it from abstract numbers and hear the story of the people themselves, the damage done and the suffering the TNV inflicted on its victims before they died, was another thing altogether.

Maybe her people should have broken the anti-nanotech treaty with the other Wyrd Worlds and helped.

Kayla turned down another offer of food and made idle chatter with an older man whose name she couldn't bother to remember. She'd never see him again anyway. Over his head she spied the Clanestas Warren. Based on stats alone, these two sisters would be among her toughest competitors. They hailed from Clan Warren in the Dhovmir Province on

Kokomar, where clan warfare in Dhovmir was a way of life. The Clanestas, or Clan Daughters, ruled Clan Warren jointly. It was rumored that neither had ever lost a fight except to each other.

The older, Sovein, had a ten centimeter height advantage on Kayla—and she was the smaller of the two. The younger, Urveina's, sleeveless tunic showed off arms thick with enough strength to wield a tree as a weapon. Her shoulders surpassed both Trinan's and Vid's for width. The Clanestas spoke to their companions with their hands, their language being half verbal, half somatic. Their palms could have been bear paws for their surface area, but their gestures were graceful, the fingers quick and agile. When they strode by with steps of matching lightness, Kayla knew their holovids had undersold them.

The Clanestas studied Isonde as they passed. They assessed and dismissed her in a heartbeat, and only a nod of Sovein's head acknowledged their fellow combatant in the Game.

Kayla surrendered.

She made her apologies to Bishop She-Had-No-Idea-Who, murmured her intention to Isonde, then slunk to a free chair she spied along the wall. She kept the princess in sight as she sat gingerly, easing stiff legs with a sigh. Her throat rasped when she laughed at her own predicament: bested by diplomats. The roar of endless conversation washed over her, nothing but babble at this point. The chair's cradle beckoned sleep. Her mind drifted.

Her eyelids fluttered closed, only to flash open when a smell piqued her senses: old-fashioned imperial soap.

"Enjoying yourself?" Malkor's voice, familiar after so many strangers'. He smiled down at her with an amused chuckle.

"What unholy hour of the night is it?" she asked.

"I do believe it is morning, and has been for some time." He glanced over his shoulder at Isonde before returning his attention to her. "Let me escort you back. Isonde's likely to be at this another three hours and you look ready to drop." He held out his hand to her and Kayla took it without thinking, letting him lift her from the chair.

She meant to slide her hand from his but somehow it just stayed there, skin resting against skin. How many times in the last five years had she touched a person like this, not because she had to, but because she wanted to, because she liked it. Someone who wasn't Corinth.

Had it always felt this nice?

On the heels of the unexpected thought came another as she studied his gray eyes. *Did you harm my people with this hand?*

"You shine tonight," he said, unaware of her turmoil. "Every time I saw you, more courtiers were forming a line for your attention. Soon you'll have as devoted a following as Isonde does."

"If they are devoted, it's to convincing me to schedule some of Isonde's time for them." Which was to be expected. "Apparently having Isonde's ear, and perhaps an influence on her calendar, makes me one of the most engaging females in the empire."

"Not so. Archon Raorin didn't even spare the princess a glance when he spoke with you. And the elder Mister Vauhn had to be pried from your side. Lord and Lady Anto looked simply delighted to be speaking with you. I can't remember the last time I've seen them so animated."

"That was animation? I thought they might expire on the spot." So he'd been keeping an eye on her, even if she hadn't seen him.

"Trust me, they were positively giddy. Let me—" The arena-wide voice system kicked in, burying his words under the blare of the latest arrival's presentation.

Who would arrive at this hour?

The Master of Ceremonies echoed out a hated name. "Master Dolan of the Wyrd World Ilmena, Imperial Officer of Astronautical Advancement, Grand Advisor of Science and Technology to Emperor Rengal and Ambassador for the Wyrd Worlds."

Ambassador? Traitor to the Wyrd Worlds, more like. Opportunistic, amoral criminal of state who should have died during the Kalichma Ritual.

Thankfully she was hundreds of meters from the presentation stairs. He'd never lay eyes on her among the crowd.

"It looks like Master Dolan and his special party have finally arrived. Now the mystery can be put to rest," Malkor said.

"What mystery?"

"Who Master Dolan is sponsoring in the Game. He's sequestered Aronse and Gio to act as diplomats for his special party's admittance onto Falanar—neither has reported in since the assignment."

A woman stepped onto the upper landing of the presentation stairs, flanked on each side by a shorter gentleman. Another woman paused behind them. Light caught the radiance of their lavender hair and illuminated their absolute disdain for the entire gathering.

"Princess Tia'tan and the Ambassadors Noar, Luliana and Joffar, of the Wyrd World Ilmena."

In the stunned silence that followed, Malkor's voice hit her like a blow.

"Apparently the Wyrds have arrived."

13

Kayla slept off the shock of seeing Princess Tia'tan and the rest of the Ilmenan Wyrds arrive as the *kin'shaa*'s allies. She awoke in the late afternoon with a throbbing headache and a bone-deep sense of betrayal.

She didn't know the Ilmenans. Hundreds of royal houses inhabited the four Wyrd Worlds; she couldn't recall most of the family names, never mind individual members. Interplanetary relations between the worlds were fairly quiet and uninvolved.

But as Wyrds they should have been her allies. People she could trust with the truth of her identity. How could they join forces with the empire? How could they work with Dolan? He'd had his psi powers stripped for a reason. He'd raped his own people in a series of mental experiments, the details of which sickened her. He had led the empire to Ordoch, had provided the coordinates for hyperstream travel. Anyone working with him was her enemy.

Her own people, now her greatest threat.

Kayla had just enough time to check in on Corinth before she was summoned to a meeting with Prince Ardin, Malkor and Isonde. A royal convoy collected them at the Game pavilion and transported them to the imperial palace in sleek hover cars. After traveling a maze of corridors and passing through more than three ID stations, Kayla and the rest were escorted into one of Ardin's private studies.

The blue tones of the woven reed floor blended into an ever-lightening scale of color that spread up the walls. The blue paled to white when it reached the domed ceiling, and star-shaped skylights poured sunshine down. The windows along one side of the oblong room showed a view of green and blue foliage. Against the far wall, water trickled down an aquamarine crystal larger than Kayla. The chime of water droplets falling a short space into a pool below was the only sound as Kayla took her seat with the others at the table.

No psi powers were needed to sense the tension from each. No one relaxed comfortably in a chair, no one reached for the refreshments offered. Ardin's sigh as he took his seat said it all.

"Now what?" The prince looked to Malkor as if the IDC agent had a plan. Clearly they were all thinking the same thing: what to do now that Wyrds had arrived to compete in the Game?

"Now? Same plan as always, I suppose."

"That's it? That's all you have? Princess Tia'tan will be impossible to defeat with her Wyrd training and psi powers."

No kidding.

"What do you want me to say, Ardin?" Malkor pushed a hand through his hair. "It's not like we can just ask the Wyrds to leave. Did your aides find out anything?"

Ardin shook his head. "They've been burning through datapads reading the Rights of Succession since the Wyrds showed up. There's no stipulation against a princess from a nation outside of the empire competing in the Game. It wasn't an issue before."

"Surely there's some rule we can exploit to get them disqualified," Isonde said. She looked as well put together as always, despite the crisis.

"If there was a way to bend the rules of the Rights of Succession to meet our own needs," Ardin said, "my aides would have found it a year ago and we would already be married."

The tiny voice of the fountain filled the gap Ardin's words opened in the room. Kayla caught both the buried longing in the prince's tone and the glance Isonde shot Malkor's way.

Malkor ignored both, all business. "What about their psi powers? There's no precedent. Can we get them classified as unsanctioned weapons, or some kind of inequitable advantage?"

"Can we prove that they intend to use their powers in the tournament?" Isonde asked.

"Why wouldn't they?"

She shrugged. "Maybe they also think it's unfair to the other contestants and don't plan to use them. Then again, how would we know if they did?"

"That's why they should be disqualified," Ardin argued. "There's no way to tell."

"What, and accuse them of cheating before the Game even starts? Talk about a political nightmare." Isonde tapped two fingers on the table. "We could probably get their powers classified as unsanctioned weapons, for the matches at least. That's the best we can do. We'll have to *hope* they agree not to use them."

Kayla couldn't keep quiet any longer. "The Wyrds didn't come all this way to lose."

"I'm not sure if they *can* use their powers in the middle of a fight," Malkor said. "All of the IDC received a rudimentary lesson on the Wyrds from Master Dolan before the whole Ordoch. . . situation. He explained that it took some concentration to use their psi powers on other people. He gave us a crash course on forming the outer layer of the mental shield-things the Wyrds normally have. He said they would be sufficient to protect us during a skirmish."

True. The effort required also increased with the target's shield sophistication or in some cases, sheer force of will. A powerful sense of self could be just as hard to overcome as constructed defenses. One problem, though.

"Princess Tia'tan might not use her powers while fighting," Kayla said. "There are, however, at least three other Wyrds in attendance who will not be similarly distracted."

"Just the three others," Malkor said. "Dolan confirmed it."

"And two of them males. They'll have been chosen

specifically for the strength of their psi powers." While the difference wasn't so marked outside of the ruling class, within the royal houses of Wyrd nations the men were traditionally stronger psionics.

The others all turned to stare at her.

Damn. Did the IDC know that? "That's the going rumor, isn't it?" Surely Dolan had told them.

"Yes, but. . ."

Malkor leaned forward, his eyes full of questions. She waved off any inquiry with a sharp motion of her hand. "The Game complex is ablaze with rumors about the Wyrds. I've also heard they suck the life from their victims with a stare and can levitate objects." That was a no and a yes. "Surely some of it is based in fact."

Malkor's intent stare promised a reckoning later that she wouldn't be able to escape. Fabulous. Fobbing him off with a story of rumors would be impossible. Maybe she could avoid him—for the rest of her time on Falanar.

"How do we combat them?" Isonde asked.

Ardin sighed. "We can't."

"We're back to the same plan," Malkor said, gaze still on Kayla. "Lady Evelyn wins the Game. Wyrd or no Wyrd."

If Kayla could have slipped away from the others and returned alone to the Game complex she would have.

No such luck.

When Isonde and Ardin turned the conversation to the political machinations from last night, Malkor listened for about five minutes before standing.

"I'll leave the council plans to you two. Lady Evelyn? Perhaps you could accompany me back."

Kayla didn't know who disliked the idea more, she or Isonde. The princess's lips compressed into a thin line. Isonde opened her mouth but one look at Malkor had her closing it without a word. She nodded as if he needed her permission.

Apprehension coiled itself in Kayla's midsection. "Maybe I should—"

"You can catch up later. I'm sure you want to check in on your brother."

Trapped. She could hardly say, "You go on, I'll just check on him later," and Malkor knew it.

She rose, fussing with her skirts, stalling as if that would save her from the inquisition. All it did was buy time for her anxiety to rise.

He led the way to their waiting hover car. They climbed inside and the weight of the door sealing shut locked them in. Silence lay thick in the metal cocoon. He gave their direction to the navbot, then kept his gaze ahead, seeming to study Falanar's towering architecture, but she felt his focus on her.

Did she want his questions now, while she couldn't escape but there was a time-limit on their conversation, or later, an ambush at a time of his choosing?

The silence congealed, stilling her lips when she might have spoken, holding her limbs in place to avoid a disturbing rustle of fabric. He was similarly still and they rode like statues, the air tense and tight between them. Already she imagined his voice in his head.

Who are you? Why are you hiding? Who are you hiding from?

Questions she couldn't answer.

Answers that had kept her prisoner for years.

Secrets that, so easily buried in private, now wanted to burst from her skin at the tentative friendship from another.

Freedom.

She wanted it.

She didn't fear his questions. She feared herself.

The hover car delivered them to the Game pavilion and the steps of her building. They rode the maglift to her floor without conversation, everything not said dragging behind them. When she would have walked right past her door to the IDC wing beyond, he stopped her with a hand on her arm.

"I need to talk to you."

"I know." She looked at her door. If she stepped inside but blocked the entrance with her body, would he let the door slide shut between them?

"Now."

"My brother—"

"You checked in on him right before we left and Rigger has been with him the whole time. He's safe. He's probably having more fun than the two of us combined."

Despite the situation, she chuckled. "Likely three times as much, if Rigger really is letting him modify the hologram."

"No putting this off then." He still had his hand on her arm, and a determined look that didn't bode well. "Don't make me wait outside all day."

"Fine." She thumbed the print scanner, then scanned her lithodisc ID bracelet. Malkor entered after her. He didn't step any farther into the room and she stopped somewhere in the middle, waiting.

He studied her across the space, his gaze tracing her features. "Who are you?" he finally asked.

"You know who I am."

"No. I know who you pretend to be."

"That's all that there is." Was it? Had she become Shadow Panthe in truth? What did she do with her life but fight in the pit?

"There's more." He watched her with those gray eyes, impatient but implacable. He wouldn't be leaving without answers.

"I have nothing else." That was certainly true. "I fight for credits on Altair Tri and I keep my brother safe."

"From whom?"

"Everyone."

"Why?"

"Why not?"

"Damnit, Shadow."

The title irked her.

Really irked her. Scratched at her skin in a raw spot.

"You can leave any time," she said.

He took a step toward her. "I'm staying until I get my answers. If I have to camp out by the door, so be it."

"Isonde won't like that."

"To the void with her." He took another step. "Tell me."

Kayla shook her head.

They stared at each other, their breaths linked, each tense and ready. She got lost somewhere in the silent fight, her mind telling her "keep silent," over and over while she wrestled the sweet urge to lay her burden on someone else.

"You're Wyrd, aren't you."

She couldn't even scoff with the breath caught in her throat. He had bluffed, guessed wildly. He couldn't know. They wouldn't be standing here like this if he knew.

"How could I be?"

"I don't know. I don't even think it's possible." His hand ran a furrow through his hair. "No Wyrd vessels have been detected entering Imperial Space since the first series of contacts generations ago, excepting Dolan's."

"There you have it."

"But it's true, isn't it, Shadow?"

"You just told me it couldn't be." She tightened a hand in the hidden fold of her dress. Stars, this was worse than she feared.

"I used to think you were a spy of some sort. Working for someone high up, maybe even someone in the Council of Seven. That you were stationed on Altair Tri for some deep mission, or hidden there while a situation cooled down. Even your obvious fear of Dolan could be rationalized if you were working against him. He's a powerful man in the empire now."

"I do not fear the *kin'shaa*." Venom crept into her voice on the last word.

Malkor snapped his fingers, the sound ricocheting. "There. See? You know things."

"That's what he is."

"I know that. The Ordochians revealed that to us. But how do *you* know that? And for that matter, how do you know being a *kin'shaa* makes him worthy of reviling?"

This time she hoped her scoff sounded believable. "Corinth got bored on the ship. He cracked your file archives."

"No. Your response was too authentic. Too automatic."

"You're being ridiculous."

"Am I? What about the rest? The knowledge of the Ordoch situation? Of male Wyrds in the royal family being stronger psionics than the females?"

"Haven't you read the IDC files?"

"What about Corinth," he pressed. "I've seen you with him. I know he talks to you. Somehow he communicates."

"You couldn't—"

"What about his technical knowledge? Sure, he's bright, but he's a kid living in a swamp. Where did he get his advanced understanding? He knows more than Rigger does."

"He likes to study."

"Stop playing with me, Shadow."

"That's not my name!"

Her breath tore chunks from the silence that followed her outburst. Frutt. Frutt her pride and frutt Malkor for pushing her.

"I know that," he said softly after a minute.

She needed to sit. Life spun while she took two steps and sank onto the nearest couch.

"You're so much more than who you pretend to be, why do you want me to keep believing the lie?"

She leaned her head back against the couch, eyes closing, and felt him settle beside her. She needed more strength to withstand this onslaught than she had today, after the shock of the Ilmenans' betrayal.

"I'm just a woman fighting in a tournament for you."

"Your identity could endanger our plan."

She opened her eyes and found him close. "My anonymity worked just fine for you before."

He took a breath, clearly forcing himself to patience. "You can trust me with this."

"Why?"

"My life is in your hands. Isonde's as well. You have enough evidence of our intent to fix the Empress Game to have us both executed. You know cheating at the Game is considered treason." He held himself so still beside her, as if any movement would set her to flight. "What more do you need from me?"

I need you not to be IDC. I need you not to have possibly been involved in the death of my family.

"Don't make me find out some other way."

He would, too. Now that he suspected, he would hunt the information down. Corinth was a popular name on Ordoch but he couldn't know that. They wouldn't have a population database of her homeworld. All he'd find is the Corinth on record with the royal family. That coupled with their secrecy would be all he needed.

"Kayla," she finally said. The name was rusty, her lips having abandoned it for years. "Kayla Reinumon."

"Reinumon? But you're—"

"Dead? So we learned." Corinth had found that official report buried amid the files he'd cracked on Ardin's starcruiser.

"Your bodies were identified after the incident, confirmed by Dolan."

"And you had no DNA profile of us to compare a scan to," she added.

"I thought the entire family. . . Holy shit."

A shudder ripped through her. Pain and relief. A heartbreak of freedom from silence so deep she couldn't breathe.

Malkor put a tentative hand on her shoulder.

Vayne. Corinth. Two lives, past and present. She drew the edges of her soul together until it finally merged. Vayne-and-Corinth.

The world settled on her once more, but lighter this time. She was distanced from it, floating almost, released from the anchor of her secret. She was free.

"Kayla."

She wanted to laugh at the sound of her name. Ask him to say it again.

It was a beautiful name.

Where did they stand now, now that he knew her identity?

"How did you escape the coup?" he asked.

She let the unanswerable questions lie. "It's mostly a haze. I remember—" she cut herself off. Did she? Did she even want to? She and Corinth never spoke of that night, never shared their memories of what it felt to have each of their twins die, and their family, their whole life, taken from them. It had been enough to know the other felt it. But now? She needed to expel the words that had built up at his question. The memory had risen and she couldn't get rid of it any other way.

"It was one of the rare times I was away from my *il'haar*. Vayne and a host of others in the palace were with a visiting master learning about levitation. He was safe, surrounded by the strongest psionics in my family, so I spent the afternoon with some of my untwinned sisters." Her sisters. It made her guilty to look at them, every time thinking how incomplete they were, women with no *il'haars*, knowing she had been granted what they would never have.

On Ordoch, when the royal family conceived it was always a set of male–female twins or a single female. Males, the stronger psionic half of the pair, were never born without a twin to protect them physically. It was only that way in the upper reaches of their society, though. Most Wyrds lived and died untwinned, unknowing of an *il'haar–ro'haar* bond.

"I knew he was safe and hadn't worried. When the explosion came I didn't even understand it. It decimated our courtyard. I was flung against the wall, something broken. At the time I thought it an accident, then I heard Vayne screaming for me in my head. Screaming and screaming and screaming."

That scream still woke her some nights.

"I left my sisters there, dead or not, and limped my way down corridors to him. He screamed and then—he stopped. Nothing. Silence. On my way I began to realize that charges must have been set throughout the palace, that I'd heard other explosions. I was almost there when I saw them. Saw him."

Malkor looked so pained by the telling that she almost stopped. But she couldn't, not now. She couldn't think past her memory. The words tumbled out as his hand fell from her shoulder.

"Teal and indigo and soot and blood. Imperial military dragging charred bodies from the chamber, counting them. I tucked myself against a piece of debris and watched. They dragged him out. My Vayne. By his leg." The fury washed up in her. The helplessness. The screaming bloodlust hatred for the men who touched him. For the *kin'shaa* who approached him.

"He twitched. In my mind I felt him grope for me. 'Where?' he asked in a single instant. I need you. His last words. 'Kayla. I need you.' I—" She choked, panted at the recall. "Dolan came up, studied my Vayne. Vayne twitched again, fighting the damage to his body. The *kin'shaa* shot him."

Vayne's burnt body had jerked like a broken puppet, then lay still. Dead, like so many others in the palace.

She had reached out with her mind then, everywhere silence, every ally gone. Every voice absent but one. She had been a microsecond from hurling herself at the pile of bodies to join Vayne when she'd heard it.

Her littlest brother. A terrified voice. Too untrained to know that in his fear he mentally shouted at the top of his lungs.

"I found Corinth in one of the practice rooms. He was hiding under the bodies of our aunt and his twin, both having died killing the soldiers who had been sent for them. I don't know how we escaped the palace. It has a million ins and outs, we must have taken one of the hidden routes. We intersected with two others fleeing. Somehow we ended up on a ship. A trade vessel." She fought for the memories. "We were nearly shot down on launch. I can't remember it all. Something about a damaged navconsole and star compass. There was a jump to hyperspace." She'd been unconscious most of the time, delirious from the pain of untreated injuries and Vayne's loss. Any lucid minutes were spent staring at the catatonic Corinth with a mix of desperate need and fierce hatred. He wasn't Vayne. He was all she had left. She had failed, but she had saved.

"Without a navconsole we'd taken a hyperstream blindly and it deposited us in the outer atmosphere of one of the empire's most distant planets."

"Altair Tri," Malkor said.

She nodded, lacking the energy for anything else. "The ship had been torn up in the firefight and the trip through hyperspace. It crashed somewhere outside the Slums. We survived the crash. We did not, however, survive the slavers and scavengers that reached the wreck almost immediately. Corinth and I were taken, the others killed as they were too old to fetch a price to cover their medical costs. The slavers didn't know who we were, only that the ship could be used for scrap metal and that we were young enough to fetch a fortune of credits on the pleasure slave auction blocks with our exotic blue hair and eyes."

"They didn't—"

"No. The slavers splurged for the best healer the slum side had to offer, first. Corinth and I were worth it, apparently. My body healed well. The slavers didn't live very long once the healers were finished. The rest you know." She shrugged a shoulder. "I found a way to support us, to keep us hidden in case the IDC and Dolan were searching for two members of Ordoch's royal family who escaped the coup."

"That's why you agreed to help us, in exchange for passage anywhere you asked," he said. "You need to get back to Wyrd Space."

She had no words left. The telling had drained them from her. Repercussions would come later. For now, only one thing mattered. "I need to see Corinth."

Malkor was immediately all action, as if desperate to get away. "Stay here, I'll bring him to you." He ducked his head, not meeting her eyes, and fled.

Malkor barged out of Kayla's room.

He couldn't listen to any more recounting of the attack he'd knowingly, if unwillingly, aided. Those soldiers had been allowed planet-side on Ordoch because of him. The charges placed in halls of the palace on Ordoch—the soldiers had had access to those areas because of him, because of his negotiations with the seneschal.

Frutt.

True, he hadn't planned the attack, hadn't placed the charges, hadn't killed anyone. Not directly. But he'd helped to put all the pieces into place, even if he never thought the empire would go through with the coup. Willfully naïve, or just plain stupid?

And now, Kayla. Her name suited her.

"Good talk, then?" Isonde's voice brought him up short. She stood just down the hallway from their door.

"Not now, Isonde." He recognized the jealous look she couldn't quite hide. Not his problem. She had chosen Ardin and the empire over him two years ago and right now he couldn't care less.

He worked to order his thoughts as he strode away.

Kayla and Corinth—Wyrds, psionics. Had they been reading his mind this whole time? That brought a cold wash over him. What the void had he said? What had they heard?

Damnit. He had to protect himself.

He recalled Dolan's lessons for mental shielding and began visualizing layers of plassteel wrapping his mind, the sections of a wall forming, edges fusing together. He reinforced the image over and over. Once the shield was in place it was natural to maintain it unconsciously. Ideally, it would remain until he decided to lower it.

Ideally.

He entered the IDC wing and halted outside Trinan and Vid's door. Shields. Steel. Focus.

He commed the room and Rigger let him in. His gaze immediately fell on Corinth. Was he reading his mind right now?

The boy's eyes widened and his hand froze mid-action.

He was so small to have survived. And he'd been even smaller. Malkor took a step into the room and Corinth's hands tightened spasmodically on the biostrip and tactile probe he held. Malkor felt the lightest touch, the pressure of a palm in the center of his chest, nothing more than that. The boy looked terrified. Hunted. How was he going to get him to Kayla?

The probe and biostrip fell to the table. In two seconds Corinth was up and pushing past him. Corinth burst into the hall and took off at a run. Malkor could barely keep up. They sprinted into the main corridor separating the housing wings, and Corinth slammed his ID bracelet against the lock on Kayla's wing when they reached it. Her door was already open and she waited just inside. Corinth catapulted himself at her and she caught him, rock-steady.

Over his head she murmured, "Thank you," to Malkor before leading Corinth into her sleeping chamber. The door shut behind them and Malkor found himself standing awkwardly in the common room of their apartments once more, alone with Isonde.

"Is he. . .?" Isonde made a vague motion toward Kayla's room with the datapad she held. "Is everything okay? He looked. . ." Concern shadowed her voice. She glanced at Kayla's door then back to him. "Evelyn looked worried like I've never seen. What did you say to her?"

Malkor took a deep breath. "I think they'll be okay now." That was a lie. How could they be?

He checked his mobile comm. About a million messages waited for him and a flashing indicator told him he'd missed a meeting. He sat down on the couch opposite Isonde. "Nightmares, I think."

She nodded, her gaze drifting to Kayla's door again.

Silence lengthened between them. There was no reason to stay, but he couldn't go.

"You'll be at the extravaganza tonight?" he asked.

"With Evelyn, hopefully. If she's up for it. Malkor—" she paused, as if choosing her words. "You did well finding her, she was the right choice for my body double." Kayla must have really impressed Isonde with her dedication to the plan for

Isonde to admit to any such thing. "She was impressive at the party last night. Natural. I had some doubts, but after seeing her charm Priestess Ush. . . She's a real asset to our cause."

Gee, couldn't imagine why. The exiled princess of Ordoch wanting to build alliances that would lead to the freeing of her homeworld. "I'll tell her."

"Well, don't get *too* carried away." Isonde turned her attention back to her datapad.

He recognized her dismissal when he saw it. He'd never liked that about her.

He should check on Rigger's progress with Isonde's hologram. He should review the list of the most likely candidates for cheating the Game with his commander. He should check the healing progress on Janeen's ankle, debrief Gio and Aronse after their time with the Wyrds and circle back with Hekkar. He should do. . . something. Anything. Anything to avoid the truth of Kayla's identity and problems that knowledge caused.

As he walked back toward his octet's wing he focused on questions he could answer, such as why Kayla and Corinth had been declared dead instead of missing by Dolan or the IDC leaders, and why a giant manhunt hadn't been launched. That was simple military coup tactics. Announcing that two members of the family had survived the coup and were at large among the populace offered hope. Hope sparked rebellion. Even if Kayla and Corinth were never found, their people would have mobilized around the idea of them, catalyzed into trying to retake their birthright.

The assumed death of every member of the family left the people with no leader to rally behind. And if the two had in fact survived and surfaced later? The IDC could deal with them then. It would not be their first or last political assassination.

He knew now how Kayla and Corinth communicated, and what trauma had left him mute. He knew why Kayla was so determined, inhumanely so, to protect her brother, and he knew how she had learned to be so deadly. His mobile comm pulsed and he pulled the unit out to see his commander's ID flash on the screen, driving home the question he couldn't avoid.

Now that he knew who Kayla was, what was he supposed to do with her?

14

The next morning Kayla stood on the edge of the sparring ring, trying to catch her breath. Her opponent stood on the other side, trying not to cry.

Kayla almost felt bad about beating the girl.

Almost.

Barely out of adolescence, Maiden Frolova had clearly nurtured hope of winning the Empress Game. That hadn't stopped Kayla from winning a best of three series of best of three matches 2–0 and 2–0. It was poor luck for the girl to have drawn Kayla on her first day or she might have made it farther. Judging by Frolova's father's thunderous look, it would be a long time before he let her forget her failure here.

Kayla turned her back on the pair and walked to where Isonde waited, wearing her skin.

I need to eat more.

Isonde, in her Kayla hologram, handed her a towel. "That was easy."

"From where you're standing, maybe." Kayla wiped sweat from her face.

"Three down."

Kayla scanned the huge pit that made up the floor of the arena. "Three million to go." The pit had been divided into thousands of sparring circles; she could barely make out the far end of the arena through the mass of contestants present. Security on the tournament floor was extremely tight. Contestants were only allowed their one attendant with them, and both had to consent to full identification procedures before entering the pit. Security officers were stationed at regular intervals along the perimeter and IDC agents circulated throughout the maze, randomly re-verifying contestants. She herself had already been re-print and DNA scanned twice.

The switch Rigger and Corinth engineered worked perfectly. With her hologram biostrip active, Kayla's print, DNA and iris scan data linked to Isonde's profile, and vice versa. No need for a DNA-laced cell spray on her hands or the rigid optical filters for her pupils.

The only other people allowed on the tournament floor were imperial officials overseeing the matches, and servers who provided the only allowed beverages and food. Everyone else was relegated to the stands. Today, on the first day of qualifying, the arena was only half-full.

"Where to next?" she asked Isonde, rubbing the back of her neck with the towel. She glanced at her defeated opponent. Yep, definitely crying.

The princess checked the schedule pad. "Ring 1A-731-BXD."

They wove through the crowd to reach the site. The previous series hadn't wrapped yet, and it looked intense. The combatants wielded staves, a choice Kayla hadn't seen often this morning. Fights at the Empress Game occurred either unarmed, or else a particular weapon was chosen for both to use. The allowable choices were staves, swords or knives, the blades being metal with dulled edges. The choice of which weapon to use was given to the contestant with the best record to date, or the one with the highest randomly assigned number if their records matched.

One of the women had a height advantage, but was smart enough to recognize her opponent as quicker. She had wisely chosen staves to make the most of her reach and keep the faster opponent at bay.

Kayla watched the combatants, absently rubbing a sore spot on her forearm. She hissed as she brushed over a deep bruise. Her fingertips came back with a smear of blood. Little Frolova had had a wicked side-piercing kick, and apparently the force of one had split the skin on Kayla's forearm. She wasn't the only one sporting such bruises. While the medical staff had been kept busy this morning, most of the contestants chose to bear their minor—or even major—wounds rather than suffer the numbness that accompanied a medstick's ministrations.

She wiped her forearm on the side of her black tank-top and turned her attention to the contestants. It was easy to tell them apart from their attendants. All of the contestants wore officially issued outfits in black, a tight-fitting tank-top tunic paired with leggings and bare feet. Attendants were also issued official outfits, a loose-fitting combination of pants and a tunic in white.

"I'm surprised to see you here."

The words came in a child-high voice from a spitfire-looking thing beside Kayla. The woman's head reached her shoulder, if that, but she had a stare that made her twice as tall.

"Oh?" Kayla couldn't place her.

The diminutive thing turned to study Kayla full on, her hazel eyes smug. "After the Councils had rejected your proposal to marry the prince without a Game being held— what, three separate times?—I figured you would be back on Piran, sulking."

She would have a suitably scathing retort if she actually knew who the woman was.

"Perhaps you didn't get the hint that you weren't wanted as empress."

Isonde cut in. "This from the woman who failed to secure the council seat that was all but hereditary for her family." Kayla didn't recognize herself with that superior expression, or that tone of disdain.

The woman turned her attention to the princess. "I'm sorry, but who are you again?"

"Lady Evelyn Broch, of the Ishimi province, Piran."

"Never heard of it. Though who can keep track of the minuscule provinces Piran insists on recognizing as sovereign nations."

Isonde nodded as if she agreed with her. "And you must be just absolutely overcome with work as the assistant junior undersecretary for the Protectorate Council, I imagine." She managed to make the position sound as though it ranked below being a sanitation bot. "No time to study such things as politics."

Color stained the woman's cheekbones, but a mix of groans and cheers saved her from answering. The series had ended, the taller contestant's decision to choose staves paying off. The short woman slunk away without another word.

"The Domina Ridea," Isonde said once she'd left. "You and I need to do more studying this afternoon."

Great. "I doubt she'll come near us again."

"Probably not, but only fools rely on chance. Preparation separates the successful from the failures."

Kayla inclined her head in agreement as she had seen Isonde do. "You're right." She liked the look in her own eyes just then: implacable determination. She and the princess were on the same page. "For now, I'm going to win another fight."

What Kayla wanted when she finished fighting for the day was a full-body soak in Varaguda effervescent simmer salts. What she got was a hurried sonic shower and an invitation to a caucus on today's tournament data.

Now she sat, or rather half-lay, on the couch next to Malkor in Trinan and Vid's room, studying the notable matches of the day. Both forearms were numb in a variety of spots, as were her forehead and left knee. She had cooling skins adhered to each to reduce swelling and her leg was elevated to try to speed her knee's recovery from the medstick treatment. Her hands throbbed but she refused to risk the numbness there. Pain she could handle—losing, she could not. It had taken Malkor fifteen minutes to convince her to let a medical technician he trusted with their ruse treat her knee. She would have refused that as well but he made a good point that the inflamed ligaments would only get worse with each match if she didn't mend them now.

Through it all Janeen sat with a look on her face that said, "*I* wouldn't have gotten injured if *I'd* been the one doing the fighting."

Kayla sank into a more comfortable position on the couch, wincing when her knee tweaked with pain. Malkor held himself stiffly beside her. What did he think of her, knowing who she was?

She felt an odd connection to him now that she'd shared her secret—as if it had bonded them somehow, tied their futures together. It was an awkward push-pull. With the truth out, was he her fellow conspirator or the man who would bring her down? Had she gained an ally or sealed her fate?

She'd lain awake last night, horrified by what she'd revealed, but at the same time knowing there could have been no other way. She'd waited to be taken into custody, waited to be delivered to Malkor's superiors at the IDC, to someone in the military, to the emperor himself. To Dolan. Waited, but it hadn't happened. Malkor hadn't revealed her identity to anyone and she'd lain safe through the night.

Safe, but for how long?

Malkor needed her right now. He couldn't risk her being taken away before she won the Game. After that? Would he keep her identity a secret, knowing she had her own bargaining chip about his cheating the Game? Would he honor their deal and return her to Wyrd Space? Or would she and Corinth be fleeing for their lives once again?

Around her, Vid, Trinan, Janeen, Malkor and Hekkar sorted through a galaxy's worth of tournament reports on everything from scores and weapon choices to techniques and injuries from the morning's matches. They adjusted their initial assessment of who the major players were, and updated reconnaissance on each contestant's strengths and weaknesses. Kayla focused on reading screen after screen of hard stats and scanning vids of her top opponents' matches. Gio and Isonde were there too, gathering intelligence from every news source possible about the political fallout of today's wins and losses.

Amid it all sat Corinth, alight with interest in the activity. He drank in the details as datapads passed back and forth and the octet called out things of note to each other. Despite her repeated warnings to stay out of their heads, he still dabbled on the edge of Trinan's and Vid's minds. As much as it scared her, it was useful. When they brought an opponent to her attention for a closer look, Corinth helped her identify which opponents they thought *could* beat her and which they thought *would* beat her.

Kayla watched tournament footage from this morning on one of her strongest opponents, the Ordinal Divinya. The woman flowed like smoke through the air, subtle, fluid, with positional shifts you couldn't anticipate. The opponent that Divinya fought couldn't have looked more flat-footed had she been fighting on mud. The series ended before Kayla could learn much of Divinya's technique. She passed the footage to Malkor. He kept their "priority targets to watch" list, but more than that, she wanted his analysis of the Ordinal's style. They hadn't expected her and Kayla had no background on her. Several unexpected quality opponents had surfaced. It was tricky to judge on day one—the mediocre could be paired with the terrible and come out looking brilliant. Divinya, however, was clearly a genuine threat.

She scanned the woman's specs while Malkor watched the series.

"Wow." Malkor whistled. "How did we miss her?"

She caught him replaying in half-time the end that had surprised her as well. Kayla read the brief bio. "She's from the Protectorate Planet Ged, southern hemisphere, a low population city on what looks to be a minor continent."

"Ged?" Malkor's gaze went to Janeen. "That's your homeworld and you haven't heard of her?"

"Who, the Ordinal Divinya?" Janeen shrugged, her gaze

sliding away from his. "Most of the people across the Southern Belt have heard of her, but beyond that she's not famous. I don't remember her being all that impressive." Her tone was a little too blithe for Kayla's liking.

"Well she certainly upped her game for the tournament."

"Who hasn't?" Janeen answered. She held out a datapad to Malkor. "Looks like the Wyrd princess is making a name for herself."

Kayla resisted the urge to grab for the pad. She'd been avoiding the report on Princess Tia'tan of Ilmena as if ignoring her might change the fact that a Wyrd had come to win the Empress Game as an ally of Dolan. Her curiosity ate at her, though. Had her kinswoman made a respectable showing? Kayla leaned in close to Malkor, reading over his shoulder.

Her pride rose at the sight of Tia'tan's record. Flawless. She'd not only won every series without it going to a third match, she'd won every match without it going to a third point. Better than Kayla herself had done. She couldn't deny her satisfaction that Wyrd training had proved itself superior today.

::You're discomfiting him.:: Corinth's voice was much too amused for her taste. She pretended to study the datapad Malkor held as she schooled her thoughts into separate compartments before lowering first her outer shields, then with more effort, her median shields. Corinth rushed inside her head like a puppy bounding onto a bed.

Too much.

Corinth withdrew slightly. His presence still filled her brain, but at least her head didn't threaten to split apart.

::Better?::

Some. We talked about controlling the rush, remember?

::I know, we just don't practice enough.::

She felt him split his focus, easing the compression on her brain.

::You've got him all mixed up.::

Who?

::Malkor. He thinks you can read his mind.::

I thought you said he was shielding now?

::Eh. Mostly. He's actually pretty effective, for an imperial. But he's so nervous about this it's shouting from him.::

Corinth, do NOT try to read him.

::I don't even have to, I swear. It's right on the surface, I'm barely probing.::

She knew better, but. . . *what is he saying?*

::It's a loop between "Can she read my thoughts? Is she doing it right now?" and "Shit! Don't think that! What if she heard it?":: She felt his humor. ::You're so messing with him.::

I'm not doing anything.

::He doesn't know that. He thinks you— Oh. Oh, wow.:: Corinth's amusement turned awkward. ::He definitely doesn't want you to hear that.::

Now she really didn't want to ask.

::I'm not sharing that one.::

I don't want—

::Yeah you do.::

Damn psi powers. She glanced up at Corinth to see his face flushing red.

::Um. . . maybe you should give him a little space.::

She jerked away from Malkor like he'd shocked her with two hundred volts.

Malkor gave an awkward cough and shifted in his seat without looking at her. The others quirked brows at her weird behavior.

::Now he definitely thinks you can hear him.::

Stars burn it, Corinth. Get out of his head. From the look on Corinth's face, and the fascinated but horrified-at-his-reaction embarrassment she felt emanating from him, she'd guess that he'd already retreated from Malkor.

Do NOT do that to the others. Just because Malkor knows who we are—

::He's not going to tell them.::

That doesn't mean they won't guess if you keep messing with them.

She felt him pause, gathering courage to say something he feared she wouldn't like. A better trained psionic could have shielded his thoughts while still inside her mind. Corinth would be able to, once she got him back to Wyrd Space.

::Would that be so bad? They like us, Kay.::

They might like you, and they might keep us safe for now because it suits them, but they are IDC. They could turn us over in a microsecond. They are not *your friends, Corinth.*

She felt the hurt she'd dealt him but there was no shelter from that truth. He pushed away from her, withdrawing in silence.

With a morning spent fighting and an afternoon spent researching both opponents and diplomats, the evening already felt long by the time Kayla and Isonde arrived for the dinner banquet. She let Isonde carry the conversation with two junior members of the Protectorate Council—who clearly had more interest in Isonde herself than her political agenda. Isonde played the two smoothly, knowing that some alliances were won with trade agreements, some with charm.

Kayla spent the majority of the meal speaking with the Director of the Interplanetary Alliance of Croppers. He had no official standing on either council, but as head of the organization that unified the farmers and corporations that provided much of the empire's food supplies, he had a position of great influence. Piran was a powerful member of the organization, and Kayla knew Isonde hoped to leverage that position to get the Croppers to take at least a leaning stance toward withdrawing from Wyrd Space.

They discussed the possible introduction of a non-native wheat variety into the Croppers' Alliance shared fields. The bioengineered species showed excellent production capability, but a full scale roll-out was beyond the means of the Croppers alone. It was easy to turn the conversation to a discussion of how withdrawing from Ordoch would leave imperial assets free to perhaps subsidize such a project, considering its potential benefit to the population of the empire. Another member of their table, a colonel in the imperial army, joined in when the subject of withdrawing from Wyrd Space came up. He went so far as to hint at the futility of the military's actions in Ordoch, and that the army itself might consider the funds better spent elsewhere.

"Even from a tactical perspective," the colonel commented, "it's time for a change. Our actions did not produce the desired result, and continuing this course, pouring more resources into it, is poor field management." The conversation returned to less contentious topics, but Kayla marked the conversation as a win. Seeds had been planted. She'd be sure to touch base with the two of them throughout the tournament to cultivate their opinions.

Kayla was still riding high off her dinner conversation when, a few hours later, she spotted Prince Trebulan. The tables had been cleared away and guests divided their time between strolling, dancing and drinking. Isonde set aside her powerhouse agenda to enjoy a turn about the floor with Prince Ardin, and Kayla enjoyed a rare moment alone. She couldn't, however, pass up the chance to meet Prince Trebulan.

He was the leader of Velezed, the planet on which the Tetratock Nanovirus originated. It was his people who had first suffered the plague, his world was the first to be devoured by the nanites. The microscopic robots' hunger for all organic material had left Velezed near-lifeless. Only a handful of people survived on each of its continents, and the TNV wasn't finished there.

Trebulan himself was one of the few survivors of the TNV. Somehow his body had fought and defeated the nanites that infected his blood, but not before they nearly killed him. Willing to do anything to save his people, Trebulan had submitted himself as a test subject to Velezed's scientists in their futile efforts to find a cure. Kayla couldn't imagine what he had been put through. Here he was, though, a walking reminder of what was at stake for each world in the empire if the spread of the TNV couldn't be contained.

His once healthy frame was devastated, wracked and twisted until he walked like a short-circuited bot that couldn't control its direction. While he gathered looks of pity aplenty, few people stopped to have a word with him.

And no wonder. Most people didn't know what to say to someone so heroic and destroyed at the same time.

"Your highness? Prince Trebulan, do you perhaps have a moment?" Kayla moved into what she thought might have been his path. It was near impossible to tell where his spasmodic steps were meant to take him. His head swiveled as if the joint were rusty, and his good eye focused on her.

"I intended to withdraw for the evening, but I have a few minutes." His voice was perhaps the only undamaged part of him, and it poured out so smoothly as to be almost freakish. He stopped an awkward distance away. Kayla closed the gap, uncertain if to smile at him was even appropriate.

"I wanted to meet you, to introduce myself. I have much sympathy for your plight," she said.

His lips quirked sardonically. "You and everyone else. Sympathy I have in abundance."

"Of course you do. The TNV is a horror. The devastation your world has suffered is incalculable. I'm sure everyone sympathizes."

Trebulan and his counselors had been circulating among the parties so far, each dressed in crimson ceremonial robes of mourning and causing a sensation. The topic of the TNV trailed in their wake.

"Perhaps if everyone was less sympathetic and more prone to action, my people might not continue to suffer."

She nodded. "There's much the empire could do for Velezed if the Councils would address more proposals related to relief efforts."

He scoffed at the mention of relief efforts. "That won't

happen unless the Sovereign Council looks beyond their self-interests."

"What you need are more allies," she said.

He raised a brow. "I'm sorry, I didn't catch your name."

"Lady Evelyn Broch, of Piran. Eradicating the TNV is a concern for all of the empire, and we're especially dedicated to the cause."

His cool manner chilled further. "What my people need most right now, Lady Evelyn, is food. Medicine. Generators. We need help incinerating our dead. Eradication of the nanovirus is a long-term goal; my people need immediate help."

"I understand that, and Piran has been committing aid since the beginning of the TNV disaster. We're pushing a bill for a bigger relief package through the Sovereign Council, but the need for a cure can't be underscored enough. We're trying to build support for a plan that will lead to the eradication of the nanovirus."

"I have heard of Piran's, and especially Princess Isonde's, 'plan' for chasing a cure. She doesn't know a thing about getting results."

His response surprised her. "Do you disagree that the Wyrds are our best hope of finding a cure before the TNV consumes the rest of the empire?"

"Not at all. But withdraw from Wyrd Space? What, *apologize*, to them?"

"With their freedom as a bargaining tool, we hope to gain their cooperation."

"You want to get their cooperation?" he asked with some venom. "Unleash it."

"Excuse me?"

"Unleash the TNV on all those heartless freaks. Let it decimate their people, devour their world. Let their dead pile in the streets because no one is left to deal with the bodies. I guarantee that'll get results. They'll bend their oh-so-superior minds and psi powers to a cure faster than a static discharge."

Her hand clenched empty air where her kris should have

been. "After all you and your people have suffered, how could you wish that on someone else?" On my people, you frutting sociopath. *I will kill you before that happens.*

"It is *because* of what we have suffered that I vote to release the TNV on Ordoch. Those—" He cut himself off. "The Wyrds had the option to help and they chose not to. They burned whatever sympathy I might have had for them with their inaction." The tremor that shivered his head intensified and he paused to breathe.

Good, she thought. *I hope it hurts.* It took everything she had not to defend her people's choice, to play her role as Lady Evelyn.

Isonde would be equally horrified. They had assumed Trebulan and the Velezed council members would be among the strongest of their allies, not their opponents.

In a quieter voice he said, "We appreciate the aid Piran has given us thus far and hope to remain on friendly terms. I cannot, however, support a plan that relies on naïve belief in the altruism of the Wyrds. Withdrawing from Ordoch would certainly be a mistake. Now, if you will excuse me." He spurred his crippled form into his disjointed walk, leaving her staring after him.

Holy shit. Could the Councils actually vote to unleash the TNV on Ordoch? Was that possible?

Trebulan had a surviving heir who was entered into the Empress Game. If she won and controlled a vote on the Council of Seven. . .

Kayla's hands tightened to fists. She would grind that little bitch into dust.

Dinner party be damned. Time to study more fight tactics.

15

An insistent beeping woke Malkor from much-needed sleep. Damnit, hadn't he just lain down? He groped for the mobile comm on the bedside table and flipped on the screen.

Senior Agent Rua,

Glad to see you made it to the Game safely. An unplanned visit to the Mine Field is treacherous enough, never mind if the visit is less than coincidental. As I'm sure you've guessed, I know about your jaunt to Altair Tri. Dangerous business, that. You might have made your plans with the best of intentions but it's clear someone doesn't share your views. Perhaps you should choose your allies more carefully.

I suggest we meet.

You have your ends and I have mine, but both can be achieved, depending on who claims the throne. I might have some insight into your particular situation, and you might have a way to repay my generosity.

I'm easy enough to spot around court, but the best way to reach me is to approach my people. What a spectacular and sensational delight their arrival at the Game has been, don't you agree?

Annoyance melded into suspicion. He'd received a steady

flow of anonymous, cloak and dagger messages on his public terminal since assuming his duties at the Empress Game, but this was the first to reach his private ID, shooting straight through to reach him on his IDC-encrypted mobile comm. He scanned it again, slower, and the hairs prickled on his neck at the wording.

He sat up in bed, blinking bleary eyes. Sleep had apparently become a luxury he couldn't afford.

He'd been awake last night with an emergency with one of the contestants he had under surveillance. The night before that the inaugural ball kept him up. Before that it had been meetings with Commander Parrel and fellow octet leaders until well past bedtime.

. . . and every night it had been Shadow Panthe. Kayla. Ricocheting through his thoughts like a well-aimed projectile.

He pulled his sleep-fogged mind together. What hour was it? A glance at the chronometer confirmed his suspicions: three in the morning. Nonetheless, he paged Hekkar with a non-urgent request. If Hekkar was sleeping, it wouldn't wake him.

"Yeah, Malk?"

So much for sleeping.

"What are you doing up?"

"Just finished meeting with an informant. Real dead-of-night, back-alleyway type. You?"

"Something similar. Got a minute?"

"Sure, I'm headed back to our wing, be at your room in ten."

Malkor considered lying back down for five, but rose instead.

The inference that Ardin's starcruiser's close call in the Mine Field had been more than bad luck matched his own thoughts too closely. And how in the void had the sender gotten that information?

Time for another look at the incident report.

Malkor poured a glass of water and settled in front of his complink terminal. He opened the report Ardin had sent him with the starcruiser's full damage assessment. He read through the catalog of sections and systems affected by the attack, then went through the defense detail of the report, pausing at the estimation of the "pirate" ships' probable weaponry. Fancy. And pricey. Too pricey for pirates scavenging the edge of the Mine Field for stream-tripped vessels.

"Let me in," came Hekkar's voice through the comm.

Hekkar entered, looking every bit as shady as the character he'd been meeting. His vibrant red-orange hair was tucked beneath a black bandana, the collar of his duster was pulled up to his cheekbones and the gray-black motley of his outfit said "street-tough" without words. Hekkar could do a fair bit of hulking when the situation called for it, and right now he looked rough enough to make a person wait for the next magchute.

"Good meet?"

Hekkar sloughed off the duster and tossed it on the coffee table. "We'll see. He claimed to have a source inside the service staff that swears one of the contestants is using some kind of organic-bionics. A substance injected subcutaneously that toughens the flesh into a pliable armor of sorts, and allows for adhesion of carbon-based bionics to the bone."

"I've never even heard of such a thing."

"Me neither. He of course wouldn't say who the source was, who the suspect was, or why they suspected anything in the first place, but he did refer to the contestant as 'the deaconess.' Figured I'd start by running down a list of which contestants can claim that title and go from there." He shrugged a shoulder. "Probably a waste of time, but, hey." Hekkar made himself comfortable on the couch, feet propped on the table. "What has you up in the middle of the night?"

"Have you read the reports on the damage to Ardin's ship?"

"Haven't had a chance yet. Something good?"

"Good? No. Interesting? Yes." Malkor enlarged the schematic he'd been studying.

"By 'interesting,'" Hekkar said, "you mean worrisome, don't you?"

"Is there any other kind of interesting for the IDC?"

Hekkar sighed. "Just once I wish there was."

"No, you don't. I saw you making the rounds at one of the banquets tonight. You love this shit. The intrigue, the drama, the intricate dance of diplomacy. Admit it—you live for this."

"I'll admit it when you do."

Malkor grinned. "Guilty." This was why he joined the IDC, to affect politics without sitting through hours upon endless hours of Council sessions. To get to know the people behind the politics and achieve the best outcome for the empire without being limited by "the rules." Backroom deals? Undocumented concessions? Last-minute saves of potentially catastrophic situations between nations? Anything and everything for the good of the empire.

"So what are we looking at here?" Hekkar gestured to Malkor's screen.

"Damage to the engines. The ships took pot shots at the drives, but didn't attack with anything too heavy. One of the hyperspace drives had the thrust output channel collapsed and the venting tubes on both sub-stream drives were riddled. None of these shots, though, hit the fuel cells or reaction chambers. Not even close."

"They wanted to disable us, not blow us up."

"True, and sensible for space pirates. But look." Malkor touched the screen to explode a section of the still-functioning hyperspace drive's reaction chamber. "What's this here?" Minuscule fractures lined the casing, barely visible on the schematic. They ran the length, irregularly spaced and branching out from a single point.

Hekkar came to study the screen. He leaned past Malkor to manipulate the image, first zooming the display in, then widening to view the overall damage to the rear section of the ship.

"Are you seeing what I'm seeing?" Malkor asked.

"Mhmm. Those stress fractures don't look like they could have been caused by any of the other damage." He bent in for a closer look. "Janeen reported that the captain had wanted to drop out of stream right before the attack, didn't she? She'd said the drives were 'twitchy.'"

"Power couldn't be equalized with those structural weaknesses, no wonder it was twitchy. Sure, power generation vibrates the shit out of casings and will eventually blow them apart if left alone, but"—Malkor tapped the central point in the fracture spokes—"no way this is standard degradation."

"So what are we saying?"

"Someone on board Ardin's starcruiser didn't want us making it to the Game."

Hekkar whistled. "Damn. Weaken the hyperspace drive so we're guaranteed to drop stream in the Mine Field, then have associates clean us up once there."

"They'd only need to delay us until the Game was over. It runs with or without Ardin's presence, once it's been called. But if Isonde wasn't there to compete. . ."

"Never thought I'd be thankful for the rooks. We'd never have escaped without their interference." Hekkar shook his head. "Couldn't have been another contestant, no one knew we were even out there."

"No one but Ardin and Isonde's inner circle, and they'll vouch for every one of them."

"Yeah, but I won't." Hekkar took his place back on the couch. "What even made you look at the reactor casings?"

Malkor read him the message he'd received. The wording struck him again.

Wait—

Malkor reread the last line. ". . . *the best way to reach me is to approach my people. What a spectacular and sensational delight their arrival at the Game has been, don't you agree?*"

Hekkar frowned. "Only one person could expect to be known just by referencing his people's presence when the entirety of the empire had arrived on Falanar."

"Yeah." The unease the letter generated kicked in triple at the conclusion. "Dolan."

16

Kayla sat on the arena floor with both legs stretched out in front of her. She leaned over them, breathing into the stretch, feeling her muscles liven. She was early, but hundreds of women and their attendants were on the floor doing the same already.

Her body hummed, energy banked until her first fight. Isonde, in her Kayla hologram, chatted with another of the attendants.

I hope she's not making an ass of me.

Every time Isonde spoke, every time she stepped with her Kayla-feet, every time she waved her Kayla-arm, Kayla's skin crawled. From deep within came the aversion to seeing herself walk apart from her soul. *She's stolen my body*. It was nothing to her to wear the Isonde hologram. She knew who she was inside, the program was just a costume. But seeing herself walk around without her. . .

Isonde–Kayla walked over and took a seat in the chair beside Kayla. She hadn't issued one complaint at the early hour, and had come to the pit like it was natural to show up two hours before the fighting was due to start because Kayla said she needed to be here. She didn't question the necessity, trusting that this was Kayla's arena, that she knew what needed to be done.

Just like Kayla had put herself in Isonde's hands when it came to politics, Isonde gave over full control of this aspect of their charade to Kayla, recognizing Kayla's skill. Two pros, two talents, one goal.

It was surprising and gratifying to be thus respected, even silently.

The arena began to fill. Contestants appeared in greater numbers and the air's charge intensified. Everywhere Kayla looked she saw determination, trepidation, focus and resignation. All had come to fight, but not all had come to win.

"There's Countess Æther," Isonde said.

Her first opponent—an easy fight: rush, overpower, score a point, repeat.

Assuming Kayla's rating was higher and the choice of weapons hers, dual knives, of course, Countess Æther, who had chosen unarmed combat every time, had zero chance. No telling who Kayla might face afterward or what they'd bring to the fight, but she would be ready.

"You've been beating them handily," Isonde said with approval, as they crossed the immense floor of the arena on their way to Kayla's fourth series of the day.

Kayla chuckled. "Kicking ass."

"Excuse me?"

"It's 'you're kicking ass today.' And thank you, I have been." She hadn't dropped a point yet, never mind lost a match. Three flawless series.

Isonde gave her an amused smile. "If you say so."

Kayla might gloat a little more if this morning's matches hadn't been fairly easy. Which wasn't all that surprising, considering that most of these women shouldn't even be in a tournament like this. The prize was just too good to pass up, though. Anyone with a claim to sovereignty on her homeworld and the ability to hold a weapon was at the Game, trying to win the crown.

None of her competitors this morning would have lasted five minutes in the Blood Pit.

"Who's next?" she asked.

"Looks like. . ." Isonde scanned the datapad with their

schedule on it. Her good humor melted into a look of distaste. "Arcanist Zerustae."

"Who?"

"Elder sister to the Low Divine on Falanar." Isonde looked even less pleased at having to mention the Low Divine.

"The who?"

"The Low Divine? Third in power to only the Mid and High Divines within the church of Aih?"

Religion? Bah. Who the void cared about that.

Isonde must have read her thoughts on her face. "You know, the church that 'you' belong to, the dominant religion among the Sovereign Planets. . .?"

Kayla rolled her eyes. "Right, right. So. You and this Arcanist don't get along?"

Isonde's lips quirked into a slight grin. "Let's just say I want you to kick her ass."

Kayla returned the grin. "I shall endeavor to beat her handily."

She paused when they approached the ring and saw the choice of weapon: swords.

Well, that's unexpected.

She'd yet to fight with swords in the Game. Good thing she'd been able to brush up on her technique on the way to Falanar. Swords weren't her favorite weapon. They lacked subtlety. No one had ever been sneak-attacked by a sword, you couldn't fail to see it coming. Daggers were so much quicker, so much more. . . personal.

Sure, she could kill someone with a sword in about fifteen seconds. She was a *ro'haar* after all, weapons were the tools of her craft. Didn't mean she enjoyed using one.

The official sword of the Game was a rapier, a thrusting weapon of finesse and control. If it had to be swords, that would have been her choice. It was still a dangerous choice, though. Even with a blunted tip, the blade, which started near the hilt as a flattened diamond shape and tapered to a fine point, could still pierce flesh if too much force was applied. No wonder most combatants chose unarmed combat or staves—much less risk of injury.

So, Arcanist Zerustae was confident in her skill. Excellent. Let's see what a confident imperial could do against a *ro'haar*.

The official called them to the center of the ring and handed them each their weapon. The rapier was light, weighing about a kilogram, and had a compound swept hilt. Several steel knuckle guards swirled down from the quillon to the pommel with an artful twist. She would have liked to have a kris in her off-hand, but the Game only allowed for the rapier. Kayla shrugged. Rapiers had very little cutting edge, being mainly a thrusting weapon. She could parry with the flat of her palm just as well.

Zerustae favored her with a smug smile. Kayla was becoming used to the expression, as most of her series began that way. Apparently the world hadn't quite discovered yet that "Isonde" was the one to beat at the Game, and everyone assumed the princess couldn't hold her own in a fight. Kayla grinned right back. They'd learn soon enough.

Zerustae sooner than most.

Kayla whipped the blade through the air a few times, listening to it sing, getting a feel for the grip, the heft of it. Zerustae's smile sagged a little.

Oh yes, Arcanist. You're about to get way more than you bargained for.

Kayla studied the woman as the ring official conferred with the official scorekeepers. Zerustae was around the same height as her, long-limbed with an excellent reach. Her face said, "You might think you're ready, but I'm still going to beat the shit out of you." Likely she had been trouncing people soundly with a sword all day.

Kayla saluted her with a flick of her wrist and settled in for the fight. Zerustae, seeing Kayla's perfectly angled L stance and low guard, apparently decided to take the match seriously, and likewise readied herself. Her stance looked competent and she held the blade comfortably.

Kayla should probably take it slow to start, wait for Zerustae to offend, develop a sense of her style. . .

But when the official called "begin!" and Zerustae attacked right off on a high outside line destined for Kayla's heart, Kayla made up her mind in a nanosecond.

Caution be damned, let's show a little style.

Kayla lunged full out in a passata sotto, dropping under the attack, front knee bent, back leg fully extended, empty hand flat on the floor to balance her while she thrust upward with her sword. The blunted tip kissed the fabric of Zerustae's tank-top square in the mid-section.

"Point, white!" called the official.

Zerustae couldn't have looked more stunned if Kayla had simply chucked the sword at her head like a rock. She hung a second, arm still outstretched, as if replaying the point in her mind.

The passata sotto was a risky move, leaving Kayla much too vulnerable to counter-attack if it hadn't succeeded—she'd never use it in a real swordfight—but as far as statement pieces went. . .

Welcome to my arena, Zerustae.

Zerustae got set for the second point with a much more cautious expression. They went around the circle, Kayla forcing herself into the less comfortable heel-first movements proper rapier footwork demanded, watching Zerustae's mirrored steps with some respect. The woman knew what she was doing.

She had apparently decided Kayla was as rash as her opening move declared her to be, and offered a series of feints designed to draw Kayla in. Subtle moves, but too obvious for her. Kayla wouldn't be drawn into an attack not of her choosing.

Seeing Kayla's unwillingness to leap into an easily countered attack, Zerustae switched tactics, becoming more aggressive. She struck with a thrust to Kayla's face and Kayla applied counter-pressure, smoothly forcing Zerustae's tip out and to the left as she slid forward with her own thrust that would have pierced Zerustae through the oral cavity had Kayla not checked it.

"Point, white!"

One match down, one to go. No way Kayla would let her take this series to three.

Kayla opened the second match on the offensive, offering inside cuts from the elbow that Zerustae dodged adroitly. Apparently her defense was better than her offense. Zerustae seemed content to dodge and parry as Kayla brought more and more pressure to bear. She parried a low thrust with her palm and caught Kayla off-guard with a counter while Kayla's sword tip was still low. Zerustae thrust high, her blade stopping three centimeters from Kayla's cheek and only a centimeter below her left eye.

"Point, red!"

Kayla froze, holding herself stiffly as Zerustae pinned her there. Despite the woman's harsh breaths, the rapier's point was steady, perfectly controlled. Well, shit, the woman had actually scored on her. The official turned to confirm the point with the scorekeeper and Zerustae leaned forward just a hair, flicking her wrist and tip-cutting Kayla across the cheekbone.

Fire burned along the mark, the blunted tip still sharp enough to score the tender flesh. "What the frutt!" Blunt tip or not, one centimeter higher and she'd have lost an eye. "You—"

Zerustae had already turned away, walking back to her start marker as if nothing had happened, as if she hadn't taken an illegal after-point shot.

That bitch! An "honorable competition" for the crown, hah.

The official returned and asked if she was ready to continue. Oh, she was ready.

The points fell to Kayla after that like wheat before the scythe. Zerustae left the ring beaten, embarrassed, and with a matching welt beneath her left eye.

All's fair in love and the Empress Game.

* * *

Kayla brushed at her temple, rubbing away a dusting of salt crystals that had formed in the wake of her evaporated sweat. She mingled with the other similarly fragrant, damp and battered contestants who had finished their fights for the day, all gathered around the ring where the elder Clanesta Warren towered over her opponent in an unarmed series. Sovein Warren looked like a walking oak tree, with shoulders broader than Hekkar's and legs that could bear the weight of someone twice her size. Knocking her over would have been impossible, and avoiding the reach of those arms and bear paw-sized hands just as tricky.

Kayla had finished her last series flawlessly against a princess whose strong defense had dragged things out. Now she wanted a nap and a shower. In that order.

Actually first she wanted to strip off the Isonde hologram and wear her own skin again.

All of those could wait, though. Some of her strongest competitors had matches still to fight today and she couldn't miss this opportunity to study them in person. She wouldn't be allowed re-entry to the pit once she left for the day so she stayed—tired, sweaty and aching in more than a few spots. Isonde had already headed back to their rooms to prepare for the evening's dance of politics.

Kayla saw medsticks, wraps, braces, dermal regen patches and more among the crowd of fighters. She'd already had her hand scanned and wore coolant ribbons on two jammed fingers to reduce the swelling.

In the ring Sovein Warren rushed her opponent, leading with her shoulder, barreling into the other woman with the force of a launched maglev train. They caught at least a meter of air before crashing to the ground. The impact had probably hurt Sovein at least half as much as her opponent, but the Clanesta showed no sign of this and had her flipped over and pinned before the other woman could regain her breath.

"Point, red!" called the official. Sovein jumped to her feet, her grin huge and aggressive. She called something to her sister, Urveina, that probably only the two of them understood, combined as it was with the gestures inherent in their half-somatic language. The meaning was clear, though, and her sister hooted in approval. Sovein strutted before noticing that her opponent, a Maude-something as Kayla recalled, hadn't risen.

Maude rolled to her side, an arm curled in against her ribs, her face white. She breathed shallowly, panting in pain. Sovein bent down to speak to the woman. Maude glared at her and said something Kayla didn't catch, but she heard Sovein's reply.

"If ya' are too weak to fight in ta Game, ya ought not ta be 'ere." She rose and stalked away, passing the medic on his way into the ring.

The diagnosis came: cracked ribs. Maude remained prone while the series was called and Sovein declared the winner.

Kayla glanced at the triumphant Sovein one last time before heading off. Damn, the Clanestas were big.

The last few series were wrapping up and Kayla had two opponents she needed to watch in action: the Wyrd Princess Tia'tan from Ilmena and the Ordinal Divinya from Janeen's homeworld. Divinya's series was yet to be called so Kayla followed the crowd to the ring where Tia'tan circled her opponent like a tireless snake.

She had flawless form, which was no less than Kayla expected. Tia'tan held her sword with perfect balance, the blunted tip at exactly the right angle, her edge precisely controlled when she struck. She executed each technique in a classic style Kayla would love to watch—if Tia'tan wasn't a Wyrd traitor and in major contention for the crown. She studied Tia'tan's footwork, her approaches, her favored retreat patterns. The woman was efficient and controlled, but Kayla saw something she hadn't expected to see: flair.

It was in the flick of a wrist after a parry, a toss of her head after a dodge.

Tia'tan enjoyed this.

The almost-smile on her lips clinched it. Tia'tan enjoyed

dancing around these imperial women, showing them what a Wyrd-trained fighter could do.

Kayla switched her gaze to Tia'tan's attendant, a male Wyrd standing silently on the sidelines. Noar, she recalled. If Tia'tan was intent, he was a laser, watching with eerie focus. They never spoke to each other between points, at least not out loud, but certainly they said plenty.

Kayla drew her ever-present shields tighter.

Tia'tan's opponent slipped unexpectedly, her heel scuffing out farther in front of her than she intended, throwing her off-balance. Tia'tan backed off and allowed her to recover, rather than attacking. Annoyance crossed her features and she glanced at Noar, giving him an almost imperceptible shake of her head.

So. The Wyrds were not above using their psi powers to influence a match. At least Noar wasn't. Frutt. How could she combat that? Tia'tan was already her equal in the ring without outside influences.

Kayla looked to the stands ringing the arena. The other two members of the Wyrd contingent sat as close as possible to the edge of the pit, each watching with smooth expressions but equal focus. Mental shields alone would not protect her from their combined telekinetic efforts, should they choose to frutt with her.

Tia'tan's impressive display ended the series shortly thereafter without a single point scored by her opponent. Again.

Kayla hustled to the last series of the day being held all the way across the arena—Ordinal Divinya, battling a solid contender for the crown, Lady Glennis.

Along the way people glanced at Kayla more often than she was used to. Much more often. Inquisitive, assessing glances. Was her hologram malfunctioning? She glanced down at her hand. Smooth skin, free of scars—definitely not her hand. What were they whispering about?

By the time she reached the ring, she'd heard enough snatches of conversation to piece it together. The standings had been released and the tournament brackets were set for the next day. Her first opponent tomorrow morning would be the winner of the Divinya–Glennis series.

Great.

A challenge was one thing, and normally she'd welcome it. With her and Corinth's future on the line—not to mention the potential turn of imperial politics on the Ordochian situation—was it too much to ask that Divinya and Sovein clashed in an injury-ridden bout that knocked both of them out of the running *before* she had to fight them? At least one of them. That would be nice.

Divinya's ebony skin blended with her fighter's garb until she looked like a living shadow. A shadow with glowing yellow eyes and a flash of white teeth.

She shifted about the ring with the unpredictability of shade formed and dissolved under the wind-blown leaves of a tree. Her unorthodox timing, combined with her quickness, clearly threw Glennis off. Glennis tried to dodge when she should have blocked, was caught retreating even as an attack dissipated. Hands and feet connected, ground was given and taken, but Divinya ruled the ring.

Kayla tried to predict Divinya's moves, but the sense of the woman's ceaseless flow escaped her. Forward, back, tiptoe turn, flat-footed double-step, shifting L stances, planted parallel stances. . . Kayla had never seen such a style. Just as unpredictable were her weapon choices: knives for this fight, staves this morning, swords yesterday.

Though Glennis tried her best, the series was quickly done.

Divinya looked over and made eye contact with Kayla, a feral grin spreading across her face.

Ready or not, it said, *here I come*.

Kayla rode the magchute to her floor in blissful silence. After a day spent in the arena with so many people she was ready for a few hours in a sound deprivation chamber. The tiny *whoosh* of the lift carrying her upward acted like a sedative, soothing and bringing her back into her own headspace. She leaned against the organoplastic wall and closed her eyes, enjoying the hum. These would be her few quiet moments of the day. Next stop—a hurried shower and a meeting with the octet to discuss the outcome of today's series. Then an orchestral presentation and whatever else for the evening.

For this moment, she let the world of the Empress Game bleed away and just drifted.

But when one concern faded from her mind, another rose to take its place, and even the peace of the silent magchute couldn't keep the question of Malkor's past at bay. Corinth had been unable to penetrate the highest reaches of the IDC's electronic security and the mystery of Malkor's involvement on Ordoch loomed large in her mind. Who was she working with? It was dangerous to go on as she had been, trust growing between them, falling into the hope that she might finally have an ally. They couldn't be on equal footing until she knew his past, as he knew hers. There was nothing for it, she'd have to confront him.

The maglift slowed and she pushed Malkor to the edge of her thoughts—back to work. The octet would want to know what she'd learned about Tia'tan and Divinya.

How had Janeen failed to bring Divinya to their attention? That question nagged at Kayla. Each of the agents had compiled a list of contestants from their homeworlds that they thought bore watching. Kayla had drawn from them to form her own list of top competitors. A fighter like Divinya didn't get that talented practicing in her backyard. By all accounts Janeen was good at her job, Divinya shouldn't have escaped her notice.

Of course, knowing about Divinya two weeks ago might not have been enough time to adequately prepare, considering all the other contestants Kayla had studied on their trip to Falanar. It would be a tough fight in the morning.

Too tough?

Never. She would beat every last woman in the Game twice to earn her ticket to Wyrd Space.

The magchute deposited her in the main hall that ran perpendicular to her corridor. Isonde better still have her Kaylagram active, or security would be here in about two minutes when a second Princess Isonde tried to gain access. She scanned her lithodisc bracelet at the entrance to her corridor and pushed through the door once it unlocked.

Maybe she could still get a nap in. The others could do the heavy lifting on researching today's fights while she slept. She could—

The doors to her room slid open just as she reached them. Janeen burst out, slamming full-force into her. Kayla sprawled backward on her ass.

"What the frutt, Janeen!"

Janeen looked more stunned than Kayla felt. "You—" She looked back over her shoulder while Kayla sprang to her feet. "You're supposed to be—" Beyond her, Kayla could see herself lying face-down on the floor near the kitchen area, motionless.

She didn't even have time to form a question. Janeen lunged, jamming something into her shoulder with severe impact. Skin punctured and a flood of angry venom shot into Kayla's shoulder.

"It wasn't supposed to be like this," Janeen muttered, as Kayla crumpled to her knees in pain. She caught a glimpse of Janeen's indigo boots through squinted eyes as the woman sprinted away.

17

It burned.

No, burned was an understatement. It seared Kayla's flesh like the molten touch of a star and ravaged her shoulder into an amalgam of pain. Kayla couldn't even breathe past it. Dizziness hit and she braced herself with her other hand against the floor, trying not to pass out.

Something's. . . happening. . .

The fire contracted, pulling, pulling; dragging on her muscles, tightening them, screwing them into something unyielding. Her shoulder hardened as the burning contracted to a point. Everything screamed in pain and the heat winked out, leaving her shoulder as rigid as stone. The lower half of her arm hung loosely from her locked upper arm. She could still feel it, still wiggle her fingers a little, but it was at the very edge of her awareness.

Isonde.

She tried to push herself to her feet with both hands, but the second she applied pressure on her left hand pain ripped through her rigid shoulder like she'd been impaled on a spearhead. She heard a distinct and horrifying snap. Kayla forced herself up with her good hand and stumbled into her room.

Inside, Isonde, still in her Kayla hologram, lay face-down on the floor like a toppled statue. It appeared as though she'd taken a header from one of the high chairs by the kitchen island.

Kayla knelt and leveraged her good hand to flip Isonde's rigid body onto her back.

Her Kayla-face was a mess.

Blood streamed from a smashed in nose. The jagged edges of broken teeth could barely be seen in her mouth beneath more blood. Kayla ripped the biostrip off of Isonde's neck and the hologram faded, but not the damage. Isonde's eyes were screwed shut and the frozen mask of her face looked as much in pain as Kayla.

Kayla pressed a hand to Isonde's chest. Weak heartbeats met her palm. *Breathing?* She listened. Shallowly. Barely.

Every instinct she had told her to call an emergency med team in—every instinct but one: self-preservation. An official investigation of the attack would be launched. They'd know when it happened, know that "Princess Isonde" had not been keyed into the room during the incident. Isonde's plot to fix the Game would be uncovered and execution would be the result. For both of them. Kayla scurried to the comm unit and punched in the code for the only person she could trust.

"Malkor—I need you. My room. Bring your medic, and for frutt's sake hurry."

She didn't dare say more than that.

She hugged her left forearm to her body. A red-hot spear of pain ground itself to a point against her shoulder whenever she jostled it. The fact that her skin, muscles and ligaments in that area seemed to have solidified into a flesh-colored stone was the least of her worries. She had torn or damaged *something* in there when trying to get to her feet and it screamed for attention. Kayla ignored it and grabbed a cloth from the kitchen before returning to where Isonde lay.

Isonde's unconscious face remained frozen as Kayla gently wiped at the blood. Her squeezed-shut eyelids didn't twitch when Kayla cleaned her cheek, and her mouth gaped, the jaw locked open. Isonde's body was more rigid than a corpse. If Janeen had injected the same thing into Isonde and it had locked up her body the way it had solidified Kayla's shoulder,

Isonde's face must have broken the fall when she couldn't raise her arms to catch herself. What the frutt was it, though?

And why had it affected the whole of Isonde's body but not Kayla's? Dosage? Blood chemistry?

More importantly, how did they counteract it?

::Kayla!:: Corinth's voice screamed in her head. ::What's wrong? We're coming! Kayla?:: His psi voice begged a response she couldn't give. Instead she partitioned her mind as best she could in a quick fashion, boxing off the pain in her shoulder, and lowered her mental shields where he flailed against them like a dying fish. He couldn't pour into her mind from this distance, and she wouldn't have let him anyway, but he could glean enough of her thoughts to know she was all right.

She listened to dozens of shallow huffs as Isonde's lungs fought the paralysis to force what air they could into her body. Her heart beat just as weakly, its thump almost indiscernible at the pulse point on her wrist.

Her door hissed open.

"I'm here. What happened?" The sound of Malkor's voice brought a flood of irrational reassurance to her. He, Trinan, Vid, Hekkar, Toble the medic and Corinth all tried to rush to her and Isonde at once.

"Don't touch me." She held up her good hand, freezing them. They halted as one, Toble grabbing Corinth by the arm when her *il'haar* would have rushed forward regardless. She realized her mistake from the horrified looks on their faces. "I'm not contagious, I just have an injured shoulder." The men converged, careful not to touch her. "Help Isonde. She's barely breathing."

"Daughter of All," Malkor uttered, looking stricken. "What happened to her?"

Toble knelt beside Isonde, immediately checking pulse, respiration.

"Janeen injected her with something."

"Janeen? You're certain?" Kayla nodded. Malkor's uncertainty cleared to action in a nanosecond. He whipped out his mobile comm, thumbing it to life. "Janeen, report." Everyone in the room held their breath. Nothing. "Agent Nuagyn, status report. Now." More silence. He punched a sequence into the comm and spoke again, his voice low and hard as stone. "You have five minutes to respond to this page before I file an insubordination charge." His fingers tightened around the device and he closed the link. "Vid. Trinan."

"On it, boss." The two agents slipped out of the room, both pulling their comm units as they left.

"Do you know what she was injected with?" Toble asked. He had his case open and a scanner already drifting over Isonde's stiff form.

"No idea. If it's the same thing Janeen hit me with it's nothing I've seen before. It solidified my tissue somehow."

Malkor tore his gaze away from Isonde. "You too?"

"Nothing like what's happening to Isonde. Just my shoulder."

Malkor knelt beside her, eyes on Isonde again. Hekkar stopped awkwardly behind him.

Kayla got to her feet, pain radiating outward in a hot throb from her shoulder.

::Are you all right, Kay?::

She nodded at Corinth and took herself out of the way, perching on the edge of a sofa. Corinth joined her, careful not to jostle her. They waited in silence for Toble to finish his scans.

"Solidified is the right word for it. All of her tendons, ligaments and muscles are locked up. The rigidity is affecting her heart as well, it's no wonder that it can barely beat." Toble fished a pressure syringe from his case, dialed up a dose and injected it into Isonde's jugular. "How long has she been like this?" He activated his scanner again and let it hover over her heart.

"I'm not sure. Five or ten minutes at least, that's when I got here," Kayla said.

Minutes passed as Toble stared at his scanner. She read the results on his face—whatever he'd tried hadn't worked. "I need more information. We have to transport her to one of the medical facilities in the pavilion."

"What? No." Malkor shook his head. "Can't you treat her here?"

"I have no idea what's wrong. I need to run blood and tissue analyses before I can even guess what I'm working with. I'm hesitant to try anything else before I know more."

"I'll get you whatever you need. Tell me what."

Toble's brow furrowed. "I need the databanks at the med center and several stationary scanning workstations. We need to get her out of here. Now."

"We can't even move her, if it's as bad as it looks," Malkor argued.

"We're going to have to. What's your issue, Malk?"

Malkor didn't look away from Isonde's face. "No one can know."

Isonde lay there, unconscious, frozen to stone, maybe even dying, and he wanted to keep up their charade? "You have to be kidding me," she said.

"You're out of your mind," Toble said harshly. "You can't compromise treatment for the sake of your espionage."

"It has to stay secret," Malkor said, vehement.

"She could be frutting dying. Her heart's beating but it's working too hard to do so. She can't keep up under this kind of strain and the muscle relaxant I tried had zero effect. I need to—"

"No."

"Malk—" Hekkar tried, but Malkor cut him off.

"It's my call."

The man was nuts. He had to be.

"The plan is and always was for Isonde to win the Empress Game. If anyone knows she can't compete anymore, it's over." He frowned, clearly liking it less than the rest of them, but he didn't back down. "This is the choice she'd make for herself."

"There is no way she'd—" Kayla started.

"You don't know Isonde at all," he snapped. "She stays. That's final." He rose, giving them each a stare that said his word was law. "Toble, work me up a list of what you need right now so I can acquire it. We'll say Lady Evelyn's had an accident, easy as that. You—" he stabbed a finger at Kayla. "Keep that damn hologram on. From this moment on you *are* Princess Isonde." He strode to the door. "I'm gathering Aronse and Rigger. I want that list in three minutes, Toble. Or less."

Hours later, Kayla held herself still by sheer strength of will while Toble manipulated her shoulder nanometer by nanometer. She gritted her teeth to keep from moaning at the piercing pain.

"It'll help to work the stiffness out, I swear," he said. The medic sounded apologetic while he tortured her. Beads of sweat formed on her brow with the effort to withstand the procedure and Corinth dabbed at them, his cloth coming back yellow-green. Her body had begun metabolizing whatever toxin Janeen had used—they still hadn't narrowed it down precisely—and the remnants of the drug oozed out of her pores with each drop of sweat. At least she was improving, which was more than could be said for Isonde.

Kayla looked across the space of their shared apartment to where Isonde lay in a specialty medical pod-bed contraption. She'd been pumped so full of muscle relaxants she should have been a puddle of human limpness. They'd had a mild effect, enough to smooth the horrific grimace from her face and ease some of the constriction on her heart. Her lungs drew fuller breaths, but even still, she needed a mask to provide sufficient oxygen.

"Toofartoofartoofar," Kayla said, as Toble stretched her arm. They walked a fine line between working the joint to speed up the metabolic breakdown of the toxin and forcing the still stiff muscles to the breaking point. Corinth squeezed her good hand.

"I need to get your shoulder to loosen up more before I can do a full exam. You said you heard something snap?"

Kayla nodded.

A half-hour later they were seeing real improvement. Her shoulder throbbed like techno bass and she was more than ready for the pain meds Toble said he would administer once they could be sure it wouldn't interfere with the toxin, but she had some range of motion back. He wrapped her arm and shoulder in gel pack coolant cells to reduce the massive inflammation and went to check on the multitude of tests he had running in the makeshift lab he'd set up in her kitchen.

Malkor, who'd been at Isonde's side like a sentinel, wandered over. "How are you feeling?"

"How do you think I'm feeling?" She swiped a hand across her brow, smearing the yellow-green fluid that oozed through her pores. "It hurts like a bitch, but I'm in better shape than Isonde."

"You need to be, you fight Ordinal Divinya in the morning."

The preposterous nature of the statement warped her mind into stupefaction. "What did you say?"

"You heard me." Malkor looked disturbingly resolute.

Kayla gestured to where Isonde lay comatose. "That pretty much answers the question of whether or not I'll be fighting in the Game in the morning. Or at all." She shook her head. "We're done here."

"We're not done until I say so."

Toble came back over then, saving her from replying.

"I've got a better idea of what we're working with," he said, "based on the results of the blood and tissue analysis, and information Rigger was able to dig up on Janeen's complink terminal. It looks like she used a synthetic polymer designed to combine the paralytic effect of the coinsis flower with the muscle stabilizer known as RDU-7. The results were supposed to be extremely localized and, from what Janeen's supplier had told her, meant to mimic a severe muscle pull."

Toble sighed. "Rigger found a communiqué Janeen had sent to an anonymous recipient. Her plan had been to inflame the knee Lady Evelyn injured yesterday with the toxin, to the point of making her forfeit the series with Divinya. Ideally, if she could administer the dosage with some subtlety, none of us would have even known the injury wasn't natural."

"Did you find a corresponding injection site on Isonde's left knee?" Kayla asked.

"I did. I can only assume that Isonde had an allergic reaction to the toxin, and that yours was more along the lines of what she intended."

"Janeen had said something like, 'this wasn't how it was supposed to be.' At the time I thought she meant only that she'd attacked the wrong one of us, but maybe she'd meant Isonde's reaction to the toxin." Kayla looked at Malkor. "What was her plan, even?"

"Rigger's only started going through Janeen's files on her complink, but it looks like she and Divinya are in cahoots to fix the Game and put Divinya on the throne."

"Wouldn't take much fixing, Divinya can get to the top all by herself."

"Janeen knows how good you are. She couldn't take the chance that you'd beat Divinya." He switched his gaze to Toble. "How bad is Evelyn's shoulder?"

Toble peeled back the coolant cells and activated his scanner. Her skin flamed without the gel packs; she'd be slapping those back on pronto. She braced for the bad news, and noticed that Malkor seemed to be holding his breath while he watched Toble. Concern for her, or the mission?

Toble's frown deepened, as she'd known it would.

"What's the word?" she asked.

"Rotator cuff injury. You have a partial tear in one of the tendons. Actually, it's more like a fracture. The at-the-time brittle tendon snapped halfway across, and the injury is sheared, rather than fibrous. That's going to make it harder to treat." He switched places with Malkor to do a full three hundred and sixty degree scan. "You're lucky that's the worst of it. The other muscles and ligaments are strained, but you have no other acute tears." He finished the scan and wrapped the coolant cells back on.

Partially torn tendon and an extremely strained rotator cuff. Not nearly as bad as what could have happened, given the situation, but no small injury for a fighter. That effectively rendered Malkor's insanity moot.

"How long will it take to heal?" Malkor asked.

"Cellular regrowth on the dermis is tricky enough. Internal accelerated healing is even more complex." Toble considered a moment. "If we could have her in a three hundred and sixty degree, finely calibrated shoulder reconstruct sleeve, I'd say the cellular material could be replaced safely over a period of three days, maybe four. After that she'd have to get the new material up to strength with the rest of her body. She'd need physical therapy for a few weeks."

"Unacceptable. How much can you get done before the match tomorrow?"

"It doesn't matter, Malk, I'm not letting her fight."

"You have no say in the matter."

"But I do." Kayla glared up at him. "There is no way I'm fighting like this. I couldn't win, even if I cared at this point about landing your princess the crown."

"This is not just about winning Isonde the throne." Malkor looked ready to say more, but snapped his teeth shut. "I need a word with you, Evelyn. In private." He walked toward her bedchamber without waiting for a response.

"He'll see reason," Toble murmured, trying to sound encouraging. "Just give him a few. . . hours." He adjusted the setting on the syringe he carried before injecting her. "This should take the edge off of the pain. We'll put a stabilizer cuff on as soon as you get back from 'the talk.'" He returned to Isonde's bed-pod.

Corinth seemed unwilling to release her hand.

"I'll be fine."

::He is serious about this.::

She nodded to show she understood.

::We'll find another way to get home. I don't want you hurt worse.::

"I'll be fine," she said again, and pulled her hand away from him to stand.

She followed Malkor into her bedroom, cradling her left arm with her right to take some of the weight off of her shoulder. She went straight to the chair and sat down. She'd prefer to keep on her feet for the impending confrontation, but she was still slightly ill from the forcible loosening up of her shoulder, and she knew that the pain meds Toble had given her would kick in soon, adding a fuzzy brain to the mix.

"You won't convince me to do this."

"I shouldn't have to," he snapped. "You should be as much on board with this insanity as I am."

"Insanity's the right word for it," she shot back.

Malkor looked as intense as she'd ever seen him. Intense and harrowed. Isonde was one of his closest friends. They'd grown up together, and he'd come on board with her and Ardin's scheme partly out of love for the two of them. To see Isonde as she was now must be devastating.

"Have you told Ardin yet?" she asked.

Malkor gave a tight shake of his head. "The last thing we need is him down here, freaking out, taking control of the entire situation and ruining us." He pierced her with his gray stare. "You *will* continue to act as Isonde."

"The Game is over. Who knows when she'll come out of that coma, if ever."

"She will."

"You can't know that. I did my part. I came to Falanar, fought in the Game, and did my best to win. Now you do yours. Corinth and I want passage to Wyrd Space, arranged by tomorrow."

"No."

The word hit her like a slap. "No?" She'd expected that response. Feared it. She'd had only his word to rely on in their bargain. Apparently that wasn't worth what she'd thought it was. "You promised—"

"You can't leave now. I need you."

"To win the crown for a woman who might never be able to wear it? What the void do I care about the crown?"

"Frutt the crown," he said in a harsh voice. "This is about so much more than that. You of all people should understand."

Time to eject from this critical failure of a mission and get Corinth out of harm's way.

He made a sound of disgust. "You're being obtuse on purpose. I know you want to go home, but what of your people? Isonde's influence on the Council of Seven is the *only* way to pass a motion to withdraw from Wyrd Space. Without her in power, the Ordoch occupation will drag on for who knows how long."

He paused, watching her, his words hanging in the air.

He was right. He knew it. And stars be damned, she knew it, too.

"It was one thing to fight as her," Kayla said, "to act as her attendant when she was there to guide me through the politics, but take over her life?"

"You have to."

She hated every word he said. The truth of it. The pain meds kicked in with a fogging effect on the edge of her mind, but she pushed it back. "When I win the Game, what then? Will you let me go?"

"Not if she hasn't woken up yet." At least he didn't lie about his intention.

"And how long do I keep this up? Am I supposed to marry Ardin? Receive her coronation? Take her seat on the Council?"

"If necessary."

"I am *not* Princess Isonde," she said vehemently. "This will *not* be my life."

He took a step forward, looming over her. "It is now, and will be until I say otherwise."

They stared at each other, Kayla trapped, furious—Malkor looking hard and regretful but implacable. Damn him for being right.

"Don't make me use Corinth as a hostage," he said softly.

That stabbed straight to her heart. She couldn't even speak past the shock.

His hands fisted at his side. "Don't look at me like that. You know I don't want to."

"But you will."

His expression left her in no doubt. "I need you to be on board with this. I need to know you're committed."

She glared up at him. A thousand angry words threatened to tumble out, but the reality of the situation stayed her tongue. Everything he said was true. Every action he demanded was the best hope for her people. And he had Corinth. . .

"I'll be your princess," she finally said, "but you promise me, *promise me*, that you'll keep Corinth out of it."

He sighed in obvious relief, his shoulders relaxing for the first time since the conversation began. "As long as you're with me, he's safe. You have my word."

What a useless bargaining coin that was.

18

Stretching on the arena floor the next morning, Kayla felt as terrible as she'd expected to feel. Maybe worse.

She'd slept in fits overnight, dozing when she could in between stimulating jolts from the cellular repair cuff wrapped around her shoulder. Toble had alternated that with a cortisone shot and layers of coolant gel cells to reduce the inflammation as much as he could. The result was a partial regeneration of the tendon to heal most of the tear—which her body hadn't had time to become accustomed to—a thoroughly numb, weak-feeling shoulder and uncertainty in the strength in her left hand because of it.

Perfect.

Add to that Malkor's willingness to use Corinth's safety against her and she was pissed off. Really pissed off. Ready-to-rip-someone's-head-off pissed off.

Divinya had arrived even earlier than she and now waited at ease, joking over something with her attendant.

Kayla hated her.

She hated her for her obvious health and smug attitude, but even more so for her collusion with Janeen. The full extent of Janeen's plan hadn't been uncovered yet, but she and Divinya had conspired to the series of events that had nearly cost Isonde her life and *had* cost Kayla her freedom. How dare she smile.

The official called the contestants to the ring. Kayla took a deep breath, hoping her shoulder was strong enough, that it could do what needed to be done. Pain was only an obstacle, not a wall. She could push past it.

What damage would she do in the process?

It didn't matter.

Beating Divinya mattered. She'd worry about the rest of her opponents, the treatments she'd need in between each series and the final damage later. For now?

Let's fight.

She approached the center where the official waited with a box. Divinya smiled when they arrived at the same time, her teeth flashing white against her ebony skin. She looked as friendly as Kayla felt.

"Ladies, your weapons." The official opened the box, revealing a pair of knives for each of them.

"I hardly expected to see you this morning," Divinya said, as they selected their weapons and the official deposited the box outside the ring. The Ordinal eyed her up and down, a slight smirk on her face. "How's the knee, by the way?"

Clearly Janeen had not caught up with Divinya about their plan going awry.

"Fine as yesterday. Better, even." That dimmed Divinya's smirk. "Surely you hadn't expected otherwise?"

Divinya shrugged a shoulder. "Some fighters are careless with their injuries."

"And some are just careless. Come," Kayla said, with a grin of her own. "I'll show you how well my knee feels."

The official sounded the chime and the dance between them began.

Kayla lunged immediately, closing the distance in two running steps. She darted straight into Divinya's space with no subtlety, attacking with lightning strikes.

Her right-hand knife thrust to the throat met Divinya's forearm block. Her-left hand knife overhand downward strike to the shoulder met with a high rising block. Right knife in an undercut to the ribs? Hit.

"Point, white!"

First blood—Kayla.

Kayla ate up the incredulity on Divinya's face. She had seen enough footage of Divinya to know she liked to control the tempo of the match. Her unpredictable style was designed exactly for that reason.

Apparently she didn't like to be rushed.

"Ready now?" Kayla asked.

Divinya twirled one knife. "Amateur technique."

"Seems about right for your amateur defense, then."

The official came between them, calling the point to be recorded and lining them up for the next go ahead. The chime sounded and things settled in more slowly. They paced around each other, gauging footing, defense and seeming weak points. It was test and strategy and acting in one. Here and there Divinya darted around, leaving Kayla one step behind. Her breaths came in short, focused bursts, ready always to be the last before some great drastic action. Kayla watched Divinya's yellow eyes, waiting, waiting.

The circling became rhythmic, lulling. Step step feint, step step feint step. Kayla hung on the edge of action, waiting, watching.

Divinya circled, launched two low strikes and an upward sweep. Her knife was at Kayla's throat before Kayla had finished processing her last movement.

"Point, red!"

Frutt.

Kayla huffed out a breath, releasing her body from the waiting game, shaking off the edge of hypnotism Divinya's feint and fade style gave her. She couldn't shake the pain out of her shoulder as easily.

::Fight, Kayla. You are the sea that swallows her river, the sky that absorbs her smoke. Absorb her flow. Make it yours.::

Kayla froze as the psi voice invaded her mind. *Who in the—?*

::It begins again.::

The chime sounded to start the next point.

The circling continued. As the mesmerism crept in, the grace of Divinya's steps convinced Kayla that waiting only led to defeat. The longer you gave her, the greater Divinya's chance of not only scoring on you, but utterly embarrassing you.

Kayla lunged, feeling the seconds ticking by as a countdown to her defeat.

This time Divinya anticipated. She drop-stepped and opened to the right, Kayla's attack brushing past her like wind over a fern. Divinya followed up with an elbow to Kayla's unprotected back. She hooked an arm through Kayla's flailing arm, knocked her knee out from under her and flipped Kayla to the mat. She twirled her knife once for flair before jamming it downward, stopping just above Kayla's heart for another point.

"How's that knee feeling now, Princess?" Divinya broke loose and turned her back as she walked away.

The fall had stretched the tendons in Kayla's shoulder and the abused muscle screamed. She pushed angrily to her feet. If Divinya took the next point she'd win the first match. Kayla would have to win both of the other matches to be declared the victor of their best of three series.

::She is flow without substance, style without weight. She uses your own strength against you and waits to make your effort her own.::

The psi voice in her head—unfamiliar. But the feel of it, its silent touch, mimicked Vayne's presence in a way that made her chest ache. How?

Get the frutt out of my head.

The chime sounded.

Kayla stepped in circles with Divinya, offering a few hesitant attacks here and there. Time melted out of existence. Circles. Patterns. Her body screamed to break form and attack but her mind feared another miscalculation, and kept Kayla dancing to Divinya's tune.

I need another point. Another point. The first match was crucial. She needed to steal away the momentum. She needed—

The whirl of black that was Divinya shifted abruptly, back-pedaling herself while Kayla drifted into the next pattern she'd thought Divinya would make. They were off-set, her strong to Kayla's weak side. She pressed her advantage, coming for a head strike that Kayla barely ducked. Once they closed, time roared back to life and Kayla came up to speed.

She rose with a cross block that trapped Divinya's wrist between her own. She twisted and stripped the dagger from that hand before launching a thrust kick to Divinya's midsection that sent her sprawling back a step. Divinya switched her remaining dagger to her lead hand but could do no more before Kayla was on her. Kayla attacked with both knives, a double strike to the chest, and Divinya blocked one while trying to grapple Kayla's other arm.

She had an awkward grip on Kayla's elbow while they fought each other one-handed. The blades struck once. Again. A third time.

Kayla swung her trapped arm down at the elbow with all her might, connecting the pommel of her dagger with Divinya's forehead. Divinya swung wildly with her remaining dagger. Kayla knocked the arm aside and laid her dagger at the base of Divinya's throat.

"Point, white!"

Damn, that felt good.

She shook her shoulder out, trying to ignore the burn. She could do this. Just one more point. And. . . then one more whole series. *Then* coolant cells and a pressure syringe full of pain blockers before her next opponent.

Assuming this opponent didn't finish her first.

The chime sounded for the final point of the match. Divinya seemed off and Kayla pressed the advantage without letting up. A continuous series of attacks had Divinya stepping back and back, ceding control of the floor to Kayla and leaving her with uncertain footing. They neared the edge of the ring, and with nowhere to go, Divinya raised her hand and abdicated the last point to Kayla, rather than letting Kayla score the point herself.

Sore loser.

They each stalked to their own sides for a mid-series break. From the corner of her eye, she saw Divinya brush past her companion, ignoring whatever the woman had to say. Kayla had no one. Not that Isonde had had much advice to offer mid-set in the way of fighting styles and techniques, but it had been nice to have someone honestly on her side who was looking out for her. Now that same person lay comatose, mind and body frozen, all because of the woman across the ring.

Frutting Empress Game. Isonde should have become empress-apparent as soon as Ardin had made his preference known. Instead they had to go through this bullshit, where a simple, "fair" tournament had put Isonde into a fight for her life.

Soon the official called them back to the ring for the second match. Divinya seemed much her former self, and even had a smile and a joke for the official as she made her way to the center.

It quickly became clear as they danced around the ring— here slowly, there with rapid, complementary steps—that Divinya had regained her center. Her focus had doubled, if anything, and her form looked more fluid. She once more had full control of the fight, and she knew it.

She offered fewer attacks, letting Kayla come at her time and again, doing nothing more than evading and watching Kayla tire herself out. Kayla couldn't wait forever. The woman clearly had more stamina. Divinya might be happy prancing in a circle all day, but Kayla wanted to lunge across the space and beat the woman like she deserved.

::Be as quiet as she, see how she flows. You are the spool she winds her thread around; she has no shape without you. Bend her dance to your tempo, guide her feet with your steps.::

By the vacuum of space, if you don't shut the frutt up—

Divinya caught her split attention and struck, gaining a point before Kayla could think to block.

The loss of a point only made Kayla more cautious, more careful about her footwork, more choosy about her opening before attempting an attack. The match crawled by as Divinya ground her down.

"Come at me," Kayla demanded.

"When I can clearly make you come to me?" Divinya grinned, changing pace and stance so rapidly that Kayla had to hop to keep up or be left in a vulnerable place. "See?"

Kayla growled.

The match closed in the same way, Divinya leading Kayla around by the nose and finally striking when Kayla made a misstep on an attack.

Three points to none.

Kayla sat on the edge of the ring again, gulping water, frustrated to be a puppet on Divinya's string. And who the void was *speaking* to her? She'd scanned the stands. The Wyrd contingent was nowhere in sight at this end of the arena, and Princess Tia'tan fought at the far end. It obviously wasn't Corinth. He'd never say anything so heavy or useless as "be the sea that swallows her sky, the spindle that tangles her up," or whatever.

You want to do something useful, whoever you are? Spew your nonsense in Divinya's ear.

Frutt Divinya's pacing. Frutt her smoke and mirror games and her melt away defense.

This was Kayla's fight, no one else's. She wasn't going to win it by mimicking Divinya's style or by waiting for Divinya to give her an opening. If she let Divinya control the fight, she had already lost.

Kayla might be an Ordochian princess, but she was also a pit whore. It was time to drive the fight, Kayla-style.

She stared at Divinya as they both entered the ring. Watched the smugness, the arrogance of someone who thought the series was already over, of someone who thought sabotaging an opponent to beat them in the Empress Game made them anything less than the worst kind of coward.

Kayla would flatten the Ordinal to the mat, face-first, and enjoy it.

The chime sounded.

Kayla rushed in but Divinya expected it. She back-pedaled and opened to the side to give herself coverage from a body shot. Instead of backing off to reset, Kayla sidestepped to match her, then vaulted backward away. She caught Divinya with a kick under the chin as she flipped, feet over hands, and landed a body-length away in a front stance. Divinya shook her head, momentarily dazed. She regained composure and slid away with a series of L-stance shifts, once again studying Kayla from a comfortable distance.

Kayla was anything but comfortable. She was up on her toes and ready for a real fight. She sidestepped, zigzagged, sidestepped, zigzagged, minutely eating up space and forcing the momentum of the fight. When she had the right distance, she took a running step, straight into a slide across the mat, one foot tucked, one foot extended. She slammed into Divinya's knee and Divinya crumpled atop her in a heap, unable to switch her weight off that leg fast enough.

Kayla kneed her in the gut, sending a *huff* of air rushing from her lungs. Kayla scrambled out from under her and rose just high enough to drop both knees square onto Divinya's lower back. She laid her knife alongside the Ordinal's throat one heartbeat later.

"Point, white!"

Point one.

Divinya rolled and shoved her off. "What the frutt is this, a back-alley bar fight?" She got to her feet and stared at the official, incensed. "You can't call that a point! That's brawling."

The official looked unshaken by her outburst. "The rules state that a point is granted when one opponent holds the other at mortal advantage by knife. That's it. The manner in which they arrive at that point is not specified."

Divinya gaped at him.

"What's the matter, Ordinal, can't hang in a real fight?" Kayla wiped at the bloodied split lip she'd gotten when Divinya landed on her, elbow accidentally to the mouth. So worth it.

"You fight like street trash."

"Maybe, but I still kicked your ass right there."

"Bah. We'll see." Divinya stalked off, sulking. She limped a little on one leg.

The chime sounded.

Kayla rushed, unwilling to give Divinya time to make sense of it all. She'd thought to catch her off-guard, but Kayla was the one who was surprised—Divinya seemed to remember something of her hand-to-hand skills. Instead of just melting back she turned and blocked Kayla's left arm with both forearms, pushing the arm away before issuing a swift backhand that nearly cost Kayla her nose.

Kayla brought her right arm across her body to block, then spun into her for a fraction of a second. She jerked a backward elbow hard against Divinya's ribs and stepped away before she could be vulnerable to her knives.

Divinya reset quicker than expected, and waited in a front stance with a look of pure hatred for Kayla to advance.

To her surprise, once forced to employ it, Divinya looked like she had a solid core defense. Kayla took a forward step into Divinya's space, shot for her throat, and stepped back when Divinya dodged. She tried two more variations of the step and strike, then made her real move. She took a long double-step and trapped Divinya's leading foot beneath her own. She ducked, coming up beneath Divinya's forward arm, keeping herself safe with a rising block over her head. She punched Divinya's other arm in the wrist, forcing her to drop the blade, and thrust her dagger in a strike straight to Divinya's heart.

Point two.

Divinya limped to the side line, yelling something furious to her attendant, who merely shrugged. The official called them together for the next point. Kayla came to the center, out of breath, sore in quite a few places, and smiling—now *this* was a fight.

The chime sounded.

Divinya lunged, a shadow flashing from one side of the ring to the other. Kayla did the only thing she could: dropped to one knee and extended her other leg out, tripping Divinya over it.

The Ordinal rolled and regained her feet with ease, both knives up and ready. She twirled one while Kayla turned to face her.

Divinya spat. "I can fight your fight."

"Badly."

Divinya charged again, fury in the yell she launched with her attack. That passion for blood Kayla could understand. Divinya struck twice with her blades in rapid succession, then shifted her weight for a thrusting kick that thudded into Kayla's thigh. Kayla came right back at her. She reversed her grip on her knife for an overhand, and when she could see the block coming, changed her angle and punched Divinya square in the face. Divinya bent over in reflex, one hand going to her nose, and Kayla lifted her knee to connect with the Ordinal's chin, straightening her up.

She let the point of her dagger kiss the base of Divinya's throat.

Point three.

Series: Princess Isonde of Piran.

Divinya threw her knives down in obvious disgust.

"Now who fights like trash," Kayla said over the cheering of the spectators, "and who's one step closer to the crown?" She let her knives fall to the ground beside Divinya's and gave her a mock salute.

That one was for you, Isonde.

::Well done.::

"Is this how you run an octet, Senior Agent Rua?"

"No, Commander."

Commander Parrel towered on the other side of his desk, staring Malkor down with tangible force. Malkor kept his eyes straight ahead, hands clasped behind his back while the director of all Falanar-based IDC octets went on.

"Is this what we trained you for, to have an agent turn traitor right under your nose?"

"No, sir."

"You've been her superior, what, three years?" He glanced down at a datapad. "It says here you specifically requested Agent Nuagyn for your octet. What does that say about your character assessment skills?"

Malkor kept quiet.

"What about your investigative skills? How did she plan her assault while working for you? Are you running a daycare over there in the Oxyard sector? Letting the children run wild doing whatever they want?"

"No, sir."

"Don't 'no, sir' me," he snapped. "I want answers. She attacked Evelyn Broch, a woman your octet personally escorted to the Game. How the void are we supposed to keep the contestants safe if you can't even keep your prized pigeons safe on your own watch?" Commander Parrel made a sound of disgust. "If it gets out that we not only failed to keep a contestant's attendant safe, but actually attacked her ourselves, there'll be panic." He pointed a finger. "You'll be personally responsible for the riot that breaks out."

"Yes, sir."

"Bah!" Parrel sat down at his desk, his chair creaking in response to the abrupt motion. He lifted the datapad that contained Malkor's report of the event. The altered report of events.

"This toxin. Has it been identified yet?"

"Doctor Toble believes he has it narrowed down to a combination of two. Both of which he's treating for now."

"And where did Agent Nuagyn acquire the substance?"

"We're still tracking that down, sir. I believe it was off-world, during our last mission to Ocha." More than likely she'd acquired it on the slum side of Altair Tri when the octet had landed for the start of this horrific debacle. Then again, their official travel log hadn't included a stop to Altair Tri.

Damn you, Janeen.

When he caught up with her, there would be some swift,

immediate and severe retribution exacted on Isonde's behalf.

"Agent Nuagyn is as yet unaccounted for?"

"Yes, sir. But the majority of my team has been reassigned to search for her."

"And what of the victim?"

"Lady Evelyn is currently stable, but her body is still experiencing a moderate amount of rigor. All of her minor wounds have been treated."

"Is she still comatose?" Parrel continued to scan the report, clearly down to business despite his fury.

Malkor swallowed hard, imagining Isonde lying like an out of order bot in her bed, bandages covering her recently reconstructed nose, teeth and jaw. "Yes, sir."

Parrel skimmed the details, tapping a finger on the desk and leaving Malkor standing in silence. Minutes ticked by before he slapped the datapad back down. "What's our story, then?"

"Last night Princess Isonde issued a statement saying that Evelyn had contracted the Virian flu and might be unavailable for engagements for some time."

"Good. At least you did one thing right. We'll stick with that. The IDC and Agent Nuagyn are not to be mentioned in any of this. I want her involvement strictly classified by my authority.

"As far as everyone on Falanar knows, Lady Evelyn has a bad case of the flu and will be resting in her quarters, understood?"

"Yes, sir."

"I want the rest of your team on board with this ASAP." He eyed Malkor from head to toe, a gaze that doubted the worth of what he saw. "If, Senior Agent Rua, you can trust the rest of your octet members?"

"I vouch for each of them."

Parrel frowned. "And doesn't that give me comfort." He slid the datapad to the side amid a stack of others and reached for the next. "Do you have more to report?"

I found her, the last princess of Ordoch, heir to the throne we usurped. I know where she is, I could bring her to you. Think of the leverage we'd have. What if we offered the Wyrds not only withdrawal from their planet, but also the two survivors of their sovereign family? What if we used them as hostages unless they helped us?

Or what if instead, we did the right thing by her, after ruining her life so spectacularly? Kept her safe, like we hadn't her family. Brought her home to her people like I'd promised. Stopped using her as a tool.

"Rua?"

"Nothing, sir."

Malkor slammed a fist against the wall once back in his quarters, venting the frustration and embarrassment the dressing down from Commander Parrel brought.

He admired Parrel, looked up to him. He'd studied Parrel's career while a junior agent, had modeled something of his own techniques and ethics after what he had found there. Parrel had nominated him for octet leader, and had pinned the eight-box on Malkor himself the day of the promotion.

They'd formed a friendship over the years, and in conversations with him, Malkor had heard things said between the words that indicated Parrel was man who understood the need to work outside of the IDC's rules and regs sometimes, if it meant doing what was best for the empire. He might almost, *almost*, understand Malkor's current plans and his reasons for going against the direct orders of upholding the validity of the Empress Game.

What Parrel wouldn't stand for, though, was someone doing sloppy, half-assed work. Someone so caught up in his own plans and machinations that he failed to uncover the betrayal of one of his own agents. Someone in command who wasn't fit to lead.

His door chirped at him. Stars, not now.

The panels slid apart and Hekkar strode in without a hello. He gave Malkor a once-over. "Visit with Parrel went that well?"

Malkor blew out a breath. "Better." He scrubbed a hand

over his face then thrust the conversation to the back of his mind. Time enough to worry over it later, say, when he should be sleeping.

Hekkar held out a datapad. "I have something that might cheer you up."

"Word on Janeen's whereabouts?"

Hekkar's lips tightened into a hard line. "Not yet, but that'll come, I promise."

Malkor nodded. He reached for the pad. "What have you got for me instead?"

"A date with the *kin'shaa*."

"I thought you wanted to cheer me up."

Hekkar loosened up enough to offer a half-grin, something of his typical humor returning. "Hey, when one problem's too big to deal with, you know what you need? Another problem. Boom. See? I'm here for you."

"Gee. Thanks." Malkor thumbed the power switch. "Tonight, Yerlany Gardens, nineteen hundred hours."

"He may not actually be expecting you. At all." His grin developed full-out. "It's less of a date than an ambush. He'll be there with his Wyrds."

Malkor brought up a display of the gardens, familiarizing himself with details of the layout. "Good work."

"You know me, only the best."

Hekkar turned to go, but stopped when he reached the door, his grin fading. "I know you think you should have seen it coming, with Janeen. We all feel like that. Truth is no one could. We didn't fail her, Malk, she betrayed us. Remember that."

19

"I'm not saying the trade sanctions were completely unwarranted. Xhido admits to exercising poor judgment during our attempt to subdue rebel forces two winters past."

Kayla arched a brow, letting her silence answer the Paramount Ruler of Xhido Province's statement. The weathered skin of his forehead crinkled as he searched for words.

"We could, perhaps, have been more restrained in our use of force on certain rebel installations." He swallowed, but was quick to add, "Force that was deemed justifiable at the time."

Most terrible ideas seemed justifiable at the time.

"The deaths that occurred in the Qinqian Steppes incident, atop the imprisonment of hundreds of innocent civilians at Rhihadri, weigh heavily against you," Kayla said. Isonde's voice still sounded odd coming out of her mouth. It was like an echo, hearing her words in her mind in her voice, then speaking them with Isonde's. "I find it hard to consider a lessening of the trade sanctions levied by the Sovereign Council."

In truth Isonde had found it fairly easy to consider abolishing the sanctions altogether, she'd told Kayla. Part of her strategy for winning the Paramount Ruler's support had been to imply that agreeing to vote down the sanctions was a great compromise for her, one she was only willing to make if the favor was returned. The civil unrest in Xhido had gotten out of hand, but the Sovereign Council had overreacted by laying down such heavy trade sanctions against the province. The country's economy, crucial to the stability of the entire planet, threatened to collapse under the weight.

"If you would allow me to outline some of our latest efforts to reach peaceful accord with the outlying districts. . ."

His voice blended into groups of syllables. Damn, her shoulder ached.

She'd come home from the arena this afternoon and collapsed in her bed, still fully dressed. That bliss had lasted no more than five minutes before Toble came to torture her. He had her sitting up with a cellular repair cuff latched onto her shoulder for too long. At least he had the decency to shoot her up with a massive pain blocker first. She'd dozed in that state until he finally released her, then she'd passed out in bed, sleeping despite the fiery throbbing in her shoulder. Then he woke her up to do it all over again.

Minus the second round of sleeping. She could have used that.

No matter how her body felt, though, it was too important to be here tonight, walking in Isonde's steps, tangoing with the influence-peddlers of the empire.

Despite the focus of her political agenda and her plans to win alliances, Kayla found herself surrounded by a different sort of crowd than she was used to, people she could only term as admirers. These people couldn't care less about her politics. They did, however, find a surprisingly ass-kicking Princess Isonde fascinating, and for once Kayla had spent more time discussing the fights than her politics.

"Ah, but I see I am boring you." The Paramount Ruler of Xhido Province's voice brought her back to him with a start. She laid the tips of her fingers on his dark arm.

"No, not at all. My mind wandered but a moment. It has been an. . . exciting day." She offered a sheepish smile.

He nodded, a half-bow that was all understanding. "Of course. Perhaps it is time to take a break from politics and just enjoy the evening in the company of so many." He glanced past her shoulder to where hundreds of people danced to a multi-orchestral collaboration. "I see others about to descend upon us, I think I have stolen enough of your time." He took her hand and pressed the back of it to his forehead. "May Jovannah's laughter lighten your steps."

As he walked away the nearby pocket of people shifted. Several had seemed engaged in conversations, each enjoying the company of others, but as soon as an opening presented itself at her side they looked ready to pounce on her. On Isonde.

A server passed by with a tray full of delicate glasses and she snagged one. She didn't even glance at the liquid before downing a swallow. She had people to see, Isonde's agenda to follow, but the evening felt relaxed. The jovial mood of the crowd entranced her. She was hopped up on pain meds and feeling somewhere between fuzzy and sharp, a place where her brain power slipped and her mind decided not to listen to the burn in her shoulder, the ache in her knee, fingers, foot. . .

She took another sip of the pink liquid. It was delicious, whatever it was.

::Delicious.::

The mind voice, same as earlier, came from nowhere, hitting her in the chest like a blow.

Vayne.

It *felt* like him. The slip of the word against her mind had his imprint, his scent almost, but the voice was wrong.

She studied those nearest to her. Who was it? A man and a woman approached from her right, the regents of Bostra come to discuss a border dispute, no doubt. Her gaze spread wider. Who?

She saw Vid resting against a pillar, a smile on his face while Trinan leaned toward him sharing a jest, hand braced on the pillar near Vid's head. They looked so comfortable, so at ease. Then Vid glanced at her, the merest brush of an eyeball in her direction, but she knew. Guards.

::A woman like you, Princess, should not be alone.::

She turned a slow circle, searching the sea of strangers for a sign, an intentness that would give the Wyrd away. One of the Ilmenans? No, they weren't here tonight.

::Look at this crowd. Who are you to these people but a symbol? A tool of power, a chance to climb.::

An invisible hand stroked a finger down her cheek, raising a shiver. The caress was familiar and foreign.

::I know you as they do not. Will you *speak* with me?::

Tears stung, taking her by surprise. *Why do you feel like my Vayne?* she asked in a voice no one could hear. The person must be nearby. Their mental presence hung in the air beside her, radiating expectancy and want. Vayne had never felt interested in her this way, but his essence imprinted itself on her. Weakly. A stamp made in ash instead of ink.

"I hate you," she whispered, her lips barely shaping the words. She wanted him, this person who was almost her twin yet so far from him.

The regents of Bostra arrived and the stranger melted away.

Malkor crossed under the delicate glass arch that marked the entrance to the Yerlany Gardens a little after 19:00. The courtiers and councilors milling inside the entrance spared him a glance as he passed the twisted metal columns that outlined an open-form entranceway of sorts. Beyond that the greenery took over, covering the ground like a carpet and rising toward the sky. On his left, spindly ornamental trees hinted at a loose network of paths. They created a trail through the horticultural symphony, allowing visitors to stroll through the most diverse garden in the empire. Malkor had no interest in the display this evening, and headed instead to the right.

Here the garden opened into a large pavilion, complete with fountains, refreshments, music and a wild array of blossoms. Flowers, some the size of dinner plates or larger, bloomed in clusters around the edge of the paved pavilion, sprang from the dozens of sculpted metal and glass planters set throughout the open space and floated amid the showering falls of the fountains. Paths lined in pebbled stone meandered off from the center and led guests to quieter, secluded areas that offered privacy and intrigue aplenty. How would he ever track down Dolan in the maze of secret ways that spread out from the pavilion?

An unnecessary worry. A somber group clustered near a fountain. A bank of open space surrounded them and no one crossed the invisible barrier. Alone amid a crowd of milling guests, the Wyrds made for a striking quartet.

They were each dressed in various tones of blue. The younger of the two men, and also the shortest of the group, wore trousers of the darkest shade paired with a form-fitting vest of the same color over a white blouse with loose sleeves. His chin-length lavender hair looked casual and artfully precise at the same time. His elder wore a similar outfit, only his shirt was silver with a flare at the cuff and his pants were tucked into short boots. The tallest of their group, a woman, looked less formal than the two men in a lighter colored bodysuit and wide silver sash. Light rippled across the fabric's sheen when she turned to silently scan the crowd.

Among them, only Princess Tia'tan smiled. She was dressed almost flamboyantly compared to the others in a floor-length gown of midnight blue. The neckline of the gown spread wide to her shoulders, barely hanging on, leaving her back bare. Her skirts flared in layer after layer of fabric. Silver edging lined the bottom, and mid-length sleeves left her muscled forearms on display.

Out of nowhere came a laugh from Tia'tan. She chuckled, purple eyes dancing as she bent to scoop a handful of pebbles from the fountain in front of her. No one else's lips moved and none of the Wyrds spoke aloud, but she laughed again after a second, and the younger male grinned.

Looking completely unamused, Master Dolan stood beside the elder Wyrd male with his hands clasped behind him. He let the merriment die down, then continued the conversation he'd apparently been having with the Wyrd. Princess Tia'tan ignored him, idly tossing the pebbles to land one after the other in the fountain. The taller female angled away from the group, eyes never resting in one place.

Before Malkor could decide if he should approach Dolan now or later, their attention shifted to him. Tia'tan's smile dimmed, then vanished, painted lips coming together in a neutral line as she glanced in his direction. The other Wyrds looked to be a mix of vaguely curious and disinterested. The bodyguard sized Malkor up with her piercing stare.

Now it was, then.

The Wyrds gave no indication of welcome when he approached, merely held their silence and looked at him in a way that had him attempting to reinforce his mental shields.

Dolan arched a brow, the permanent half-smirk present on one side of his mouth. "IDC afoot in the gardens, how unexpected."

Malkor tried not to stare at the blank red orb of the man's ruined eye or the web of scars that started at his temple and spidered out across his right brow and cheek.

"We have been known to take the odd hour or two off," Malkor said.

"So this is a social inquiry, then?" Dolan waited for the lie.

"A not-so-chance meeting, perhaps." He nodded to the Wyrds, who had yet to do more than look at him.

Dolan gestured with an elegant hand. "Have you the pleasure of my guests' acquaintance?"

"Not yet," he replied, though he knew every one of them. Noar, the youngest male, accompanied Tia'tan to the pit. Joffar, the elder male, and Luliana, the female bodyguard, spent every series just above the pit in the stands, their intent stares following the Game's progress. Dolan made the introductions and the Wyrds unbent enough to incline their heads when named. Tia'tan opened her hand in the stilted silence that followed and a stream of pebbles splashed into the fountain with a loud *sploosh*. She dusted her palms with her fingertips, first one then the other, while watching him. Her gaze traced his uniform, touching briefly on the pin he wore to signify his rank as an octet leader—the outlines of eight overlapping silver rectangles fanning out to form a ninety degree arc.

Tia'tan didn't say a thing, but Luliana cracked a smile, Noar ducked his head with a slight cough and Joffar tried not to look amused. A glance at Dolan's face showed he felt as much frustration as Malkor at not hearing the silent exchange, though he quickly hid it.

"Could you leave your charming guests to their amusements for a few moments?" Malkor asked him.

"Of course. I find I am quite ready for a diversion."

Malkor headed toward an unattended fountain across the way. From there he'd spot anyone who approached to eavesdrop, and the waterfall would provide white-noise cover from any listening devices.

He stopped a meter from the fountain. Hopefully the polite mask he wore hid his distaste, not only for the *kin'shaa*, but for the whole situation he found himself in. It should—he'd been perfecting it for years.

There were a dozen ways he could hint at his true reason for being here, things he could say whose double-meanings would lead to a conversation within a conversation that might, just maybe, save him from an admission of guilt. He ignored them all. The fact that he met with Dolan by choice said they were past that.

"I received your message."

"Excellent." Dolan inclined his head. "I'm glad you decided to seek me out."

"It was thought-provoking, if ambiguous." Malkor studied the man's scarred face, judging intent.

"One can't be too careful, given the situation."

"And just what situation is that, exactly?"

Dolan chuckled. "Surely you're aware of your own predicament, Senior Agent."

Malkor forced a smile in response. "Humor me."

"You have friends in high places. Good friends. That's well-known, but what isn't as clear is how far you might go for them." Dolan clasped his hands behind his back, looking perfectly at ease in lavender robes, despite his shorter stature. "You, I and your friends know exactly how far. Far enough to see a woman you once coveted married to another man, far enough to compromise your career in the IDC and, in fact, risk your very life. It's because of those friends that you find yourself here, fixing the Game you were meant to police."

There was no point in denying it.

Dolan continued. "Your plan is sound, I'll give you that. With your means and resources it might almost have succeeded."

"Almost?" Surely the man didn't discount Kayla's skill and her ability to win the Empress Game.

"You have two problems, the first being that your plan relies too heavily on people whose loyalty you misjudged."

Janeen. How had he known? Suspicion bloomed in his mind. Dolan *could* have been involved, could have helped Janeen secure the toxin, or might be hiding her even now. "And the second?"

"The second is, of course, my guests. Not your fault, though, you couldn't have predicted the allies I would bring to bear at the Game." Dolan looked a touch too satisfied for his liking.

"Isonde can defeat Princess Tia'tan."

The *kin'shaa* surprised him by chuckling. "It's charming that you refer to her as 'Isonde.'"

"Should I not?"

"Call her what you like, I only find it amusing that when you and I know the truth, you still act as though nothing untoward is occurring."

"Your Wyrd princess is talented," Malkor said, "but not unbeatable."

"You are discounting her unique set of assets, I think. And those of her companions."

So they did intend to cheat. Understandable. They wouldn't have come all this way to lose. Then again, neither had Kayla and Corinth.

"It might be too much to automatically assume their psi powers will tip the balance in Tia'tan's favor," Malkor said. It was nearly a certainty and he knew it. Still, he went on. "You yourself taught the IDC that some individuals have inborn defenses, and others can be instructed to develop them." A junior IDC agent crossing the pavilion caught his eye, and Malkor forced himself to smile in a friendly fashion and offer a nod of hello to her, silently wishing the young woman on her way. Dolan had the good sense to keep quiet until the agent passed out of earshot.

"That is true, but how effective do you think those defenses will be against four expertly trained psionics?"

How effective could Kayla be? She was a Wyrd princess, surely as well-trained as the Ilmenan bunch, with well-established shields. Could she withstand any pressure they might put on her? For that matter, how many Wyrds would she have to worry about? Tia'tan wouldn't be doing anything more than fighting, but Noar was in the pit with her, more than ready to attack Kayla with his mind. And the others? How far could a Wyrd extend his influence? He was overdue for a long talk with Kayla about the nature of her psi powers.

Malkor forced himself to maintain his polite tone. "I appreciate the enormity of the advantage your people seem to have. It can't be that easy, though. If their combined psi powers could win Tia'tan the crown and a seat on the imperial Council of Seven, you wouldn't have requested a meeting with me."

"It is that easy, I assure you. However, my friends are coming to understand the nature of the political system in the empire. While they could use their skills to win the Game and the throne, they're beginning to question whether that is the best outcome they can achieve."

Malkor arched a brow. "They have loftier goals?"

Dolan smiled privately at the thought. "Perhaps, but in this instance I believe they are looking for a more effective outcome than putting Tia'tan on the throne."

"Such as?"

"The real power of having a seat on the Council of Seven comes from being the deciding vote that controls which way the Council goes on any major issue. Without the influence to sway half of the other votes, the Empress becomes less effective." Dolan made a vague motion with one hand, delicately emphasizing the point. "My people lack allies."

"I can't imagine why," Malkor said. "It's not as if they refuse to help us while millions of our people are consumed alive by the Tetratock Nanovirus."

"We are not your enemy, Agent. Ilmena was not consulted by the empire about designing a cure. In any case, that's not what we're here to discuss."

It might as well be. The entire Game, as far as he was concerned, was a battle for control over the empire's next move with regard to the Ordochians and a cure for the TNV. A battle he, Ardin and Isonde couldn't bear to lose. He took a deep breath, unseating the tension that had grown between his shoulder blades.

Dolan continued. "Princess Isonde is a formidable and growing force in the empire, with strong allies in the Protectorate and Sovereign Councils—not to mention she all but owns Ardin's vote in the Council of Seven. She has the political cachet to see her agendas progress. If her agendas allied with those of my guests, they *might* consider aiding, rather than defeating her in the Game."

Malkor blinked, uncertain what he'd heard. "Did you just offer to help put Isonde on the throne?"

Dolan inclined his head. "Possibly. They are considering it. Though it is hard to ignore the fact that they would still have much power if Tia'tan won."

The water splashing in the fountain filled the silence. Could it be that simple? With the Wyrds' aid Isonde was all but assured the crown. Their logic was reasonable—Isonde would fight for Ordoch's freedom, and could accomplish ten times the amount the Wyrds would be able to in the Councils. The councilors would oppose Tia'tan's agendas every time. She'd have a hard time accomplishing anything more important than a lunch order.

"What's your angle?" Malkor asked.

"My guests would of course stay on as advisors to Isonde, and be given prominent positions within the government. She would take their input on certain matters, and—"

"Not theirs," Malkor interrupted, "yours. What do *you* get from arranging this alliance?"

He expected to hear a line about how proud Dolan was to be able to assist his countrymen, to try to mend relations between the empire and the Wyrd Worlds, or even something about doing the right thing for no reason other than that it was just.

"I want the princess."

Malkor didn't wonder for a second which princess he meant. "Not happening."

"What use will you have for her once 'Isonde' wins the Game?" Dolan smiled, a look that set Malkor on edge. "I dare say she's a liability, someone you couldn't trust to wander around freely. Let me look after her."

"And by 'look after her' you mean. . .?" The *kin'shaa* knew. Frutt. He *knew*, and he wanted her. Malkor eyed the entrance to the garden. How quickly could he find Kayla if he sprinted out of here this instant, find her and assure her safety?

"Perhaps I think she'll make a good wife."

He'd suck vacuum first.

Dolan arched a brow, giving him a slow once-over. "Maybe you mean to 'look after' her yourself."

Fine job he'd done of it so far. Malkor didn't bother to answer.

"The princess will be safe with me," Dolan said, "I assure you."

Malkor drew himself up, and his tone, when he spoke, was polite, if a touch frosty. "Thank you for your generous offer of aid, but I'm afraid we must decline."

"For now, perhaps. We'll speak again soon, Agent Rua." The *kin'shaa* offered a short bow and made his way back to where the silent Wyrds waited.

Malkor headed for the exit as quickly as he could without knocking people down.

Kayla must have spoken to everyone at the party this evening. Certainly everyone seemed to have approached her. Everyone, that was, except Malkor. He had arrived at the dinner hall over an hour ago and hovered on the edge, in sight but too distant to engage.

For the best.

After their conversation yesterday and his insistence that she remain as Isonde, she didn't want to speak to him. Something was on his mind, though. He had an intensity about him that unsettled her.

What—did he think she meant to flee? Rip the hologram off and declare to everyone that she was a fraud, that the real Isonde had been struck down? Or was something else afoot?

The head of state for Terra Prime descended on her with a gush of smiles and congratulations. She fully expected him to immediately turn the conversation to their mutual trade agreement. When instead he discussed only her success in the arena that day and his well wishes for her continued good fortune, the truth of the situation struck. He expected her to win. He hadn't come to discuss a sticky political situation with Princess Isonde, he'd come to make the first inroads with soon-to-be Empress-Apparent Isonde, one half of the couple set to inherit the throne on the emperor's death.

The party grew by one, then three, then six as others, sensing room at her side, joined their circle. Isonde, already a star in the sea of power-players, was a constellation unto herself now. Kayla was deep in a conversation with senior members of the Sovereign Council when the satellite that had orbited all evening was pulled in by her gravity.

Malkor. Approaching her, clearly on a mission.

The governor to Kayla's left frowned, turning her head to murmur something to her lieutenant governor. Beside her other murmurs arose. Here a nervous gesture, there a bracing gulp of a drink. The senior councilors broke off and their stares turned chilly, but no one looked in Malkor's direction. Instead, the uncertainty focused on someone behind her.

Intriguing. Kayla readied a polite smile, curious about the prejudice against whomever approached. The smile froze on her face when a gentle voice she recalled too well spoke Isonde's name.

"How lovely you look this evening," the *kin'shaa* said. Conversation halted and people shifted away from the Wyrd, trying not to look like they recoiled even as they gave ground.

As Grand Advisor of Science and Technology to the current emperor, Dolan was too important to ignore. That didn't stop her companions from looking like they wished to be elsewhere. At least she knew now why Malkor had been trying to come to her rescue.

"Master Dolan." She didn't bother to nod in greeting.

"White is exquisite on the princess, don't you agree, Sir Jahvier?" Dolan looked directly at a man who'd attempted to sidle away from his company.

"I— but of course. Princess Isonde is as lovely as ever." Jahvier smiled weakly.

No one offered small talk to fill the awkward void in the air.

Dolan's lips quirked, his sarcastic smirk deepening. "I'm sure I've interrupted a stimulating conversation. I wonder, though, if you've had enough of talking for one night, Princess?"

"I was enjoying my company greatly, to this moment."

"No doubt." His lavender robes stirred as he angled himself to more fully center his attention on her. "Surely it is exhausting to be always speaking politics, though."

Kayla flexed her fingers, itching to shove him away from her with all her strength. As Isonde, she could not. He and Isonde had a working, if not warm, relationship. Isonde had told her that they interfaced from time to time, mostly during social affairs at court.

"Come. Enough work." He held out a hand to her, palm

up. She made no move to touch him.

They had everyone's attention now. The look in his good eye said it all: he wouldn't back down.

You were there, she wanted to say. *On Ordoch. I saw you, I remember. You killed my Vayne.* She wanted to spit in his face. Her fingers curled around the spot where a kris dagger should have been strapped to her thigh. She would jam it up under his ribs, punching with all her force, her hand making a hollow in his stomach as she drove it in. Then she'd withdraw and do it again.

But Isonde never would.

Instead, with everyone watching her and a burning in the back of her throat that was loss and rage and hatred, she laid her hand on his.

"Where to?"

As he led her to the dance floor her gaze connected with Malkor's. He'd stopped near Vid and Trinan, all three equally worried. She shook her head when he started to come after her. She could do this. One dance with Dolan to maintain appearances, then she'd quit the evening before the elite of the empire witnessed the impeccable Princess Isonde commit murder. The last thing any of them needed was Malkor making a scene. Vid laid a hand on Malkor's arm, halting him as well.

"You seem to have something of a watchdog, Princess," Dolan murmured, leading her into the crowd and away from her guards. Astute bastard.

He might have been handsome once, in the Wyrd way, before the Kalichma Ritual scarred him. The thought stopped her. *In the Wyrd way?* When had she decided there was any other way to be handsome? He was short, coming to her chin. It was said that in Ilmenans especially, the height (or lack thereof) of a man marked his power. He must have been an impressive psionic once.

No longer. Now he was as ruined as she.

He drew her through rings of dancers and into an empty pocket near the center where Malkor couldn't see them. A pocket that subtly widened. They had privacy in the middle of it all, and an audience large enough to guarantee her best behavior. He turned to face her, that permanent half-smile on his face, and brought her closer by gently tugging on her hand. She tried not to flinch when he reached for her other hand. At least the dance required no more than this, intermittent hand-holding between turns and a series of steps that would bring them around each other.

She forced herself to look into his eyes, both of them, the healthy and the blank one.

"I'm here. What did you want?"

He didn't miss a beat, even with her brusque opening. "Your company."

"And what else?" They stepped apart before coming back together. He was younger than she remembered, younger than her own father but still older than her eldest brother and his twin sister had been.

"That isn't enough?"

"Not for you."

Was Isonde this rude with him? Not for the first time she felt at a loss when trying to play Isonde's relationships. She'd blanked on someone earlier who had apparently been a long-time confidant of the princess. She softened. "I mean, you are very busy after all, with your guests."

"They have little interest in the general amusements of the Game, and I found myself craving the company of someone who spoke aloud, if only for a short time."

"And so you sought me?"

He smiled. "Who better?"

Perhaps someone who doesn't intend to kill you before the Game is over.

"You're quite possibly the most influential woman in the empire."

She relaxed a fraction. This she could handle.

"So you *do* have an agenda." She opened up as much space between them as the dance allowed. "Let's hear it."

"Didn't I claim a lack of interest in politics this evening?"

"I doubt you ever tire of politics."

He inclined his head. "Tonight, though, I prefer to dance."

She stepped to the side as he did, bringing them shoulder to shoulder, their gazes in line.

Kin'shaa. Exile. And with good reason. He should have been executed for his ethical violations against his own people. Well before joining the empire, well before coming to Ordoch as a supposed emissary of peace and betraying her family, he had been a scientist. A neuroengineer. Every Wyrd had read the account of his crimes.

She spun around him and he again took her hands, smiling as he watched her, no doubt sensing her tension. Reveling in the power of it.

Dolan's cutting-edge research had been funded by the Ilmenan government. He'd developed an advanced AI, a synthetic brain that could interpret commands sent telepathically. It was rudimentary, he'd reported, but reliable. It would revolutionize the service and machine industry. Bots of every type—domestic, educational, constructional, militaristic—would be able to receive and act on commands through a psionic link with the user. His work was so advanced, with such a widespread potential for good, that he'd been allocated unlimited funds to improve the design.

And he'd improved it.

His quest to refine the psionic AI outstripped that of his peers, and unbeknownst to them he began his own research project in the other direction. He developed an AI not only capable of receiving telepathic commands, but sending them.

Kayla stepped away from him, trying to picture the slight man before her as the orchestrator of such a heinous experiment. He looked like any other councilor or advisor here. Understated lavender robes, zipped from toe to jaw, said he eschewed any vanity about his form. His only adornment was a series of rings, and his smile was polite, if a bit mocking. It would be hard for those gathered to imagine that he had raped an entire group of people mentally. Repeatedly, for years.

He'd set up a group of test subjects for his AI. She couldn't recall what the cover story was, but all of his test subjects believed they were brought to live in a community for some other reason. He had one goal: override the minds and personalities of others on a protracted basis to see just how far he could push them beyond their natural inclinations. While a powerful Wyrd could, with enough force or surprise, inflict mind control on someone, it was severely limited—by proximity to the victim, the strength of the perpetrator's psi powers, and of course the perpetrator's need to be conscious the whole time.

An AI capable of sending sophisticated telepathic signals, however, with a direct and unflagging power source, could send those signals indefinitely. Dolan, using that AI as an amplifier, had controlled each and every member of the community, warping them into someone else. He made the peaceful violent, the shy gregarious. He manipulated love and hate, fear and loyalty. He controlled them down to their basic moral impetuses, determining their compass of right and wrong. He violated them on every level, using them as tools against each other. Who knows how far he would have taken it if he hadn't been caught.

He clasped her hand, one of his thumbs moving over her skin in an almost-caress. The music pulled her toward him, away. Toward, around.

He deserved death. But even for a criminal who had tormented the souls of so many, Ilmena had no death penalty. The Kalichma Ritual should have killed him. Instead, like a festering supervirus that resisted every antibiotic thrown at it, he'd survived.

Survived to kill her *il'haar*.

Screw it. Scene or no scene, she had to leave.

Kayla pulled her hands from his with a snap. He stopped as well, a brow arched, looking amused.

"You must excuse me, the tournament begins early again tomorrow."

He gave her a deep bow, eyes on her the whole time. "Of course."

As she stepped off, he stopped her with a raised hand. "Princess? I should have mentioned this before, but. . . How like your brother you look. The resemblance is striking." He bowed again. "Sleep well."

The offhand comment shouldn't have raised the hair on the back of her neck except for one thing—Isonde didn't have a brother.

20

Kayla collapsed back against the doors to her room as soon as they slid shut behind her. Her chest heaved and the breath echoed in the dark room. He knew. Dolan *knew*. She'd fled on slippered feet all the way to her room, too panicked to wait for the maglifts to free up. She'd taken the stairs in leaps, all the way feeling someone running her down.

Five years of hiding. For nothing. What the frutt had she been thinking, coming to Falanar? Bringing Corinth here?

Corinth—

Her doors hissed apart without warning and she fell back into the hallway, into someone's arms. Before she could struggle the man wrapped her up hard, immobilizing her.

"Kayla, stop. It's me." Malkor leaned back, squeezing the air from her lungs, and carried her inside. The doors slid shut again, leaving them in blackness. He set her down before her mind could right itself.

"What are you doing here?"

"I had to make sure you got home all right." He hit the touchpad, bringing up the lowest light.

Her body still wanted to run. "Dolan—" That was all she could get out past her throbbing heart.

Malkor sighed, sinking down on the couch like a deflating balloon. "I don't know how long he's known. I wasn't aware he did until meeting with him tonight."

"It could have been from the beginning, if he took an interest in Isonde's attendant. He would have recognized my ID photo for sure."

"Does he know about—"

She nodded. "He mentioned Corinth. How does he know I'm playing Isonde now, though? Why didn't he think it was her?"

"I have a pretty good idea where he got that piece of information." His voice roughened on that, giving the answer away.

"Janeen?"

Malkor nodded. "I think it's safe to assume he knows all."

Kayla ripped the biostrip from her neck and dropped it to the table. Damnit.

Malkor's gaze centered on her in the low light, tracing her features.

"What did he want?" she asked.

Malkor watched her still, seeming to reacquaint himself with speaking to Kayla instead of Isonde. "He made us an offer."

Dolan had plans. He had plans for *her*, her and Corinth.

"I hope you told him to frutt himself."

"I was more diplomatic than that."

"Pity."

"He's too dangerous to ignore."

"Don't you think I know that?" Kayla reined herself in, strangling down the fear that had her all but scrambling for Corinth and hunting down someone—anyone—to fly them off Falanar. She forced herself to unbend and sit on the edge of the couch opposite Malkor's. "What did he propose?"

"He offered to allow us to win the Empress Game."

"What about his precious Wyrds?" Her tone sounded bitter even to her own ears.

"He claimed they would help."

"That's bullshit. Those traitors didn't come for any reason other than to win."

Malkor shifted, leaning back into the couch as if finally releasing the tension that had gripped him all night. "He made a good point that even controlling the empress-apparent's seat on the Council of Seven wouldn't guarantee they'd gain their ends. Whatever they are."

"They probably plan to give up state secrets to the empire and lead the imperial take-over of Ilmena next. Those frutting bastards."

"Dolan intimated that they might agree to put Isonde on the throne *if* she makes them certain promises and agrees to carry their agendas forward."

"*Put* her on the throne? What are they, puppeteers?"

"You tell me." The words had come off casually but she could tell he meant it. "They're Wyrds. Psionics. Can they control us?" His voice dropped lower. "Can you control me?"

Once upon a time, if I were that kind of person.

"It's less likely they'll try, now that you have rudimentary shields in place. You'd be harder to control because you're on watch for the manipulation."

"That doesn't answer the question."

"You'd be safe from Dolan," she said. "He's had his psi powers stripped."

"Kayla, answer me."

He'd thought to control her, threatened to use her responsibility to Corinth against her. Even if he had the right reasons for wanting to continue their charade, he had manipulated her into staying. Let him think she could do the same, *would* do the same. That he might be in her power as much as she was in his.

She met his gaze, silence her only answer. *Chew on that, Malkor.*

"So," she said instead, "the Ilmenans intend to use their telekinesis and telepathy to hinder their opponents, including me."

Malkor watched her a long time before answering. His voice was neutral when he finally spoke. "That's the plan. Unless we agree to Dolan's terms."

Four well-trained psionics were more than she could

handle. She could keep her mental shields in place but she couldn't create any physical barrier to protect her body if they tried to attack her telekinetically. She had no way to dissipate any shield they might place around her opponents, either. And even her shields, as honed as they were, might not be able to withstand the combined pressure of four minds attacking at once.

Dolan's pet Wyrds could control the outcome of the entire Empress Game.

"Damnit." She banged her fist against one knee. The truth of the situation pressed in on her. The reality of her world, the only way to win, stood out black and white against her denial. She couldn't.

She had to, she had nothing else.

"I need Corinth."

The next morning, Kayla was keyed-up and anxious about the day's fighting schedule. It was nearing the finals, the brackets closing down, with the empire's toughest fighters in her queue. The competition was ramping up and she had a tough day ahead. Tougher than she wanted.

The arena was filled to bursting with spectators. With so few combatants left, only the fighting rings at the very center were being used, every eye trained on them. She felt like a bug under a microscope as she warmed up.

In her mind she was ready to beat the shit out of every opponent thrown her way and climb to the very top. Her body, however, had other ideas.

I can do this.

Shoulder or no shoulder, she could do this. She had to.

By mid-morning she was sitting on a stool in the middle of the arena, leg propped up, a doctor applying a medstick to the split skin of her shin. Corinth filled much of her mind and she heard him mentally hiss at the cold burn of the medstick's dermal regenerator.

::Are you sure you're okay?:: Corinth asked for the hundredth time.

I'm fine. She wasn't. The morning's fighting had already undone all of yesterday's healing on the shoulder. More than that, though, she could never be fine with her *il'haar* among all these imperials, in plain sight, vulnerable. She wanted to shield him, hide him—anything to keep him from so many curious gazes. Anyone who took a marked interest in him rocketed to the top of her threat list.

He had come to the ring with Vid, whom he officially accompanied. The two of them "happened" to be near the ring where Kayla fought for every one of her matches. She stayed away from them, but Corinth had been in her mind or close to it since he had arrived shortly after her.

It gave her the headache of a lifetime.

How are you holding up?

::I'm fine.:: He matched her tone perfectly, which meant he wasn't fine either. His weariness expressed itself to her. He hadn't worked this hard with his psi powers since fleeing Ordoch.

The medic gave her a smile and a pat on the knee. "You should be all set, Princess. I'd tell you to stay off that leg, but. . . Good luck out there."

"Thanks." They'd need it if the Wyrds decided to get serious.

::I need to rest a few minutes.::

Go. She squeezed Corinth out of her head. She'd had him channeling a physical shield around her and her opponent each time she'd fought, blocking any outside interference from the Ilmenans. It was a median-level skill, but still the most complex thing Corinth had learned before going into exile.

The Ilmenans had challenged it.

Not heavily. They tested here and there, dabbling, prodding. They pushed to gauge his strength, but also just to let her know they were there. That they could mess with her. Corinth reported back on each encounter. So far, none of the attacks had posed any real threat.

So far.

Kayla got to her feet, careful not to jostle her shoulder. She scanned the crowd in the arena and mentally tried to conjure the Wyrd who seemed to have taken a fancy to her. She had no way to contact him, and naturally now that she actually wanted to speak with him he was silent.

She held no illusions about Corinth's ability to block out the combined efforts of the Ilmenans once they decided to meddle in earnest. What they needed was an ally. What they had was a mysterious stranger who had made no threatening moves against them and so far seemed to want to help. Someone Wyrd enough to contact her and cautious enough not to reveal his identity. Despite their desperate situation, she would never in a hundred light-years ask for his help if he didn't remind her, in a watered-down way, of Vayne.

But she couldn't even do that on her own. Whenever he decided to drop in, she'd need Corinth to *speak* for her. She forced that frustration away and focused on her next series. Her opponent must have drawn the luckiest fight schedule so far because she had no business advancing as far in the tournament as she had. At least this fight wouldn't push Kayla's stress level farther into the atmosphere.

The sword vibrated, a living extension of Kayla's arm as she thrust with a strike that would have penetrated her opponent's left lung.

"Point, white!"

The Blessed Matron Hilla pushed the sword away from her chest in obvious frustration as Kayla withdrew. As suspected, Hilla had not been up to the challenge of a *ro'haar*. This was the easiest of Kayla's series today, which was for the best since her shoulder burned with unholy fire.

Kayla stepped back to her starting mark. One point left. One point and she'd bury this imperial's dreams. One point and she'd prove Wyrd superiority. Again. There was a delicious satisfaction in that.

Could Corinth hold out for one more point, shielding her from telekinetic interference?

Better make this quick.

Hilla slipped into an L stance, by all appearances ready to fight Kayla to the bitter end. The chime sounded to begin the bid for the next point. Kayla advanced, trailing foot following the leading foot as she maintained her L stance, minimizing the target she presented. Hilla's retreat matched Kayla's movements perfectly, keeping them two sword lengths apart.

Hilla dodged Kayla's first attack and advanced with her own, a thrust low to Kayla's outside. Kayla circled her blade over Hilla's and forced the thrust down and out from her body. She gave ground as she parried, avoiding the backhand cut Hilla followed up with.

Hilla wasn't content with that. She ate up the space between them with a cross-over step and thrust outside again. The strike came at a height above her guard. Kayla circled her blade under Hilla's and easily guided the strike up and away, looking for the moment to counter-attack, but it wasn't there.

Patience, she told herself. Rapier is all about control.

The words did little to ease the pounding of her blood.

She offered her own attack that Hilla dodged, though she caught the woman across the upper arm with a forehand cut that would have drawn blood with a sharpened blade. The strike enraged Hilla. She came with a lightning-fast thrust to Kayla's high inside. It was too quick for Kayla to sidestep, all she could do was parry with the flat of her left hand, thrusting furiously out and up. Her torn shoulder screamed in protest at the motion. Kayla gasped at the pain. A point-blank ion blast to the rotator cuff would have hurt less.

She missed the opening in Hilla's guard that should have been her last point and had to fall back several steps to reset. Hilla gave her no time to do so, she must have scented blood.

She advanced with a series of feints, then committed to a thrust aimed at Kayla's face.

That was her undoing.

Kayla brought her blade up to high, using an attack with counter-pressure. She forced the line of Hilla's tip out and to the left even as she thrust. Her sword connected just barely with Hilla's chest at the height of the second rib.

"Point, white!"

Match. Series. Win.

Kayla let her sword arm sag, the pain in her body outweighing the feeling of victory. One fight left today, one more fight before she could get her shoulder into the repair cuff.

And then?

She'd do it all over again tomorrow, only harder. Faster. Better.

The eighthfinals in the morning and the quarterfinals in the afternoon. The enormity of what rested on those fights was too much to bear at the moment. All she could hear was the slowing pulse of her blood and her own unending chant: *I have to win, I have to win, I have to win.*

Kayla took a tired step away from the ring, searching the arena for Corinth.

::Flawless.::

The mind voice whispered into her brain, raising shivers on sweat-dampened skin.

::You executed the final point perfectly.::

Kayla pulled up the edge of her tunic to wipe sweat from her brow, attempting to make eye contact with Corinth.

Now, she wanted to shout, *get in my head now!*

Corinth sat with his head bowed, Vid resting a concerned hand on his shoulder. The Wyrds must have been more direct in their attempts to meddle during her fight with Hilla.

Corinth, I need you.

He couldn't hear.

::Rest.:: The concern coming through was perfectly Vayne, but it was an unknown voice that urged her from the sparring

ring. ::Your next series isn't for a while. Rest, and perhaps *speak* with me?::

If only.

She lifted her left shoulder, the stretch screaming through tortured ligaments. This next series would be her last of the day, one way or the other. She gritted her teeth and walked from the ring, aiming for the nearest medic. She needed a deep-tissue regen sleeve, anti-inflammatories and unconsciousness. With one series left she'd have to settle for a massive dose of pain blockers.

::You're weakened, or your thoughts wouldn't be coming through your shields to me. Please don't take the pain meds. Without the feedback from your body you'll push yourself too hard and cause irreparable damage.::

She didn't have a choice.

Malkor intercepted her on the way to the medic station, not quite making eye contact. He had the injector in hand.

"Thought you might need this," was all he said. He passed her a syringe full of respite. Good man.

She shot up immediately. The Not-Vayne who stalked her psionically with Vayne's touch sighed, disappointment coming through. Kayla gripped Malkor's arm to steady herself as a wave of sensation flowed downward from her neck.

"You don't kid around," she said. It equalized a moment later, the pain blockers settling into place.

He watched her with those gray eyes, clearly doubting his own judgment. "Too much?"

When she thought it wouldn't send her into a spin, she shook her head. "Just right." She forced herself to let go of Malkor and stand straight. "I need Corinth but I don't want to approach him."

"His strength's flagging, are you sure?"

She nodded. He pulled out his mobile comm and spoke to Vid.

::Kayla?:: Corinth's voice. She waved Malkor off and went to sit alone in a chair. She closed her eyes and forced herself to open to Corinth.

He's here, can you speak to him?

::I don't feel him.::

Wait for it.

The stranger's voice slipped along her senses. ::What does a warrior like yourself think of when she closes her eyes amid a battlefield?::

Corinth's shock rocked through her. She'd warned him, but— ::Vayne?:: he said to her, with so much hope it ached in her chest.

No. She couldn't hide her pain and the bleeding ache of loss. Not-Vayne had so familiar a feel, entwined with the foreign. *Can you speak to him?* she asked Corinth.

She felt Corinth struggling to compose himself, reorient himself to this new reality.

It's not Vayne.

::I know that, Kay.:: He paused, gathering what strength he had. At last she felt his focus split. Part of him separated from her consciousness.

::Who are you?:: he asked the stranger, and she heard it as if he were beside her, having a normal conversation.

::What's this?:: the stranger said in her mind. ::You have another admirer?::

Inside her head as he was, Corinth heard Not-Vayne's words. ::I am her ally:: Corinth replied. ::You seem to come as a friend, and we have need of those.::

::I am the princess's friend.:: The stranger sounded cautious. ::Not necessarily one of yours.:: She felt him near to her, with Vayne's warmth and desire for connection, paired with something stronger. A telekinetic finger brushed along her cheek, then the stranger spoke again. ::Who are you that she lets you in?::

::It matters only that she has need of me, and I am here. As you are as well.:: Corinth sounded older than she expected, but she cringed at how untrained he felt in his communication.

::Why do you let this young one speak for you?:: The stranger's voice carried a current of displeasure. ::I would hear your voice on this, not the pup's. Do you require my aid?::

Corinth forged ahead. ::If you are to be trusted then yes, we do.::

The stranger made a sound of exasperation. ::Be gone, she can speak for herself.::

::Meet with us, and then she'll speak to you. The interests of three Wyrds cannot be so dissimilar. We could form a mutually beneficial alliance.::

::The last thing she needs in so delicate a situation is the "help" of a rough, untrained, clumsy psionic as yourself.::

She felt every centimeter of the barb's penetration. Her desire to shield Corinth mingled with his shame.

::It's not working:: Corinth said just to her.

We need his help. You and I can't stand against the Ilmenans alone. If we can persuade him to do no more than shield me during the fights, it'll be worth whatever it takes.

::If you want my help:: the stranger said ::then all you need to do is ask me, Princess. Seek me out. Alone.::

::How will we—::

The stranger cut Corinth off, speaking only to her. ::Open your eyes. You will know me.::

Kayla shook off the lethargy the pain meds had brought and forced her eyelids apart. A crowd swirled around her, everyone intent on their own business. It could have been anyone. Then her eyes collided with his ruined gaze. He held her, his red and lavender stare across the arena like an icy spear in her chest.

It could have been anyone, but she knew it was him.

The *kin'shaa* smiled at her.

The last series passed in a blur. All Kayla could remember was a group of people congratulating her at the end and asking what her plans were for the evening. Somehow she'd broken away, promising to be at an engagement she couldn't remember the location of, and made it to the magchute bay. She waited in the giant lobby among people too polite to approach her when she no doubt looked like shit. Conversations floated past here and there.

Dolan had psi powers. And he felt like Vayne. *Vayne*. How? How did the *kin'shaa*, whose powers had been stripped from him, *speak* like her twin? And where the void were her powers? How was she still so useless?

The doors to the magchute in front of her opened, revealing a sparsely populated tube that no one else tried to enter. Odd. She took a step forward, then froze when the occupants' identities registered. The Ilmenan Wyrds.

Frutt it. She was too tired to wait for another lift and way past caring. One of them pushed the button to close the door but she strode inside before the mechanism completed its task. The doors shut behind her with a *whoosh*.

She met four hostile stares with one of her own, then turned her back on them to contemplate the seal of the door in silence. They could go frutt themselves.

::We know what you are:: came a female voice.

Kayla stiffened, holding her breath to listen. Had she imagined it?

::Traitor.:: The word's venom leached into her wounds.

Kayla whipped around. "Excuse me?" She stared at Tia'tan, knowing exactly who would have the balls to say something like that.

::You're Wyrd, but working with the IDC.::

"Speak out loud when I'm talking to you," Kayla snapped. She clearly caught them all off-guard.

Tia'tan tilted her head back, staring right into Kayla's eyes. "Traitor." Her tone dared Kayla to challenge her.

"Who the void are you, to call me a traitor?"

"You're not Princess Isonde, no matter what you pretend." Tia'tan's gaze raked her from head to toe. "You are Wyrd trained. You and whoever shielded you today."

"You don't know what you're talking about." Useless words. There was no hiding from other Wyrds.

The shortest one, Noar, scoffed.

"You're helping one of the empire's strongest to win the Game. You're an embarrassment to our people," Tia'tan said.

Kayla's temper shot through the red, outrage provoking her past caution. "I am *helping* my people."

"Liar," Tia'tan spat back at her. "You probably helped the IDC in the Ordoch coup."

Kayla shoved Tia'tan as hard as she could. Tia'tan slammed against the chute wall and bounced off it. She grunted, dazed for one second, before she lunged at Kayla, fury on her face.

The other Wyrds swarmed them. The tall female grabbed Tia'tan by the arm while the two males force-projected, wrapping Kayla's limbs with invisible weights. Kayla snarled but backed off, raising her fingertips to show she meant to stand down. The invisible weights evaporated when Tia'tan regained her composure.

"How dare you call me a traitor," Kayla said. "*You* came here to ally with the *kin'shaa*. He raped those people. Your people. Like they were nothing but toys. He's the emperor's ally and you're *helping* him."

Tia'tan looked furious. "We would *never* help the *kin'shaa*."

"You are here as his guests," Kayla said, taken aback somewhat. Her blood still sang with the need for violence.

"As was our design. We—" Tia'tan cut herself off, her gaze flicking to the elder male. They debated something in silence while the other Wyrds held their breath. When Tia'tan finally resumed speaking, she sounded no calmer. "Our plans are our own." She straightened, shaking off Luliana's hand. "But we are *not* traitors like you."

What in space was going on here?

The doors behind Kayla hissed open and the Wyrds filed out, pushing past her. Tia'tan's accusation filled Kayla's ears.

Traitor.

21

Malkor found Kayla in Trinan and Vid's room. The two agents were out on assignment and she sat on the couch in silence, Corinth asleep beside her, his head in her lap.

"He's exhausted," she said, before Malkor could ask. Had she read the question in his mind? What else had she read? He shook off the thought, uneasy.

His concern for Corinth paled beside his worry for Kayla. She had a discreet dermal regen patch on her chin and a haunted look in her eyes.

"Toble said he'd be fine, he just needs rest," Malkor said.

She nodded, not taking her eyes off of Corinth.

"As you do," he added.

She nodded again.

"You look terrible." That got a chuckle out of her.

"Thanks."

He hung in the doorway. Was he intruding? Probably.

To the void with it. She can mind-control me away if she wants to.

The truth of that possibility gave him a shiver.

Still, he needed to check on her, see how she felt. Not her injuries, he could imagine those. It was her mental state he couldn't gauge, not with all she was going through. He needed to know that he, Isonde and Ardin hadn't, in their selfishness, damaged her spirit.

He could imagine her throwing that concern back in his face. *"Save your pity, Agent, I don't need anything from you."*

He took a seat on the far end of the couch, at Corinth's feet, bracketing the boy between them. "How does he seem to you?" he asked softly.

She smoothed her hand over Corinth's hair in a continuous motion. "He's only sleeping. He'll be. . . he's fine." The protective way she sheltered him told Malkor how worried she truly was.

Malkor contemplated the boy he'd initially regarded as merely a liability. Corinth was intelligent, startlingly so. He'd impressed even Rigger with his tech savvy and his improvements to the Isonde–Kayla hologram design. Without speaking, Corinth had somehow bonded with Vid and Trinan. He'd overcome his sheltered background and faced what must be a terrifying amount of people to protect his sister in the arena. His *ro'haar*, Malkor reminded himself. More than sister. A connection stronger than blood.

"I don't think they did anything to him," Kayla said, her voice barely audible over Corinth's snores. "He said nothing about an attack, only that they tried to penetrate his shielding. They found the gaps he couldn't see and exploited them. He—" She stopped, choking up a bit. "He apologized. As if he'd failed me."

She finally looked at Malkor then, her Isonde-blue eyes full of pain. "As if I wasn't the one who had put him in the situation."

And Malkor had put them both in that situation.

"Take the hologram off," he surprised himself by saying.

Kayla's holographic Isonde-brow furrowed.

"I need to see *you* when we speak of things as important as this," he said. "She doesn't know about protecting *il'haars* with your life, or risking everything to win a Game you don't care about. She isn't you, Kayla, and I don't want her expressions. I want yours."

Kayla peeled the biostrip from her neck. "Even when it adheres to my skin and all but disappears, I feel it, feel the weight of wearing her body."

He reached out and curled her fingers over the biostrip so he didn't have to look at the shackle he'd given her.

"I know you hate to risk Corinth, but it's necessary," Malkor said. Not that that made it any more bearable for her, or her any more willing to forgive him for it.

He couldn't remove his hand from hers, and they both pretended not to notice they were touching the other. "Can he hold out for another day of fighting?"

She hesitated as if debating something.

"What is it?"

"Nothing. There's no one else I trust to help us, Corinth will have to do his best again tomorrow. It's our only possibility for blocking the Ilmenans." She smoothed her hand over Corinth's hair again, her gaze full of concern as it rested on her brother.

"Kayla— I never wanted to use him as leverage."

She flipped her gaze back to Malkor, eyes narrowed.

"I was desperate the day Isonde got attacked. I couldn't think straight, and I said the one thing I knew would force your compliance."

"But you *meant* it," she said. "You threatened my *il'haar* to get what you wanted."

Had he meant it? "Yes," he acknowledged. "It's too important to give up despite what happened."

"I agree with you. I would have then, too, if you'd given me time to consider."

"I didn't have time."

She frowned. "You had enough. You should have trusted me to make the right decision."

He hadn't. She had trusted him with her life and Corinth's and he hadn't given her the consideration she deserved, hadn't allowed her a choice. "I'm sorry, Kayla."

"I understand why you did it. And," she said, cutting him a glance that promised dire consequences, "that you'll never do it again."

"My word."

She nodded, satisfied, and something regrew in the silence

between them. The damaged bond strengthened, reaffirmed itself. They were back on the same page.

She stood and tried to lift Corinth in her arms, but got no farther than lifting his shoulders from the couch before hissing in pain. The regen cuff on her left shoulder had started its work, but it would need many, many more hours before she would begin to see any improvement.

"Let me." Malkor scooped Corinth up before she could answer, and carried him to his bedroom. Corinth slept through being deposited in bed and covered tenderly with blankets by Kayla.

It was odd to see hands that could be so ruthlessly effective with sword, dagger and staff deal so delicately with one exhausted boy.

They returned in silence to the couch. It was the first quiet, tension-free moment he'd had all day. She settled close to him, her thoughts turned inward, and he relaxed back against the cushions. He studied her face obliquely. He wasn't just looking at the Kayla he knew, the pit whore, the *ro'haar*, he was looking at Kayla Reinumon, Wyrd Princess, heir to the throne of Ordoch. One of the last survivors.

The peace that had lasted mere moments was replaced with the familiar guilt.

What would her reaction be when she learned he'd been involved on Ordoch? Would their truce hold? Would she understand his reasoning, his concern for his people, why he'd agreed to the mission to Wyrd Space? Or would she come after him with a dagger?

"This partnership we have," she said, "if I am to trust, if we are to succeed together, I need to know." She turned, squaring her shoulders to him. "What role did you play in the coup on my homeworld?"

The question had been coming since they'd met. She, more than anyone else alive, had the right to know. She was also the last person he wanted to confess his culpability to.

"I need the truth, Malkor." Her bright blue gaze held him still, demanded an answer. "After all I have done, I deserve that."

She did. If he wanted her trust, he'd have to earn it.

More likely, though, he'd earn her enmity. "You're certain?"

"You were there. On Ordoch. You weren't just part of the planning process, were you?"

"I was there."

"In the palace? When they—"

"No." He shook his head. "No, I was recalled to the ship before the actual coup began. Most of the IDC agents were. But that doesn't mean I wasn't involved." Memories, imperfectly buried, bloomed to full life. "I was part of the diplomatic team sent to negotiate assistance with the TNV from your people. I knew the military had planned the coup as a last-ditch backup plan if all diplomatic channels failed, never expecting it would be necessary.

"I agreed to the Ordochian mission believing that diplomacy would win the day, as did most of the IDC agents involved. We felt the need of our people was so great, our risk so high in traveling to Wyrd Space, that the Wyrds—that you—would agree to offer what assistance you could. I believed the trickiest part of the mission would be defining the terms of an alliance between our people."

She rose, putting distance between them. She looked away but he knew he had her full attention.

"I wasn't among the agents working with council members who'd been sent as emissaries. My role was more basic. I liaisoned with the seneschal of the palace and with your security forces. I negotiated the day-to-day terms of our presence on your planet: how many people were allowed in our delegation, how many shuttles we could land on your planet, how many military people we could bring as protection 'just in case,' what ordnance they could carry. There were a million things to negotiate—access to the palace, where our people could go, how supervised they had to be, if they were allowed into the city proper to see part of your world, how many personnel changes we could make, where the diplomats who stayed planet-side would be housed. . . The list was endless."

As had been the frustration. While the seneschal was almost generous in his concessions, not believing the empire advanced enough to be any sort of threat, Malkor heard from Commander Parrel that talks at the top level were not progressing. The frustration of being relegated to a minor role, unable to help in the most important negotiations of his lifetime, had eaten at Malkor even as he excelled at his own negotiations.

"Talks stalled with your leaders and everyone grew tense. We'd traveled with our military's two strongest, most heavily armed ships. Our commanders were getting antsy and plans aboard the ship kicked into a new gear. Everyone was on edge but I honestly thought we could convince your people."

Did that in any way absolve him of his part in the coup? he wondered.

She gave no reaction to his words, standing robot-like a meter away from him, her gaze fixed on the wall.

"Then the IDC was ordered off the planet. We were to turn our visitor passes over to military personnel from the ship. The councilors and senior IDC staff were pulled from negotiations, changed out for the colonels who would lead the coup. I knew it was happening."

He'd known and he'd— what? Protested strenuously? Stayed planet-side to the last possible second? Threatened to warn the Wyrds? All of that, but what did it matter?

He'd known, and in the end. . . "I followed my orders." That was the truth of it. He'd followed his orders, start to finish. "The coup took place a few hours after I returned to the ship."

There. The words were out, the damage done.

No. The damage had been done five years ago.

She nodded. The movement was so slight he might have imagined it, but it was there. She nodded to herself, the silence lying heavily between them.

How did they go on from here?

Her shoulders relaxed, but still she didn't face him. Her fingers uncurled from the fists he hadn't noticed, her chest filled with a deep breath.

"Did you kill my family?" she asked softly.

He had never been so thankful that the answer was, "No."

"Did you place the bombs?"

There the blame lay on him heavily. "No, but I negotiated the terms that allowed those who did to be there. They were able to do so because of my actions."

She shook her head. "It's not the same."

"I—"

"It's not the same."

She finally looked up, meeting his gaze steadily. Instead of the rage he expected to see in her expression, the hurt or hatred, he saw relief.

"Thank you," she said, "for telling me, but mostly for being the man I thought you were."

"But—"

"There are two sides to every tragedy," she said. "It took my coming here to see it. My people are not blameless. The damage of the TNV is catastrophic, I understand that now. We hid behind old laws and our suspicions of you, refused to help even though billions had already died. Whole planets of people—decimated. There's no guarantee that we could have stopped it, but we could have at least agreed to try."

The breath sighed out of her and she took another, seeming to gain strength. There was the nod again, to herself, as if an understanding shifted inside of her and she accepted it.

He was not proud of his actions five years ago but had owned them, finally. Owned them before the one person most likely to judge him harshly.

"You surprise me," he said. Listening had to be even more painful than the telling had been. Understanding even more so.

"Am I supposed to hate you personally for everything that was done that day? Hold you accountable for the actions of hundreds of others, decisions that weren't yours to make?"

"A lesser person might."

"And so I might have, in the last five years. Before meeting you, meeting you and Isonde and Prince Trebulan. The IDC was nothing but a symbol to me. An entity to be feared, hated and reviled. Now?" She stepped forward slowly, determinedly, and took her place beside him on the couch once more. "I can't forgive what was taken from me, but I can begin to understand. And to move forward."

"We can make this better, Kayla, if we work together. If we fight for it."

Her closeness said it all. "We will."

Kayla limited her social activity to a single event that evening—a banquet celebrating all of the contestants that had progressed to the eighthfinals. It was a raucous affair, the mood full of celebration and cheer and anticipation. The guests of honor were easy to pick out, surrounded as they were by groups of admirers, and each looking a bit weary in their own way, herself included.

She wore a sleek, high-necked gown with no sleeves and an open back. She'd shot up with a pain blocker before the event and wore the regen sleeve on her shoulder. Even a minute less of her cellular regrowth and rest routine was more than she could afford with tomorrow's fighting ending in the quarterfinals. Besides, thousands of commentators and analysts had watched every second of her fights, they'd identified her shoulder injury based on the differences between her earlier and later fights. Everyone here knew her weakness, no reason to hide the cuff.

Her most prominent fashion accessory? The emperor-apparent himself, Prince Ardin, on her arm. What better way to say "the Game is mine."

It couldn't have been more awkward.

Malkor had yet to tell Ardin about Isonde's condition and coma. Kayla trusted that Malkor knew what he was doing when it came to Ardin, but damn if it wasn't uncomfortable to pretend to be Isonde with him. She could stand the warm smiles and adoring looks, it was the discreet touches he managed to sneak in amid all the guests that made her skin crawl.

Archon Raorin caught Ardin's attention and Kayla used the moment to escape him.

It's only for a moment, she told herself. The political cachet it gave her to be seen with Ardin was too great to pass up for long.

Malkor managed to fight his way through her admirers to gain a place at her side. He made his apologies to the crowd, citing official IDC business, and led her away to a quiet space of the room, his fingertips warm on her bare back. No one else would have dared touch her there, not even Ardin.

"You should be resting," he said, dropping his hand. She suddenly missed the gentle pressure.

"Isonde needs to be here tonight. Strutting. Gloating. Preening. A show of confidence can psych out more than one opponent for the morning." Her eyes scanned the room. "Let them know the Game is mine."

"Tia'tan and Clanesta Sovein seem to have the same idea."

True. The Clanestas Warren were celebrating with abandon, the two of them drinking, eating and dancing the night away. Sovein, the elder Clanesta, might be celebrating winning the whole damn tournament, based on her good cheer. Tia'tan, by comparison, looked like a block of ice among the guests. An arrogant and altogether superior block of ice. *It's only a matter of time*, her attitude said.

Kayla's regen cuff gave a double beep and shut down.

"You've done enough tonight already," he said.

She nodded, willing to be convinced to leave the party. "It's time for a round of anti-inflammatories and coolant packs anyway." She gave him a smile. "Wish me luck in the morning."

The morning of eighthfinals closed out as expected. Princess Tia'tan finished her three matches flawlessly, becoming the number one seed. Clanesta Sovein and Kayla tied records for second, but a point-by-point comparison put Kayla in third. The last competitor in the quarterfinals would be President

Devon DiMasta, but it didn't matter who had that spot—Tia'tan would eliminate her.

After a two-hour break for lunch and rest, the quarterfinal series began: Tia'tan vs. Devon and Sovein vs. Kayla.

"Frutt!"

Kayla dropped her front hand from the staff reflexively after Sovein Warren slammed her staff into her opponent's fingers. The tip of Kayla's weapon dipped toward the floor as she shook out her probably cracked appendages, and Sovein darted in. She struck with the butt of her staff, stopping less than a centimeter from Kayla's throat to claim a point.

A far as opening salvos went, it was damn effective.

Kayla shook her hand, flexing her fingers one last time before getting a solid grip on her staff. She was two steps from the crown, two steps from winning it all. The winner of this series would go on to fight in the championship bout after a rest day. All Kayla had to do was defeat a hulking woman who could give two men a fair fight at the same time and she'd be on her way. Simple, really. Especially with a group of Wyrds simultaneously channeling enough psi power to stagger her poor *il'haar* as he tried to hold them off.

Sovein grinned, brown eyes sparkling with the excitement of battle. "Got hold a' it now?"

Very funny.

::I don't know how long I can do this.:: She barely heard Corinth's small voice. ::Hurry up, Kay.::

Right. How in space was she supposed to do that?

Sovein started circling and Kayla mirrored her. The woman presented such a big target she should be easy to hit. Not the case. Sovein blocked every attack Kayla tried with intense force. Each block sent reverberations through her, stinging Kayla's already hurting hand and jarring her shoulder. The woman could wear her down simply by maintaining a solid defense.

They traded blows, the wood of their staves clacking

together. Here a shot got through, there Kayla got lucky. They split points and Kayla somehow took the first match. She doubted she had the strength to best this woman in an actual fight. She scored sparring points because they relied on position and potential for damage rather than actual damage, but Sovein would clobber her in real battle.

As the second match began, Kayla felt oddly sluggish. She *might* have slowed a fraction due to fatigue, it was possible. But certainly not enough to miss the opening under Sovein's arm that she lunged for. Definitely not.

She backed off, warding against a flurry of blows from Sovein that felt like hammer strikes. When Kayla ducked under a swing and came up for an open shot at Sovein's unprotected chin, the air thickened around her. Her arms swung through slush and the butt of her staff slowed to a halt before it found its mark. To observers it might appear that Kayla wouldn't commit a full extension to finish the strike for fear of leaving herself open.

::I'm sorry.:: Corinth said. ::They're—::

She retreated and felt something behind her heel before she tripped backward. She dropped her staff to catch herself on her hands and Sovein hit her dead-on in the chest, knocking the breath from her.

Point, Wyrds. Those bastards.

Kayla coughed up something and regained her feet.

::Better hurry.:: The water-weak Vayne—no, Dolan—urged her with concern.

If you're so concerned then help, you frutter. She glanced over at Corinth. His eyes were clamped shut in concentration and his skin shimmered with sweat.

Hurry, hurry.

The official confirmed she was ready before resuming the match.

A strike. Another. Two steps, a strike-block-block-strike-block combo. Back-pedaling, and then Sovein had her against the edge of the ring with what would have been a crushing blow to the skull. She took a third point quickly after that and it was second match, Sovein.

The third match started cautiously, neither willing to drop a point. Kayla let openings slide by, afraid to chance anything less than a sure thing, wary of the Ilmenans breaking through Corinth's spotty shield.

Sovein came across with a swing that should have landed square on the center of Kayla's staff. Instead Kayla's weapon dipped against her will and the strike cracked across her abused knuckles. She clung to the staff with a numb hand as the air turned gelatinous around her. She couldn't raise her arms fast enough or dodge quickly enough. A blow glanced off her block and Sovein's staff slid along Kayla's until it crashed into her chin.

"Ya' all right?" Sovein drew back, concern overshadowing the bloodlust for a second. Kayla pressed a hand to her throbbing chin and it came back scarlet. One didn't expect to get bloodied in a match with staves.

"I'm fin—"

Sovein hooked her staff under Kayla's ankle and flipped her onto her ass. She loomed over her with a stylized head-smashing pose and claimed her point.

Kayla spat blood from the bite she'd given her tongue.

::It's too much, too much. . .:: Corinth's voice trailed off and he passed into unconsciousness. Vid scooped him up and carried him from the arena.

Rage surged through Kayla, roared from the depths at the sight of her *il'haar* falling victim to anyone. These Ilmenans, Wyrds who should have been her allies, had done this. They'd forced Kayla to use Corinth like a tool.

They could not be allowed to triumph.

Her body trembled with the force of her hatred. She climbed to her feet, determination providing its own sort of certainty. Ilmenans or no, she *would* win this.

Just then psi energy hummed around her, stroked like a finger down her cheek. *Dolan.* The air's unnatural thickness vanished.

Holy shit, he was shielding her, and doing a much better job of it than Corinth could. He freed her from the Ilmenans' interference, protected her.

She had no time to consider further as the chime sounded to start the next point. The fight narrowed to a single technique at a time. She no longer saw points or series or combinations. She saw a strike. A twist. A shift in position. Only one motion mattered at a time, one after the other. She was focus, she was precision. Sweep, twist, strike. Dodge, drop to a knee, upward hanging block. Vault, ox kick, swing.

Point.

Point.

Point.

Sovein snapped her staff over her knee with the roar of an enraged bear. The crack of wood splintering fractured the cocoon around Kayla and reality caught her in its rush once more. The world swelled, sights and sounds and everywhere the cheering of the crowd that crowned her in victory.

She had won, but she hadn't done it alone.

She glimpsed Dolan haunting the edge of the crowd. He caught her eye and smiled, a secret between the two of them.

Late that afternoon, Malkor stared down at Isonde in her medical pod. He wrapped his hand gently around her wrist, wanting to let her know he was there but unwilling to do more for fear of hurting her.

Stars, he felt powerless.

"You'll be okay," he murmured. To her, or himself? The muted beeping of the console at the foot of the pod told him that—for the moment—she was stable. How long would that last? Her body couldn't maintain this state for long without deteriorating. Toble had been able to reduce the strain on her heart and lungs but not alleviate the rigor entirely. Janeen's poison, or what had to have been Isonde's allergic reaction to it, still held her in a stony, comatose grip.

He gave her wrist a slight squeeze. "I'll find her."

Janeen had been his responsibility, his agent. He should have seen her plans taking shape and neutralized her before they had come to a head. She never should have been allowed near Isonde—or Kayla.

Malkor withdrew his hand from Isonde's arm, swallowing the bitterness of his failure. He couldn't do anything for her here—time to get back to work.

A table full of datapads greeted him when he entered his room. His complink bleated notifications and his mobile comm, once he turned it back on, chirped with a slew of incoming messages. He scrolled through the headers on each, skimming and mentally organizing, then tossed it on the bed. The complink promised better intel. Rigger had cracked a deep level of encryption on Janeen's complink and sent over the data packets retrieved from her secured storage—real private stuff, data it would have taken a tech team months to ferret out. Thank space for Rigger. Malkor dialed up a serving of water from the food synthesizer and settled at his table with his stack of datapads.

Malkor reviewed his notes. He'd done an in-depth reconstruction of Janeen's schedule since they'd arrived on Falanar, a rougher sketch of her engagements during their trip to Altair Tri, and pulled together a list of her official activities on Falanar before that.

The timeline had more gaps than he would have liked. Had he been monitoring her moves it would have raised his suspicions, but he had had no reason to watch over his own octet, not when he trusted them and knew them to be responsible and good at their jobs.

Everyone had been pulled in a million directions since they had arrived for the Game and his own reports were spotty, considering he usually had two to four things going at any one time. But here—Janeen had nothing written during the fighting on the second day. No reconnaissance done, no issues logged, no event attended. . . nothing. Same for dinner that night. She'd had the Inquini Gala on her assignment sheet but he didn't remember seeing her there. Plus the affair had broken up before too long due to political tensions and she had nothing else on her schedule after that. How had she been spending her time?

He pushed that aside and accessed the files Rigger had sent him. They looked like mission reports, going back at least seven years. Wait— He grabbed another datapad and pulled up her service record. Seven years ago she'd still been in the academy, and for two years after that she had been a junior agent working other agents' cases. Why did she have mission reports for that time?

He opened up the oldest batch, definitely during her time at the academy. The first one he skimmed wasn't a mission file at all, it was a profile. It was a full report on one of her fellow classmates, and not just the public details. She had notes on his schedule, associates, love interests, family background, grades in the academy, vices, political affiliations, public—and not so public—society associations. The profile was followed by notes on observed behaviors and a discussion of possible strengths and weaknesses.

The subject wasn't an ordinary classmate. He belonged to the ruling cartel in the Protectorate Planets' Trade Federation. Malkor opened other reports. All similarly detailed, all persons of influence.

It was the kind of file an agent would set up for an assignment involving a tense politico-military-economic situation where leverage made all the difference.

He flipped ahead a year, once Janeen was out of the academy, curious what he would find. Her reports continued. She had mission reports now, the standard kind he'd been receiving from her for the last three years they'd been working together. Then she had secondary, unofficial reports. The same situations covered in much greater detail. Contacts she had made outside of IDC channels, unofficial assignments completed outside of the mission scopes, the kind of back-room, under the table dealings the IDC was infamous for, and exactly the kind of behavior he wouldn't tolerate.

So whom did she work for? Who pulled the strings on these black-op missions completed while on valid IDC assignments?

And what the void had she done while she had been working for him?

He called up her files from the last year. There they were, profiles on the entire octet, including him. His file was embarrassingly detailed, full of observations of his character based on every command decision. It even included a timeline of his brief, bitter, and—he'd thought—ultra-secret affair with Isonde. The one even Ardin didn't know about.

Leverage.

He started going through her files more seriously, searching her most recent reports for indicators. These reports had definitely been written for someone specific, not just for general note taking. She favored a conversational style in these reports and clues popped up here and there. He couldn't underline them all directly, but he saw hints. Enough to learn that whoever orchestrated her clandestine assignments was themselves IDC.

Someone very powerful. Someone who had to have been less than pleased by the failure of her mission to neutralize Kayla. No wonder Janeen had gone into hiding.

He had to bring this to Commander Parrel.

Kayla commed his door, catching him by surprise. She entered his rooms and stripped off the Isonde hologram almost before the doors shut behind her.

"We can't shield my fights from the Ilmenans," she said without preamble.

He set the datapads aside, shifting gears after a look at the seriousness of her expression. "It worked today," he said. Thankfully. They had no other weapon against the Wyrds.

"You saw it yourself, they overwhelmed Corinth and I wasn't even fighting Tia'tan. Imagine how much more intense their pressure will be in that final series."

"He's overtired. You'll both have a day to rest, tomorrow's an off day for the combatants to prepare for the final round. Surely that's enough time."

She shook her head. "Not for him. And even at full potential, he couldn't be expected to hold off that many trained psionics when he's only a boy."

"But what of you?" he asked, as she sank into the chair opposite his desk. "You must have almost a decade's worth of training he hasn't had."

"It won't be enough," was all she said.

"You managed it today. Corinth passed out before the end of the fight."

She sighed. "I didn't manage anything." A cloud crossed her face.

"What?"

"I—" She hesitated. Wrestled with something.

"Kayla, just tell me."

"You won't like it."

"I don't like any of this. What are you avoiding?"

"It's Dolan." She spilled the story of him contacting her psionically, and his apparent willingness to help her.

"He must have helped me today," she said. "Once Corinth was carried off, the Ilmenans didn't interfere again. I don't think he touched the Clanesta, but I think he shielded me."

"I thought he was powerless. Isn't that the definition of being *kin'shaa*?"

"He is. Or, he was. Now. . ." Her voice drifted off, her thoughts turning inward.

She came back to herself slowly, a slight shake of her head, a frown, then her flame-bright eyes focused on him.

"I think we have to deal with Dolan."

"As in. . .?" He had images of her sneaking through an air duct in the *kin'shaa*'s room to stab him straight through his ruined eye.

"As in take the deal he offered. His help for the throne." She sounded more willing to kill him.

"Absolutely not."

"I have more reason to hate the idea than you do, but I can't win otherwise. Corinth can't protect me." She glanced away, her voice falling into disgust. "I can't even protect myself."

"What do you mean?"

She seemed to wilt in on herself. "Not that way. Not anymore."

She had no psi powers? The pressure of holding a million forbidden thoughts behind mental shields at all times nearly burst his eyeballs and she couldn't read his mind?

Something deep within him relaxed. She couldn't mind-control him, couldn't compel him. He didn't have to defend his thoughts or his very soul from her.

He let his shields drop, feeling strangely naked and relieved. "How long?"

"Not since the attack on Ordoch. Since. . . Vayne."

"Why didn't you tell me?"

She snorted. "Would you tell me if you didn't have all your faculties? That you'd lost one of your senses?"

He understood the rest of it. She'd let him think she could control him to regain some power in their relationship, to push back on him for blackmailing her to remain as Isonde.

"I'm not whole," she said. "Corinth deserves better than a handicapped, psionically dead *ro'haar*."

"He's lucky to have you."

She took the words in as if hungry to believe them.

"We need to ally with Dolan," she said.

"Not happening."

She pushed her fingers through her dye-blackened hair, disheveling the loose strands. "I just don't see any other way out of this."

"I refuse to meet his terms."

"He wants power, so what. He wants to give the Ilmenans power, big deal. As long as we have the empress-apparent's seat on the Council of Seven, it'll be worth it."

"He wants *you*, Kayla. He doesn't just want power or influence, he wants you, and I refuse to make that trade."

"What does the bastard want with me?"

Malkor could imagine more than a few things. "He didn't say. He only made it clear that his required payment would be you."

"We could always agree, and then—"

"No."

"Damnit, Malkor. My people *need* Isonde on the throne. I've seen enough to know that's the only way a bid to end the Ordochian occupation can be successful."

"What about the other Wyrds. The Ilmenans?"

"What about them?"

"Can we approach them directly?"

Kayla looked away. "They won't help us."

"Why not? If they're willing to deal through Dolan, maybe they'll deal with us directly. They can still get what they want."

"Assuming we even know what they want."

That brought him up short. He paused, waiting for more, watching her in silence until she continued.

"I spoke to them. They. . . I don't think Dolan knows the whole story. They have their own agenda."

"Damnit, Kayla! Why didn't you tell me?"

"The conversation was. . . somewhat personal."

"Frutt personal. These are things I need to know." He wanted to reach across the space between them and shake the shit out of her.

She sighed. "The Ilmenans won't deal with us."

"We don't have a better option." He held up his hand, ticking off points on his fingers. "You can't shield, Corinth isn't strong enough to shield you, Dolan will only help us if he gets you as a prized who-knows-what, and I'm useless to you in this situation." He marked off that last point with frustration. "They're all we've got, Kayla."

22

Kayla drummed her fingertips against her thigh. She stared out the night-darkened windows of the atrium and forced herself not to pace as she waited for Malkor. One would think that, "I'll see you in ten," meant minutes, not half-hours.

She propped a booted foot on the edge of a sill and studied the faces she saw in reflection. The lobby thrummed with activity, people coming and going through the building on their way to or from the million social events taking place that evening. No one paid attention to the woman in the dark gray jumpsuit who had tucked herself into a quiet corner of the atrium and turned her back on the crowd.

Kayla glanced at the atrium's chronometer in reverse. Where was he? If they were going to meet with the Ilmenans she wanted to get it the frutt over with. Corinth would wake soon. She expected him to call to her when he regained consciousness and she wanted to be close by when he did.

Kayla patted the top hem of her left boot, checking for the fifth time that the pressure syringe full of sedatives she'd stolen from Toble's equipment was ready to go. She didn't have many weapon choices in the Game complex. That hadn't, of course, stopped her from stealing a fork at dinner and tucking it into her right boot. Better than nothing.

She didn't know what to expect from the Ilmenans, if they even agreed to meet. If it came down to a fight, she'd be ready—as ready as she could be with a fork and a dose of sedatives against four psionics.

Malkor came into view at the other end of the atrium. He caught her eye and nodded back the way he'd come. Kayla adjusted the fit of the fork in her boot and followed him out of the atrium.

"They agreed. Reluctantly," he said, when she caught up to him in the hallway. "Ready for this?"

Ready? To meet with her people, who considered her a traitor, and who more than likely were traitors themselves? Not at all.

"Listen," she said. "If this goes to shit—"

He chuckled. "I know, it was my idea."

"True. Also, take out the smallest male first, he's the strongest."

He glanced at her sidelong as they made their way down the corridor. "Expecting things to go that well?"

"We need a game plan. In case." In case the Ilmenans were the traitors they seemed. In case they let Dolan in on the meeting and the double-dealing bit them in the ass. In case Kayla had to stick a fork in someone for calling her a traitor one more time. "Just be ready."

Malkor patted the ion pistol at his hip. "Always." He wore his IDC casuals, black pants, gray T-shirt. Well-worn and practical. He looked tough and confident, able to handle himself in any situation. They navigated busy hallways and crowded magchutes and arrived at the level where Tia'tan and her one allowed attendant, Noar, were housed.

She halted him just short of Tia'tan's door. "Let me do the talking."

"I thought your first meeting didn't go so well?"

"We *might* be able to convince them that I'm here to help my people, not as a traitor. They might not hate me, but you. . ." There was no nice way to say it. "You'll always be IDC."

She saw the words strike him, caught the tightening of his lips in response. She opened her mouth but he chimed the door, and they waited an awkward minute in silence before the panels slid open.

Tia'tan occupied the center of the room, dressed almost identically to Kayla and looking as ready for a fight. Noar stood beside her, his stare locked on Malkor.

"We agreed to meet with her," he said. "Alone."

Malkor followed Kayla into the room. "I come with her."

Noar's gaze flicked to Kayla. "I bet you do."

Kayla sized Tia'tan up, judging her stance, her positioning in the room, her mood. Lightning crackled between them as Tia'tan returned the favor. "Where are the others?" Kayla asked.

"Busy," Tia'tan said. "We decided not to bother them with this."

Interesting. She'd bet her best daggers the bodyguard would blow a hyperdrive if she knew Tia'tan was meeting with an armed IDC agent. Malkor shifted a step closer to Kayla while still leaving her room to maneuver, if it came to that.

"This place is secure?" she asked Tia'tan.

"A child could reprogram imperial surveillance tech," Tia'tan said. "Joffar did it in his sleep."

"Good."

"Why are you here?" Noar asked, giving Malkor a final look before turning his attention to her. "Your IDC agent insisted it was important." Noar looked elegant and precisely styled in a scarlet suit with a black shirt, the top button undone. The polished points of silver shoes peeked out from beneath the cuff of his pant legs, and cufflinks of plascrystal caught the light. How strong a psionic was he? If she had her powers still, could she take him?

Unlikely, judging by his ease.

"We came to discuss the offer you made through Dolan." Kayla's words were met by blank stares. "For an alliance."

Noar laughed. "You have to be joking."

Tia'tan did not look so amused. "You're spaced if you think we offered any such thing."

Kayla made eye contact with Malkor, who nodded.

"He was indirect about it," she said, remembering Malkor's recount of the discussion, "intimating you would stop interfering in my matches so that I could win the Empress Game, in exchange for an alliance between us."

"Why would you think for a nanosecond we'd want you to win the Game?" Tia'tan asked.

"Because we want the same thing." *I hope.* "And I can do it better."

Malkor coughed, but whether he meant "cool it with the attitude," or "damn, you're sassy," she couldn't guess.

"Did you mean what you said?" Kayla asked Tia'tan. "In the magchute, you said you'd never help Dolan. That you had your own reasons for being here."

Tia'tan didn't answer immediately. In the ensuing silence Kayla felt the weight of a conversation between Tia'tan and Noar. She held her breath on the debate.

"Who are you?" Tia'tan finally asked. "We know you're Wyrd, and we know Dolan has his theories. We've seen your picture, but. . ."

Now it was Kayla's turn to silently confer with her partner. Malkor's expression said "we're all in now, just do it." He eased closer, ready, protective almost. The sense of security provoked her out of the cautiousness she'd nurtured for the last five years. She reached up and peeled the biostrip from her throat, letting the hologram die.

"I am Kayla Reinumon, rightful heir of Ordoch."

The Ilmenans stared. Kayla imagined that Tia'tan relaxed a fraction.

Noar nodded. "Told you."

"So," Tia'tan said, "Kayla Reinumon lives." Her gaze flashed to Malkor. "And she's working with the IDC."

Kayla frowned. "It's complicated. If you're truly Dolan's enemy, what are you doing here?"

"We're here to win the Game," Tia'tan said.

"I get that." Kayla focused her attention on Noar. "Why?"

"Why else?" he asked. "To influence the empire from the inside out to free Ordoch."

"That is our plan as well."

Tia'tan snorted. "We might believe that if you had enough honor to fight in your own name. Instead you fight as one of them. You're not trying to win the throne for Ordoch, you want to put one of their own princesses on the throne."

"Princess Isonde wants freedom for Ordoch as well," Malkor said.

Noar frowned at him, clearly not pleased to be reminded he was in the room. "So you say."

"We have only your word to go on as well," Malkor countered.

Noar's frown deepened.

"We each have little proof but our word," Kayla said. "You look to be in league with Dolan, we look to be working purely for the Empire's interests." She met Tia'tan's purple stare. "Appearances are not always truth."

"What now, then?" Tia'tan asked.

"Now? We work together. We put Isonde on the throne."

Tia'tan shook her head. "No way."

Kayla stifled a sigh, tired already and not in the mood for a long argument. "She has more clout among the other council members than you could hope to have. She will fight for Ordoch's freedom, and has the power to make it happen."

"We are not without our own leverage." Tia'tan sounded a touch smug.

What in space did that mean? They couldn't hope to telepathically influence everyone on the Council of Seven. It wouldn't be possible, not with Tia'tan being the only psionic in the room and all of the council members on guard against her.

"What could you have that comes anywhere close to matching Isonde's influence?" Malkor sounded as cautious as she felt.

Tia'tan smiled. "A cure."

23

The words impacted Kayla with the force of a shockwave. "A cure? For the TNV?"

"It's not ready yet," Noar said, giving Tia'tan a look.

"It's close," she returned, her grin smug.

"How is that possible?" Kayla asked. The Ordochian scientists refused to produce a cure while under imperial control.

"A group of Ordochians escaped during the attack and fled to Ilmena. They brought samples of the nanovirus with them."

"But, the pact," Malkor said. "I thought all of the Wyrd Worlds had a standing interplanetary law forbidding the development and use of nanotechnologies because of the galaxy-wide destruction of the Nanite Wars?"

"The experiments are being very carefully controlled," Tia'tan said. "Our scientists will not make the same mistakes that yours did, Agent."

"Our people are dying," Malkor snapped, taking a step forward. "If you had any decency, you'd turn the cure over now."

"*Our* people are suffering," Noar said, unintimidated by Malkor's aggressive stance. "At the hands of your empire. You have no right to be in Wyrd Space."

Kayla put a hand on Malkor's arm, speaking to Tia'tan. "They need the cure."

"We know," she said. "And Ordoch needs freedom. We're willing to bargain."

"It's not complete, though?" Stars. But even the thought of being close to a cure. . .

Noar shook his head.

"So at present you have nothing to bargain with," Kayla pointed out.

"We will," Tia'tan said.

Malkor's forearm flexed beneath Kayla's grip. She tightened her fingers, sending him a message of support.

"You can't guarantee that, Tia," Noar said. "The last round of tests produced unstable nanites that couldn't be controlled after prolonged contact with the TNV nanites."

"It was a step in the wrong direction," Tia'tan replied. "They will reverse the latest programming."

"How long will that take?" Kayla asked. "Months? Years? And what happens to Ordoch in the meantime?" Isonde was still their best bet, especially if a cure existed. Isonde could push treaty legislation through the councils faster than Tia'tan. Surely the Ilmenans realized that.

::Kayla?:: Corinth's tired voice reached her, faint at first, then growing stronger. ::Where are you?::

Judging by the looks on their faces, the other Wyrds heard it too.

::Are you all right?::

"Who is that?" Noar asked.

"Corinth Reinumon. My youngest brother and, I suppose, the second heir to Ordoch."

Noar exchanged a glance with Tia'tan. Tia'tan shook her head but Noar spoke anyway. "That. . . might not be true."

Kayla's hand fell away from Malkor's arm. "What?"

"Winning the Empress Game is only half of our mission on Falanar."

Tia'tan made a sound of disgust but Noar continued.

"We've received intel over the years from refugees escaping Ordoch that some of the ruling family, your family, might have been captured instead of killed," Noar said.

Vayne.

But it couldn't be.

"You think Dolan has them," Malkor said, a statement, not a question. Who else could it be?

Kayla's knees threatened to buckle.

Tia'tan nodded. "We don't know who or how many, but, yes. We think he kidnapped members of the ruling family to..." She glanced at Kayla then refocused on Malkor. "To experiment on. Because they are the strongest psionics on Ordoch."

"We're here to rescue them," Noar said. "The Game offered the only opportunity to visit Imperial Space or we would have come sooner. We will not suffer our people to be at the *kin'shaa*'s mercy any longer."

The room spun around Kayla. "My parents? Vayne?"

Tia'tan's voice softened for the first time. "We don't know. We have only scattered reports of what happened. Enough people claimed to see prisoners being led, alive, to an imperial starcraft that we have to credit the information."

"We plan to rescue them as soon as the Game's over," Noar said.

Vayne. In Dolan's hands. Her sisters. Her mother.

"I will help," Kayla said.

"We don't—" Tia'tan started.

"I will do it without you, then. Tonight."

"Kayla—"

She shot Malkor a look when he tried that warning tone on her.

"If you jeopardize the outcome of the Game before one of us can win the throne," Tia'tan said, "I'll kill you myself."

Kayla stared her down, hands fisting at her sides.

Noar turned his attention to Malkor. "Would you be in on the offer of help?"

"No, he's not." Tia'tan frowned at Noar.

"It's important to Kayla. I will be there, *if* you wait until Isonde wins the Empress Game."

"I will not work with the IDC," Tia'tan said.

Kayla could guess the gist of their silent argument going on.

He can't be trusted. But if he could, the IDC's help offered so many more options. Is it worth the risk?

Finally, Noar turned to Malkor. "We'll discuss your involvement later."

Could Vayne truly be alive? If so, how could she wait one more second to rescue him?

Simple—she had no idea where he was, no means to free him, and no means to get him off of the planet and back to Wyrd Space. Allying with the Ilmenans was the only answer.

"We'll finish this," Tia'tan said, "after the final series."

Kayla lay awake on her bed, staring unseeing into the blackness of her room. She'd turned off every light, shut down every console or panel that could illuminate the weakness of her fledgling hope. In the darkness she let it fly. The possibility that Vayne might still be alive filled the room. The certainty. The desperation. *If any had survived, please let it be him.* To be this close, to learn some of her family might still live and for Vayne not to be among them, would be too much. Hope had raised him from the ashes in her mind—she couldn't bear his death a second time.

Tomorrow they would start the search for Dolan's prisoners, learn if any had survived whatever tests, research or torture he had put them through. Her dreams would be made whole or dashed.

Tomorrow they would have answers, but tonight she still had hope.

Kayla woke early the next morning after only a few hours of sleep and tiptoed into Isonde's room. The princess still lay comatose in her medical pod. Her nose and teeth had been reconstructed after her fall on her face and she at least looked more like herself while the tissue healed. She should probably have her Kayla hologram on, in case Game officials busted into the room for any reason, but it was too disturbing for Kayla to see herself like that.

Not that it was any less disturbing to see Isonde lying stiffly, unconscious but not at ease. There were signs of Toble's presence in the room, he'd been here late last night working on a cure for Isonde, to no avail. Her rigor continued unabated.

"We'll get her," Kayla said in a low voice. "But you have to fight. You have to beat her toxin."

If only it were that easy.

"We're down to the last series in the Game. I'll win you that damned crown, but you need to wake up. I can't be you for much longer." Not if her family, her twin, were alive. "I can't be you, Isonde. You need to fight."

Isonde gave no reply.

By breakfast Kayla was sitting on the sofa in Malkor's room, which had been turned into a base of operations for the massive investigation into Dolan's affairs of the last five years. She'd already seen every agent in the octet save Aronse, and she hadn't even finished her hot cereal yet.

She was useless in the search for the missing Ordochians in its current stage so she did the next best thing: prepped for her final series with Tia'tan tomorrow. That amounted to resting on the couch like an invalid and letting the regen cuff on her shoulder work its slow, painful magic.

"I understand you're very busy with the number of guests staying in the royal pavilion for the Game." Malkor spoke into his comm unit. His tone, which had varied from cajoling to authoritative, took on a seriously short-tempered note. "Yes. I know that. Sir, this is not a polite request, this is an order from Senior Agent Rua of the IDC. I require a list of every permanent and semi-permanent resident of the palace and their quarters locations." He gave the man only a second to reply before barking, "I expect to see it within the hour, or you will be hearing from my commander, do I make myself clear?" He switched the comm off and leaned back in his chair. "Damn bureaucrats."

Kayla scooped the last of her now lukewarm cereal out of its bowl. "No doubt running the emperor's household during the Game is a once in a lifetime nightmare."

"I'm going to be that man's lifetime nightmare if he doesn't get me that list in a half-hour," Malkor said, already reaching for a datapad and moving on to his next contact. He looked ragged around the edges. His brown hair fell haphazardly into his eyes and his IDC casuals were creased.

She gestured to the multiple datapads lying about, all in mid-read or with their screens covered in notes. "Did you sleep last night?"

"Did you?" He gazed at her, assessing her appearance. She'd tried to dress as immaculately and elegantly as Isonde always did, but she hadn't quite hit the mark this morning.

"How could I?"

He nodded. "Exactly."

His words of yesterday rang in her head. *It's important to Kayla. I'll be there.* He hadn't hesitated when Noar asked if he'd help.

Malkor returned to flipping through screens on a datapad while comparing them to something on his complink. It felt right to be here together, both focused on the same goal, bending their efforts in the same direction. He might need her for the crazy Empress Game scheme but she needed him just as much. More, even. She wouldn't be able to find her family without him, never mind rescue them or get them off the planet. She needed him, and she didn't mind the feeling.

Something was definitely wrong with her.

"Can you stop staring at me like I've grown a third eye?" he asked without looking up. "It's disconcerting."

"Sorry." She gestured to her injured shoulder, feeling suddenly awkward. "I should get back, time to switch over to coolant packs."

Concern crossed his features. "Kayla, I'm—"

The doors to his room slid apart without warning and

Malkor shot to his feet. "Commander Parrel. Sir."

"Are you running a circus in here, Senior Agent?" Commander Parrel's voice carried into the corridor before the doors closed behind him. "A damn scavenger hunt?"

"No, sir."

"Could have fooled me. I got a dozen alerts this morning, alarms pinging me from all different sectors about unauthorized access to sensitive files." He stopped short, seeming to notice her for the first time. His frown deepened. "I guess that answers the question of who's behind this inquest."

Kayla froze. An IDC commander, here. Two meters from her. She glanced down at her hands to make sure the hologram still held up.

"You are aware, Agent Rua, that you still report to me, correct? That you don't get to spend IDC agents and resources on investigations instigated by friends?" Malkor flushed a dull red. "I see that's coming back to you now."

Commander Parrel turned to her. "If your business here isn't pressing"—and his tone put a world of meaning on the word "business"—"I need to speak to my agent. Alone."

Malkor watched Kayla leave, wishing he could slink out after her.

"That woman's your one weakness, Rua," Commander Parrel said, before the doors had even finished closing.

Kayla? With her strength, fighting spirit and loneliness? How true that had become.

"You and Isonde are too close, always have been." Parrel's words drew him back to the situation. Isonde. Right. "You're a good agent, one of my finest. I know you want what's best for the empire and I depend on that, but your first loyalty is not to the IDC."

A swift denial should have followed that statement, but Malkor couldn't form the lie. "I serve for the good of the empire," he said instead.

"Is that why you're digging into all these files this morning?

For the good of the empire?" Skepticism laced Parrel's words.

"Yes and no, sir."

Parrel frowned. "Which is it?"

Could he trust the man that far? He respected Parrel, they'd always been on the same side. But this. . .

"There's what's good for the empire, and then what's right," Malkor said.

"Don't lecture me about gray areas," Parrel snapped. "I've been making these kinds of decisions since you were toddling. And stop standing there at attention like a damned recruit, you look like a fool."

Malkor sat without relaxing. Parrel crossed the room and grabbed another chair. He thunked it down opposite Malkor's desk and perched—a bird of prey, waiting to strike.

"Well?" he prompted. "What has you so riled up about five-year-old files at this hour?"

"Master Dolan."

Parrel nodded. "I suspected as much. His people are about to beat your lady in the Empress Game and suddenly you need something, anything, to catch him on. I get that, but why the Ordoch coup files?"

"How did you know?"

Parrel gave him a guarded look. "Every file on the Ordochian coup is classified highest security. We're talking the Emperor, Council of Seven and senior IDC officials. Information like that isn't left unguarded. I'm not the only one who set up protocols to be alerted in the case that someone breached the encryption and attempted to access the files." Parrel looked as serious as death. "You're lucky my protocols are touchier and it's me that came looking for you."

"I need access to those files, sir."

"Why?"

All in. He was all in or he was done. Either Parrel would get him the access he needed or he would fire him. Kayla needed to know. *He* needed to know. Had the IDC allowed Dolan to take prisoners from Ordoch for experimentation?

"I have reason to believe that Master Dolan removed prisoners from Ordoch. Members of the royal family that were, as a matter of semi-public record, reported deceased. Prisoners that may still be alive and under his control."

Silence.

That Parrel didn't instantly deny it, or deny knowing one way or the other, confirmed it.

"That would have been against imperial wartime policy." The standard response sounded stale coming from Commander Parrel.

Malkor nodded. "And a host of other humanitarian laws. That doesn't mean it didn't happen." He stared Parrel down. "I need to know." He needed to rescue Kayla's family. Not just for her, for himself. To begin to repay, in some small part, the debt he owed to the Ordochians.

Not that it could ever be paid in full, but he could start. Here. Now.

Even without that, his honor as an IDC agent would not let this rest. Had the institution he served sanctioned Dolan's actions?

"Who suggested this to you?"

"The Ilmenan Wyrds. They traveled light-years on the strength of this information. That's enough for me."

Parrel clearly teetered on the edge. He appeared as implacable as always on the surface. His eyes, though, said it all. He had doubts.

"I had been recalled ship-side when the coup went down," Malkor said, "but you were there. You saw what actually happened on Ordoch. Let me read your report."

Parrel shook his head.

Malkor splayed his fingers wide on the desktop, frustration building. "I *will* track this information down, Commander." Nothing would stop him from learning the truth. If Ordochians had been taken from their home and given to Dolan for experimentation, Malkor wouldn't rest until he'd found them and freed them. What torture had they been through in five years as lab rats? Had any even survived? It was unthinkable. Anyone involved in such an action, be it the IDC or the imperial army, had damn well better start running now. What's more, Kayla's family could be alive. The twin she still mourned daily could be here, on the same planet with her. Malkor could return someone to her she thought she'd lost forever.

"You don't want my official report," Parrel said.

"Sir—"

Parrel raised a hand. "You won't find what you're looking for in official reports." He sighed, closing his eyes for a minute. When he finally opened them, the look he gave Malkor was part resignation, part respect. "I'll tell you what I know, but only if you promise not to use the information to get yourself killed."

"Thank you, Sir."

"Don't thank me, you pain in the ass. I'm the nicest of the guys who will come looking for you if you insist on pressing this." Parrel gave a wry smile. "If I'm lucky, they'll shoot you before you can involve me any further."

24

Kayla stood at attention in the center of the arena the next afternoon. Only the length of one sparring ring separated her from Princess Tia'tan, and every ounce of her concentration should be on the final fight of the Empress Game.

It wasn't.

Instead she heard Malkor's words when he'd come to see her late last night.

"He was alive, Kayla. Vayne was alive when Dolan evacuated him from Ordoch. What you think you saw. . . Dolan had them all stunned, each of the Wyrds he planned to take with him. He shot them with a stunner that interrupted their brain function and numbed their psi powers, essentially taking them off the psionic grid. That's why you couldn't reach Vayne, why he went silent and you thought he'd died. No one but Dolan's own men was supposed to know."

Malkor had held her when relief and grief brought her to her knees, and had known enough to back off when the rage followed.

"What he's stolen from me," she had said, *"from Vayne, from all of us, I will make him repay."*

In blood. Nothing else would slake her thirst for retribution.

Now here she stood in the arena, ready to burst apart from the force of her hatred and pain. Did it show?

She knew it wouldn't.

She was Princess Isonde, who never looked anything less than perfectly composed. Tia'tan glared at her from across the ring, similarly stoic.

In the center a historian droned on, extolling the accomplishment of the emperor's family line. The last series of the Empress Game was apparently a time for lengthy patriotic speeches that emphasized how lucky one of the two women competing would be to join the Soliqual family and rise to the Council of Seven. The enormous crowd was into it. Thousands of people hung on the orator's words, cheering so often that the speech took twice as long as it should have.

Even as he seemed to wind down, his words transitioning to a discussion of the significance of the Empress Game and the ferocity of the battle about to occur between her and Tia'tan, all Kayla could see was Vayne. Her last image of him, prone, bleeding, begging for her help, before being shot by the *kin'shaa*. She heard his voice, felt the touch of his mind. Not that weak imitation Dolan had somehow managed to create, but the real strength of him. The vibrant personality that influenced those around him.

Her true *il'haar*.

If he had somehow managed to survive what Dolan had done to him the last five years, she would save him, as she hadn't before.

She would not fail him again.

But first, her series with Tia'tan. One fight. Such a small thing, to control the entirety of her planet's destiny.

::I'm ready to shield, Kayla:: Corinth said in her mind. No, he wasn't. He couldn't possibly be. The Ilmenans would hit with the force of a starship's core detonating.

The historian in the ring turned the voice augmenter over to someone else whose voice boomed through the arena with enough force to shake the floor. "Princess Tia'tan of Ilmena, for whom do you fight this eve?"

Tia'tan stepped into the ring, looking serious and oddly

introspective for such a moment. She spoke without hesitation, her eyes on Kayla the whole way. "I fight for my people."

It must not have been the answer the crowd expected. Half-hearted cheers and booing broke out, no one seeming to know how to respond to such a statement.

"Princess Isonde of Piran, for whom do you fight this eve?"

Kayla took her place in the ring, separated from Tia'tan by a few paces of synthetic flooring and an unaccepted offer of alliance. She held her gaze, willing Tia'tan to listen to her.

"I fight for *our* people." Her words drew a thunder of ignorant cheers from the arena.

Finally the others quit the sparring circle, leaving Kayla alone with Tia'tan and the official who would distribute their weapons.

Tia'tan, with the better record, had chosen the weapon.

Double daggers.

Kayla wanted her own wavy-edged kris daggers back, but accepted the standard-issue ones from the official. They were useless to her—she had only one way to win this fight.

"We found them," she said, not caring that the official looked at her funny. There was no time left for secrecy. Tia'tan halted in reaching for her daggers. "We know where they're being held." Kayla willed the urgency of her voice to convince Tia'tan.

Tia'tan shook her off, grabbing her blades and stepping away to begin the match.

Frutt. How to convince her?

The official left the ring and Kayla settled into a crouch, daggers ready. Tia'tan looked as tense as she felt, muscles rippling up her bare arms as she flexed her fingers around the handles of her daggers. Neither moved when the chime sounded to begin the match.

She expected Tia'tan to shift to her right, begin the slow circling dance she had employed in her other fights. It was the style the princess favored for her opening. Instead she held her ground, daggers ready, waiting. Tia'tan's gaze burned into her, suspicion and wariness paired with determination.

Kayla advanced, raising her weapons. "I will fight for this. You know Isonde will make the better empress." *Even if I have to play her part.*

"I disagree." Even as Tia'tan spat the words, her head cocked to the left as if someone demanded her attention. She frowned, eyes flashing away from Kayla for just an instant. "But the others do not." She took a step toward Kayla, then another.

Kayla crouched lower, ready to spring. Maybe if she went for an immediate injury to her leg, hampered her mobility. . .

Tia'tan took one last step, within striking distance, then raised her arms, hands out to the side, palms facing Kayla. She knelt and laid her daggers on the ground at Kayla's feet.

She rose, squaring herself off. "Your princess had better be every bit as noble as you say she is, or you have doomed us all."

Cheering broke through the stunned silence in the arena. The sound gathered strength as one after the other of the spectators realized that Tia'tan had forfeited the series. The roar drowned out the furious beat of Kayla's pulse, the rasp of her breath, the bleed off of her adrenaline. She grabbed Tia'tan's arm before the woman could step away.

Kayla knew the heart of the woman she pretended to be. The woman she *would* be, if necessary. Her voice was steel when she said, "We will not fail."

Isonde had been so confident in her plan—or so unwilling to accept any other outcome—that she'd had her engagement dress made already. Kayla felt as though she slipped into Isonde's skin as she pulled on the opulent bronze gown.

She stepped in front of her mirror, trying to ignore the way the neckline of the gown choked, and the fabric twisted as if to say, "you are not my body." She didn't belong here. She belonged with her family in whatever holding cell Dolan had locked them in for all these years. She belonged with people who knew her for herself. Instead, she wore another's skin and prepared for her engagement feast with that woman's soon-to-be husband.

Kayla hadn't fully disappeared yet. Her face looked back at her from the mirror, the hologram's biostrip on the desk waiting for her like a collar. Her lightless black hair coiled around her head in a series of braids designed to mimic a crown. Her blue eyes blazed from their place in the mirror.

I am Princess Kayla Reinumon, of Ordoch, she reminded herself.

But for how long?

She should have been free. She'd delivered on her end of the bargain, she should be going home now. She and Corinth should be packing their things, stopping only long enough to rescue their family from Dolan—killing him in the process.

She shouldn't be worrying what would happen to the people of the empire with her absence, thinking about the logistics of manufacturing and distributing a cure for the TNV. She shouldn't feel responsible for the fate of her entire people, or have to worry about crafting the political agenda that would lead to their freedom. Most assuredly, she should not be wondering where Malkor would go from here. She should be home, in Wyrd Space, trying to build a life with just her *il'haar*'s safety to worry about.

Only, she didn't have just one *il'haar*, not if Vayne lived. And she didn't have a home, not without her people's freedom.

And she did care what Malkor decided to do next.

Kayla fussed with the seams leading down the front of her bodice, tweaking the slippery fabric a nanometer to the right. She had to meet Prince Ardin soon. As was proper, he would escort her to the celebratory engagement banquet where he would name her as his future wife.

The thought made her ill.

Malkor had finally told Ardin the truth about Isonde's condition, and even though Ardin knew she wasn't Isonde, he sent enough adoring glances her way to make her wonder how often he forgot. Was she even a person to him, or just a placeholder Isonde? He never saw her out of hologram; maybe Kayla had ceased to exist for him.

Not for Malkor, though.

He saw her. He looked through the hologram and never forgot for an instant. She was real to him.

She was real, and she was doing the right thing.

Kayla applied the hologram and studied herself in her Isonde costume.

This *was* right, she told herself.

Déjà vu hit Malkor when he entered the banquet hall. He'd done this dance before.

His best friend, Prince Ardin, strode about the throng with the gravity of a star, pulling admirers along behind him as he made the rounds of the room. On his arm, sparkling and smiling and breaking hearts all at once, was Isonde. Just like always, they made a striking pair, and just like always, a wave of bitterness washed over him at the sight.

But this wasn't the same Isonde.

And it wasn't the same jealousy—it was worse.

He banished the irrational thought. He hadn't lost Kayla to Ardin, she had never been his to begin with. The only reason she was even at the engagement banquet with Ardin was because he had forced her into it.

He should spend the night observing the guests at the engagement dinner. With the Game settled, nascent alliances would crystallize and a new political landscape would arise. Every available IDC agent would be circulating through the multitude of parties happening across the planet tonight. The IDC counted on him for his report on the latest shifts in diplomacy.

The IDC would have to wait.

He had a meeting with an informant regarding Janeen's whereabouts in a half-hour. Finding Janeen, and extracting the exact formula for the toxin she'd used, took precedence. Only by healing Isonde could he give Kayla her freedom.

And if a back-alley meeting with a criminal got him away from watching Kayla become engaged to Ardin, he'd welcome it.

What, though, would save him from the wedding in three days' time?

A half-hour later found Malkor deep in the heart of Falanar's Pleasure District. He skulked down the narrow alley separating the Velvet Whip from Sex By Design. He couldn't say the Pleasure District was a favorite meeting spot of his, but it was dark and anonymous.

He slowed as he neared the end of the alley and sidled up to a half-hidden door. A series of knocks met with a sliver of light as the door cracked open.

A guard sized him up. "We're at capacity. Try Rookie's across the street."

"Ramjet's is all right, if you like that sort of thing." Malkor pulled a quad-credit from the fold of his watchcap. "Me, I'm more of a program 'n' play kinda guy."

The guard's gaze flicked to the credit chip. "You like bots, eh?"

Malkor pulled out a second quad-cred and idly slid the chips along each other in a circle between thumb and fingertip. "They do what they're told and they don't talk back."

"Ain't that the truth." The guard hesitated, no doubt debating Malkor's ability to pay for services and likelihood to cause trouble. "We have room for one more."

Malkor grinned. "Thought you might."

The door widened just enough to admit him. Malkor slipped the bribe to the guard who accepted it without acknowledgement. "See Mandy, up front. They'll get you settled."

The hallway he entered was barely brighter than the alley. A diffuse indigo glow shimmered across the ceiling, providing just enough light to avoid walking into the wall. It drew him farther into the establishment. A bass beat thrummed through the walls. A sharp slap, followed by cackling, sounded from a door he passed.

This had better be some usable intel.

He reached the inner lounge. The lighting was vaguely brighter here, so he kept his eyes strictly on the proprietor of the house and avoided the patrons getting cozy on the couches, in the booths and on the bar.

"I'm looking for love," he told Mandy, when he reached the androgynous owner of the brothel.

S/he looked him over head to toe, black duster to watchcap, boots to vest to. . . pistol. "Aren't we all, hon." His/her white painted lips smiled, eerie in the violet dark of the room. "But what speed are you? Hot and heavy, slow and easy, yes ma'am no ma'am, or something in between?"

"I'm an all night, low light, take it fight or flight kind of guy," he said in response, hoping Mandy knew the code.

S/he nodded once, almost too quickly to notice. "If you're looking for love, I can point you in a direction. Follow me." S/he glided past with a gait too smooth to be biologic in origin and led him to the upper levels. S/he stopped outside a door and flashed a lithodisc bracelet across the panel to open it. "Payment's been arranged," was all s/he said, before s/he turned and walked away.

"You're late," said a male voice inside the room.

"Lights," Malkor ordered, still standing in the hallway.

He heard a raspy chuckle, then a lightstrip on the back wall illuminated the room's one occupant. "Happy now?" Rutcker looked surprisingly refined for the environment. His blond hair was pulled into a smooth ponytail. His goatee, a shade darker, was trimmed with razor precision, and emeralds glinted at each earlobe. His overcoat hid most of his outfit but the shoes said, "I've got credits to melt," as loudly as his metallic incisor did.

Malkor strode into the room and closed the door with his heel. "What have you got for me?" His eyes scanned the saferoom but nothing seemed out of place. There was no space to fit anyone else and his informant didn't look armed. Of course, appearances could be deceiving. The ion pistol Malkor had on his hip was only one of three weapons he carried with him this evening.

"Did you bring it?" Rutcker asked. A big-time extortionist with more enemies than Malkor had friends, he lounged in his chair. He eased his weight back, tipping the base of the seat off the floor.

Malkor withdrew an iden chip from his vest pocket. He pulled a reader from his other pocket and plugged the disc into the slot. Credentials came up on the display, a complete suite that Rutcker could use to access a million places currently off-limits to him.

Malkor flashed the screen Rutcker's way for five seconds. "That's all you get until I have my information."

Rutcker balanced the chair in its off-kilter position. "I've seen your missing agent."

"Where?"

He shrugged. "Here and there, running missions for some higher-up, but she's in town."

"Rutcker, these credentials could practically get you into the palace. Either you have something useable for me, or. . ." Malkor ejected the iden chip and made as if to drop it on the floor. The sensitive trinium circuitry wouldn't last a nanosecond beneath his boot.

"Okay. Okay. I know where she's been staying. Mostly. Some days."

Malkor slid the reader back into his pocket and held up the chip. "Either you want it or you don't."

"She's got friends. Better friends than you. She's keeping low in Shimville but someone's supplying her."

Shimville, a neighborhood in the Mercantile District where the illegal import/export business was real lucrative. "Where in Shimville?"

"That's all I've got." Rutcker grinned. "Hey, it's more than you had."

"That's not worth a new chip, Rut." Malkor pinched the iden chip between his thumb and forefinger, ready to snap it into uselessness. He applied the slightest pressure to the chip and Rutcker's chair landed with a thud. He stared at the chip as if it was his salvation. Who knew? In his line of crime, it might be.

"Fine. She's topside. Left leg. The shop by the Nadarians."

"What else can you tell me?"

"What am I, one of your junior agents?" Rutcker rose slowly. He adjusted the fit of his coat, straightening his lapels and aligning the zip-up. "She's there alone, my guy says. No backup, but heavy tech."

"Low or high?" Malkor asked.

"We're talking tip-top. Whoever's spotting her, they don't scrimp." Rutcker pointed to the iden chip Malkor still held for ransom. "Speaking of, that piece isn't going to get me flagged for a bad forgery, is it?"

Malkor gave him a flat stare. "Maybe, maybe not. Depends if your intel checks out."

"You know my drop's always good."

True, but he wasn't usually tipping on something so heavy, and Malkor knew he recognized that. Malkor took the chip's protective sleeve out of his pocket and slid the thing home before holding it out to the extortionist. "All yours."

The instant Rutcker took possession of the chip it disappeared, flitted away in a sleight-of-hand technique Malkor couldn't follow. If he wanted it back, he'd have to roll the man's body for it.

Malkor turned to go, thoughts already churning on a plan to check out Shimville without spooking Janeen. Rutcker's voice stopped him at the door.

"I'm going to give you something else," he said, and the words froze Malkor in place. It wasn't in Rutcker's nature to be generous with intel. "Not for free, let's put this in the category of 'you owe me.'"

Unease prickled across Malkor's skin. "Will I?"

"If the rumors are right, you're about to." Rutcker regained his confident air. He had what he wanted, and more than that, he had something Malkor needed—even if Malkor didn't know what that something was yet. "I've got a tip for you, friend to friend."

"Yeah? What's that?" Rutcker was the best kind of

informant: high enough in the criminal element to have access to useful intel, and smart enough not to waste Malkor's time. If he had something worthwhile, something Malkor hadn't even asked around about yet, it had to be big.

"When I say your agent's working for someone well-connected, I don't mean on my side of the fence." His lips quirked in a grin. "You want to find her handler? Look at home, first."

Rutcker adjusted the fit of his cuff. "Things aren't as cohesive in your little org as you'd like to think. There's a split coming, and man," he chuckled, "are you on the wrong side." He made his way past Malkor, giving him a clap on the shoulder as he went. "I'd ask your commander about it."

25

The next morning, Kayla followed Malkor silently through the corridors on their way to the Ilmenans' quarters. She had too much on her mind to talk and he looked equally troubled. Seven Wyrds had been taken from Ordoch according to Parrel, Vayne among them. In her heart she had already known. How else could Dolan have mimicked Vayne?

More disturbingly, how had Dolan regained his psi powers, and stamped them with Vayne's essence. . . and what had happened to Vayne in the process? Her head swam with scenarios. If Vayne still lived, she couldn't imagine what state he was in after five years as the *kin'shaa*'s prisoner.

Kayla pushed those questions to the back of her mind when they reached Tia'tan's quarters. All four Ilmenans awaited them. Joffar, the eldest male, sat apart from the rest, perched at the breakfast bar with the look of overseeing things. The bodyguard, Luliana, had been leaning against a wall, but pushed off to stand behind Tia'tan, who was seated on a couch next to Noar.

Awkward quiet ensued while the two sides sized each other up. The Ilmenans had committed to trusting her in a big way at the Game yesterday, it was time to show she was willing to trust as well.

"Thank you," Kayla said, "for allowing us to win the Empress Game. Putting Isonde on the throne is the best way to free my people, and that's all I want."

Tia'tan nodded, seeming to relax. "We believe you. . . now."

It was more trust than Kayla might have given, were their situations reversed. It had taken watching Isonde in action, hearing her speak about her plans to convince the empire to withdraw from Ordoch, to win Kayla over to their side. "Malkor and I are willing to share our intel on the Ordochian prisoners with you. *If* you agree to work with us on a rescue mission."

Until that moment, the Ilmenans had seemed content to pretend that Malkor wasn't in the room. Being forced to acknowledge his presence displeased the whole lot of them.

Tough.

Malkor was the only reason they even had a chance of rescuing her people. He'd spent hours yesterday digging into off-limits files, calling in favors from all ends of the empire, putting himself and his career on the line to track down their whereabouts.

"How can we trust him?" Tia'tan asked.

Malkor kept his silence, letting Kayla speak for him. She could offer a dozen examples of his loyalty. The fact that he stood here now should be proof enough. She had a dozen reasons, but only one mattered.

"Because I trust him with my life." The truth of the words sank in, filling her with certainty. She trusted him, without hesitation. He was her partner, had been from the beginning, even though she hadn't realized it.

Her words caught him off-guard, judging by the way he stilled. Then he smiled the slightest bit, and she knew he felt the same.

Tia'tan's gaze went to Malkor and back again before she nodded. "That will have to be enough."

"For me as well," Noar said. "So. What have you learned?"

Kayla made herself comfortable on the opposite couch with Malkor.

"Our intel indicates that Dolan kidnapped seven people from Ordoch," Malkor said. "All seven were presumed alive at time of capture. Only three of their identities are known: Vayne—Kayla's twin—and Erebus and Natali, their older twin brother and sister. The rest are unknown, as is their current status. I haven't gotten hard and fast confirmation of where they are being held." Malkor glanced at Kayla, looking apologetic. "If any survived this long."

"They did." Tia'tan sounded certain. "Our people endure. We will find them."

"Dolan had been granted funding to establish a laboratory on Falanar shortly before his return from Ordoch. He keeps offices in the palace, but does all of his research from that laboratory on the edge of the royal city."

The idea of Vayne being that "research" infuriated her. Dolan's death couldn't come soon enough to suit her.

"We believe he's holding the Ordochians there." Malkor laid the datapad he'd brought on the table, calling up a schematic. "I lifted these plans for the facility. Based on layout, conduit placement, electrotech relay wiring, ventilation clearance and so on, I was able to eliminate a number of zones from our search."

Joffar came to peer at the floor plans. "That still leaves a lot of area. How many agents do you have at your disposal?"

"Those of my octet, and some have business elsewhere and can't join the mission."

"How many other octets can you enlist? We could use more manpower."

The guarded look Kayla had noticed earlier came back into Malkor's eyes. "It will be just my octet."

"If you don't have the authority to activate at least another octet, perhaps your commander—"

"No." Malkor's abruptness silenced the room.

What was that about? Had Parrel forbidden him from further action against Dolan, despite the fact that taking prisoners of war violated imperial wartime laws?

"The details of this raid will not go beyond my octet. Period." His frown forbade further argument.

"We'll narrow down our search, then," she said, bending her attention to the schematic. "What are these shunts, here?"

The conversation turned to common architectures and the likely use of each possible space in Dolan's facility. They whittled it down to a handful of possible areas. Assuming, of course, they were even correct about the location in the first place. *It's our best guess*. What other options did they have but to try it? They'd never find her people, else.

"My men and I will have a secondary objective while on the mission," Malkor said, pointing to the spaces defined as tech/lab rooms. "We'll access Dolan's databanks and retrieve the files on his experiments to date."

"No frutting way," Tia'tan snapped. "Dividing our team lessens our chance of success. Anything jeopardizing our rescue of the Ordochians is unacceptable."

"That's why it's called a secondary objective. Look. Dolan's had your people for five years and he didn't kidnap them for their company. Also, he has an unholy fascination with Kayla. With. . . obtaining her. He's been planning something for longer than five years."

"What?" Joffar asked.

"I don't know, that's why we need to get into Dolan's files."

"Our people—"

"Believe me," Malkor said, "rescuing the Ordochians is my first priority, but I have to think of my people as well. Whatever Dolan's plans, they can't be for the good of the empire, no matter that he presents himself as our ally." Malkor paused before adding, "I don't think he's working alone, either."

That set everyone on edge.

"We go tonight," Kayla said. "It can't wait any longer." Two days from now she'd be married to Prince Ardin and up to her eyeballs in protocol and official engagements. These were her last days of freedom. "Let's pin down the details."

*　　*　　*

Kayla prowled her rooms in the Game complex. She and Isonde would be housed here until the wedding, until she moved into the palace with Ardin. They were familiar rooms and normally comfortable, but today they felt like a cell.

Her thoughts looped over and over, incessant spirals that led one into another. They ground her down with their relentless voice, set her pacing the confines of her room in a futile effort to escape the weight they bore.

Hours remained before the mission and already she felt like she could snap.

She had to get out of here, get out of her head.

All she could hear was: *Is Vayne still alive?* He had to be. *What if he wasn't?* Who else had made it? What if she were searching the wrong location? What if Dolan found her there? What if she found Vayne there? *Is Vayne still alive?* He had to be. *What if he wasn't?*

She pressed the heels of her palms to her eyes, trying to calm herself, trying to calm the voice.

Breathe. Just breathe. She could do this. She would do this.

But what if—

Breathe.

Tea. Tea would help. Tea or tranquilizers.

Kayla punched in the selection on the food synthesizer unit and peeled the coolant packs off her shoulder as she waited. The damage was finally beginning to heal, now that she'd had several days of rest without fighting. She tested her range of motion. A spike of pain jabbed into her shoulder at the top arc of her rotation, but it disappeared as soon as she swung through.

Better. Much better.

The same could not be said for Isonde. Kayla perched on a stool at the breakfast bar with her tea. Toble had broken the news when she and Malkor returned from the meeting with the Ilmenans this morning. The toxin resisted all efforts to flush it out. Even though he kept Isonde as relaxed as possible, her vitals had begun to destabilize. Toble couldn't say how much longer she might last.

Malkor had stormed from the suite upon hearing the news, rage and pain and fear scrawled across his face. Now Kayla waited alone, with the best hope for her people dying in the next room.

Worry ramped up again. She sipped her tea, trying to ignore the rising flood. She'd visited Corinth earlier in hopes that some time with him would soothe her. It hadn't. Corinth's worry over her part in the rescue mission had been a living thing, filling the room and fueling her stress. In the end she'd had to leave, and Vid had taken Corinth for a walk to get his mind off things.

She knew she should probably try to sleep, but even sitting still this long taxed her nerves. The immediate crisis of the rescue mission consumed most of her thoughts, but she couldn't ignore the realization that one way or another, tomorrow would come. Then, the day after that. Even if they rescued her people, even if she was reunited with Vayne, with her family, one truth remained: she was locked into playing the part of Isonde. Her chances of escaping that fate faded with each of the princess's weakening breaths.

Her people would return to Wyrd Space. She would be alone. Truly alone, for the first time. She'd send Corinth back to Ilmena with Tia'tan and her people. She needed him safe, needed him to have a whole life, not the pathetic half-existence she'd made for him these last five years. He needed training and family and. . . everything. She could give him everything by sending him back, everything except a *ro'haar*. She'd stay behind, play her part as Isonde. The needs of her people could not be set aside no matter what she wanted.

Every day she'd have to don the disguise, the voice, the politics, the morals of Isonde. She'd lose herself little by little. The charade would suffocate her until the lines bled. Choices made, relationships cultivated; who would she decide as, Kayla playing Isonde, or Isonde? Where would one end and the other begin? She'd lose the ability to tell.

She felt like she was drowning under the weight of her responsibilities, suffocating from the frustration of being choiceless. Kayla gripped her mug of tea and flung it against the wall. It smashed in a splash of brown liquid and crystal but the violence couldn't satisfy her. She hopped up and grabbed her chair with both hands, knuckles white. Her rage burned so hot and fast that she couldn't breathe. She lifted the chair, ready to do. . . what? She wanted to slam it against the floor a hundred times until she'd slaked the violence of fear inside. She wanted to hurl it full-force across the room. Her arms shook from the effort of standing still.

Hot tears pricked her eyes, stung, spilt over. The chair slipped from her fingers and clattered to the floor. Her life was being pried from her, her choices, her future. The dream of what she might have had slipped away. She sank to her knees and covered her face in shame at the tears she couldn't stop.

Her door sounded, then slid open before the chime had faded away.

"I commed you—" Malkor's voice. "Kayla?" He crossed the room in a second to kneel beside her. "What's wrong?" He touched her, his hand landing gently on her back.

His murmured words, his touch, it was too much. It was all too much. She turned into him, her heart aching for everything she couldn't have.

"I don't want to be Isonde," she whispered.

He gathered her tightly to him but said nothing. There was no other choice and they both knew it.

She cried against his chest, hungry for his comfort.

"I'm sorry," he murmured. His lips brushed her hair and she wept harder. "I'm so sorry." His voice sounded as ragged as her emotions.

Time passed but his grip never eased. Even when her sobs subsided into quiet and her tears began to dry, he held her. She finally tilted her head up. He looked pained and reckless, something wild haunting his eyes while he gazed at her. So close. Before he could move, before the moment could pass, she kissed him.

He held perfectly still as he had that first time so long ago in the Blood Pit. He waited as if to say, are you sure you want this? She cupped the back of his neck and pulled his lips more firmly against hers. He made the slightest sound against her mouth, then he kissed her back. His arms tightened, melding her to him even as she pressed closer. His mobile comm buzzed and he stripped it from his hip to toss aside.

He kissed her with strength and passion, and she met his force with her own, needing it. Their lips met over and over, parting only long enough to grab a rough breath before their next kiss. She couldn't stand to be even that long from his mouth. She threaded her fingers into his hair, fingertips spearing along his scalp.

More.

She needed more.

This connection, their closeness, awakened every part of her. She'd craved it without knowing. Five years of isolation had burrowed into her and only Malkor could rid her of it.

Kayla pulled back just enough to look into his eyes. To see him, really see him, and let him see her. No defenses, no shields, just truth.

She needed him.

His fierceness stilled. He lifted his hand, hesitated, then gently stroked a finger down her cheek as if she were made of spun glass. The touch undid her and she kissed him again.

Kayla urged him backward by the shoulder, moving with him so they never lost contact. She pushed him to the ground, lying atop him with her knees along the outer sides of his thighs and her breasts crushed against his chest. She claimed his mouth again and his hands clamped on her waist. He slid her up his body until their hips met.

"You don't know how long I've wanted you like this," he said.

She flicked her tongue over the hollow of his throat. "Tell me." A dozen images of him flashed through her mind, fantasies she'd woken to but hadn't admitted to herself.

In answer he clutched her to him and rolled them both over.

"I'd rather show you." He worked a hand between them to grip the pull of her zip-up, opening her bodysuit to the waist. He peeled one edge open and half off her shoulder.

The door chime sounded.

"Ignore it," she pleaded, pulling his mouth to hers. The chime rang again.

Again.

And again.

"Something's wrong." Malkor pulled her bodysuit back together and she tried to zip it as he leveraged himself off of her. She worked with shaking hands, suddenly adrift without him. Dread rose to the back of her throat as her thoughts coalesced. Something was definitely wrong.

He paused at the door as if collecting himself, then thumbed the control. Hekkar waited in the doorway.

"Report," Malkor barked.

Hekkar wouldn't look at her, couldn't make eye contact. He focused his attention on Malkor and she knew what was wrong. Blood roared in her ears so that she barely heard his words.

"Corinth's missing."

26

"When?" Malkor asked.

Kayla's heart stuttered, hearing the words replayed. *Corinth's missing.*

"Some time in the last hour," Hekkar said, still unable to look at her.

"How? Vid and Trinan watch him like he's their kid."

Worry sat heavy on Hekkar's expression. "Trinan was running down leads on Dolan's business associates. Vid was alone with Corinth in one of the outer gardens when it happened." Just the way he said "it happened" froze her blood.

"Vid?" she asked.

"He's hurt. Badly." Hekkar made eye contact for the first time. "Burns on thirty percent of his body, seared tissue in his trachea and lungs, and two ion pulse wounds—shoulder and lower back. We don't know how long he lay there until Trinan found him."

"Prognosis?" Malkor asked.

"It's not good, Malk."

Malkor took a deep breath, clearly trying to absorb the information. "How is Trinan holding up?"

"He's a mess. Won't leave Vid's side. I couldn't even understand him when he first commed in." Hekkar's gaze darted briefly to Malkor's discarded mobile comm lying under her still upended chair.

"Damnit." Malkor kicked the chair out of the way and scooped up the mobile comm. He flipped it open. "That frutting bitch."

"What is it?" Kayla asked.

He thumbed the screen and a familiar voice spoke.

Janeen.

"I'm sorry about Vid, I really am. If he'd just given up the kid none of this would have happened. Frutt!" Janeen took a shaky breath in the recording. "I never wanted any of this. You should have let me act as Isonde in the Empress Game, then I could have controlled things without having to hurt anyone." The recording paused. When Janeen came back she sounded more composed. "I guess it's gone past that now, hasn't it? I don't know how much you know about the new lines being drawn and the power shift within the IDC. Presumably something. In any case, I have my orders.

"The boy is of marginal use to us. We're willing to trade him, but only for his sister. I know you've got plans for her so you'll have to decide. His life for her. We don't intend to kill her, she'll be safe with us.

"And Malkor, if the boy isn't enough incentive for you to make the trade, we'll find someone who is. Janeen out."

Two hours later Vid still wasn't out of surgery and they had no new information. Malkor had reluctantly left Kayla to rework their plans for tonight's raid on Dolan's facility with Hekkar. He'd intended to be by Kayla's side when they rescued her family, but now Corinth needed him and Malkor was the only person in a position to help.

New plans laid, he returned to Kayla's room to find her pacing.

"I need to find him," Kayla said, as soon as he entered.

"We will." They had to, Kayla wouldn't survive otherwise.

"You don't understand. I *need* to find him. Now."

"Kayla," he gently cupped her arms, "I understand. I know what he means to you."

"No, you don't." She brushed off his hands, pacing away. "He's my *il'haar*, I should never have let this happen." She stopped, her eyes full of fear. "How could I let this happen?"

"It wasn't your fault—" he started, but she ignored him. She went to her tactical pack, checking and rechecking the contents. He had provided her and the others with standard IDC gear for covert operations, including weapons. She had her daggers, an ion pistol, stun grenades, electromag cuffs, a stunner and a few other tricks in the lightweight pack she strapped to her back. They were due to meet the Ilmenans in bay 21 where they'd change into tac-suits and head out.

"I'm going after him," she said, heading for the door.

"You can't."

"You said you had a lead on where Janeen might be hiding him."

"I need you on the Ordochian mission." And he'd take an ion pulse to the brain before he let her walk into Janeen's trap. He played the card he knew would stop her. "You have another *il'haar* to think about."

Her face twisted, pain flashing openly across her features.

"You can't help them both, Kayla." He felt like a jerk for pointing out what she'd see as her greatest failing. "I need you to go after Vayne."

"The octet—"

"Vayne knows you, he trusts you. The other Ordochians will also." Malkor prayed she saw his logic. "I need you to convince them we're there to help them." And he needed her as far away from Janeen as possible.

"How can you ask me to choose between them?" Her whisper shot him straight through. "I am their *ro'haar*."

She was so on edge he couldn't tell what she might do and that scared him. There was only one thing he could offer, but he knew it was right as soon as he spoke the words. "I will be Corinth's *ro'haar*."

Her blue gaze locked onto him. "What did you say?"

"You can't be in two places at once. Let me become Corinth's *ro'haar*." He didn't think twice about what he offered. "I'll rescue him while you save Vayne."

She said nothing, only stared at him.

"Let me do this for you. I'll bring him back safe." *Please, Kayla*, he silently begged. "Corinth is likely being held in a safehouse in Shimville. It will take stealth and covert ops training to get in without raising alarm and get him out before we're captured. That's training I have. You're an excellent bodyguard, but I'm better suited to the mission."

He could see he was getting through to her. Her need to do the best for her *il'haars* would convince her to leave the mission to him. She had to.

"You will protect Corinth with your life?"

"Yes." Nothing would stop him from keeping this promise to her.

He held his breath while she searched his face. The moment stretched out and the length of their relationship, from the Blood Pit until now, ran through his mind. Had he earned her trust? Could she depend on another person, when she had been alone for so long?

"I hereby relinquish my right as *ro'haar* of Corinth Reinumon to you, Senior Agent Malkor Rua. He is yours to protect at any cost."

Malkor bowed his head. "I am honored to take my place as his *ro'haar*."

She nodded to herself, then again, as if confirming something. "He will be lucky to have you." Her voice gained strength and her focus seemed to crystallize. She tightened the straps on her pack. "Let's rescue our *il'haars*."

Kayla leaned against the side of the building, sweating in the comfortable evening air.

The tac-suit she wore covered her with flexible microarmor. It was agile, responsive and as hot as Altair's sun. At least she had daggers strapped to her thighs again. That and the ion pistol at her hip made her feel secure. She waited alongside Tia'tan, Luliana and Noar on one corner of Dolan's laboratory, keeping watch on the street out front while Hekkar, Aronse and Gio watched the back. Meanwhile Rigger sabotaged the window leading into the facilities area of the building. Something about resonant frequencies and harmonics compromising the integrity of the otherwise shatter-proof window.

Hey, as long as it worked.

"What's the holdup?" Hekkar asked over their linked comms. He'd been put in charge of the mission with Malkor tracking down Corinth.

"This is more refined than just blowing it up. Give me a minute," Rigger answered.

Less than a minute later she reported success and everyone converged on the window.

"Any word from Joffar?" Kayla asked Tia'tan.

"They're just sitting down to dinner." Joffar was tasked with keeping an eye on Dolan, and the two were having dinner with officials from Joop. Should take most of the evening, knowing Joop customs.

Rigger scanned the interior of the room. "Ultrasonic motion detector. There." She pointed to a spot diagonal from the room's door.

"On it," Noar said. He climbed onto the window ledge with a leg-up from Aronse. He summoned a refractor shield, a technique Kayla used as a child to sneak around the palace on Ordoch. It refracted the motion detector's ultrasonic waves away from him, thereby avoiding their pinging off his moving body.

Kayla's thoughts turned to Malkor while Noar crept across the room. She couldn't believe she'd abdicated her duty as Corinth's *ro'haar* to Malkor. . . and she couldn't believe how relieved she felt now. There was no one else, from her present or past, she would feel comfortable leaving Corinth's safety to except Malkor. As soon as he had proposed becoming Corinth's *ro'haar*, she knew it was right. And while worry for

Corinth still loomed in her mind, she was able to focus more fully on Vayne and her mission.

Thank you, Malkor.

"The motion detector's down," Noar reported. "I'm moving to the main control panel in the next room."

Everyone waited in silence for the shriek of alarms.

Nothing.

Minutes passed, marked by drops of sweat rolling down between Kayla's breasts.

Finally Noar's voice broke the tension. "Should be all clear to here. Rigger, I could use your help disabling these other systems."

Aronse helped Rigger up, then they followed one by one into the facilities room. Aronse pulled herself up last.

"Looks like the strongest security is on level seven." Rigger tapped a section of the control panel's display. "Right where we thought they'd be."

Hekkar studied the schematic. "Double chamber doors on either end of the section, separate ventilation system. . . what's this, here?"

"Piraphoric gas cylinders," Rigger said. "Looks like they can anesthetize the entire unit with the push of a button and keep the air supply quarantined from the rest of the building."

"Lovely."

Rigger manipulated the console. "Okay, I've got the motion and IR detection systems deactivated everywhere, I've shut down the automatic lockdown features of the security doors, killed the circulation fans in case we need to climb through these ducts here, and managed to get the outer doors on each end of the prisoners' ward unlocked. The inner doors are up to you."

Hekkar clapped her on the shoulder. "Better than hoped for. The lab?"

"One floor down, but close by. Noar and I will head there."

They had initially argued about who would go where, Tia'tan wanting all of her people with her, but Noar made the point that Dolan's research systems would be a mishmash of Wyrd knowledge and imperial tech. It might take Rigger and Noar's combined know-how to crack Dolan's databanks.

"Gio, with them," Hekkar said. "Aronse, monitor our signals from here and hold the egress. This will be our primary exit."

"Kayla, Luliana, Tia'tan and I will head to the prisoners' quarters. I want status reports every five minutes, and we'll rendezvous here in forty-five. Anything goes to shit, you get out and we'll meet at the safehouse. Understood?"

Everyone nodded.

Hekkar waited until Rigger's group headed off before taking point in the other direction. They crept down the hallway and reached the entrance to the stairs without incident. That didn't slow the racing of Kayla's heart any. Her shallow breathing echoed in her ears as she took step after step, expecting any minute to be discovered. She wasn't made for this kind of subtlety. Luckily, the IDC agents were. She wondered again what the Ilmenans' plan would have been without the octet's help.

They climbed the stairs on silent feet, preserving stealth at the sake of speed. Three flights up they heard men enter the stairwell one floor above them. Kayla drew her ion pistol but Hekkar put a hand on her wrist, stalling her. He shook his head, holding up the hand stunner he had. Tia'tan's voice interrupted their wordless debate.

::We will go. Wait here.:: She and Luliana left before Hekkar would stop them. Kayla could tell he was pissed.

Seconds passed. Twenty. Thirty. Surely they should be there by now. Hekkar started forward when feet could be heard scrambling against the floor.

::It's safe:: Tia'tan called.

Kayla rushed after him up the stairs. Two guards in Dolan's lavender uniforms were pinned to the wall by unseen hands, red-faced, with bulging eyes.

::Should we strangle them unconscious?::

"That's too inexact for my tastes. One of them might die."

Tia'tan shrugged as if to say, "so?"

Hekkar stunned the immobile guards and the Ilmenans let the bodies drop. Kayla helped Hekkar bind and gag them after stripping their comm units, lithodisc creds and weapons.

"We're at the lab," Rigger said. "Breaching door security now."

"Noted," Hekkar replied. They climbed the rest of the floors uninterrupted and paused outside the door to the hallway that ran parallel to the prisoners' ward. He slipped the door open, inserting a tiny mirror in the crack to peer down the hallway.

"Nothing, come on."

The short hallway ended on both sides in solid quadtanium doors. She'd seen less secure hatches on spaceships. According to the schematic a chamber lay beyond each that would hold them until the doors shut. The inner door would release if the right code was entered, but the inner and outer doors could not be open at the same time.

Beyond that waited Vayne.

Kayla started toward the one on the left.

"Luliana, go with her. Tia'tan, you're with me," Hekkar said. "We'll breach at the same time and take the security out from both sides." Kayla was surprised when Luliana followed the order, but apparently the Ilmenans understood the wisdom of having a psionic at each entrance.

Kayla had her hand on the outer door before Luliana caught up. "Let's see if Rigger's as good as I think she is." The latch released with a hiss of pressure locks disengaging.

Luliana followed her into the nine meter square chamber, sealed on the other end by an identical door. Kayla waited impatiently for the portal to swing shut and across the length of the hallway Tia'tan and Hekkar did the same.

The door shut with a vacuum-sucking sound and the interior lights of the chamber came on. A soothing female voice prompted them to enter the security code and Kayla's breath lodged in her throat—her mother's voice. She withdrew the scrambler device from her pack with shaking hands. Luliana had to take the scrambler from her and affix it properly to the palm scanner–keypad device when her mother prompted them again to enter the code.

"The scrambler's working through algorithms on our side." Hekkar's voice pulled her out of it, grounding her in the here and now.

"Same," Kayla commed back. The scrambler flashed a digital light show as it ran through possible unlocking sequences. The interfacing lasted a minute. Two. Three.

"How long does this take, Hekkar?"

His voice came back worried. "Should have found the code by now."

::Let me see.:: Luliana pried the faceplate off of the keypad, pulled a case of instruments from her pack and selected a diode modulator. The circuitry beneath the plate flashed green-blue as data zipped back and forth. Luliana manipulated first one pathway node, then another, realigning the current flow.

Kayla glared at the door. Her family waited on the other side. Her twin. If she had to beat the door down with her bare hands, she would do it. She reached out and touched the quadtanium surface, splayed her fingers against the cool metal. This close. Eighteen centimeters of quadtanium were all that separated her from Vayne, now, after all this time.

Luliana spoke into the comm. "I've got the code entered and Tia's got it on your side. Give the go and we'll pop the locks at the same time."

"Rigger—we're about to make entry, things are likely to get hot. Status on the data upload?"

"Slow, but making progress."

"Okay. Get ready to bug when I give the word," Hekkar said.

"Got it. And good luck. Rigger out."

"Kayla?" Hekkar asked.

"I'm good," she said, drawing her ion pistol. "Let's do this."

Luliana flipped the workaround she'd rigged and the pressure locks on the nearside door released. She and Kayla flattened themselves against the wall, letting any guards announce their presence with a blaster shot before they offered themselves up as targets. When nothing happened, Kayla crept forward in a crouch.

The corridor she entered was nothing like what she'd imagined.

Instead of stark and sterile it was painted a muted coffee color with dark and light accents. The floor was carpeted in a soft synthfiber of contrasting cream, and sconces every few meters gave the walls a warm glow.

Kayla padded forward, wary of an ambush. Three steps past the door and a glance to the left showed her that while the ward might have been decorated like a hotel, it was most certainly a gilded cage. A hallway led off that way, and looked to contain a series of apartments. . . apartments with glass fronts and electrically charged doors. She started down the hallway.

The first apartment stood empty. Glass lined the front of the living room and revealed a sofa, complete with spotless matching pillows and end tables, a bookshelf with nothing on it and vases with no flowers. Nothing inside marked this as a place where someone had lived for five years. Maybe someone *had* lived here, only they hadn't made it five years.

A chill spread over Kayla's skin and she picked up the pace. "Any sign of guards?" she whispered into her comm.

"None from here," Hekkar replied. "We're fanning out down a secondary hallway."

"Same."

She passed a second empty apartment, decorated differently than the first but equally as abandoned. Light shone from the apartment just ahead, painting the cream carpet golden yellow.

Kayla halted.

"We found one here," Hekkar said, tense excitement coming through the comm.

"Who?" She couldn't breathe past the hope in her chest.

"Natali. She doesn't look well."

Thank the stars, her older sister was alive.

Luliana tapped her shoulder to get her attention. ::You investigate this one, I'm going on ahead to scout the guards.::

Luliana walked right past the front of the lit apartment as if Kayla's life didn't wait inside. Kayla forced one foot to move, then the other. She crept forward, slipping into the pool of light as if it would burn her. She froze when she reached the middle of the glass wall.

She saw him in profile.

He sat at a high, elegantly structured table, a fork held absently in one hand while he read from a datapad held in the other. A half-full wineglass was just within reach and a curl of steam escaped from his dinner server. The top half of his cobalt hair was pulled into a stubby ponytail at the back of his head. The rest was down and looked to be about jaw-length, but it was tough to tell with the slight wave it had. His pale skin made his lips look more violet than red, and they moved as he read from the datapad.

Her soul realigned. Every last fragment shifted and found a new configuration.

Vayne lived.

She wanted to bang on the glass to get his attention. Couldn't he feel her standing here? His presence called to her so strongly she thought her atoms would stream through the glass to reach him.

Sweet Mother, he's alive.

She ran for the door and fumbled with the control to deactivate the electric bars. All the while she kept one eye on Vayne, afraid that if she looked away for even a nanosecond he would disappear. The bars dissolved and the door split open. She pushed the glass aside when it didn't slide fast enough for her. Five years he'd been taken from her. Five long years.

A trillion thoughts and emotions ran through her in a hyperstream but all she could get out was, "Vayne."

Nothing happened.

Had Dolan damaged his hearing? She stopped short, a strange awkwardness creeping in.

"Vayne?"

He sighed and set the datapad down on the table with a snap. He finally turned his attention to her, looking her over from head to toe with an annoyed expression.

"This again?" He lifted his chin and pitched his voice as if talking to the ceiling. "Haven't you hit this note enough lately?"

He reached for his wineglass and spoke to the ceiling again as if she wasn't there. "I know you have a hard-on for my sister, but really, what's with that suit? She looks ridiculous." He took a sip of his wine, his posture saying, "I couldn't care less," but his aqua eyes told another story. Harrowed. Piercing. "I'm in the middle of dinner, so maybe you could save your mind-frutting until after dessert, hmm?" He turned back to his meal.

What the frutt? He thought she was one of Dolan's mind-games? She stared at the cold turn of his shoulder, more muscled than she'd remembered. What had Dolan done to him that he wouldn't trust his *ro'haar*?

"It's really me, Vayne. I came to free you."

He lifted the datapad again and resumed reading.

"We have to get moving. Now."

Her words had no effect.

Damnit. They didn't have time for this. She reached for his arm. "Vayne—"

He jerked back like she meant to cut him. "Don't touch me." His voice snapped like a whip and his furious stare pinned her in place. "You are *not* my twin. You might look like her and sound like her, but you are *not* her." He raked her with his gaze. "I don't know what void Dolan brought you from to play 'Kayla' for me, but you had better run your ass back there this instant, or I swear I will rip her face from yours."

::Found two guards in an office midway between the corridors. I need help with them:: Luliana said in her head.

Hekkar's voice sounded low in her ear. "We found Ghirhad, and two other empty rooms. Luliana, I'm coming to you, do not engage the guards yet."

Kayla grabbed Vayne's arm. "Come on."

He twisted free of her grasp as he shot to his feet. His chair screeched across the floor behind him and toppled.

"I warned you not to touch me." He squared his shoulders to her, stepping toe to toe and staring slightly up at her with blazing aqua eyes. His body was thicker than she remembered, padded with muscle he'd never had before.

"Kayla, what's happening down there? The guards are up," Hekkar said.

"I am your *ro'haar*," she said vehemently to Vayne, "and I am doing this for your safety so you will come with me *now.*" Once, the words would have resulted in instant acquiescence.

Instead they raised a low growl in his throat. It was pain and rage and hatred in one sound. He struck before she could react, shoving her away from him so hard she rebounded off the glass front of the apartment.

Alarms went crazy.

"Kayla, report!" Hekkar said.

Pistol fire sounded down the corridor.

That stopped Vayne short. "Well, this is new." Another ion discharge seared the air and someone screamed. He half-smiled. "At least you brought something fresh to the table."

Kayla whipped out the hand-tranqer. "Don't make me stun you and carry your ass out of here like I did at the Gorgent fiasco," she said over the alarms, "because you know I'll do it."

The air left his lungs in a rush as if she had kicked him in the gut. "Kayla?" He stared at her, seeming to see her for the first time.

"It's me." Relief flooded her system but it was short-lived, cut down when another blast sounded in the hall. "We have to get out of here."

"Luliana's been hit," Hekkar commed her. "We neutralized the guards but they managed to call for backup. Do you read me, Kayla?"

"I hear you."

"We've rescued two Ordochians, that's all we could find. I'm calling this mission, everyone to the exit, now."

Rigger commed in. "We're not quite done."

"Now, Rigger. That's an order."

"I've got Vayne," Kayla said, "we'll meet you in the stairwell." Only three Ordochians rescued, out of seven. She wanted to rush down the hallways and check each apartment herself, just in case he'd missed someone.

"Do you need to bring anything with you?" she asked Vayne. He looked at her like she was out of her mind. Or a phantom. Maybe both. "Come on." She was almost through the door when his hand gripped her shoulder and yanked her backward.

"What the—" The hairs loose from her ponytail rose up and brushed her face a nanosecond before blue-green bolts of energy shot from the doorframe and connected with the floor, locking her in. Her comm link went dead.

"Trust me," Vayne said, "you don't want to touch those."

"Hekkar!" She banged the butt-end of her hand-tranqer against the glass, trying to make as much noise as possible. "We need help!" Thirty seconds of that with no response convinced her it was too late. The others had either been captured or escaped out the prison wing through the quadtanium doors, putting them beyond earshot.

"Get back." She grabbed her ion pistol and fired at the glass wall. The discharge dissipated across the surface harmlessly.

Fear bloomed as the reality of the situation crystallized. Trapped. In one of Dolan's prison cells. She turned to Vayne. "Do you have any ideas?"

"If I did, do you think I'd still be standing here?"

"Psi powers?"

He shook his head. "Dolan keeps us dosed so we can't access them. Besides, he harvested mine too recently. Try yours."

"Mine are dead." Like she would be if she got trapped here. Dead or worse.

The alarms cut out. The sudden silence unnerved her. It was as if the empty hallways waited for something.

"I truly hope that is not the case, my dear."

Dolan.

His voice piped in through the room's comm system. "In fact, I'm counting on it."

Her tongue felt fuzzy. Fuzzy and swollen. Her mouth was. . . humming. Buzzing. She swallowed, tasting something sweet in the back of her throat.

"What—"

Vayne seemed to be fading away, or maybe she was fading away. The room stretched out away from her. She heard Vayne from a distance of light-years.

"You should lie down."

Her stomach rolled with a space-sick flip, then the floor rushed up to meet her.

27

Malkor lay on his belly on the rooftop of a building in Shimville. Across the distance of an alley sat the building Janeen was holed-up in. Even for Shimville, this wasn't a good part of town. The buildings were more like two-story shanties than real warehouses, and bars on the windows was about as high-tech as it got.

Except for Janeen's place, of course.

Rutcker hadn't lied—she had some sweet gadgets installed. The data array on the roof could send and receive transmissions not only planet-wide, but galaxy-wide. The scanner tucked under the overhang on the front of the building was a PLuA-4100, capable of reading the credentials embedded in any lithodisc bracelet within fifty meters. Not only was it recording appearance and biomass data on everyone who walked by, it was IDing them as well. Definitely not standard IDC-issue.

Of more concern to him, though, was the automated perimeter defense system. It bore the mark of Hundin tech, which meant it had micrometer precision targeting capabilities. It could be programmed to trigger on any number of mechanics, such as movement, proximity, body heat and so on. The trick was finding the trip. Janeen wouldn't want to shoot everyone who walked down the alley for a black-market deal. The bodies would stack up. Maybe a tight-range proximity? One or two smugglers get too close to the building and soon word gets around to avoid this section of Shimville. In any case, that beast would have to be disarmed before rescue could be attempted.

Initial thermal scans showed the presence of two adults on the first floor and one child-sized on the second. Had to be Corinth. He couldn't guess who the second adult heat-signature belonged to. Who would a rogue IDC agent have over for dinner at her safehouse? A hired merc for security? Another rogue agent? Or someone higher up on the food chain?

The cynicism that had stalked Malkor for years over IDC's misuse of power solidified. What kind of element within IDC would have recruited and trained Janeen for her position as a double agent—and how large was that element?

Malkor pushed the thoughts aside and focused on the mission.

He'd take out the data relay first, then the automated defenses. The scanner on the front of the building could stay. He readied a spider dart with an electromag tip and fitted it into the barrel of his backup weapon, a versatile hand-launcher that fired any number of projectiles. He had a few gems loaded into it already and a couple of special-occasion goodies in a pocket of his tac-suit. Nothing beat the spider dart for surveillance, though.

He fired the dart square into the center of the relay's casing. Electric shocks shot from it and wrapped around the casing in all directions.

One data relay—fried.

Perimeter defenses next.

The weapon nodes for the defenses were affixed halfway up the exterior of the building, and the main control unit would be inside. He'd have to shut it down the hard way, node by node.

The nodes covered the building evenly front-to-back, making neither the front nor rear exit a more attractive option.

Rear exit it was, then.

He made his way across the roof until he was parallel with the back of Janeen's building. He spotted a node on each corner and one directly above the door. The others wouldn't wrap around the building so he had three nodes to disable.

Gee, was that all?

He pulled a datapad from his pack and set it to scan, angling it for the closest node on the corner. A close-up look with zoom lenses showed two points of weakness: the ratchet clip locking the node in place and the trinium sensor. Ideally disabling the sensor would prevent the node from going off, no matter what the trigger was. Assuming, of course, that disabling the sensor wouldn't trigger it anyway.

What a pain in the ass.

Damn you, Janeen.

His scan showed what he already suspected: the node was hardwired to the mainframe, meaning a spider dart wouldn't be able to short-circuit it. That would have been too easy.

He could target the ratchet clip. The acid in a widow dart could, if placed correctly, liquefy the component, dropping the node to the ground. Of course, that might also set the node off.

Trinium circuitry was notoriously delicate, and shooting out the sensor with a pellet projectile would be a lot quieter than sending a fist-sized node crashing to the ground from one and a half stories up.

Disabling the sensor it was.

Malkor spun the chamber on his hand-launcher to align with the pellet and aimed at the closest node. Praying that the node would go down without a fight, Malkor took a deep breath, let it out, and fired.

The node didn't fire back.

Thank the void.

Another glance through the zoom lenses confirmed the hit. One trinium sensor—annihilated. He disabled the other two quickly.

At least, they had better be disabled. Either that or he was about to get shot.

His tac-suit would absorb two to three blasts from an ion pistol and had enough body armor to provide protection in a hand-to-hand combat situation, but who knows what punch those nodes packed. He was looking at a serious maiming if he'd been wrong about the sensors.

Malkor selected two web darts from his pocket and loaded them into the launcher. The dart, once fired, would blow its tip and shoot a plasma web at the target, big enough to wrap an adult from shoulder to hips. Once the center of it touched something, the web would spread and wrap around the object before adhering to itself at the edges into a nearly indestructible plasma cage. Handy for trapping prisoners you'd rather interrogate than kill. Or interrogate, *then* kill.

Downside? It launched at a low velocity, and a target with enough presence of mind to make a dive could dodge the web. Hence the backup.

He messaged Hekkar that he was breaching the perimeter, then climbed down to land boots-first in the alley behind Janeen's place.

He grinned at the silent nodes. *Take that, Janeen. Still not as slick as your octet leader, no matter who's backing you.*

He crossed the alley to the back door. No visible alarms from outside but there wasn't a chance she'd left it unwired. She was too cautious to rely solely on the defense nodes, and, sadly, too clever to give him something to disable from this side. Ah well, he was tired of the stealth technique anyway.

He drew his ion pistol and hand-launcher and took the direct route—boot-heel to door. The thing burst inward and set off a pulsing alarm. He caught the backswing on his arm as he sprinted into the building. The short hallway had doors on either side, but scrambling came from straight ahead on the main warehouse floor. The speed of his steps brought him into the open area before Janeen and an IDC agent he recognized as Thack could respond.

They were about three meters apart and froze when Malkor came into view, a weapon trained on each of them. The warehouse had an open space in the center where Janeen had set up a command post. Stacks of crates took up the rest of the two-story space, and to his left a set of stairs led up to a loft.

Thack cut his gaze to Janeen, clearly looking to her for a sign of what to do. Malkor shot an ion blast at the floor beside his left foot. "Don't move."

"You can't be serious," Janeen said. She held her hand away from the weapon at her hip, but looked ready to draw. "You came alone to take the two of us on?"

"The rest of the octet's here."

"You wouldn't be kicking in back doors if they were." Still, she glanced over his shoulder to the hallway behind him, then at the window to her left.

He gestured with his gun. "Looks like I'm doing just fine."

"What, with one pistol and a hand-launcher?"

"That's more than you have in hand."

"Where's the princess?" Thack asked.

Janeen answered for him. "He didn't come to trade. He thinks he's here for a rescue."

"Oh, I know I am," Malkor said.

"Give us the girl. This doesn't have to get messy."

The slow boil of anger in his chest kicked up a notch. "Tell that to Vid. And Trinan."

She frowned. "You know I didn't want that. He should have just handed over the boy."

"Where's Corinth?"

She didn't answer.

"You—"

She bolted toward the nearest stack of crates, drawing her weapon on the way.

"Frutt!" He got off a shot with the launcher but she dove to the floor and the plasma web sailed over her head. She scrambled for the crates while Thack darted in the opposite direction. Malkor nailed him in the back just as Thack made it to the cover of a cargo pile.

Malkor ran for cover himself when he heard Janeen's ion pistol drawing charge.

The stairs. He had to get between her and the stairs. If she made it to Corinth first and used him as a hostage they were done. He was Corinth's *ro'haar* now, he'd die before he let anything happen to him. . . and that might be exactly how it went down.

A blast splintered the crate near his head.

At least it was only one blast. Hopefully Thack had been too injured to do more than lie there and try not to die.

Malkor crept toward the stairs, keeping the containers at one shoulder while he rotated the cylinder on the launcher to dial up the next web dart. Another shot, from closer to the stairs this time. Damnit. He came to a break in the cargo and peeked through to see her desk area. Malkor took a second to shoot out the mainframe for the perimeter defenses. Who knew what exit he and Corinth would be leaving by in a hurry and he'd rather not get killed on the way out.

He hustled across the opening, taking fire as he crossed to the next stack of crates. He narrowed in on the stairs, but based on the direction of her shots she was getting there quicker. He couldn't afford to fire back. No way he'd risk killing her when she had a billion pieces of information he needed. He needed to get her out in the open so he could use the plasma web on her.

Only one chance for that.

Malkor glanced at the rickety metal stairs leading to the loft. If he let her reach them first and she thought she could get to Corinth before him, she'd be channeled in a straight line while she climbed them. Nothing would impede a shot with the launcher from the base of the steps, assuming he could get there quickly enough. And assuming he hit her before she could shoot him from her higher ground.

Of course, if he missed, she'd have Corinth and he'd be dead.

She took the decision out of his hands when she hit the first stair and started to back her way up them, pistol trained on the spot she thought he'd emerge from. She'd underestimated him, though, and he was one stack of cargo boxes ahead. Not that it would help him much once she spotted him, which she would if she reached any higher.

Now or never.

He stepped from behind his cover and aimed the hand-launcher. He took a shot to the shoulder that his suit absorbed, then one to the chest that started to burn through the material. The dart launched with painful slowness and when the web sprang open Janeen grabbed the stair rail as if she meant to vault over it. The web hit her side on and she crashed to the metal steps as the plasma wound around her. The *thunk* of her head striking the edge of a stair was as satisfying as her grunt of pain.

Something punched into his shoulder blade and fire erupted across his back. The impact doubled him over and the next shot grazed his ear.

Thack. Apparently the frutter hadn't died.

Malkor looked back and saw Thack standing across the open space, one hand wrapped to his ribs, the other aiming a pistol at Malkor's head.

So much for Corinth's rescue.

Malkor couldn't even stand against the burning pain so he turned, still at a crouch, and faced the man down. At least he'd have to look in his eyes as he shot him.

Thack gasped, clutching at his ribs and taking several shallow breaths. Malkor smiled. *That's what you get, you double-agent bastard.*

The spasm passed and Thack straightened, aiming his weapon again.

SSzzzt.

An ion blast seared the air and Thack's head whipped forward. Blank eyes stared at Malkor as his dead body toppled face-first to the ground. Smoke rose in a crooked waft from the back of his head. Malkor raised his eyes to the man standing behind him, weapon still pointed in Malkor's direction. Beyond that the front door of the building stood open to the night.

"Sir."

Commander Parrel held the pistol trained on him.

"Are you going to shoot me as well?" Malkor asked.

Parrel chuckled. "Don't be an idiot." He holstered the pistol and came forward to help Malkor to his feet. "Who am I going to blame for Thack's death, otherwise?"

Malkor gritted his teeth against the pain and straightened as best he could manage, uncertain if he should thank the man or shoot him.

"You can put the guns away, Agent Rua. I'm here to help." Parrel held his gaze, waiting patiently for Malkor to decide which side he was on.

Malkor didn't sheathe his weapons. "I'm here for the boy."

Parrel nodded. "I know you are. You did excellent work tracking down Agent Nuagyn, we've been looking for her too. You've got your reasons for being here and I think we're on the same side."

Malkor fought against the pain in his shoulder. "Right now, I don't give a damn why you're here, as long as you don't plan to shoot me in the back."

Parrel shook his head.

"Good." Malkor dropped the pistol from his near useless left hand and sheathed his launcher before making his grueling way up the stairs. "Corinth?" he called up into the loft. "Corinth?"

Janeen moaned as he passed.

The loft was sparsely furnished with a bed, dresser, table and a food synthesizer. Corinth lay on the bed, bound hand and foot by magcuffs. He looked pale as death in the weak light coming through the windows and didn't twitch when Malkor touched his neck, but he had a pulse.

Malkor sighed out the tension that had been strangling him, and sank to the bed. He rested his hand on Corinth's forehead. So small. Too small to have been through so much. Malkor felt a need rise up inside him, a need to keep Corinth not only safe, but sheltered. To provide him not only protection, but happiness.

Corinth's eyes fluttered open, irises focusing on Malkor's face. ::You came for me.::

"Of course," Malkor said. "Can't have anything happening to the junior member of my team."

Corinth smiled, his lids drifting shut again.

Kayla's throat clogged like a gummed-up pipe when she tried to swallow and she choked on her own saliva. That brought her sputtering awake. She coughed and spat, fighting to clear her throat and draw a full breath.

"Easy, Kayla, easy." The soothing words, spoken in Dolan's voice, had her coughing all the harder. She leaned her head forward, the only part of her she could move, and spat a clump of mucus on his shoes. She instantly felt better.

What had happened?

She had a debilitating pain in her skull and weakness in her limbs. She was strapped into a comfortable chair—chest, wrists, hips and ankles—and seemed to be a prisoner in his laboratory. The room was all smooth-paneled drawers, neatly organized work stations, foreign instrumentation and flashing digital consoles. Events of the last few hours cascaded through her mind.

The rescue.

Vayne.

She looked wildly about.

"Don't worry, he's here."

Her heart broke to see her twin seated nearby, similarly restrained. He looked resigned, almost to the point of apathy.

"I'm sorry," she whispered, wishing she could touch him, reassure herself that he was still alive—for the moment.

Vayne shook his head. "Not your fault."

She spat again, and this time Dolan dodged. The bastard had anesthetized her, that's how she'd ended up here, locked down, weaponless and pissed.

"How are you feeling?" Dolan appeared beside her chair, concerned. "I apologize for the rough treatment, but I couldn't have you stabbing me."

The haze fogging her brain made it tough to concentrate. She met Dolan's stare, focusing on his good eye. "Release my brother. Whatever you want from me, you can have it."

Dolan's permanent half-smirk cocked up. "I know I can." He touched her cheek and she forced herself not to recoil.

"If you release Vayne, I won't fight you." She swallowed hard against the words, squeezing them out. "I'll do whatever you want."

"Kayla—" Vayne started.

"Will you?" Dolan arched the brow ruined by the spider web of scars. He glanced over at Vayne. "He means that much to you?"

She nodded.

Dolan's half-smirk turned into a smile. "Good. I had heard that on Ordoch, the bond between *ro'haar* and *il'haar* was much stronger than on Ilmena, and I have experienced Vayne's memories of you. You do not disappoint."

"If you don't let him go, I will do much more than disappoint you, *kin'shaa*. You have my word on that." She'd been stripped of her tac-suit and wore nothing more than a light gown, but she gave him the stare of the warrior she was.

Dolan walked behind her chair and out of sight. "You are lucky to have such a fierce champion, Vayne."

Kayla twisted her wrists, testing the strength of her bonds. How long had she been unconscious? Had Rigger and the others made it to safety? Did they know what happened to her? Even if they did, what could they do?

Her bonds proved immovable. Organoplastic cuffs with an infused gel lining that conformed exactly to her wrists. She studied the room, trying to ignore the sound of Dolan working on something behind her. The one door she could see looked as sturdy as those on the prisoners' ward, and there were no windows.

She jumped at a touch on her temple. Dolan affixed something there, then one on the opposite side. The things hummed to life and pressure built in her skull as they seemed to squeeze inward toward each other.

"Don't do this," Vayne said. "You still have me, that's enough."

"If you were enough, we would not be in this situation," Dolan replied. "I need her." He stroked the hair back from her forehead gently before affixing another device there. It was small, no bigger than a credit chip, and blinking with electrical impulses. He forced her head forward and attached one underneath her hair at the nape of her neck. The pressure intensified as those two devices started to pull on each other.

A console on the wall ahead of her lit up and revealed a neural scan of her brain. Dolan moved to study the screen. His lavender robes swirled around his ankles, giving him an oddly elegant appearance.

"As I suspected, your psi powers are intact. Look here." He enlarged a section of the scan. "The cartaid arch is entirely undamaged. There's no scar tissue or signs of past hemorrhage. You should have full access to your powers, but there's no activity." He tapped a finger against his lip. "I think it's a mental block rather than physical." Dolan turned to look at her. "You're no good to me like this."

Vayne sighed with such relief that her heart ached. Whatever being of use to Dolan meant, Vayne had clearly suffered the result of it many, many times.

"Let her go, Dolan. She's useless for your plans."

"I never said she was useless. She just needs to re-form the pathways between the cartaid arch and the rest of her brain."

"How would that help you?" she asked. The constant squeezing on her head edged out the effects of the anesthesia.

He smiled. "I thought that was clear. I plan to control the Council of Seven."

"With one vote on the Council?" That explained why he wanted Tia'tan to win the Game, if he thought her on his side, or why he might have helped Janeen in her attempt to fix it and put Divinya on the throne, if he could have used her as a pawn.

"Not one vote. All of them."

Thoughts crawled over each other in her sluggish brain. Something about Dolan and mind control. On Ilmena. His experiments? The pieces clicked together haphazardly. An artificial intelligence, constructed to generate its own telepathic output. Something about keeping it constantly powered to maintain indefinite control over a group of people.

"You rebuilt your AI." The only explanation. No Wyrd could achieve the level of sophisticated mind control on a consistent basis needed to control the Council otherwise.

"It took years," Dolan said, "with only the empire's rudimentary tech to work with. The invasion of Ordoch finally gave me access to the materials I needed."

"How lucky for you," she snapped. "So you've been, what, experimenting on my family these last five years?"

Dolan walked past her again, and when he returned to view he was affixing electrodes to Vayne's head. He was less gentle about it and Vayne hissed when the last one locked into place.

"It was necessary to have test subjects while I refined the AI."

"You did more than just test your AI on us," Vayne said, his words echoing with contempt. "We've been your frutting playthings." His aqua eyes blazed with hatred, and a betraying twitch in his hand showed how he struggled to sit still while the *kin'shaa* touched him.

Dolan lowered his voice. "Lie to her. Tell her you hated every second of it. Look her in the eye and tell her I never gave you joy, or happiness, or pleasure."

"You took the choice from me."

"I gave you so much more in return." Dolan's certainty made her shiver.

Kayla couldn't bear the conflict of hatred and self-hatred on Vayne's face. "Leave him alone." His body might be stronger physically than she had ever seen, but looking at him now she knew he'd been destroyed on many levels.

She was going to tear the flesh from Dolan's body while he still lived.

"What do you want from me?" she demanded.

Dolan looked over his shoulder at her, his ruined eye seeming to peer into her soul. "Many things, in time." Again the certainty, and with it came a sick roll in her stomach. "First, though, I need your powers."

"You just said I don't have any."

"You will. It takes only the right emotional trigger to convince your brain to re-form the connection to your cartaid arch. Vayne knows all about it." Her twin wouldn't look at her.

"What then? Once I have my powers—"

"He'll harvest them," Vayne said. "The AI doesn't grow its own psi powers, they are grafted onto the neuroface. Once there, the machine can sustain the psi powers for a period of time, but eventually the grafted energies die, and," he looked up at her, "more need to be harvested."

"He's been. . . farming you?"

"It's slightly more complex than that," Dolan said. A second screen lit up on the wall beside hers, showing Vayne's neural scan. The area he'd indicated as the arch looked twisted and scarred. "As you can see, it's not a forgiving process."

Understanding clicked into place. "That's how you got your powers back, after the Kalichma Ritual. You stole them from Vayne."

"The ritual did much more damage to my brain than this—" he gestured to Vayne's misshapen cartaid arch. "But yes, I was able to graft the energies from his psi powers onto my brain. He was the strongest of the Ordochians that I. . . acquired."

Vayne cut in. "I told you—I am stronger than Kayla. If my powers are not enough to feed your AI then hers will be of even less use to you."

"Alone, perhaps, but I did not capture Kayla to use her alone."

Her head throbbed from the pressure on her skull and the anesthesia's aftereffects. "What does that mean?"

"The energies of twins are complementary in a way that no two other psionics working together can be. I theorize that if I harvest the psionic energies from each twin, overlay them and splice them together *before* attempting to graft them on to the AI, I'll be left with something greater than either of you could achieve on your own." He frowned, looking grave. "I meant to try this with Erebus and Natali, but—"

"Erebus is dead." Vayne's words lanced into her. "And Shyla and Kuutu and Mother." Each name was a blow to her heart. Erebus, her eldest brother, Shyla and Kuutu, her aunt and uncle, and. . . her mother. . .

"Enough. Now is not the time." Dolan came to stand beside Kayla and she fought the urge to struggle against her restraints. "Are you ready to re-form the pathways to your psionic powers?"

"Only if you free Vayne."

He sighed. "Kayla, this is going to happen either way. Even though I've recently harvested Vayne's powers I might still need him. I'm afraid I can't release him." He lightly touched her shoulder, a caress through the thin fabric of the gown. "Maybe in time, if it means that much to you, I will consider it."

She tried to shrug his hand off but only succeeded in shaking the chair that held her. His hand trailed down her bare arm before he stepped back. "We'll need something to. . . expand your consciousness, before we get started."

She felt the pinch of an injector in her neck. She saw in Vayne's eyes the same frustration she felt. He couldn't help her any more than she could help him. She held his gaze until the room started to slide.

28

"What do you mean she didn't make it back with you?" Malkor's near-shout silenced the room. He stood in the open living area of the safehouse the Ordochians had been brought to and stared at Hekkar. "I trusted her to you."

"Malk, I'm sorry, but—"

"You're sorry?" He practically spat the words. "Kayla's been captured by Dolan and you're sorry?" Corinth still lay unconscious in his arms or he might have grabbed his second-in-command. "I trusted you."

He scanned the room's faces. Gio, Aronse, Tia'tan. Luliana lay on one of the beds, tended by a medic. Same for two other people he didn't recognize. Two rescued Ordochians, two lives for Kayla's.

An unacceptable trade.

He strode to the nearest bed and lay Corinth down as gently as the fury racing through him allowed. He turned on Hekkar. "I'm going after her."

"We can't, you know that. Dolan's on alert now."

He pushed past Hekkar but the man grabbed his injured arm. "Malk, think, for frutt's sake."

Malkor yanked his arm away, breathing hard as the burn across his shoulder and back stung. "Do you know what Dolan wants with her?"

"No."

"Neither do I, and that scares the living shit out of me."
He forced a hand through his hair. Kayla, in Dolan's clutches.
Think. He had to think.

"She's with Vayne," Hekkar said. "At least, she was when—"

"Vayne's alive?"

Hekkar nodded.

Stars. Was she happy to know he wasn't dead, or devastated
to know he'd endured as Dolan's prisoner for the last five
years? Which was worse?

"I'm going after her."

This time Hekkar let him go, but Malkor didn't make it
three steps.

"Frutt." Hekkar was right. He couldn't charge back there,
couldn't break in alone. He couldn't do anything. It was on his
tongue to curse Hekkar again but it wasn't his friend's fault.
Kayla had willingly risked herself in order to save her people.
She would happily become Dolan's prisoner, he knew, if the
action would save her brother.

Only it hadn't.

Now they were both trapped, and Malkor was utterly
useless to her.

He faced the door, trying to get his breathing under control,
trying to master the fear-born rage.

"Malkor?"

"I'm fine," he said, when he could speak without shouting.

"Judging by your tac-suit you've been shot. More than
once," Hekkar said.

Malkor turned around with a sigh, giving up on rescuing
Kayla. . . for the moment. "I'll heal."

"Not well, with the armor melted into the edges of the
wounds. Let one of the medics look at it."

He consented and took a chair by the door. Hekkar cut the
melted tac-suit away from the wound on his shoulder blade,
reporting on the mission while he worked. Apparently they'd
rescued Natali, Kayla's elder sister, and Ghirhad, one of her
uncles. Both were in bad shape, but it seemed to be the mental,

rather than the physical kind. Natali confirmed that the rest of the Ordochians were dead.

"So Parrel's got Janeen?" Hekkar asked, when Malkor related the details of Corinth's rescue.

"He promised to get the formula for the toxin out of her first thing. Toble's with Isonde, ready."

"They'll get it in time."

"They'd better, or I'll kill Janeen myself." And enjoy it. Immensely.

"You might have to get in line behind Trinan."

"Shit. I haven't even asked. Vid?"

"Finally out of surgery. He's got a long road of recovery ahead, including another surgery, but the doctor said he should regain full mobility and functionality eventually."

Another thing Janeen had to pay for. Or was it Dolan? She'd kidnapped Corinth to trade for Kayla, clearly a plan designed by Dolan—no one else on Falanar had the slightest interest in Kayla. Who did Janeen work for, exactly? And if it was the IDC, was some faction of the IDC aligned with Dolan? The idea made him ill.

What had the IDC come to? Who did *he* even work for these days?

"Noar and Rigger?" he asked, to distract himself from questions he didn't want answers to.

"They're at Rigger's quarters in the Game complex, decrypting Dolan's files." Hekkar sat in the chair across from him to give the medic access to Malkor's back. "We'll discover his plans."

"In time to help Kayla?" Malkor lowered his voice. "I can't sit here like this, not with her out there. With him."

"We'll get her," Hekkar said. Malkor met his gaze and knew neither of them believed it.

Kayla relaxed in her comfortable chair, feeling the world spin. She'd been sliding in and out of consciousness and only now felt coherent enough to form words.

"This chair's wonderful."

"I'm glad you like it." She knew that voice. Dolan? He came into her view, smiling at her. Where was she again?

"But my bracelets are tight." She wiggled her fingers, looking down at the white cuffs. Not bracelets. Restraints. Right? Or were they bracelets? The closer she looked, the more they seemed to shine like jewelry. Had he given her jewelry? That seemed odd.

"Kayla," someone called. "Focus on me. Focus on what's real."

She looked over at the man. Aquiline features, vibrant turquoise eyes, stern mouth. So intense. Why did he look so upset?

"Vayne?"

The man nodded. "That's right. Focus on me. Ignore everything else."

Dolan swiveled her chair until he filled her vision. Elegant lavender robes. Full lips. A strange thing to notice, with the scars on his face, but his lips caught her attention. So red. His lips curved into a smile. "How are you feeling?"

How *did* she feel? Light. Weightless. Happily sliding through a dream while sitting in a comfortable chair. She looked at Dolan, feeling strongly for him. They shared something, something powerful. What was it?

"Lovely," she finally said. That made him smile more. He touched her hand where it lay in her tight bracelet. Restraint. Bracelet.

He stroked her fingers, then intertwined his with hers.

It felt good, touching someone, being touched. She hadn't been touched in so long, not like this. And she wanted to touch. . . someone. She'd had a need. Her body had needed someone, needed his touch. She looked up into Dolan's eyes, one a blank crimson, one purple. Was it him? Had she longed to touch him?

"I've gotten to know you, these last five years." Her attention was drawn again to his mouth. To that half-smirk he couldn't help. "Through your brother. He's shown me a million memories of you, and I came to love you over the years."

"Love me?" Was that right? Did she love him, was that this feeling pressing against her chest, demanding release at his touch?

"It's not fair to say I truly loved you before we met. Vayne's memories of you are filtered through his experience of being your brother. He does not see all of you, the way another man would. As I do." He tilted her chin up. "Now that I've met you, however. . ."

He bent those full red lips down to hers and kissed her. It was a long moment before he raised his head again. "Vayne's memories did not fully do you justice," he whispered, "but I will." He kissed her again, and while the room spun around her, something grew within. Passion? Was it desire she felt?

No. Something was wrong. Something was wrong in his kiss. Suddenly she wanted to be free of his hand, of his mouth.

He lifted his head and glanced past her, to a screen embedded in the wall. "Perhaps this is not what you need." The words, spoken lightly, didn't match the disappointment in his eyes. He released her hand and walked away.

She felt a feather-light touch at the base of her skull. A feeling she knew she should recognize but didn't. A man came into her sight.

"Perhaps this is more what you need," he said, in a voice that slid along her skin like rough velvet. She knew this man, this voice. Malkor. She felt the smile that came to her lips.

"Ah," he said, smiling in return. "Is this what you want, my dear?"

"Whatever you see, it's not real," Vayne said. "That's not who you think it is."

How could it not be Malkor? His palm curved over her cheek. His touch, not as gentle as Dolan's, was possessive, strong like Malkor. He claimed her lips, sealing his against her own.

Yes.

This was what she wanted. This man.

His hand slid to cradle the back of her neck, holding her mouth to his. Her heartbeat kicked up and something beeped, far off, in response. Malkor deepened the kiss and she tilted her head back farther to receive it.

Yes. This.

"Kayla, stop!" someone demanded. Why wouldn't they leave her alone?

"Ignore him," Malkor said against her lips, sounding breathless. "He wants you for himself."

He kissed her again and she drank him in. Why were her arms tied down? She wanted to hold him, grip him. She wanted to— Why were her legs tied down? What was going on?

"Malkor, why can't I move?"

"Shhh," was his only reply. She breathed in his scent. Heady, woodsy. It was smoky and. . .

. . . and not at all like old-fashioned imperial soap.

She turned her head away and his next kiss smeared against her cheek. It wasn't Malkor. Malkor never smelled like that.

Focus, Kayla, focus.

That lab. She was in a lab.

Dolan's lab.

It wasn't Malkor. She was being held here to. . . to. . . She twisted away when the man tried to kiss her again, and a ruined red orb of an eye came into view.

She remembered.

Kayla slammed her forehead forward, smashing the bridge of his nose when he tried to kiss her again.

"Gah!" Blood spurted through clenched fingers as he covered his face. It splashed into her mouth and she spat it back in his face.

"Get the frutt away from me," she growled.

Dolan backed off, hand still clamped to his nose. He sat at one of the workstations, gauging the damage in a mirror before grabbing a medstick from a nearby drawer to treat the injury. That he had a medstick so readily available made her uneasy. How often had his work here required immediate medical attention?

Kayla tried to find her mental footing, but whatever drugs he'd administered played havoc with her mind and emotions. Dolan approached. Blood dotted his lavender robes and his nose showed considerable swelling.

"I had hoped," he said, and she had the insane urge to giggle at the change his injured nose had wrought in his voice, "that a warm emotion like love might be trigger enough for you to rebuild the pathways in your brain. Looks like we'll have to try something different."

"Don't do this, Dolan," Vayne said. "She's not like me."

Dolan spun Kayla's chair so that she faced Vayne. Fury at Vayne's imprisonment flamed through her chest, hotter than she could hope to control with the drugs in her system.

"Your brother responds quite well to a different stimulus." Dolan selected a benign-looking tool shaped almost like a massager from a tray. Vayne's look of horror flipped her emotions.

A cold howl of fear snuffed out the fury. What was that thing? Terror blossomed, pushed high by the drugs, paralyzing her.

Vayne struggled in his chair. "Don't do this." His pleading tone shot her fear through the roof. "Please, Dolan."

Dolan approached her with the massager and her breath came in sharp gasps. She scrambled for any way to stop him, drawing on the space where her psi powers had always been, begging for the strength to push him away with her mind, to shield herself.

Come on, come on.

She fumbled for the connection like a blind man for his cane. *Help me!* she silently screamed at Vayne. His own pathways had been severed just recently, Dolan had said. He was as powerless as she.

At the first gentle touch of the instrument her body arched off the chair in a giant spasm. A trillion nerve endings flared to life in a burst of pain that ripped through her body like an electric shock. She would have screamed if her jaw hadn't locked down tight. Dolan lifted the tool from her arm and she could breathe again.

The reprieve lasted only a second before he touched the instrument to her skin again and her entire body seized in a fit. Pulse after pulse after pulse of utter agony streaked through her body, tearing her apart.

When he released her again she gasped and choked. The instant he pulled the tool away the pain evaporated. That didn't save her body, though, from sweating and gasping and twitching in the aftermath. Every muscle ached from the spasms and her heart threatened to burst from her chest.

"More?" Dolan asked. He extended his hand again and she screamed as he neared. She fought with every fiber to reach her powers. It was like scrambling bare-handed to climb a glass wall. Then the tool landed and she couldn't even scream anymore.

When he released her she heard sobbing. It took a moment to realize it came from her.

Dolan brushed at the tears on her cheeks with one hand. "Kayla," he said softly, "I don't want to do this to you. You can stop me, but you have to fight for it. Find the connection." He leaned down and kissed the top of her head. "Take your powers back."

She glanced through tear-blurred eyes at Vayne, whose lips were pinched in a bloodless line. She kept her gaze on him as Dolan touched her again and her world exploded into pain. The last thing she saw before losing consciousness was Vayne mouthing, "I'm sorry."

Voices drifted to her while she floated.

"She's stronger than you were, the first time."

"She's stronger than I am now."

"Not true. You endure a little more each time we do this, resist a little longer before the pathways re-form in your brain."

"Is that something to be proud of?"

"It's something to wonder about. I worry that you no longer want your powers at all. If I didn't force you, would you ever try to get them back?"

"Would you kill me if I had no more powers?"

A pause.

"No. I've grown too accustomed to your company."

"You know that someday I will kill you."

"So you say. But if you can't do it now, while I am torturing a woman we both love, then you'll never be able to."

Kayla fought against full consciousness. It was so warm and soft here beneath the exhaustion left in the wake of pain. No one could hurt her. She couldn't fail anyone here. She could just float.

"You know your twin would die for you. An interesting notion. Perhaps that's the trigger I need."

Their words stirred her brain, made her think when she didn't want to, wonder when she could be resting. If she sank back down, it would be—

"I need her."

Who said that? Kayla's eyes opened of their own accord and she groggily raised her head.

Vayne and Dolan fell silent, both watching her with matching looks of concern.

How bizarre. . .

"Are you ready to try something else?"

She was ready to pass out again. Her arms and legs felt like mud, and the effort of holding her head up made her want to close her eyes.

She forced herself to sit up in the chair, rather than be merely held in place by the restraints. Whatever Dolan had planned next, she could take it. It couldn't be worse than that painstick of his.

Vayne watched her with understanding in his eyes. "You'll come out of it."

She tried to nod. She trusted Vayne. He'd been through this and survived. She could do this.

Dolan walked to his tray of implements and reached for the painstick again.

"But— You said—"

"I'm not going to use this on you, you've had enough for one day." He made his way to Vayne's chair, the permanent half-smirk the only expression on his face.

"I'm surprised you waited this long," Vayne said. He gave Dolan a flat stare, not looking at the painstick.

Dolan sighed. "I should have started here but I was hoping to spare her this, as it's bound to be the most painful." He glanced at the neural scans; her cartaid arch looked as inactive as Vayne's.

"Dolan— Don't." Her voice came out sharp, stopping the *kin'shaa*. He met her gaze and she had the feeling that he truly did not want to harm Vayne. He waited, looking at her in such a way that said, "Give me some reason to stop this."

"If you meant anything you've said about knowing me, then you know what it will do to see my *il'haar* tortured." The desire to protect Vayne was so strong that she felt almost capable of tearing through her restraints to get to him. Dolan had to see that, had to feel it radiating from her. "There has to be another way."

"I *do* know you," Dolan said, with quiet emphasis. "Nothing will be as effective as this."

He touched the painstick to Vayne's wrist before she could argue further.

Vayne jerked with violent reaction. His whole body bowed outward. Hoarse shouts tore from his throat and blood rushed to the surface of his skin as if he boiled alive.

Dolan finally lifted the tool and Vayne collapsed back, broken. He panted, head turning side to side as if trying to escape the memory of the pain.

"When I get my powers back, I am going to rip your throat out," she promised Dolan.

"I'm sure you'll try, but your connection will be too weak at first." He inclined his head in the barest of nods. "Thank you for the warning, though."

She snarled at him, jerking on her restraints as he touched Vayne again. She writhed in the chair's grasp, desperate to get any limb free enough to stop Dolan. Vayne's shouts fueled her fury as he twisted under the torture.

She scrabbled against the hole in her mind where her powers

should be, clawing with mental fingernails at the edges.

Dolan backed off, giving Vayne a respite.

Even after the painstick had been withdrawn Vayne continued to tremble. His leg twitched and he couldn't catch his breath. His chest shuddered twice before he turned his head to the side and vomited.

"Vayne." Hot, angry, choking tears came.

"I'm all right," he said, coughing out the last of it. He relaxed back and closed his eyes as if about to slip into sleep... or death.

"Vayne. Vayne?" Was he breathing? His neural scan looked the same, surely something would have changed if he were dying. "Vayne!"

His lids pulled back heavily.

Dolan reached toward Vayne again and her brother flinched back like a helpless child. Kayla roared at the sight. She closed her eyes and dove inside her head, pushed against every barrier that she felt, tore at every edge and seam and crack in her consciousness. *Please, please, please*, she begged herself, *do this for Vayne. Do it.* She couldn't find anything unknown. *Be the* ro'haar *you failed to be the last five years.* She dug in the dark for nothing.

Vayne's scream forced her eyes open. She stared at her neural scan, willing her brain to make some kind of connection to the image. He thrashed in his chair, his screams turning to a strangled gurgling. He let out a horrific groan and his neural scan burst into rainbow color. Threads of every conceivable shade erupted from his cartaid arch and shot through the image.

Vayne shattered their chairs' restraints.

Kayla lunged from the chair, launching herself at Dolan. She collided with him full-force, driving him to the ground. His eyes were huge as she wrested the painstick from his slack grip. Before he could recover from the shock she jammed the painstick through his throat, staking him to the ground by his windpipe. Blood spurted and covered them both.

"Don't die on me yet," she growled. She toggled the switch

on the painstick to active, then crawled off of his writhing body. "There you go."

She looked up to find Vayne staring at Dolan with haunted eyes. He still lay in the chair, his gaze fixed. "It's not enough."

Kayla wiped the hot blood from her face and neck with her gown, leaving Dolan to bleed out in agony.

"It's not enough," Vayne said again, with more force this time. "It's not." He pushed himself to standing and she rose as well, ready to catch him if he needed it.

"He deserves. . ." Vayne's words changed into just a sound, and that sound grew into a roar. He thrust his hands out and Dolan streaked across the floor to slam into the far wall of the laboratory. Vayne pulled him back, lifting Dolan's body telekinetically to waist height, and slammed him into the wall again, destroying a cabinet of instrumentation and vials. Dolan was littered with cuts from the glass. Vayne pulled him back and smashed him against the wall again, this time cracking two of the digital displays and most of the bones in Dolan's body.

It wasn't enough.

Vayne let the body drop with a wet thud and raised his arms. He turned in a slow circle, arms outstretched, and everything in the path of his hands—glass, complinks, furniture, digital displays—shattered.

She ducked as his spinning arm would have cut across her. He spun until everything in the room was destroyed, with the exception of the two of them. Fragments covered her, stuck in the blood she couldn't wipe off, coated her hair, lanced her face. Similar cuts appeared on Vayne as flying debris hit them like shrapnel. Finally it settled in a whirl of psychotically flashing broken lights, smoke, ozone and chemicals.

He lowered his arms, then his head. He took a deep breath. Another. She wanted to go to him but was afraid to move, afraid of what he'd do.

They waited in silence, she in a crouch, trying not to even twitch, he like the statue of a lost soul. A broken soul. When he finally lifted his head she saw the brother she knew there, and she saw someone else.

"We have to go," she said softly. He nodded but didn't move. "We'll find my gear and comm Malkor. He'll come for us." She dared to straighten, watching him the whole way, but he gave no reaction. She took a step toward him, heel scuffing on debris, then another. She approached until she could touch him, and when she reached out a hand for him he met her with his own.

He squeezed her fingers gently. "You're real this time. Right?"

29

Malkor sat opposite Kayla and Vayne in the back of an IDC hover car.

One of the other octet leaders Commander Parrel trusted drove the hover car. An octet had come with him to retrieve Kayla and Vayne, and other agents had been left to secure Dolan's facility. He didn't know how Parrel had activated the agents so quickly and he didn't give a damn. All he cared about was the woman across from him and her silent twin beside her.

Kayla hadn't said anything since he'd found her and Vayne standing in the antechamber of Dolan's building, surrounded by dead guards. She seemed whole in body—the blood wasn't hers—but something had happened to her. If the octet hadn't reported finding Dolan's corpse, Malkor would have put flaying the skin from the *kin'shaa*'s body at the top of his to-do list.

All he could do now was stare at Kayla and promise himself he'd never let her out of his sight again.

Ever.

Vayne stared at the city slipping by, now painted in the brilliant colors of morning. He was paler than a pilot after a decade in deep space and looked unhealthy in a way Malkor couldn't describe.

They were driving back to the safehouse where the other Wyrds and half of his team waited. Kayla would need to see

Corinth before she could take a deep breath, and she'd need to see Vayne in safe-keeping before she'd let herself rest. From the way she lay limp against the seat cushions, he knew she needed a lot more than that.

"We're here, Agent," the driver said.

Malkor popped the latch and climbed out, Kayla nearly pushing him out of the way to get to the door, Vayne trailing along slowly. Anxious faces awaited their arrival. Corinth rushed for Kayla, knocking Malkor aside. He wrapped his arms around her waist and she held him, strong for him when he needed it, no matter what she'd been through herself.

There it was, the sigh, the exhaled breath she'd been holding ever since Corinth had been taken. Her shoulders slumped with the release. She nodded, listening to something only she could hear, and hugged Corinth tighter.

"I am too," she said. She looked up then, her eyes meeting Malkor's over Corinth's head. Her face revealed her gratitude and understanding passed between them. Malkor couldn't have done anything greater for her than to have rescued Corinth.

Corinth released Kayla and latched onto Vayne with an equally fierce hug. Vayne froze, his face showing shock. He remained stiff for a second but Corinth didn't relent. Vayne's arms came around the boy slowly as if afraid to touch him, as if he wasn't real. He wrapped his arms around Corinth, hugging gently at first, then squeezed him tighter, clinging to him. Vayne, impassive until now, broke down, tears cascading from the corners of his eyes as he hung on to Corinth.

Kayla wrapped her arms around them both and they stood in the doorway like a relief carved of homecoming and painful joy.

She had her family now.

Her elder sister, Natali, lay sleeping in a room upstairs and there would no doubt be another reunion when she woke. The same with her uncle Ghirhad. Kayla was reunited with her people, whole in a way he could never make her by himself.

Malkor left them standing there and approached Hekkar. "Any word?"

337

Hekkar nodded. "Rigger and Noar broke the encryption on Dolan's files. They're still sorting through it, but there's a lot of material tying Dolan's activities to those of several IDC commanders and generals, and even the chief-general."

It was true, then. "The IDC's been working with Dolan? How in space did that happen?"

Hekkar looked equally displeased. "Apparently they've. . . we've, been funding the bulk of his research since Ordoch."

"In exchange for. . .?"

"Psi powers. Rigger found several contracts for funds and materials, all expressly stating that Dolan's end of the bargain was the development of a method to give us imperials psi powers."

The repercussions of such a deal set in. "They knew about the Ordochian prisoners, then. That he was performing experiments on them."

"Looks like it." Hekkar frowned. "I haven't always been proud of the decisions the IDC's made, but I've always thought we had a good direction. If this is where the IDC is heading, though. . ."

"There are others like us, and like Parrel. I'm not about to let anyone, including the chief-general, corrupt the IDC any worse than it has already suffered." He looked at Kayla, wiping tears from her face and actually smiling. "If there's a split coming, you and I are on the right side."

Kayla woke in a strange place, groggy and hungover.

She lay on her back in a bed, searching her memory for details as afternoon sunlight streamed in from a window nearby.

It slowly came back. The rescue attempt last night, the capture by Dolan, getting drugged, and then escaping this morning. No wonder she'd passed out for some hours, based on the angle of the sun. She should look in on her twin and Corinth, but she couldn't make herself stir.

A knock sounded.

She pushed herself to sitting. "Come in." She'd recovered

the tank-top she'd worn under her tac-suit, and was dressed awkwardly in that and the bottom half of her suit with the arms tied around her waist to hold it up. Real classy.

Vayne eased the door open. "You awake?"

"Barely. I have a killer headache."

He entered the room and shut the door behind him. "Me too." He took the only chair and Kayla sat cross-legged on the bed. He didn't say anything more, just watched her. She wished she could reach out and touch minds. Not even speak, just share the closeness of each other's essence and pass feelings between them faster than words. She'd let him into her head if she thought he could stand it, but something told her he was too raw for that kind of link.

"Tia brought me up to speed on the situation," he said finally. "At least, the half of it she knows."

The situation. Such an inadequate word for the tangle of conflicting loyalties that had become her life.

"She told me what their plans had been, and then about finding you here, working with Princess Isonde and the IDC on your own plans."

She felt a question coming. The way he shifted in his seat, the pensive look, the slight frown on his violet lips. . . his signs were as familiar to her as always.

"What she couldn't tell me was how you got here, and where you've been the last five years." He looked up at her from under midnight blue lashes and she heard the rest of the question he hadn't asked. *Why didn't you come for me sooner?*

Maybe it was her guilt talking. Or maybe it was the rightful pain of an *il'haar* abandoned by the *ro'haar* who was supposed to protect him with her life.

Either way, the unspoken question hung between them, distancing them. He needed her answer. Needed to believe she hadn't willingly left him to his fate, even as much as he seemed to fear it was true. What answer could ever be enough to explain why he'd suffered for so long?

"I thought you were dead." She told him everything she

339

remembered about the attack on Ordoch. He listened silently, never interrupting when she paused. She told him about escaping with Corinth, and what their life had been like in hiding. The more she talked, the more she had to say. Words spilled out, one after the other, describing life as a fugitive on the slum side of Altair Tri.

When she finally ran out of words, he said, "I'm glad you were able to save Corinth." Her regret filled in the rest of the sentence: *even if you couldn't save me.* "Are you his *ro'haar*, then?" he asked in a soft voice. "Have I lost you completely?"

"It's not like that. He needed me." She shook her head. "No. We needed each other. I would have died that day if I hadn't had to save him." The truth of the words hit her. "He saved me as much as I saved him. He's kept me going these last five years, kept me fighting to get us home."

"And now?"

That was the question, wasn't it? When she'd agreed to Isonde's scheme, she never thought it would lead to finding Vayne. Was she still locked into being someone she wasn't, now that things were so different from what she and Malkor had envisioned?

Yes.

"Now. . . now I send Corinth home with the Ilmenans. And you."

"You're not coming with us." It wasn't a question but she answered anyway.

"No."

They fell silent then, he seeming to take time to absorb the words. She had nothing else to say. She couldn't change her mind, not when so much was at stake. Not even for Vayne.

"Don't stay," he whispered. "I know what you're doing. Tia told me about your ploy to be the empress, to gain a seat on their ruling council."

"Our people need—"

"Frutt our people," he snapped, his voice lancing across the room. "I don't care. I've been subjected to mental, physical and emotional experiments for the last five years. I've seen my family members die slowly, one by one, and lived with the knowledge that I would eventually succumb to the same madness, the same exhaustion and hopelessness that killed them." He stood as if he couldn't contain his intensity. "I don't care about the political situation on a planet so far removed from the life I've been forced to live. You're alive, Kayla." He spoke as if she couldn't begin to imagine what that meant. "And Corinth's alive. And by some miracle, I'm still alive. I don't care about strangers. I want my twin," he said vehemently. "Ordoch can burn."

She stood as well, not immune to his energy. "This is our best chance, not only to help Ordoch, but also to put someone in power who could save millions of people from the TNV."

He ignored her words. "Come with me."

"Vayne—" How could she make him understand? She tried to think of another argument for her actions, but in the end, it didn't matter if he understood or not, she would still stay. "I can't."

"Is it because of him?"

She didn't have to ask who he meant. She shook her head, unable to say more. She almost wished it was because of Malkor. That might be easier for Vayne to understand than the divided responsibility she felt for both the empire's people suffering the TNV and her own.

Besides, Malkor was IDC. His job would lead him onward and away from Falanar on mission after mission. And she would marry another man tomorrow morning, chained to the imperial homeworld. When, if ever, she escaped, it would be back to Wyrd Space, not to Malkor.

"He's an imperial, Kay. IDC. He's no good for you."

"Don't you think I know that?" She took a deep breath and blew it out through her nose, trying to find even footing in the broken emotional landscape.

"Do you love him?"

She broke away from his gaze, staring at the door. "It doesn't matter."

"He loves you."

The words brought pain and an unexpected longing. If there were no one else: no suffering Ordochians, no dying nanovirus victims, no *il'haars*, no IDC. Just she and Malkor. Would they chance being together?

"That doesn't matter either," she said dully. "I'm marrying Prince Ardin tomorrow morning as Princess Isonde."

"I won't stay for that. If you want to be part of these imperial politics I can't stop you, but I refuse to sit around and watch." She heard the disappointment in his tone, the anger, and it nearly broke her. "The Ilmenans are just as eager to get out of here, with any luck we'll launch tonight."

Her gaze snapped back to his. "So soon?"

"Tomorrow morning at the latest." He sighed, his eyes closing for a minute. What did he see behind those lids? What memories haunted him? He looked weary when he opened them again.

Vayne headed for the door. "You still have time to change your mind."

"I won't."

"I found it at her apartment in the palace. I'll bring it over to you." With that, Malkor ended the conversation and Kayla stared at the comm unit.

She was back at the rooms she shared with Isonde in the Empress Game complex, waiting for Malkor to bring her Isonde's wedding dress. Isonde and Ardin had been planning this a long time, of course she had the thing already made up. Isonde herself lay in her medical pod like a rag doll, the blinking lights and occasional beep proving that, while her condition was deteriorating, she still lived—for now.

Kayla's brothers were in the safehouse with the Ilmenans and some apparently trustworthy IDC agents for company/guard. Maybe Kayla could actually get a full night's sleep tonight. The wedding would take place tomorrow morning in the arena. She and Ardin would be on the floor with as many titled and well-connected people as they could fit in chairs. Everyone else would be relegated to the stands. She didn't know what to expect for the wedding, but then, what did it matter? She'd speak her lines, manage a smile if she could and stand where they told her to. Easy enough to accomplish even if she did hate the idea.

She was still trying to grasp the reality that she'd actually have to go through with the ceremony when Malkor arrived. He had the dress in a case, and if she wasn't worried about it wrinkling she wouldn't have looked at the thing until the last possible moment. It made her future all too real.

She went into her room to hang it in the closet and Malkor followed her.

"You'll look beautiful in it," he said.

She chuckled at the irony. "Actually, Isonde will look beautiful in it." She closed the door on the thing so she could pretend it didn't exist. "How did the meeting go with Parrel?"

"Meetings plural. I decided to turn over the data regarding Dolan's dealings with the IDC and imperial army that Noar and Rigger gathered from Dolan's files. It's. . . not good." He sat down on her bed and she followed, sitting right beside him. Who knew when she'd be alone with him again, if ever? Their legs pressed together, hip to knee, and he gently placed his hand on her thigh.

"There's evidence linking several high-ranking IDC officials—including the head of the IDC—to Dolan's activities. Dolan has records of what actually happened on Ordoch and who was involved. Based on violations of wartime ethics laws, they could be looking at severe judicial action. If this gets out, it could destroy the IDC. The Council of Seven would vote to restrict our jurisdiction, rights, authority. . . Not to mention that with all of those officers stripped of their positions in the IDC, the structure of our organization would be ravaged."

"What's Parrel going to do?"

"It's a tough decision. If he releases the information it could mean an end to the IDC and the good we do. If he keeps quiet for the good of the organization, they get away with their crimes and the corruption spreads." His disgusted tone told her exactly what he thought of that option. He lightly stroked the inside of her thigh with his fingers while he spoke. "I didn't come here to talk about this."

She watched his hand, feeling the slip of his skin against hers on her bare leg. The sleeping tunic she wore covered her to mid-thigh and his fingers rested just outside of it.

"How is Vayne?" he asked.

She preferred discussing the demise of the IDC. At least that subject didn't hurt. "The same and not the same. We've lost five years of each other's lives, and my psi powers are absent from our bond. It'll take time to get to know each other again." She thought of their earlier conversation. "Time we don't have."

He squeezed her leg gently in support. "I'm sorry. I heard he and the Ilmenans are hoping to leave tomorrow morning."

"He doesn't approve of my decision to stay, he asked me to go with him."

Malkor didn't give her the automatic, "you're doing the right thing" response, for which she was grateful. It was impossible to know if she was making the right choice. And even if she was doing the "right thing," what comfort was that to her?

Malkor lifted his hand from her leg only to wrap his arm around her, resting fingers on her opposite hip and pulling her closer. "He'll understand, in time." He felt warm and solid. She laid her palm on his thigh.

The silence grew comfortable as they found a new closeness in the sharing of life's troubles. Unspoken emotion flowed between them. The past weeks had melted her down and reshaped her, and time with him had altered her forever.

His breath feathered across her skin as he turned his head toward hers. She turned to meet him, centimeters away. It was as natural as dreaming to press her lips to his. One kiss led to a second. A third. A flurry of kisses.

He pulled back only far enough to rest his forehead against hers, their raspy breaths echoing each other's. "I'm selfish. It's terrible, but I'm glad you're not leaving with the other Wyrds."

He rushed on before she could say anything. "I keep hoping that, with enough time, something will change. For us."

His words echoed her own futile wish.

"What could change?" she forced herself to ask. "I'll stop belonging somewhere else, or you'll stop being needed here?" She tried not to give in to bitterness.

"It's impossible, I know, but—" He tilted his head to look at her. "Don't you feel it?"

"You know I do," she said softly. "But that's my wedding dress in there. Or Isonde's. Or whoever I am now. And you're embroiled in IDC politics no matter which way Parrel decides."

He caught her hand. "What if I wasn't? What if I resigned my commission and stayed here on Falanar with you?"

"As what, Isonde's lover? While she—I—am married to Ardin?" She looked into his eyes. "Could you pain Ardin like that? Embarrass him in front of the entire empire and tarnish Isonde's reputation? Or would you do nothing, sit by and watch me play the good wife to him?" She touched his cheek. "How could you stand that?"

How could she?

Better that she walk away now, break the bond that had formed between them.

He looked ready to argue further so she stopped him with another kiss. His duty to the IDC would carry him away from Falanar again and again. She'd be alone day after day, praying for Isonde to wake up, knowing that the microsecond she did, she, Kayla, would speed to Wyrd Space after her brothers. Her *il'haars*.

She kissed him deeper, cradling his cheek. Tonight she belonged nowhere but here, belonged to no one but him. And he belonged to her.

She drank him in. Everything else blurred until only his touch, only their connection, mattered. She shifted, their thigh-to-thigh perch on the edge of the bed making closer contact difficult. He cupped her hips, hands guiding her to straddle his lap, facing him, as they continued to kiss.

The heat of him seeped into her, softening her muscles, relaxing her against him even as the tempo of their mingled breaths kicked up. This was right, this melding, fusing.

This was *so* right.

He pulled her closer, palms feathering down her back, hands stroking her hair so lovingly, so gently, that it caused an ache in her chest. No one had touched her this way before.

She stripped his T-shirt off to place kisses on his shoulder and he returned the favor, tossing her sleeping tunic to the floor. His mouth burned everywhere it touched.

More.

She needed more.

When he scooted back on the bed, pulling her with him, she followed mindlessly, concerned only with touching and being touched. She was need and want and he answered.

His lips led her on as she followed him down to the pillows. "Kayla," he murmured, her name existing only in the wisp of a breath between kisses. Kisses alone couldn't satisfy her, not with his strong body beneath her and the edge of desperation their reality gave her. She moved against him, the friction of skin on skin exquisite. His moan sent her passion spiking and turned her movements frantic, rough.

He held her tight to him, hooked a leg over hers, and rolled. When he finally settled the full weight of his body on her, she hitched her legs over his hips and pulled him closer. "Yes," she murmured against his mouth. He wrapped her in his arms as he sank into her, erasing five years of loneliness in an instant.

The beautiful completeness of being joined brought a wash of tears and she tried to blink them away before he noticed.

When they lay quiet and blissful, tucked together like puzzle pieces, the future tiptoed in.

Not yet. Please, not yet.

Kayla grasped at the cocoon she and Malkor had built

around themselves. *Not yet, let us have tonight.*

He nuzzled her neck and she turned to kiss him, memorizing every detail of the moment. This is what a life without Wyrds and the IDC and nanoviruses would feel like. A life with him.

She had to say the words. Just once. "I love you." It didn't change anything, but it had never been more true.

His lips curved, and then he smiled like he couldn't contain it, like he'd never heard three more perfect words. She couldn't keep from smiling with him.

He brushed his fingers across her cheek, and she half-laughed with his happiness. With their happiness.

"I love you," he said, and kissed the tip of her nose. "You love me and that's all that matters. The rest. . ." He waved a hand as if the duties and responsibilities of their lives were no matter. "We'll *make* it work."

Her smile faded and she kissed him as if she agreed. There was nothing else she could do in that moment and their night was slipping away.

"We will," he whispered against her lips.

30

The wedding officiate droned on.

Kayla, uncomfortable in the heavy, multilayered wedding dress that weighed her down, let her mind wander. She stood on a dais in the center of the arena floor in the Game complex. Ardin stood across from her, the solemn, somewhat sad expression on his face making it easy to guess his thoughts: he was spending the wedding day he'd dreamed of with the wrong woman.

Kayla had glimpsed him early this morning seated beside Isonde's medical pod, whispering to her, one hand clenching the pod's edge as if to keep from touching her and disturbing her fragile state. Seeing him now was painful enough, but it was the sight of Malkor positioned behind him on the dais as his supporter that threatened to undo her.

She couldn't bear to look at him, not when he looked ready to stop the wedding at any moment, and not when she wanted him to so badly. All the emotions of last night welled up, the poignancy, the connection. It was wonderful and it was bittersweet, standing as she was in Isonde's wedding gown.

Instead, she let her gaze wander over the immense crowd that had gathered. Thousands of people—rulers, diplomats, councilors and Empress Game contestants—sat below the dais on the arena floor, crammed elbow to elbow to witness the event of a lifetime. Even more princes, mayors, oracles, clan leaders and governors filled the arena's higher-level seating to the very ceiling. People who couldn't claim a seat stood in the aisles.

She looked through the crowd, watching everyone watch her.

She saw Archon Raorin, with his passionate appeal for a withdrawal from Wyrd Space. She saw Councilor Adai, who was more concerned about the price of gallenium ore than humanitarian issues. She saw Prince Trebulan, the TNV-struck leader of Velezed, with his contingent all dressed in their ceremonial crimson mourning robes, marking the devastation of their planet by the nanovirus. Each of these imperials' needs and demands were so different from each other, but she'd have to balance them all if she hoped to sway the councils to vote her way in the coming years.

Maybe her coming lifetime.

Based on the structure of the toxin Janeen used, Toble identified four distinct formulations of a cure. Isonde's condition hadn't responded to the first formulation. The other three were very similar to the first, their molecular structures varying only slightly. Toble admitted the odds of one of the other three compounds working were very slim.

Kayla put that out of her mind and went back to scanning the crowd. The two faces she most wanted to see weren't present.

She and her brothers had said an awkward goodbye this morning at the safehouse. Vayne and Corinth would be traveling with the Ilmenans to the space dock in orbit around Falanar sometime soon, and they hoped to have clearance for departure before this evening.

It had been nothing short of torturous to walk away from them. Corinth had held it together until she'd turned to go, then he'd thrown a fit, refusing to leave without her. His powers raged out of control and he'd even launched Vayne across the room when he tried to calm him down. It took all of her energy, false calm, love and devotion to Corinth's well-being to make the case that leaving without her was best for him. He still didn't believe her, but when she'd finally begged him to agree to leave for *her*, he relented. His tears had broken her heart, and his final words still rang in her head.

You said you'd never leave me.

She'd barely made it to the wedding after that.

She struggled to keep a pleasant expression on her face as the wedding officiate lectured about the virtues of marriage. Couldn't he just declare them bonded for life and end it? Her shoulder still ached and she wanted to visit Vid in the recovery ward.

A disturbance in the crowd caught her eye—someone moving toward the center aisle. Someone as desperate to escape as she?

Crimson robes made a loud statement as Prince Trebulan and his people exited to the center aisle. Trebulan walked in front, the others arranged behind him in a stream of blood-red solemnity. The official stuttered to a halt and everyone turned to see what was going on as they made their way to the foot of the dais.

A flicker of unease laced the expectant hush that fell over the crowd. Security personnel gathered around the perimeter started filtering up the aisles.

Trebulan's voice boomed into the silence. "I see so many of you gathered in accord for such a frivolous event, and it pains me. Here you are, every ruler from every last province in the empire, coming together for a game.

"Yet when a quorum was called on a plan of action to stop the spread of the Tetratock Nanovirus and provide relief for those planets suffering, less than one percent of you came forward." He scanned the gathered crowd on both sides, his gaze blazing with scorn. "Less than one percent."

He stood as tall as his crooked form allowed, looking regal even with the ever-present tremor shaking his body. Regal and furious. A sense of foreboding crept in as their earlier confrontation came to mind.

"The TNV is the most important crisis our empire—our people—have faced, and nothing, *nothing* should be taken more seriously." He slid a hand into his robe and retrieved a cylindrical silver object. "But I can see that you won't act if your own interests aren't threatened. I'm here to make the situation more immediate for you."

Unleash it, he had said. *Unleash the TNV on the Ordochians if they won't help.*

Holy shit.

He raised the cylinder to eye level, thumb hovering over a button.

"He's got the TNV!" Kayla shouted, and the microphones on the dais blasted her words across the arena. "He's going to release it!"

The crowd exploded into chaos.

From the corner of her eye she saw Malkor rushing toward Trebulan but she was quicker. She grabbed a fistful of skirts, took three running steps and launched herself from the dais to crash into Trebulan.

They landed in a jumble of fabric and limbs and shouting. She'd aimed to knock the canister from his grip but his hands clung, claw-like, to the metal.

Did he manage to activate it? Am I covered in the TNV right now?

The horror of that possibility stunned her like a blow to the head, and only her *ro'haar* training kept her fighting.

His elbow smashed her nose and she clamped her hands around both of his, locking his fingers in place. If he hadn't released the virus yet, she wasn't going to give him a chance to move even a micron closer to the button. Someone yanked on her hair and a red-robed Velezed kicked at her hands. Through it all Trebulan shouted, but it was impossible to hear him over the stampeding crowd.

"Malkor!"

Another kick to her hands. Where was he? "Malkor!"

The sea of crimson fabric around her parted as Malkor crashed down through the tangle. Two of the Velezed staggered back creating the only opening he needed. He disabled

Trebulan with a punch to the temple and the cripple went limp beneath her. The canister felt like fire in her hands—had it been activated, or was it just the heat from their struggle?

Her instinct was to fling it as far away as possible. *Save yourself!* her mind shouted. Instead she fought the urge and knelt upright to wrap the canister in the dense layers of her skirts. Would that slow the spread of the virus if released in aerosol form?

All around her was screaming and running and terror.

Malkor gripped her shoulder, mouth at her ear. "Did he release it?"

"I don't know!" She could be breathing in the TNV right now. It could have already infected her. Infected Malkor. They could only stare at each other as around them the spectators fled

Alarms blared, overriding even the crowd's frenzied noise. Malkor cupped a hand to his earpiece. "They're sealing the doors, but hundreds of people have already escaped outside."

Her own fear of infection was nothing compared to this new possibility. "They could be spreading it! Malkor— If this gets out into the city, the planet. . ."

An automated voice came on the speakers telling everyone to remain calm, that the doors to the arena would be sealed as a safety precaution against further contamination. Someone in an official indigo and turquoise uniform came sprinting toward her, carrying some kind of equipment.

"Cover her face!" he yelled at Malkor, even as he aimed a nozzle at her. Malkor stripped off his coat and wrapped it around her head as the first freezing shot of liquid hit her.

It was over in a minute, and the officer told Malkor he could remove the coat. She was sealed from neck to floor in a foamy, sudsy green material that hardened into a solid cocoon as she watched. It crystallized her to the floor in her kneeling position, making any movement impossible.

"It's a biohazard containment foam, gas impermeable. If that canister is still leaking the nanovirus, this will seal it in."

With me.

She supposed she should feel relieved, but all she felt was horrified.

Was she already dead?

Thank the void her brothers had gotten off the planet.

"What now?" she asked, and Malkor leaned down to hear her. Ardin was nowhere in sight.

"Now we wait. They'll send medical personnel with scanners to see if the TNV is present, if it's been released."

"And if it has?"

Malkor looked at her and his gaze held regret. "Then at least we'll be incinerated together."

"You know you're a fool, right?"

Kayla had told him that more than once in the last three hours. Malkor sat beside her on the arena floor, wishing he could strip the Isonde hologram from her and see her face. This might be the last time he ever sat with her like this. Well, she still knelt, encased in the green containment foam, while he sat.

"You've been cleared," she said. "Get out of here."

It was true, he was TNV-free, but with Kayla potentially contaminated by the canister she'd wrapped in her skirts, he could never truly be free. He tucked a lock of Isonde's auburn hair behind her ear. "Where else would I go?"

The arena was empty except for the two of them. In the last three hours the building's sensor system had been realigned to scan for the TNV on a broad basis, and the space seemed to be nanovirus-free. It wasn't as refined as he'd like, but there hadn't been another way to determine safety without sending in a bevy of technicians, potentially exposing them to the nanovirus.

Reports from outside indicated chaos. The wedding spectators were quarantined in the secondary wing of the arena until they could be individually scanned, but word of the attack had gotten out. All of the Empress Game contestants and their families staying in the massive housing structures abutting the arena—those who hadn't made it to the ceremony—had poured into the streets to escape infection. Panic spread through the city like a rising tide, and even an official statement that a TNV release had not been confirmed couldn't hold it back.

"When they crack this foam open," she said, "you'll be as dead as I am if the TNV escaped the canister."

"It didn't." He tried to sound firm but it was impossible to know what had happened in the struggle with Trebulan. Images kept flashing through his mind, autopsy shots of people killed by the TNV. Body cavities, thick with a black layer of nanites, opened to reveal organs eaten away, damage that had been done while the victim still lived. Cysts of nanites erupted through the skin. Faces, bloated and distorted, each an unholy gray as the nanites infiltrated the capillaries of the skin.

"Dying a gruesome death in the name of love might sound romantic now, mister, but wait 'til—" Her words cut off with a cry of pain, and suddenly he was looking into her brilliant blue eyes.

"Stars be damned, that hurt!" She worked her jaw, one of the only parts of her body she could move. "I think the biostrip just shorted out."

"Your hologram's dropped. Shit." He grabbed his coat. "Quick—tilt your head down." He draped the coat over her head to hide her face just as a voice sounded in his comm.

"Agent Rua, I'm First Sergeant Carsov, Biomech Containment Team. I am entering the arena now."

Great. The imperial military. Just what he needed.

The IDC was still in charge of security for the Game complex due to the Empress Game and that meant they controlled the visual feeds inside the arena. Hopefully he'd acted quickly enough to hide the hologram malfunction from those agents watching live. As for playback when the incident was dissected and catalogued later. . . He opened a channel on his comm. "Rigger. I need you to do a little artistic manipulation for me. . ."

Neither of those would hide the truth of Kayla's existence from the biomech tech when he arrived. Malkor jogged out to intercept him as the man entered from the far door.

Carsov moved slowly in a copper-colored suit that looked made out of tissue-thin metal. It covered every centimeter of him, toes to crown, so that even his face was shielded. The head section bulged outward and a lens protruded where Carsov's eyes would be, the camera feeding images to him on an internal screen.

When he spoke, his voice came from a speaker. "Agent, you need to exit the building. Now."

Malkor pointed to the man's suit. "Will that protect you from the TNV if in fact it has been released and trapped in Isonde's skirts?"

A pause, then, "Probably."

"Probably? And yet you're going in." Had Carsov volunteered—or been volunteered—for the possible suicide mission?

"It's my job, sir. Now please, exit the arena. Techs are waiting in the quarantine zone to confirm that you're clean."

"I'll stay, thanks." If Commander Parrel couldn't order him from the building, no one could. "However, we need to talk about your equipment." The man had a large backpack with poles jutting out of the top and a carry case with him, neither of which concerned Malkor. "You're recording everything and transmitting data in real-time back to your team leader, I assume?"

"It's protocol."

"Cut the feed."

Carsov's gloved hand tightened on the carry case. "Excuse me, Agent?"

"I said cut the feed. And it's IDC *Senior* Agent."

"My apologies, *Senior* Agent, but I can't do that."

Malkor took a step closer. "Don't mistake this for a request. You will cease visual and auditory communication with your team this moment, or you will turn around and exit the building."

He could imagine the fit the Biomech Containment Team Leader was having on the other end of this transmission—he almost felt sorry for putting Carsov in the middle of it.

"Are you incapable of doing your job without someone in your ear telling you what to do, First Sergeant?"

"No, sir." The voice from the speaker sounded decidedly stiff. "But protocol mandates—"

"The IDC retains jurisdiction over the Game complex until reassigned by Emperor Rengal himself, and as ranking IDC agent, I am in charge." *Well, all in.* "I deem the extraction mission of the TNV canister too sensitive to be broadcast pre-screened. The information can't be tightly controlled, and therefore poses a security risk."

How's that for bullshit?

"It's not as if we're sharing the live feed on the local vidscreens," Carsov said. "We know how to handle confidential material."

They probably did it all the time. Still, this wasn't just his secret to keep.

"You will end transmission with your team or you will send someone else in who knows how to follow orders." He leaned toward the camera's lens until he blocked out all else. "Do you need my boss to explain to your boss how jurisdiction works?"

Parrel was going to kill him for dragging him into this if Biomech didn't cave. And either way, Malkor was going to pay for it later. If there was a later.

"Fine," Carsov said. "The IDC can take the blame if this goes to shit."

Malkor commed Rigger. "Can you confirm?"

A minute passed in tense silence. It was an eerie faceoff with a faceless man—hard to look a biomech containment suit right in the eye.

Rigger finally answered. "Yeah boss, his suit is no longer sending or receiving transmissions. Good luck down there."

One problem down, at least. Now there was just Carsov to deal with.

"What you're about to see is classified."

"Did you really just use that line on me?" Carsov shouldered past him and started down the center aisle.

Malkor followed him to where Kayla waited, the coat draped over her head and shoulders acting like a deep hood.

Carsov set his gear down, then pulled a scanner from the carry case. "And the reason for the coat is. . .?"

Malkor knelt beside Kayla and waited for Carsov to do the same. His coppery suit shimmered under the lights as he moved. Malkor lifted the edge of her makeshift hood just enough to reveal Kayla's face to the tech.

"That's not—" A whistle came from the suit's speaker. "No wonder you have a stick up your ass about jurisdiction and 'sensitive material.' The IDC's frutting with the entire empire."

Pretty much, yeah. Or at least my octet is.

"This is Princess Isonde's body-double. We received multiple threats against Isonde and Prince Ardin." Which was at least always true. "The wedding was deemed an unsecured situation, we couldn't risk having them exposed like that."

"Prince Ardin had a body-double too?"

"He was hurried out before the switch could be discovered. The only reason you're meeting Isonde's double is because she's braver than any of us, and jumped on the canister to try to save everyone."

Kayla grumbled. "I might be locked in crystallized foam, *Agent Rua*, but I can still talk." Her sarcastic tone couldn't cover her anxiety. She nodded at Carsov. "Evelyn. Hi. Nice to meet you. Can you cut me loose now?"

"It's a little more complex than that." Carsov flipped on the scanner he held and started a silent survey of the hardened biocontainment foam.

Malkor wanted to kiss the tightness from Kayla's lips. He wanted to switch places with her. If he'd been faster. . .

"It's not your fault," she said softly. "No one could have stopped me from going for the canister."

"I could have beaten you to it."

She scoffed. "Not in a million years, buddy."

Same old Kayla.

"No nanovirus has breached the foam," Carsov said. He stood. "Help me with the containment tent, let's get this done."

Malkor took a last look at her, then let the coat fall back into place to shield her from the vid feeds. Carsov unpacked folded sheets of the same coppery material from which his suit was made and started laying them out. He instructed Malkor on the assembly of the poles for the tent's frame.

"So, Princess Isonde using a body-double, huh? How long's that been going on?" Carsov smoothed wrinkles from the material as he spoke.

"It's protocol," Malkor said. "I figured you'd love that."

Carsov began sealing the edges of the copper-colored sheets together without comment.

They worked in silence, Malkor building the tent's frame around Kayla and Carsov fusing the sheets to the poles to form the containment walls. When it was finished, when Kayla was hidden inside, they both stood and stared at it. Carsov might be steeling himself for a delicate procedure, but after three hours of waiting, Malkor couldn't take one more second of not knowing if Kayla had been infected.

"Well?"

"Before I go in, tell me this: Was it just the wedding that was deemed too risky for Princess Isonde, or were there other parts of the Game as well?" The suit's camera lens focused on him like an unblinking eye.

"It's classified."

"Thought so." Carsov hefted his carry case of tools and entered the containment tent.

Minutes went by, too many minutes, while Malkor paced in silence, waiting for word.

Finally, Carsov called out, "Layer one is dissolved, no nanites present. Proceeding with layer two."

"Evelyn?"

"I'm fine, but damn it's hot in here. You got a fan in that case, Carsov?" The strain in her voice left her words flat. Both fell silent after that and Malkor went back to pacing.

"Layer two, no nanites present.

"Layer three, no nanites present."

How many layers could foam have?

"I'm into the hypodermis now."

A whirring sound kicked up from inside the tent and he barely held his ground. What was better, waiting and guessing what was going on, or watching every moment, layer by agonizing layer?

"Layer four—" The sound stopped. "Agent, I'm about to breach the last layer, I highly recommend that you leave the arena at this time."

"Why, what have you found?"

No answer.

"He's got a scanner," Kayla said, "but I can't read the screen."

"I'm sure everything will be fine," Carsov said, in an overly steady voice. He'd heard that tone before. He'd used it himself during incendiary negotiations. "It's just a precaution, Agent Rua, but I am asking you again to leave."

"Listen to him, Malkor. Please."

"Just get it over with," Malkor called back, nausea settling in, "or I'll come break her out myself." He should run. Carsov wouldn't tell him to leave again if his scanner wasn't picking up nanites. No reason he and Kayla both had to be infected with the TNV.

No reason except that he couldn't leave her to face the death sentence alone.

"Breaching final layer now."

Malkor couldn't breathe as he waited for the confirmation from Carsov.

Instead he heard a sharp *crack* and Kayla's groan as someone's body hit the floor.

"Kayla!"

"Layer four is clear, no nanites present. The reading is coming from inside the canister."

Malkor knocked over the containment tent and rushed to where Kayla had collapsed, his coat still veiling her face. She groaned again, and a peek under the coat showed her teeth gritted in an eerie rictus of a smile, the shards of broken containment foam all around her.

"Ha!" she finally gasped out. "Take that you frutter!"

"What's wrong?"

She gripped her legs, and it took a second to realize the sound coming from her was a raspy chuckle. "Just recirculation pain. I've been immobilized for three hours, I thought my legs were going to break off." She chuckled again. "We stopped him. Trebulan thought he was so slick with that TNV. He thought— He—"

Her weak laugh turned to gulped breath, and then the tears were flowing. They were tears of denied fears, tears of relief. He felt dangerously close to tears himself, and he hadn't been clutching a canister of TNV for the last three hours.

The tears lasted no more than a minute. She scrubbed them away before he could speak without a clench in his throat.

"Your coat stinks, by the way."

He laughed, and the sound eased the breath in his chest. She was fine, and he was fine. They were fine.

"You just saved hundreds of thousands of people, maybe millions, and the first thing you think to say is that my coat stinks?"

"Well, it does." She sat up, keeping the coat around her like a hood. Her gaze fell on the canister that Carsov was locking away in the carry case. "All those people, Malkor."

All those people, their lives so close to the edge today.

"Has the IDC discovered where he got the TNV from, or where he'd kept it until today?" she asked. The nanites in Trebulan's body were all inactive, she knew, his body having miraculously defeated them years ago. He'd need another source.

Malkor shook his head.

"So there could be more out there, more canisters to set off?"

"Exactly. The entire planet is on lockdown but it's utter chaos out there."

Carsov broke in. "Agent Rua, okay if I comm my team leader, let them know the TNV's contained?" He hadn't taken his suit off, not with the TNV so close, even if it was sealed away. A pity. Malkor wanted to look right into the eyes of the man who now had the knowledge to ruin them.

Instead, he wrapped his arm around Kayla's shoulders, the most intimate gesture he was allowed under so much scrutiny.

"Carry on, Carsov. But if the IDC learns you breathed one word of what you saw here. . ."

There was no reply from the coppery suit.

31

FIVE DAYS LATER

Kayla had seen Malkor half-a-dozen times in the week since the Trebulan incident.

Unfortunately, most of those times had been on the vidscreen.

Rigger had had a new hologram biostrip waiting for her the moment she and Malkor had escaped the arena. They'd slapped it right over the minor electrical burn on her throat from the old one and brought her out into the throng, a waving, triumphant Princess Isonde, soon-to-be empress-apparent and now the Savoir of Falanar. She'd belonged to the public since that moment.

She had barely been able to get four hours of sleep in a row, never mind have a private moment to herself, between all of the appearances and interviews. She'd done her duty by the press, as she knew Isonde would have.

Interviews about the Game:
What does it feel like to have won?
Why do you think the Wyrds abdicated the crowning fight to you?
Do you and the Wyrds have an alliance?

Interviews about the TNV:

What was going through your mind when you wrestled with Prince Trebulan?

How did you know he had the TNV?

You must have been mortally afraid! Tell us how frightening those three hours were!

The worst were the joint appearances with Ardin:

You two look so in love, you must be devastated that the wedding is pushed off.

Tell us about your love story.

Give us a kiss. Oh, don't be bashful, go on, show us how you really feel about each other!

And at each of them, the questions about Malkor:

We understand you two grew up together, tell us about him.

How long have you been friends? You must be some friends for him to stay by your side in the arena with the TNV.

Is he single? Citizens across the empire want to know!

They showed the footage over and over: she, walking unscathed from the arena, giving the military reporter a wave— "the wave seen across the stars!"—all the while gripping Malkor's hand for support.

The IDC needed a new secretary just to deal with all the proposals of marriage and bonding ceremonies that Malkor had received since then.

If her life had become a whirlwind, Malkor's had become a full-blown storm. The empire had gone crazy since Trebulan's unsuccessful attack at the wedding, and the IDC was caught up in more conflicts than they could handle in three lifetimes. Every available octet was pulling double and triple shifts to quench the political wildfires. The first few days had been the worst, when the planet was under quarantine while the search for Trebulan's possible supply of TNV had occurred. Tensions were so high she could taste it in the air. Everyone suspected everyone, alliances fractured and fear reigned. The repercussions spread outward across the system, reaching the homeworlds of everyone trapped on Falanar. The empire was mobilized in a way it never had been before.

Trebulan had gotten his wish.

Once his remaining supply of TNV had been found—a single canister, stashed in a warehouse in Shimville—the planet-wide quarantine had been lifted. The attempted mass exodus from Falanar created even more problems as people were forced to wait to receive transport to the space docks above the planet, and from there wait longer for their launch window amid millions of others.

No wonder her contact with Malkor had been limited to a handful of quick hellos via vidscreen.

The days apart had given her room to think, and time to spend in vid chat with her *il'haars*. Vayne, Corinth and the Ilmenans had been trapped by the quarantine along with everyone else. Whenever Kayla had two spare moments she commed the ship, checking in with Corinth, Vayne and her rescued family members. The connection had clarified her thinking.

Now their launch window loomed. They had been cleared to leave tonight, in a few hours in fact. She planned to be on that flight. She was only waiting planet-side for a visit with Malkor, to break the news to him.

He'd better hurry.

She left her—Isonde's—sumptuous bedchamber and strode down the hall toward the bedchamber that contained Isonde's medical pod. Isonde kept a house in the capital city and Kayla had taken up residence there now that the Game complex had been evacuated. After a week Kayla still felt like an intruder.

She slipped into the room quietly, wanting to check on Isonde one last time.

Nothing had changed.

The display at the foot of the pod glowed with the same low-level life signs it had all week. The second formulation of the possible cure didn't seem to be working.

Two down, two to go, with the odds decreasing daily.

Isonde lay like a barely breathing corpse amid the sheets of the bed inside, her lips slightly blue. Evidence of Ardin was all over the room, from the chair that bore his imprint pulled up beside the pod, to the clothes strewn about and the untouched dinner tray on a side table. He practically lived here with them, in between everything else.

Isonde's hands were arranged perfectly symmetrical to each other, which meant Ardin had been holding one of them. Kayla had seen the way he placed her hand back on her stomach before he left, delicately arranging each finger to be perfectly spaced apart. It was the only thing he could do for her, the only comfort he could give.

It felt too intrusive to Kayla to touch her, so she patted the edge of the medical pod instead. "You'll come out of it. Toble is the best."

Two chemical formulations of hope left.

And then?

She patted the pod again. "It will work."

That was all she could stand, so she made her escape from the room and returned to her chambers. The bag she'd brought from her escape from Fengar Swamp on Altair Tri greeted her at the door, packed with all her possessions.

Right. *Her* possessions.

Everything she owned in the universe was strapped to her thighs. The clothes she'd packed, even the outfit she wore, were all compliments of her double-life here on Falanar.

A comm from the security detail at the front of the house demanded her attention.

"Princess, Agent Rua is here to see you."

"Thank you, Rawn, send him up."

When Malkor entered the room minutes later, uncertainty hit her in the chest at the sight of him. Had she come to the right decision over the week?

She peeled off the hologram and cupped it in one fist.

"It is so good to see *you*," he said, and smiled as if the stress of the last five days melted away. He was three steps into the room before the import of her bag by the door hit him—she saw it in his expression. If she were going anywhere as Isonde, she would have packed Isonde's clothes in one of Isonde's cases. But the sight of *that* bag, her bag. . .

His smile faded as he stopped a meter from her.

"I'm leaving," she said, with no other words to soften the truth. Nothing could soften it.

He didn't answer, seeming without words to reply to such a statement. She held out the hologram biostrip for him but he didn't move.

"Take it."

They stared each other down, and finally she dropped her hand.

"You don't need me anymore," she said. It was the truth she had come to this week, the realization that had set her free.

"How can you say that?" His soft words inflamed her doubt, but the facts didn't change.

"You need *someone*, but it no longer has to be me."

"Kayla—"

"You needed me to win the Empress Game. I've done that, it's over. Now you need someone to be a diplomat, a politician. Any number of women with a background in such things would be a better choice, as long as their size is close enough to Isonde's to make the hologram work."

She held the biostrip out to him again. "She'll need this."

He looked at her outstretched hand, then back to her. "Am I correct in assuming you mean to leave with your brothers?"

"In about two hours' time." She tossed the biostrip toward an ornamental table but it hit the lip and fell to the carpet. Neither made a move to retrieve it.

"And just like that, you're done with this." He blew out a slow breath. "Done with us."

She would never be done with him—she never wanted to be.

But she knew where she belonged.

"You'll find someone else for the ruse."

"Where, Kayla? Answer me that. Where would I find someone I could trust with this?"

"The IDC."

"After Janeen, and what we learned from her defection?" He gave a bitter laugh. "Try again."

Though she felt anything but indifferent, she shrugged one shoulder.

His eyes narrowed on the movement. "Don't tell me you don't care."

"Of course I care. I wouldn't have stayed all this time if I didn't care." And she wouldn't be feeling like she was betraying him if she didn't care. "You took a chance on me once, you can take a chance on someone else."

"Not your problem, huh?"

Her plan to remain stoic broke down. She crossed the distance to him, laid a hand on his arm and he covered it with his own.

The neutrality faded from his expression, letting his hurt show. "How can you walk away from me?"

"How can I stay while my *il'haars* leave? I was born to be their *ro'haar*. It's who I am."

"You are so much more than their *ro'haar*, Kayla."

She pulled back a little. "I am *thankful* to be their *ro'haar*. You can't know what it's like, to be one half of a bonded pair. I am less without my *il'haars*, not more."

"Are you less when you're with me?"

She couldn't lie to push him away. "Of course not." He filled the spaces of her life in a way her brothers never could. "It is different, not less."

He brushed his fingertips over her cheek. "But it's not enough?"

"I can't have both."

"And you have chosen them over me."

She could tell him of the struggle that raged within her, heart over soul, loyalty over desire, family over lover. The urge to change her mind that gripped her even now. None of it would be explanation enough.

His hand dropped and he glanced back at her bag. "You have made the choice without talking to me, without giving me time to change your mind, or time to understand and agree." His lips tightened. "You are not the only person whose life changes with this decision, Kayla."

"But I am the only one who could make it." Even if it split her heart down the middle.

He looked furious and lost, and so achingly dear that she wrapped her arms around him and pulled him close.

"I will never see you again," he said into her shoulder. She squeezed her eyes shut. Imperial travel would never be allowed in Wyrd Space, even if the Ordochian occupation ended. And if a peaceful accord couldn't be reached, if their two sides somehow went to war. . .

"Forgive me?" she asked.

He held her even tighter. "Would Vayne forgive you if you'd chosen me over him?"

The comm chirped, and Tia'tan's voice broke them apart. "Kayla, you need to get to the ship."

She stared into Malkor's eyes, unwilling to be parted. "I thought I had another hour."

"So did we." Tia'tan's tone sent Kayla into business mode. She crossed to the comm unit by the door and hit the vid switch. Tia'tan's face appeared, with Vayne in the background, pacing the forward cabin of a ship.

"What's going on?"

"Our launch window has been 'frozen.'"

"But the flight plan was approved twenty-seven hours ago." She looked to Malkor, who pulled out his mobile comm and dialed someone up. He turned away to speak.

Vayne leaned past Tia'tan's shoulder toward the screen. "Kayla, you need to get up here now. Right now."

"I bet hundreds of launch windows have been delayed in the last few days." Surely no one would mess with the Ilmenans' launch window, though. Wyrds were the last people anyone on Falanar wanted hanging around right now.

Noar appeared. "We're getting orders from the launch deck to power down the engines and prepare for an 'inspection.'"

"There is no way I'm doing that," Tia'tan said. "Prep for embarkation. Kayla, you need to get here five minutes ago."

"On my way. Switch to my mobile comm and keep me updated." She sprinted for her bag and Malkor followed her out the door. "I need a ride," she called out, "my transport doesn't leave for an hour."

Malkor nodded, still in a terse conversation on the mobile. Whoever it was, they weren't delivering good news.

They burst through the front door and into the street. Malkor suddenly gripped her arm, halting her before she could shake him off. "We have to go—"

"Stop, Kayla. The Ilmenan ship won't get off the space dock."

She broke free and started down the street again without waiting for an answer. This time when he grabbed her she couldn't wrench away.

"The imperial military's after them. This isn't an 'inspection,' they're being arrested as war criminals."

"They're locking down the docking clamps," she heard Tia'tan say over her comm. "Get an override going."

"Kayla," there was a note of pleading in Vayne's voice that killed her to hear. "Please. You have to get here now. If we wait much longer, we won't be able to leave."

What the frutt was going on?

She struggled against Malkor as he gripped her other arm. "I have to leave!"

"Listen," he said, "listen! They found out who supplied Trebulan with the activated TNV."

The comm tucked into her ear buzzed with frenzied conversation.

Tia'tan: "Their military demands our surrender? What the void for?"

Vayne: "They're saying we did *what*?!"

Noar: "I can override the lockdown but it'll only last minutes, maybe three."

Corinth: "We can't leave without Kayla!"

Tia'tan: "Kayla, are you coming? They're starting to target us with the station's weapons."

Corinth: "I can disrupt their sensor array. Please! I'll do it right now while we wait for Kayla, to give her more time."

Foreign voice: "This is General Solcath of the Imperial Military, Prime World Division. Prepare to be boarded and taken into custody. If you resist in any way—"

Vayne: "I can NOT be taken prisoner again. I—" his voice was so fierce it shook. "I will not. I will *not*."

Tia'tan: "I'm firing up the engines. Noar, get ready with that override."

Vayne: "Kayla— I'm sorry, I'm so sorry."

General Solcath: "Power down your engines now or your ship will be disabled with all necessary force."

"No!" Kayla shouted. "Vayne, I'm coming. I'm coming! Do you hear me?" She took off at a run and Malkor let her go. "*Wait* for me!"

Vayne: "I can't, Kayla. Tia, do it now!"

Tia'tan: "Engines lit. Prepare to override on my mark. Kayla—I'm sorry. My priority is to get as many Wyrds home safely as I can. Ready, Noar? Mark."

The rest was ship noise and engines roaring and the military shouting threats and then. . .

"Vayne? Corinth?"

Silence.

She stumbled, fell to her knees, the dead air of the comm suffocating her.

"Vayne?"

Gone.

"Corinth?"

Gone.

A hand rested on her shoulder, a voice quietly said, "They escaped."

They'd left her behind. Her *il'haars*, they'd left her behind. Left her behind with the man she'd left behind.

Malkor tried to help her stand.

"Leave me alone."

"You can't be seen like this, without the hologram. Lady Evelyn has the Virian flu, she's bedridden. You can't be seen crying on your knees on the street."

"I'm not crying. And frutt Lady Evelyn."

"Kayla." His voice softened and he knelt next to her. "Kayla. Let's go back inside."

"They didn't do it. The Ilmenans, the TNV, it wasn't them." But they did leave her behind.

He was quiet so long that she looked at him, at his frown. "Apparently the evidence is very convincing. The IDC is requesting a review of it, once the military allows us access."

"It *wasn't* them." The vacuum of pain in her was so great that she thought she might implode from it. Only one thought kept her from collapsing. "This will start a war, Wyrds against imperials."

Malkor nodded.

"This could start a catastrophic war."

He nodded again.

"We have to prove it wasn't them."

He sighed. "We might discover that they *are* in fact responsible."

"Then we'll have to 'prove' it wasn't them. By any scheme necessary."

Let the game begin.

ACKNOWLEDGMENTS

I can't say thank you enough to Diana Botsford and Jen Brooks, the world's greatest writers and critique partners. They have been with me through thick and thin, and devoted an unfathomable amount of their time to helping me develop this novel and grow as a writer. Here's to many more book releases in our futures! Thanks also have to go to my mentor, Timons Esaias, who whipped me into shape in graduate school at Seton Hill University (when I needed it most!) and who continues to inspire me to do better. My most heartfelt gratitude goes to my family, and especially the other "Power of Four" ladies: my mum Beverly, and my two sisters, Rosemary and Andrea. I couldn't imagine life without you, and I wouldn't have ever made it this far without your unfailing love and support.

I may be verbose, but I can't express in words the thanks my dear husband, James, deserves. He's been through endless hours of my talking about writing and characters and plots, and he has somehow managed to appear interested through all of it. I couldn't ask for a sweeter, more encouraging, more positive partner to go through this life with.

Lastly, I want thank my agent, Richard Curtis, for taking a chance on an unpublished writer, and my editor, Alice Nightingale, for her help in making Kayla even more of a badass. I wouldn't want *The Empress Game* in anyone else's hands.

ABOUT THE AUTHOR

Rhonda Mason divides her time between writing, editing, bulldogs and beaching. Her writing spans the gamut of speculative fiction, from space opera to epic fantasy to urban paranormal and back again. The only thing limiting her energy for fantastical worlds is the space-time continuum. When not creating worlds she edits for a living, and follows her marine biologist husband to the nearest beach. In between preserving sea grass and deterring invasive species, she snorkels every chance she gets. Her rescue bulldog, Grace, is her baby and faithful companion. Grace follows her everywhere, as long as she's within distance of a couch Grace can sleep on. Rhonda is a graduate of the Writing Popular Fiction masters program at Seton Hill University, and recommends it to all genre writers interested in furthering their craft at the graduate level.

You can find Rhonda at www.RhondaMason.com.

THE CONFEDERATION

TANYA HUFF

In the distant future, two alien collectives vie for survival. When the peaceful Confederation comes under attack from the aggressive Others, humanity is granted membership to the alliance—for a price. They must serve and protect the far more civilized species, fighting battles for those who have long since turned away from war.

Staff Sergeant Torin Kerr and her platoon are assigned to accompany a group of Confederation diplomats as they attempt to recruit a newly discovered species as allies. But when her transport ship is shot down, the routine mission becomes anything but, and Kerr must stage a heroic last stand to defend the Confederation and keep her platoon alive.

VALOUR'S CHOICE
THE BETTER PART OF VALOUR
THE HEART OF VALOUR
VALOUR'S TRIAL
THE TRUTH OF VALOUR
PEACEMAKER

"An intriguing alien race, a likeable protagonist, a fast moving plot, and a rousing ending. What more could you ask for?"
Science Fiction Chronicle